"TOM DEITZ, ALREADY A
GOOD STORYTELLER, HAS
GOTTEN EVEN BETTER"
ROGER ZELAZNY

W9-BSM-348

Praise for Tom Deitz's

SOULSMITH

"A refreshingly different kind of magic.
His story and characters
capture the imagination"
A. C. CRISPIN,
author of *The Starbridge Chronicles*

"Successfully combines such disparate
elements as ancient Welsh mythology
and Southern Gothic . . .
Tom Deitz weaves a potent spell indeed"
JOSEPHA SHERMAN,
author of *Child of Faerie, Child of Earth*

"Tom Deitz is a master of
modern fantasy . . . A riveting read,
brimming with grief, ecstasy,
and the sweet pain of being Other . . .
May well be the finest fantasy of the year,
or even of the decade."

BRAD STRICKLAND, author of *Moondreams*

"Tom Deitz is trying something
more ambitious, darker,
and he's writing better than ever"
MERCEDES LACKEY, author of *Magic's Prize*

WORDWRIGHT

TOM DEITZ

AVON BOOKS • NEW YORK

WORDWRIGHT is an original publication of Avon Books. This work has never before appeared in book form. This work is a novel. Any similarity to actual persons or events is purely coincidental.

AVON BOOKS
A division of
The Hearst Corporation
1350 Avenue of the Americas
New York, New York 10019

Copyright © 1993 by Thomas F. Deitz
Cover illustration by Tim White
Published by arrangement with the author
Library of Congress Catalog Card Number: 93-90228
ISBN: 0-380-76291-9

First AvoNova Printing: September 1993

AVONOVA TRADEMARK REG. U.S. PAT. OFF. AND IN OTHER COUNTRIES, MARCA REGISTRADA, HECHO EN U.S.A.

Printed in the U.S.A.

RA 10 9 8 7 6 5 4 3 2 1

For reasons best left unstated, this book is not dedicated to anyone. I would, however, like to take this opportunity to thank Gilbert Head for *always* being there when I needed him. There are precious few about whom that can be said.

Thanks, Gil.

Acknowledgments

Thanks are due to

Gilbert Head
Margaret Dondle Head
Adele Leone
Chris Miller
B. J. Steinhaus

and especially to

Greg Keyes
for general moral support, and for sharing his expertise
on Southeastern Indians, which helped make
Chapter 12 ring true.

Prelude

Songs from the Wood

Jackson County, Georgia
Early September—midnight

His skin, he discovers, is aging—as well it might. He has sheltered in it longer than he has ever dared in one he was not born to; has dwelt with those lies convenience calls memories a greater space of days than in all the years before. Five times his rack has sprouted since it first sprang forth, full grown and out of season. Now he has become a legend: a shape scarce-glimpsed at the changing of the sun, a numinous pale goal glimmering in hunters' dreams. Twice he has been shot and emerged unscathed, though he carries seven scars 'neath the white fur of his belly, each the mark of an antler prong five years gone by. Since then he has hid in this hide alone: for contrition, for mortification of the flesh. As a sigil of how once he failed, even in the shimmer of success.

One work he wrought then, of the stuff of the Earth, though he broke the Rules at its making. And two other . . . *things* likewise felt his hand. Both were Changed; both must be tempered further—and for that he has finished waiting. *This* time, however, he will be more circumspect. *This* time he

1

will come like a thief in the night: so subtly he may even beguile himself.

But that is then; this is now.

Now his antlers itch most terribly, there in their gloves of brown velvet where they drink his own heart's blood (or is that *hart's* blood? something wonders) and grow strong and hard and lethal.

And now that he has noticed, he is aware of nothing else. He finds an oak and rubs a prong against its ancient roughness—and the itching eases. Harder, and flesh rips with a pulse of pain. Wetness warms the dome of his skull and burns into his eyes, and still he scrapes, as velvet shreds and spikes break free into the forest light.

Yet something is wrong! Never has the itching crept so far onto his forehead. And so he scratches there; and the velvet tears to tatters that fly in bloody motley 'round his ears. His head feels better now, though strangely cold and . . . *empty*.

But now it is his neck that plagues him, worse than the bites of a thousand hungry flies. He drags its furry arch along more bark, and yet the torment lingers: down his back and hips and ribs. There, too, he grinds it gone, but it merely flees ahead—to his legs. Them likewise he accommodates— to find his lips assailed. And his cheekbones. And his chin. Harder—and blood veils his vision, and still he grates his flesh against rough wood. His chest now, his hooves (strangely soft), his belly, and his pizzle. Blood patterns the leaves for acres; skin festoons twigs for a score of miles, for he has run while he assays this rubbing. He is cold too, colder than he has been in seasons. And his back hurts, thus stooped over. He shakes his head and his vision clears.

He has hands.

When he rises, something atop his skull snags a branch. He jerks reflexively. A pain, a ripping, a crack, and a weight abates. Two objects fall to rattle in the oak leaves: twelve-pointed antlers, still clad in blood and ragged velvet, where he, a man, wears nothing now but sunlight.

No longer the Beast, then—but who in the world is the Man? he wonders while he walks. *I once had a name,* he recalls, *one I can no longer remember. Perhaps the Wind will hum one to please me. Perhaps it will even hum me a life.*

He listens, and it sings with suggestions. He heeds a person's worth and makes them his own.

Color catches his eye: a flash of white, a glimpse of saffron yellow. He looks down and sees a daisy. It wakes a memory. A brazen bullet case brings forth another. Memories of Making.

Prologue

In the Midnight Hour

Cardalba Hall, Welch County, Georgia
Friday, January 17—11:50 P.M.

I
Season of the Witch

"Is she . . . ?"

The nervous edge on Lewis Welch's query made his voice too loud and jerked Ron Dillon back to confused awareness from where he'd been dozing with his mouth open, his shirt unbuttoned, and his head lolled sideways against the over-stuffed cushions of the burgundy velvet love seat in the narrow parlor outside his great-grandmother's bedroom.

"Wha—?" he sputtered, blinking the dimly lit chamber back into focus exactly in time to see two sets of indigo eyes shift his way and glare: the older from beyond a quarter-open door, the younger from a red leather lounger. Ron blushed obligingly, for in spite of having consumed enough Jamaican Blue Mountain coffee in the last twelve hours to set a small country fidgeting, he had violated the unvoiced terms of this vigil and nodded off—again.

Waiting *did* that to him, dammit! It was not an art he either enjoyed, cultivated, or practiced with conviction. And it was a thousand times worse when the delay in question was born of something he absolutely could not control—like the rate at which a certain old lady was dying.

Not that he wasn't *concerned*; he wasn't so cold-blooded as to actually wish a kinswoman dead. But the obvious outcome seemed more important to observe than the inexorable journey thereto. Napping was simply a way to expedite the trek toward the inevitable.

"Sorry," he mumbled, stretching enough to make his shoulders pop. He burrowed his slim bare feet into the thick red carpet, yawned hugely, and tried to look contrite.

From his place plugging the bedroom door, his elder uncle (for so Ron preferred to think of Dion Welch in lieu of their true relationship, which was even closer) merely shrugged noncommittally, which Ron took as a sign of forgiveness; nudged the nearest stereo control down a notch, thereby reducing the Enya CD Miss Martha Welch had ordered to accompany her demise to a whisper; and turned his raptor gaze to Ron's fraternal twin brother. His dark hair flapped about his cheeks like wings, adding to his predatory air. In his black silk shirt and black jeans, Ron half expected to hear Dion vent a raven's cry. Or, given what he did for a living, caw.

Lew—who, to judge by his wrinkled clothes, greasy hair, and dark-circled eyes, was at least as far down the road to burnout as Ron—merely lifted a dark brow into blond curls that had passed Renaissance some time back and were now breathing hard on heavy metal. His fingers beat a silent, impatient tattoo on the oxblood leather of his chair. *"Is she?"* he repeated.

Dion spared an anxious glance over his shoulder. "Not yet," he whispered. "Soon, though." Without further comment, he eased fully into the room and let the heavy oak door click shut behind him. A pair of decisive strides took him to the small ebony table at Lew's right, where a crystal sherry decanter shared space with a black porcelain thermos of coffee. He chose stimulant over depressant and poured himself a cup, then squatted gracefully, twisted around in place, and reached for the empty mug Ron had stashed beneath the love seat. A black-furred paw flashed out when he touched the handle. He jerked his hand away reflexively, the smooth, tanned skin now marred by streaks of red.

"Matty, be good," Ron snapped, reaching down to snare cat and cup with left and right hand respectively, before extending the latter for a refill. The old black tom named Matty Groves promptly twisted from Ron's grip and leapt to the floor, where he proceeded to bully a bony, long-limbed white hound from its cozy corner with a single purposeful yowl. The dog rose awkwardly and found another nook, where it resumed the exact pose it had just abdicated: head extended along the floor, paws draped across its crimson ears. Waiting too, Ron decided. Waiting, waiting, waiting. *Goddamned* waiting.

Lew giggled in self-conscious punchiness, then poured himself a sherry and bolted it at one gulp. "Any idea *how* long?" he asked seriously, not for the first time.

Dion replaced the thermos and slumped down beside the darker of his sister's unmatched sons. He shook his head again. "She can't make the night."

Lew nodded toward the door. "What about Uncle Gil?"

Another shrug. "He's running on air and imagination."

"And Luck, of course," Ron grumbled into his cup. "Let's not forget that."

Dion mussed Ron's spiky dark hair. "I wasn't forgetting, lad—much as we'd all like to."

Ron reciprocated the assault, resorting to petty play to ease tension. It was easy to forget that the elegantly handsome man sprawled lazily beside him—his late mother's brother for certain, but almost certainly his progenitor (but not Lew's) as well, which fact they both conveniently ignored— was nearly thirty years his senior: mid fifties, though he could have passed for twenty-five, and little of that clothes or hair, which tended more toward redneck or rock star than either the academician or jurist Dion had been before his jailbird phase. In *fact* he was a bum. A footloose street-person sorcerer with no home (by choice) save the alleys and abandoned buildings of Jacksonville, Florida. Whether it was penance or posture that had led him to forsake the trappings of the family wealth, Ron had never had the nerve to inquire, but the silk he now affected was a short-term concession to his grandmother, nothing more.

Silence, for a while, and then Ron chuckled grimly. "You know, there's a real irony here, guys: the last great sorceress in Georgia's dying in there, and the four most powerful . . . whatever we ares . . . in the Southeast sit around like buzzards waiting for the corpse to cool."

"But not *wishing*," Lew noted forcefully.

Ron looked up from where he'd been tying his shirttail into knots. "Yeah, but it's hard to separate the person from the role. Trouble was, she was less and less the person as she got older, and more and more just . . ."

"—The matriarchal Listener in this part of the world?" Dion supplied.

"I can't believe how much she's changed in the last few months," Lew murmured, rising and starting to pace. The cuff ties of his winter cammos threatened to foul what furnishings his flopping sneaker laces didn't. He seemed not to care, was as slovenly as Ron had ever seen him, though his compact wrestler's body was tense as a board.

"That's how it happens, though," Dion sighed, leaning back. "How it's *supposed* to happen, anyway. You guys haven't ever seen the Change progress normally, have you?"

Ron shook his head. "Not bloody likely!"

Lew padded over to join them, sat on the floor at their feet, nursing a second sherry. "But it's scary, man: seeing someone alter that much that fast. I mean, I *know* she was old. But to have all your years fall on you at once . . ." He shuddered. "Jeez!"

"That's what happens when the Luck slips away, though," Dion said tersely. "It keeps you up better than nature does, but there at the end it lets you down in spades."

"Maybe it was best the way it happened with Uncle Matt," Lew mused.

"You mean being clubbed to death by your asshole grandson?" Ron snapped. "I don't think so!"

Lew ignored him.

"But bad as that was for you guys to have witnessed," Dion inserted smoothly, "the worst thing is that Matt didn't get to pass on what he was supposed to."

"*Tell* me about it!" Lew grumbled. "I had to learn everything from scratch—and half of it I never *did* learn. God knows how many secrets *that* old geezer took to the grave."

Ron snorted contemptuously. "Well, *I* think you did fine at being Master, 'specially when you didn't even know you were a *Listener* until you were seventeen."

An indifferent grimace. "Yeah, well, you can learn a lot in ten years, even when you don't want to."

Dion checked his watch.

Ron glanced automatically toward the antique burled maple fascia of Martha Welch's very modern radio. It picked up every station in the world, courtesy of a couple of Ron's tweaks—metallurgical, not electronic. "Can't wait for midnight to roll around, can you? Time to start collecting more mojo."

Dion grinned wickedly. "We shouldn't have to, not if this morning's batch makes good."

Ron frowned, having difficulty remembering that far back. Eventually he recalled that the Near Future tune in the musical tarot this very uncle had devised and his assorted kinsmen had now adopted when they had need of auguries had been Eric Clapton's "After Midnight." "I did love her, though," he volunteered. "She was always nice to me. And when she wasn't, at least she was honest. You always knew where you stood with her."

"Generally on her shit list," Lew giggled edgily. "I don't suppose she said anything about our apocryphal sister, did she?" he added, to his uncle.

"You mean the one whose unsuspecting offspring you're hoping to foist all this nonsense on?" Dion drawled. " 'Fraid not. I doubt—"

The soft click of a well-oiled lock interrupted him. Ron looked up—they all did—to see the bedroom door ease open. A man stood there: smooth skinned and dark haired like Dion and Ron, between them in apparent age, and with a bit of Ron's Kevin Baconish tilt of nose and angle of chin. Though by no stretch of the imagination fat, Dion's brother, Gilbert, was softer muscled than his very fit kinsmen, and wore a permanently dissolute expression that had probably done him no good during the rape trial thirteen years before. His loose-knit green sweater bagged on him. His face, still pale with prison pallor though he was now on parole, looked tired.

"Ronny, Lew . . . she's asking for you."

The brothers exchanged wary glances and rose as one. Dion made to follow, but Gil shook his head. Dion shrugged and sat back down. Ron heard Gilbert rattling crockery behind him as he stuffed his shirttail into his jeans and followed his brother.

Lit only by thick white candles in dragon-headed sconces Ron had forged for her two Christmases back, Martha Welch's bedroom was even dimmer than the parlor. *Too* dim for light-loving Lew's taste, Ron knew, and definitely too old-fashioned—but *he* thought that was kinda nice. Lew had modernized the rest of Cardalba Hall and stuffed it to the gills with tech, but Martha's second-floor suite had been sacrosanct, an island of antiquity crammed with the unlikely artifacts nearly a century of globe-trotting had accumulated.

And in that vast clutter, the thin, steel-haired, iron-eyed bundle that was the Lady herself was almost lost: a stick of driftwood storm tossed into the froth of snowy bedding.

Ron held his breath as the now-familiar odor reached out to enfold him. It was not the sulfur-sweet sickroom smell of medication and excretion, though; rather, it was the warm, dry scent of old wood long gnawed by termites and opened suddenly to fresh air. There were other odors, too: obscure herbs smoking in braziers in the four corners and some kind of eucalyptus balm that was doing its best to heal bedsores the Luck had finally ceased attending.

"Took you long enough!" The voice that cut through the gloom was strong enough to make Ron stumble on his approach—which made his bad knee twinge and caused him to wish for the ornate silver crutch that often accompanied him when it got cold or damp—or when, as now, he overstressed that troublesome joint. For an instant he expected to see Miss Martha rise from the bed and stalk toward him, her wit and tongue sharper than any weapon she ever could have wielded.

But the tiny gnarled shape did not move, though a dry chuckle noted his misstep, seeming to hang in the thick air like dust before sifting down to the dense Persian rug. "I won't bite," came that voice again. "And death isn't contagious."

Lew found his social equilibrium first and continued on, to claim the single chair beside the headboard, leaving red-faced Ron to choose between bed, floor, his feet, and distance.

"How are . . . ?" Lew began.

"About *not* to be," Martha gave him back tartly. "I figure about five minutes."

"I'm sorry."

"Yeah," Ron echoed, inanely.

"No, you're not," the old lady corrected, her gray-blue eyes fixed on Lew. "And I don't blame you, either. You've done the best you could with a bad situation."

"Thanks," Lew barely managed. "I—"

"Two things," Martha interrupted. "One *I* need to tell you; one *you* need to tell me."

"I—"

"Promise! *Promise* me, Lewis!"

"What?"

"That you'll keep on. That you'll continue being Master—if not for yourself, for the folks up here."

"I've *said* I would," Lew told her softly.

"You've said you would *as long as you could*," Martha replied flatly, "which is not the same thing at all. I've listened to you carefully, and you've never *promised*. God knows I've been around enough Listeners to know an evasion when I hear one."

Lew's face was very white. "I . . . promise."

The old woman's eyes narrowed. "Promise what?"

"I promise . . . that I'll continue to be Master."

"Of *what*?"

"Of . . . Cardalba."

"For how *long*?"

"As long as—"

His great-grandmother's face froze abruptly, as if some unseen force had hijacked whatever moved her muscles and flicked the switch to OFF. She tried to swallow and failed; her breath caught, then turned husky. The air thrummed with Luck—maybe Martha using the last of her fading Strength to summon her grandnephews; maybe Lew doing the same.

"The other thing . . ." Lew prompted.

"Your sister," Martha gasped. "Your *sister* . . ."

"What about her?" Lew demanded, leaning forward. His eyes sparkled so greedily Ron had to look away. "You've never said squat about her. What—"

"Let me finish, boy! You need to know where she is, just in case."

Lew's troubled gaze met Ron's, both full of relief. God knew they'd both been holding out for this tidbit for years.

"She's—"

A coughing fit wracked the old lady. She shuddered, tensed, drew tighter into herself. Ron closed his eyes, took the three deep breaths that triggered the trance that was gateway to the Realm of the Winds, where thoughts and emotions sang like birds, murmured like breezes, or screamed like tornadoes clogged with the damned, and dared a mental probe toward her mind. And found the shields around her thoughts that had always been so indomitable still as strong as ever. He could sense Lew's presence too, assaying the same; and, from farther afield, Dion. But all that seeped through was fear: fear of dying, dread of entering the unknown with a conscience not wholly clear.

A brightening of light, a shift of air, meant the door behind them had opened. Footsteps thudded quickly forward. The smoke swirled and eddied and made knotwork in the air. In the hall outside, a clock chimed.

The cough that followed came from their great-grandmother.

It was a very long cough, too, and segued into a full-blown fit. And the longer it lasted, the more liquid it became. Until, very suddenly, it ended.

Ron did not need to feel her pulse to know that Martha Welch was dead. For there, half in the Realm of the Winds as he still was, one Voice cried out in joyous exultation, and was gone.

Lew stood first, easing aside to let his younger uncle close the old lady's eyes and cross her hands on her breast.

"*Shit!*" Lew mouthed silently, where only Ron could see. Ron nodded.

"What'd she say?" Dion asked sharply. "There at the last?"

Gil shook his head, looking as if he was trying hard not to cry, though Ron suspected it was as much from relief and frustration as actual regret.

"Nothing," Ron gritted, slamming his fist against the bone white coverlet as he rose. "Goddamned *nothing*! She was on the verge of revealing where our sister is, and then—"

"*I* . . . got something," Lew gasped shakily. "Only an image. Nothing really concrete, but maybe a starting point."

"You're a better man than *I* am, then," Ron grumbled. "Best *I* could tell she kept her blessed shields up right to the bitter end."

Dion was already steering them toward the door. "Be that as it may be, boys. If we're gonna go through with what we were talking about, we'd best be at it. Or would you rather wait 'til the coroner leaves?"

Lew's face was white—a mixture of shock, relief, and dread. "I'd rather do it now, in case there're . . . complications."

Gil's expression was troubled as he rose to join them. "Too bad about the sister thing. I know you guys were counting on that."

"Except that even if we found her, it would mean an abdication of responsibility in favor of someone else," Ron muttered from the door. "We'd just be sticking some other poor sod with our dirty laundry—which would still be a no-win scenario, 'cause there's no way we'd not feel guilty."

Lew shot him a sour glare. "Well, like it or not, it *is* our responsibility, or has been—to the people of this county, anyway."

"Who'll now have to get along without anyone more imminent than God to look after them," Dion finished for him.

"Which basically just puts them on a par with the rest of the population—and they *have* had a two-century head start," Gil added, shooing them out and shooting the bolt behind.

"Every bit of which we've discussed before," Lew sighed. "Come on, folks; let's get to it. I'll buzz Gwen and get her to tend to things here. She's been expecting it."

"How're you gonna get along without her?" Ron wondered aloud, glancing at his twin.

"Same way *you've* got along without footholders for years," Lew replied promptly, reaching past Ron's nose to touch a switch and punch a code into the keypad beneath a silver-gilt grille. "Yo, Gwen," he called. "It's, uh . . . happened. Unfortunately, me and the boys have gotta see to some stuff, like, right now. So I'd appreciate it if you could come on up and sit with the body, and, uh, kinda explain things in case the coroner gets here early. It's . . . probably gonna be the last favor I'll ever ask of you."

"What *about* the coroner?" Ron wondered.

"I'll take care of that," Gil volunteered. "You guys go ahead; I'll make the call and meet you in Lew's room. I'll try to arrange a delay or two," he added, with a conspiratorial wink.

Footsteps sounded softly outside, and the door to the upstairs hall opened before any of them touched the knob, revealing the grim round face of a girl of perhaps fifteen, the irony of whose name (Gwen was Welsh for *white*) seemed indelibly stamped on her very African features. She was dressed, with pleasingly appropriate sobriety, in black: black jeans, black sweater, black sneaks.

The girl slipped calmly into the parlor, gave each of the newly bereaved a solemn hug, and proceeded to the bedroom door. "I'll be fine," she informed them quietly. "You guys do what you have to."

And tomorrow you will be free, Ron thought, and led the way outside.

Behind them, the radio clicked on automatically and whispered the first omen of the day into the adjoining tape recorder, which had followed its example. Ron shuddered when he heard it: another tune Clapton had made famous.

"Crossroads."

A song about a man who bargained with the devil.

II
Breaking Up Is Hard To Do

Two minutes later Ron, Lew, and their maternal uncles were sharing space in the yard-square closet to the right of the low-tech fireplace in Lew's very high-tech upstairs bedroom. Or more properly, were rubbing shoulders, chests, hips, and assorted other cramped and misplaced body parts in what was normally a man-high dead space *beneath* the closet, which the careful levering of an oversized onion in the Craftsman-style cornucopia carved into the mantel had caused to appear, displacing the closet upwards as it rose. Once everyone was ensconced, Dion punched the hidden stud that awoke the century-old complex of slides and cables, cogs and counterweights that collectively made the closet descend first into the bones of Cardalba Hall, then into the bowels of the earth itself.

Ron held his breath as the musty darkness enfolded them. Only when the wooden floor thumped to a halt less than a minute later did he exhale again. Dion, who was best situated for such an undertaking, pressed the stud that slid the door open. Ron immediately caught a whiff of cool, moist air, heavy with the scent of damp, raw earth. Lew poked him in the back, and an instant later light flared as Dion flicked his Bic, then set the flame to the simple rag torch stuffed in a rusty, wrought iron sconce at the left of the door. And then Ron was following his uncle to the right: down a narrow, stone-lined corridor that led, through a series of round arches, back to the center of the house, where the terminus was marked by a massive door of rough-sawn oak, which bore, in a neat row across its ironbound surface, four large copper-and-vanadium locks Ron had made himself. There was considerable fumbling in pockets for keys before they all ground open, one key per Welch per lock. As the last corroded tumbler grumbled home (Ron had underestimated the humidity), Lew eased in front of the rest of them, and so was in the lead when they crossed that final threshold.

Once again, Ron held his breath. He had been in the place beyond but twice, once six years ago, come August, when Lew and he had met there alone in order to transfer the Binding Ritual that bound the Masters of Cardalba to the earth of Welch County from Lew, who, at twenty-two, had been Master for over five years already, to himself, who never had—and had not desired it even then.

The second occasion had come a bit over three years later, when Lew had proved as good as his word and resumed the Mastership upon completing a pair of degrees in ornamental horticulture at the University of Georgia. At that time Ron had followed his uncles' examples and formally renounced the Luck, thereby negating any claim to more than minimal use. Since then, the Luck in Welch County had never run more smoothly, more subtly, or with less hint of corruption. As for Ron himself—*he'd* been having a fine old time smithing, casting, and building exotic sports cars at his girlfriend's not-so-quasi castle up on Keycutter Knob. And their near-matching, politically incorrect uncles—well, they'd been serving out their sentences in an un-matched set of Florida "incarceration centers," Dion for embezzlement of a sort; Gilbert, alas, for rape.

Ron hoped this would be the last time he ever saw that room. If plans progressed smoothly tonight, he would get his wish. Holding his breath one final time, he stepped through.

Space bloomed around him as he blinked into the torchlit gloom. A level below the "official" basement, Cardalba Hall's Chamber of Binding was circular and easily twenty yards across, walled and domed with off-white limestone, but with the webwork of ribbed vaulting that supported both composed of hard, gray granite. The walls themselves were featureless and raw; the only illumination from the niche-mounted candles Dion was still igniting; all unusual, but not wildly so. Except, of course, that it was directly beneath a post-Victorian mansion in the wilds of extreme north Georgia.

The floor was an even greater oddity. A stone ledge completely encircled it, four feet wide, with four flights of shallow steps (each marking a cardinal direction) leading down to a surface of the same red clay that enclosed the rest of the foundations. That clay was spotted with mold, too: a suspiciously star-shaped pattern of unsavory fibrous white sprawled precisely in the center. A circular brick-rimmed hole near one edge led to who-knew-what lower depths. Whether tunnel, well, or remnant of Underground Railroad, Ron had never cared to discover.

Nor did he bother to suppress the inevitable shiver when he thought of what they were about. He was among kin, dammit! None here would condemn him for yielding to his doubt.

Lew had seen him, too, and laid an arm across his shoulders to give him a comforting squeeze. "What're *you* scared about, bro? It's *me* that's about to take the plunge."

"Except that it affects us all," Dion inserted, from where he was struggling with the last and most recalcitrant candle. "Don't forget, nobody's ever tried what we're going to—not in *living* memory."

"Let's just *hope* that's not the operative word here," Gil chuckled nervously.

Ron frowned in confusion. "But didn't you guys . . . ?"

Dion shook his head. "Oh, me and old randy-pants here renounced the *Mastership*, all right—just like you did. Very soon after you were born, as it happens. But that was before the fact; we hadn't actually *assumed* it at the time. That may make a difference."

"It did with you," Gil added, peering intently at Ron. "The Land itself rejected us; it apparently thinks *you've* got a right to hang around."

"Probably because *he* served it, at least minimally," Dion concluded. He exhaled loudly and glanced at his nephew expectantly. "Any reason not to get the show on the road?"

Lew shook his curly head—and for an instant, actually looked his age, which was twenty-nine. "Not if you're ready."

Dion nodded in turn. "Okay, then, just follow my example, guys; and do *exactly* what I say. I'll take the north; Gil, you be south; Ronny, you're east for now."

"And I'm west," Lew finished, already padding that way around the rim.

A minute passed while the men found their assigned places, which were marked by uncials rough hewn into the stone

pavement. Ron winked covertly at his twin from the top of
one flight of steps, while Lew, deadly serious, claimed the
head of its opposite. Dion cleared his throat, and Ron was
not surprised to see him begin unbuttoning his shirt. Ron
applied himself to his own buttons, zippers, and laces, continuing to take clues from his kinsmen until he was as bare
as the day he was born—watch and earring included. He
even removed the buckskin medicine bag his long-term lady,
Brandy Wallace, had given him, dropping it atop his jeans
and khaki work shirt. When he straightened from slipping
off his skivvies, he shivered, wondering where any breeze
could possibly come from to chill him this far underground,
January notwithstanding.

Across from him, Lew coughed. His eyes shifted nervously. His body was taut with anticipation.

Ron set his shoulders and watched his gracefully lanky
uncle for some new cue, noting absently that fifty-plus or
no, the man was in damned fine shape: hard, sleek, and
as smooth skinned as Ron himself. Taller, too, if not so
heavy of shoulder and arm; and like all male Listeners,
uncircumcised, scant of body hair, and free of bruise or
scar or blemish. One of the good things about even residual Luck, he supposed. Or at least not a disadvantage. If
only he hadn't trashed his knee *exactly* when the damned
stuff manifested . . .

Dion cleared his throat again, frowned them to attention,
then fixed his gaze on Lew and pointed toward the splatter
of fungus at the heart of the depression in the floor.

Lew took a single pace forward and was on the stairs,
then the naked red earth. He stopped there, dead center, and
lay down on the mold, spread-eagled, head to south: a star
within a star, the very prototype for da Vinci's "Measure of
Man."

Ron couldn't help but recall how different this was from
before. They'd *both* been down there, then. They'd used the
prescribed obsidian knives, and had carved deep, bleeding
gashes into each other's arms and legs, buttocks and backs,
before lying down so the Land could drink its fill. There'd
been more, of course, having to do with the actual transfer-
ence, most of it involving a more intimate bodily fluid; but

Ron didn't like to even *think* about that. And this time . . .

"You, Lewis Owen Welch, have given your blood to the Land," Dion intoned, the mellow voice that was equally good at singing and courtroom oratory booming formally around the chamber. Ron listened attentively. Even the candles ceased flickering, as if they too strained to hear this onetime silver-tongued liar. "You gave your blood—your *substance*—to the Land," Dion repeated. "And the Land tasted of you, found you entire and acceptable, and lent you its ancient Strength in return. But now you would relinquish that Strength, now you would sever that sacred bond—and so the Land must forfeit what it has taken."

Ron shivered again. He hoped Lew was up for whatever followed. Lord knew he doubted *he* could have gone through with it. On the other hand, Lew was getting his fondest wish—freedom forever from the Mastership. Ron already had as much freedom as he could easily orchestrate.

Besides, it was too late to turn back.

"Sit," Dion commanded—whereupon Lew sat up and folded himself into an expectant squat, his legs crossed elegantly beneath him like a particularly beautiful Buddha.

"The Land has tasted of you," Dion continued. "You must, therefore, taste of the Land. Since there is but one thing to consume within your reach, eat all you can. And with each swallow, regain what you have forsaken."

Lew looked confused—probably fatigue plus stress acting on him. No fun at all, Ron conceded, given the way he felt himself. But then his twin's fingers moved from where they'd been folded in his lap and brushed the moldy surface to his right. Some of the gunk came free—Ron could see it like a flouring across his brother's firelit flesh. And then Lew raised it to his nostrils and sniffed. He made a face, closed his eyes—and licked his fingers. Ron saw him shudder, saw his throat constrict as if he were on the verge of vomiting.

Instead, he repeated the gesture, taking a larger sample this time, leaving a raw red wound on the floor where the mold had torn loose.

And again—as Lew slowly cleared an arc around him.

At some point Dion began to sing in an unknown language.

Ron joined in automatically, harmonizing on the monosyllabic bass line, while Gil improvised across the high parts. The room filled up with sound, even as the moldy star in the center of the floor was by slow degrees eroded.

Lew had consumed half of it already—everything in reach before him and to his right. And he looked awful, had to fight to gag down each mouthful, had to pause and gasp between each halting swallow. Ron sympathized. The Road Man had forced him to sample nearly as unsavory a repast ten years before as part of the trial that had resulted in his apprenticeship to that strange wandering tinker. He'd gone solo then, forced to rely on his own resources. But Lew was not being tested now; there was no reason he should endure such torment alone.

Ron promptly closed his eyes, took the requisite three deep breaths, and willed himself into the Realm of the Winds. His elder kinsmen welcomed him there: bright solos against the oddly damped and muted murmurs that were the thoughts and dreams, wishes, fears, and desires of their fellow Welch Countians. He could hear Dion's song here too, but clearer, brighter, and this time with words that were comprehensible, though more on an emotional level than any linguistic or logical one—no way he could have written them down and had them make sense. He could also hear Lew: humming between mouthfuls, but with fear a cold beggar poised on the threshold of his mind. Ron sent himself there; joined with his twin in a bond that was deeper, far, than sex; assured him that he did not have to face his fear alone.

And so was with Lew as he ripped up the last fragment of mold within reach and—finally—gagged it down. This time, however, Ron felt his brother spasm, felt his gorge start to rise, even as his will fought it down and an awful sour taste poured into his mouth. He—they—relented, let it come. And vomited—endlessly. Cramp after cramp wracked his belly, agony burned his throat, and still he heaved, not caring that he fouled his legs and belly and manhood. On and on, and there was nothing else to spit from his stomach, no more to drip from his crossed legs to the earthen floor— and yet the ordeal continued. Lew could no longer taste air, was already fleeing consciousness, when the part of Ron that was not sharing angst with his twin sensed a shift in the song. He took it up. So did Gil. Lew froze in place, then coughed, sputtered—and fell back where he was, as a too-final darkness swept near.

Ron stayed with him, enduring the cold and the panic and the waiting. But now it came to him that as Lew emptied his gut, something less tangible had drained from him as well. Not the Luck, precisely; that came with the blood no matter when or where. But a . . . *focusing* . . . of it, perhaps? Ron could only think of it as being like his bad leg sometimes was: present and complete in all its sensations and abilities—and parts save one—yet too weak to support him unaided.

What remained—at least in Lew—was relief.

"Stand up, Lewis Owen Welch!" Dion cried joyfully, segueing seamlessly from song to speech. "Stand up—and be free!"

Ron opened his eyes—exactly in time to see Lew rise shakily to his feet. He blinked, then squared his shoulders and marched toward the steps. The *eastern* steps: west to east—sunset to sunrise. Death, Ron supposed, to life. He shifted south to accomodate, as Gil likewise moved a quarter-arc to occupy the vacant western post.

And Lew stood in the east. Lewis Owen Welch: sweaty, and firelit, and golden; dead, now, to the Land, and yet in a much more personal way, newly alive.

For more than a minute they remained there, freeing their Voices from the Realm of the Winds, gathering their Luck back into their Selves. And then Dion edged around to the well, drew up a bucket of water, and emptied it across his nephew's filthy body. Gil followed suit, so did Ron. Dion produced a pair of thick white towels.

Lew wiped himself down with one, then knotted the other around his narrow waist. "Thank you all," he whispered, between bouts of residual coughing and chills. "And thanks be to the Land of Welch County for what it has given me. Though I leave it now, I pray I have served it as well as I was able."

No one spoke again until they once more stood in Lew's bedroom.

III
Slip-Slidin' Away

"That'll be fine," Gilbert Welch said to the short, balding man in the dark blue suit—the one whose like-colored Grand Marquis bore on its driver's side door a large but elegant decal that proclaimed it property of the Welch County Coroner's Office.

Ron, who was leaning against the plain wooden rail of the lower of Cardalba Hall's double-decker front porches while he peered between gaps in the neatly trimmed hedges at the goings-on in the drive, couldn't catch more of the man's reply than a nod and a handshake, and didn't feel like using what little Luck he had left to Listen for more particulars. But whatever Gil's excuse for not calling a doctor had been, it had evidently satisfied officialdom, because the man got into the car, cranked it, and waited at idle for the pair of white-clad orderlies to slam the back door of the burgundy Lincoln hearse that served as temporary depository for Miss Martha Welch's earthly portion. That accomplished, and the attendants comfortably ensconced up front, the official proceeded to lead the way down the curving sweep of the private drive. Ron saw the wide bank of taillights flash once, and then the sad little caravan was lost to sight beyond a screen of budding dogwoods. Welch County had had a very warm winter. Ron wondered if they would henceforth be so mild.

He discovered then that his eyes were misting. A glance at Lew beside him likewise showed a bright gleam there. And though Lew still looked tired and drained, he also looked better than Ron had seen him in ages—and in a way that was not a function of clean clothes and a hasty shower. Relief did that to you, he supposed.

"You boys sure you're up for this?" Dion wondered through a yawn, appearing so quietly behind them that Ron started and Lew actually yipped.

"Might as well," Lew replied quickly, knuckling his lids.

"I'm runnin' on pure adrenaline now. I wouldn't sleep anyway, so I'd as soon rock till I drop."

Dion merely shrugged. "Whatever you want's fine with me. 'Course I'll feel *better* the sooner I'm away from here."

Lew nodded sagely. "Yeah . . . I think I can already feel the Land rejecting me. It's like . . . I don't know, a kind of nervous tingle, sort of like the opposite of a cat's purr. Makes you just wanta get away from it."

"Trouble is," Gil inserted, "it gets worse and worse until you take off or go crazy. I won't be able to shake the dust of this place off my shoes soon enough."

"Yeah . . ." Ron chimed in. "I think I can kinda feel it too, and I didn't used to. Nothing major, though." And with that he fell silent, content to let his older, more magically adept kinsmen take charge. He was the stranger here, the delta male. Which was fine. Not fifteen minutes away was a place he was alpha—or alpha *male*, anyway. What Brandy Wallace, who actually owned the locale in question, was, he had no idea. His girlfriend, he supposed. And, in a way, his partner. But not for an instant did she let him forget whose name was on Brandy Hall's deed. Dammit!

Gil's deliberate cough roused Ron from his flirtation with paranoid self-pity—and showed him Dion and Lew already disappearing behind Cardalba Hall's three-car garage. A moment later, they returned, each at the wheel of a vast Econoline cargo van. Gil backed his right up to the steps, then hopped out and opened rear and side doors alike. When he joined them on the porch, he flexed a biceps speculatively. "Four more hours, guys, five max, and this whole bloody charade'll be over."

"Not if we stand here jawing," Lew yawned, as he strode past Ron to lead the way through the front door, down the palm-filled gloom of the formal front hall, and into the bleached-walnut splendor of Cardalba Hall's library.

It took them all of the projected four hours plus a bit, working assembly line–style and with Gwen's help, to strip the floor-to-ceiling shelves that lined that eight-yard-square chamber. But in the end, every book and artifact; every atlas and dictionary; every *National Geographic, Road & Track, Foxfire, Rolling Stone*, and *Architectural Digest*; every bound

Welch County *Witness*, illuminated manuscript, and first edition had been boxed and stashed in a van for transport to Brandy Hall. It required all eight Lew had rented.

Even the vaults stood empty: the twin ones that hid behind the wainscoting to either side of the library mantel, and the under-floor job in Lew's upstairs suite as well.

Their contents were the last to be secured: scrolls and manuscripts, books and boxes, and a single ornate dagger Lew absolutely refused to touch, all too rare, precious, or dangerous to risk outside the clan. Some were deeds and personal papers, but many contained in their vellum and parchment pages virtually all that had been recorded about Listeners, Listening, and the Welches. It was nearing dawn by the time they cycled around, and Ron and Lew packed most of them—rather more hastily than was strictly optimum, to the extent that, dead-on-his-feet, Ron let a pile of priceless volumes slip from his fingers, scattering loose leaves across the floor. He hastily stuffed pages back between covers, and hoped Lew (who was making a pit stop) hadn't heard.

Not that he'd blame his bro for hollering at him; these things were too valuable to undergo such treatment, and here he was flinging them around like cordwood. If he was too tired to respect ancient artistry, he was obviously just *too* tired.

Fortunately, Ron's faux pas comprised the final load. Lew himself carried the *pièce de résistance* of the collection: the small brown volume that had shown him how to construct a lover for Ron out of flowers. More precious, maybe, than anything else on the planet. He flipped through it one final time and passed it to Ron, with the solemn line, "I know it'll be in good hands." And slammed the side door of the remaining van.

Ron did not reply as Lew climbed in and claimed the passenger bucket, leaving him to drive by default. Together they waited for Dion to finish sorting out keys with his brother. Gil would stick around another day to see to the funeral arrangements and attend to the closing of Cardalba Hall. But Dion would spend what little would remain of the night when he and Gwen finished ferrying vans with Ron and Lew up at Brandy Hall, then head back to Florida in Martha's Lincoln

Mark VIII somewhere around sunset that evening. The car would be sold within the week.

As for the remaining family vehicles, Lew's Jag convertible had just been signed over to the weeping Gwen, and the Ford Ranger that had replaced Lew's latest Sable sedan only a month before was already in residence at Brandy Hall. Presumably Gil would head out with the dogs in the gold Continental when he got good and ready.

Meanwhile . . .

Dion appeared at the open window just as Ron was considering the wisdom of dialing up a set of electronic omens. Ron gave him a hasty thumbs-up, and cranked the van.

"Well," Lew sighed, leaning back in his seat, "I guess this is it, man."

"Yeah," Ron yawned, as he navigated the first curve. "So, any idea where to now?"

"Your house, of course."

"Don't let Brandy hear you call it that," Ron chuckled. "But I meant after tonight. Tomorrow."

"Oh," Lew replied absently. "I thought I told you. I'm gonna go look for our sister."

If Ron had not been so tired, he would have argued. Had he had any sense, he would have anyway. In after years he regretted bitterly that he had let it stand at that.

When Ron awoke the following afternoon, Lew was gone. He had left no hint at all of any specific destination. And Ron, to his shame, had never asked him.

PART I

FIND THE COST
OF FREEDOM

Interlude 1

Dream Weaver

Somewhere in the South
New Year's Eve—midnight

Making a woman could only be done once, so he had thought. So he had heard. So he had read, more than once—and committed, at last, to the dark, twisted corridors of memory. But books could be wrong, sometimes; often were, in fact; books as old as *that* one had been, at any rate. Books, alas, could even lie. Books with pages like the petals of dried flowers and as easily seen through. Books with colors like blossoms, whose truth, like those colors, could fade. Books written in the juice of lemons to fool the eye, even as their words beguile the mind with subtler falsity.

And what if I chose to make a man? *he thinks. I never had a father, not as most men do; not truly. What if I took bud and blossom, root and leaf and stem and a drop of my blood and made one from those things to stand by me and tell me true? What then? Would he love me as my mother, once, did love? Or would he leave me to seek one more in tune with his soul? Suppose, too, that in my loneliness I made more than one? What if I made ten, or a score, or ten times ten?*

Or what if I made a brother?

The walls do not answer, those walls that prison his thoughts, those walls that will not let the past by.

Maybe I have made such things before, and do not now remember. Maybe I was another person then. Maybe I should make a memory.

Maybe . . .

A woman is like a song or a sonnet, maybe a poem or a game.

And a man . . .

He awakes, and for a long, long time is Making.

Chapter 1

(I Can't Get No) Satisfaction

Brandy Hall
Thursday, June 6—late afternoon

Making a set of lips was not the simplest task Ron had ever assigned himself—not to the absurdly exacting standards he'd established when he had commenced Project Oracle. The problem didn't lie in difficulty, though; he had any number of equally challenging constructions afoot in his sorcerer's den-cum-tower studio alone—never mind down at the forge. It was just that he was terminally impatient and tired of delays on the *present* endeavor. Shoot, he was on his fourth attempt in five days now, and *still* hadn't managed to produce a pair that both looked right *and* articulated properly—neither of which glitches in anywise affected functionality, only his attitude toward the completed work. And since *he* was the only one who would ever see the ultimate result anyway, he wondered why he bothered. Except that he knew: anything less than his absolute best would have grated on his nerves until he fixed it. Such was the price of perfectionism; such the curse of Welch-clan genius.

Grimacing sourly, he gave a needle-sized file one final pass around the dip in the center of the upper curve, fixed

the offending assembly with a long, critical squint, and set
the tool on the inch-thick slab of marble tabletop he'd been
hunched over for the last five hours. *Maybe* these would do,
he decided, as he pinched the left corner between thumb and
forefinger and saw the apparatus twitch reflexively. Good—
that part was cooking, anyway. He'd give 'em one final
eyeballing, stick those suckers in, and get on to something
less demanding—like, say, the brain.

Yeah, sure!

A flick of fingers flipped the lips over, revealing an array
of hair-fine silver wires, microcams, and tiny pneumatic pis-
tons (pressure activated to duplicate the subtlest nuance of
grin or scowl), all obscured when viewed from the fine
copper-beryllium mesh that formed the public surface. There
they shaped a classic Cupid's bow: nearly the color of human
lips and almost as soft and pliable.

Yeah, maybe these *would* work.

Ron held his breath as he plugged a brace of thread-thin
braided-silver hoses onto hollow chrome-gold pins at either
corner (hoses that disappeared into the gleaming complexity
of larger lines that arabesqued across the back of the table).
Okay . . . and now . . .

Another pause, and he raised the lips with both hands and
pressed them neatly into the darkly gleaming orifice that
comprised the mouth of The Head. The right anchoring
stud clicked home; the left followed. A poke at the corners made it open, revealing teeth that looked like pearl
because they were. The tongue, now safely barricaded, was
wrought of the same copper-alloy mesh as the lips; the surrounding skin, of tiny brazen scales too small for the naked
eye to see.

Somewhere in the chaos of the room behind him, a buried
CD player began Wagner's "Death of Siegfried," its heavy
percussion harmonizing with a distant roll of thunder. Ron
leaned back to contemplate his creation.

It was starting to look like it ought to now: a life-sized
male head and neck composed mainly of brass, but with a
whole metallic menagerie of obscure alloys forming bones
and muscle beneath its gold-toned skin, while even more
unlikely substances detailed eyes and ears and nostrils. And

the brain—best *not* to consider the brain. Not silicon and circuits, but gears and levers; cams, pushrods, and bearings. He could see the front part now—because The Head still lacked the forward skullplate he was beating into shape down at the forge. Eventually he'd give it hair of copper wire, maybe a beard of the same, and then—who knew?

Another prod at the edge of the left-hand orbit replaced the vacant stare with a wink—which reminded him that he needed to trim the carbon-fiber eyelashes if the thing was really going to mirror the model.

Not that he had that precise a record of the prototype, anyway; *mostly* he had one fuzzy Polaroid snapped twelve years before: younger versions of himself and Lew (though neither looked much different now, courtesy of their Listener blood), with the much taller, voluptuously muscled, red-haired fellow he'd only known as the Road Man.

The Road Man . . . the strange, wandering jack-of-all-trades who'd exposed a barely blossoming teenaged talent to the wonders hid alike in mind and metal; who'd shown that same neophyte the secrets of the alloy universe and forever changed the way Ron viewed the world.

Who'd saved his life in more ways than one—and disappeared.

Or maybe not.

Perhaps he'd returned a few years later, in another role, with a different personality, and a fresh new body.

Or maybe that hadn't been him at all who, in the guise of a cocky lumberyard foreman named Van Vannister, had completely transfigured Brandy Hall from the modest protocastle Ron's sweetie, Brandy Wallace, had then been building, into the current sprawling Baroque-Gothic keep, all in one horrible, amazing, magical night. Shoot, the four-story northwest tower, the third level of which housed this studio, hadn't even *existed* before then, never mind the terraces around it—or half the rooms.

As for the mysterious vagabond himself: he was gone now—in the flesh—but his sculpted likeness still lingered at the point of the West Terrace two floors down: cast in bronze, life-sized, and leering—a self-made reminder to Ron to resist complacency.

Sighing, he gave The Head a gentle pat on the brow, slipped off his stool, and padded barefoot across the red Persian rug that made an octagonal mandala in the center of the flagstone floor, angling toward the southwest corner, where a burgundy velvet lounger was flanked by matching pairs of narrow Gothic windows in adjoining walls. A detour to snare a bottle of Guinness from the small refrigerator recessed beneath the southern casements distracted him, however, and instead of settling into his familiar unwinding place, he hopped onto the wide windowsill. Matty Groves emerged from beneath the complex gears and pulleys of what looked like a flight of bats caught in a treadle loom, but was in fact a perpetual motion machine, to paw at a particularly long thread unraveling from the fringe of Ron's cutoffs.

"Scat, cat," he grunted, easing his pet away with a dangling foot, even as he pressed a pair of stone buttons disguised as the hearts of Tudor roses in the carved window frame. The first sent electrical charges through the glass and changed them from colored renditions of Govannon and Wotan, smith-gods of legend, to transparent portals on the present-day sky. The second slid them sideways into the adjoining walls, to admit the heavy, sweet breezes of summer. Ron inhaled appreciatively, grateful to be smelling something besides metal filings and WD-40.

A glance at the sky showed storm clouds massing to the west, and the next breeze was colder against his bare torso, and thick with moisture. Thunder rumbled, as did Wagner. For an instant he felt like Elmer Fudd in "What's Opera, Doc?" calling down tempests from his rocky pinnacle. Except that what he gazed upon was less fanciful than a cartoon landscape, but only barely.

To the right, a forested ridge thick with oak and hickory slumped down to the lake invisible to the north behind him, the former alive with deer and squirrels drawn to the old-growth timber there, the latter amply provided with trout and bream—all meat for Brandy Hall's table. A swimming hole lurked there, too—a shallow finger of lake: sheltered, cool, and still.

The edifice itself clumped to the left, its basic form—a Byzantine basilica dumped in the middle of a crenellated

Roman villa—still discernible behind the wilder spires and
buttresses Vannister had conjured up around it from the stone
of the outthrust granite knoll on which it stood.

And straight before it stretched the low, embattled prow
of the South Terrace, bisected asymmetrically by the front
stairs. Beyond them a flagstone pavement did duty as parking
lot and forecourt, with the greater mass of Keycutter Knob
rising sharply behind to Clanton Gap and the county line,
while the quarter-mile-long driveway snaked in to the right.

Along the fringe of the forest, there, where Brandy had
once parked her trailer, a covey of canvas pavilions now
gave the place a perpetual carnival air, housing shops and
studios for the various artisans and craftspeople to whom
his lady gave haven. But not *free* haven, for they exchanged
bed and board for goods and services, with each obliged
to embellish some part of Brandy Hall while pursuing his
or her personal fantasies. Ron could see one now: Sharon
Frizzelle, intent at her potter's wheel, auburn hair bound
back as she bent her small frame in concentration. Only two
other guests were in residence at the moment: John Marx
and Perry Steinway, both mosaicists, both plying their trade
in the foyer.

As for the east side of the courtyard . . . *that* was Ron's
domain. For there, beneath a more permanent shelter, stood
his forge for the shaping of metal into larger works, and by
more dangerous means, than the tower room afforded. And
adjoining it stretched the eight-door sprawl of the garage,
set into the mountainside and resembling thereby a series
of caves, though instead of dragons, it presently housed the
guests' vehicles, as well as Brandy's big Ford pickup, Ron's
inevitable Thunderbird, and his half of the almost-matched
set of Centauris he was constantly updating. A third Centauri
crouched half-completed between the garage and the forge: a
glimmering arrow of raw aluminum.

Finally, to the *extreme* left, blocked by Brandy Hall's
clerestory level, a series of stone terraces made a natural
amphitheater, beneath the lowermost of which a circuitous
trail described a zigzag path to a second lakeside cove.

Not a bad way to live, Ron conceded, taking a very long
swig—a bit ostentatious, but not shabby.

The wind shifted again, and this time it flipped a splatter of rain into his face. He sniffed and withdrew into the room, replacing the odor of oak, pine, and ozone with the spicy scent of the odd white lilies that nodded from brass urns in the corners. Their pollen made him high sometimes—and horny a lot more frequently (not that either he or Brandy ever complained). But they also gave him flashes of inspiration he could not account for otherwise.

He'd *need* a lot of that, too—if The Head was ever to fill the role for which it was fashioned.

Sighing again, Ron eased off his perch and knelt below the window closest to the room's single door. The walls there bore bas-relief interlace on limestone panels, one of which concealed the refrigerator. But a second, a yard to the left, shielded something far more precious. Using his index finger, he traced three nonsequential curves of the pattern there. A soft click meant an electronic lock had activated. A second set of gestures, a second click, and the panel slid aside to reveal a wide, shallow vault crammed to the edges with assorted ancient tomes. He chose the topmost— a warped, vellum-bound volume he'd taken to calling *The Book of the Head* for no better reason than that that was what it was about—and rose, pausing for a sneeze as his nostrils filled with dust and the odor of aged leather. And pollen, of course, which the ever-more-frisky breezes were stirring up alarmingly. His eyes watered, and he blinked, looked around for a rag with which to wipe them, and saw other eyes appraising him from the brazen head across the room. He glared at it. "*Do* you mind?" he muttered, as he returned to the workstation to snare a bandanna, with which he scoured away the tears. "Asshole," he added for no reason beyond pure cussedness, wishing it did not look so human staring back at him with that unfinished face. Finally, he could take no more, and reached to the corners of the orbits and pushed. The lids obligingly slid closed. Carbon-fiber lashes brushed brazen cheeks. He wondered if the gold-rimmed pupils were dilating under there like they were supposed to.

He also wondered if Roger Bacon had wondered the same thing when he'd used the very same book that weighted

Ron's hand to construct *his* head back in the thirteenth century.

And wondered, more to the point, if Bacon had possessed the same motivation.

Probably not, he decided, as he settled into his chair, given that it was bloody unlikely that the famous medieval friar, however talented, had been a Listener. Ron, as usual, was wishing *he* wasn't, as he found his place, took three deep (and rather hypocritical) breaths, stared at the topmost diagram on the page—and began.

Not reading, though, not in the sense most people understood it. Few folks would even have recognized the alphabet, never mind the words it articulated. And the intricate diagrams that crammed most of the thick, wavy pages would have made little more sense, though a truly astute scholar of the obscure might have recognized certain symbols from astrology or alchemy. Ron hadn't understood them either—the first time he'd glanced through. And *still* didn't, if he simply scanned one casually. But when he let himself slide into the Realm of the Winds *and* breathed the pollen *and* kept his eyes open . . . somehow it all came clear.

—To his *right* brain, which was where most of his patently unnatural genius for smithcraft lay. He could no more have articulated the underlying principles that shaped The Head than the man in the moon; he simply *knew*. He wondered idly, how whoever had composed this tome lo those many hundreds (thousands?) of years ago had managed it. Writing—explaining—required a right-brain/left-brain interface. But how could the left brain—the rational portion—possibly distill into mere language the subtlety of the relationships expressed in these complex diagrams?

As best Ron could describe them, they were like carpet pages from the ancient Irish holy books—save in three dimensions, each page a different layer, a separate cross section, a unique aspect that, could he ever understand them completely, might someday render up a brain that could accomplish what he sought.

But he dared not let himself ponder applications now. Rather, he relaxed as much as he could and let his eye ride one lazy curl of red ink across a page, absently noting each intersection in order, whether it crossed yellow or dived beneath; how many times it looped around green before curving on to blue . . .

He almost had it: the next level . . .

Except that it was continued on the following page. His eyes were still slightly out of focus as he turned the heavy sheet.

"*Huh?*" he gasped out loud. For what he found there made no sense at all.

He blinked back to the edge of normal consciousness and looked again. Yeah, he was right. Even his regular senses told him this was not the next logical page. And a closer check confirmed it; a whole sheet of diagrams had gone AWOL.

And he bet he knew when, too! The missing page almost had to be one of those that had escaped their bindings and gone frisking across the floor when he'd dumped that pile of books the night they'd stripped the library at Cardalba Hall.

But what had he *done* with the blessed thing?

Well, as best he recalled, he'd stuffed the whole lot of them back into what he had assumed to be their rightful sources. Only he'd obviously been wrong at least once.

Unless . . .

But no. A thorough check of the rest of the book showed nothing. Which he'd expected, given how much time he'd spent prowling through it since he'd begun Project Oracle early last summer. Odd that he hadn't missed that page before now, though. Or maybe not, given how similar some of the brain diagrams were.

"Argggghhh!" he growled to Matty Groves, who merely looked at him complacently—which only skewed his rapidly rising frustration in the direction of actual anger.

It wasn't as if this was a *minor* setback, after all. If he didn't find the missing page, he'd be unable to complete The Head's brain. And if *that* happened, he might as well not have started—which meant he'd have wasted a whole year of his life. He'd have a trifle more metallurgical experience and an interesting, if useless, toy—nothing more.

"Argggghhh!" he said again, as he returned to the vault and wearily continued his search there.

"Arrggghhh!" he repeated a third time fifteen minutes later, this time with far more force, when it became obvious that the delinquent document was not inclined to be found. "This is a real bitch, ain't it, Matty?" he added, as he rose and once more (though more sullenly) padded toward his chair.

It was times like this, when he was wired and frustrated and out of balance, that he needed someone to blow off steam to. Brandy wouldn't do (even assuming she was present, which she wasn't, courtesy of an impending Chamber of Commerce meeting—what else was new?). Specifically, though he hated to admit it, it was times like this he needed Lew.

God, how Ron missed him! That brother he'd wanted unaware for seventeen years, the one he'd shared a normal adolescence with for a brief few months and had finally lost, at least in part, when Lew assumed the Mastership. And then had to give up all over again when his twin embarked on his so-far inconclusive quest for their elusive sister.

Speaking of which, it was just about time . . .

Ron took a sip of Guinness and grimaced, then set the bottle down and evicted Matty from the back of the lounger. That accomplished, he reclaimed his seat, closed his eyes, and relaxed, letting every muscle and tendon go slack— more so than he'd done while reading. He hated this ritual, as he hated the reason for it; but the alternative was ignorance and apprehension, where this, at least, admitted a modicum of security and hope.

Taking three deep breaths, Ron triggered the trance and Jumped.

Not merely into altered consciousness, as he had done while reading, but fully into the Realm of the Winds—that place where thoughts dispersed when they had served their original function, a place of Voices that were not voices, of emotions tangible as sound.

He Listened there for a moment: centering, sorting the nearer Voices first, so as to establish a base—and found nothing beyond the ordinary. Mostly just Sharon, because she was most mentally active at present. He tried not to eavesdrop, but couldn't help noting that she was recalling rather fondly how he'd looked with his shirt off when they'd met outside the kitchen at breakfast that morning. The other two guests, John and Perry, were indulging in a late-afternoon nap in the Celtic bedroom—legacy, probably, of a hard night's partying. Perry was starting to stir into wakefulness; John was simply snoring. Not for long, though; it was past five o'clock, which meant they'd be rising momentarily to adjourn to the kitchen to whip up dinner, which they always did to thunderous heavy metal.

All of which was business as usual. Ron tuned them all out as soon as he identified them; went further, caught the town—much more faintly than Lew would have done. And *far* more faintly than Lew with the amplification of a footholder.

Nothing new there either; all the Voices were familiar. Fleetingly, he sought out Brandy, found her not unexpectedly sharing a croissant and a cup of coffee with her buddy Weedge at the Cordova Dunkin' Donuts prior to the meeting.

Further, then, to what he thought of as the fringe of the Winds, though in fact it was only the range beyond which his Strength would not carry him, save to his closest kin.

He waited there, no longer searching *for* Voices, but Shouting his own with all the Strength he could muster. The intent was to provide a beacon, a means by which Lew, who was more adept at such affairs, might locate him. Unfortunately, Lew sometimes did not respond—not often, but occasionally. Other times—like last fall and winter, when his twin had been in Europe (Ron thought, for Lew was obsessively secretive about such things), and thus far out of range—there'd been letters, untraceable phone calls, and secondhand reports via the network of Masters.

Which bugged the bejesus out of Ron. It was *one* thing, dammit, to want to be on one's own, pursuing some noble quest wherever it might lead; it was quite another to be so furtive and sneaky about the process that it put one's sanity at question. All Ron knew—all Lew would tell him besides that he was alive and healthy (and how *else* would a Listener be?)—was that he was narrowing the search for their missing sib.

Last week's report had been optimistic but inconclusive. (Again, what else was new?)

Tonight . . . ? Anybody's guess.

And then there was no more time for speculation, for someone had called his Name.

Ron?

Lew?

Metal Man?

Flower Boy?

I'm getting sick of this, you know, Ron replied, unable to dissemble, irritated as he was, and with his Self necessarily laid bare by this form of communication.

Of what?

Of having to play this stupid game! Of us having to use bloody code names to identify each other 'cause you're so fucking afraid I might accidentally look down deep and find out where you are that you even close off the part of your Voice that identifies you as You!

You're just pissed 'cause you can't do the same. (Lew sounded calm—he always did.)

Bullshit!

We've been over this before, Ronny.

And we'll be over it again, too—if you don't cut it out and start leveling with me! Seventeen months is long enough for anyone to get his act together.

I don't trust you not to interfere.

Wisely!

You don't understand.

Bullshit!

A pause. *I don't have time for this now, bro.*

The hell you don't!

No, really. Listen, guy . . . I've found her! Our long-lost sis! I—

You're kidding!

I can't kid like this, remember? Voices can't lie.

As closed off as you are? I'm not so sure—but go on.

Another pause. *Okay, but listen close, 'cause this is exactly as much as I'm going to say until I know what's going on. I . . . got hold of her on the phone yesterday. We're supposed to do dinner tonight. In fact, I'm waiting for her now.*

And of course you won't tell me where.

Of course not. I wouldn't have checked in at all, until it was all over, except that I knew you'd go ballistic if I didn't get in touch exactly *on schedule.*

I resent that!

It's true, though.

Ron paused to reorder his emotions. *So . . . what's she like?*

I'll know in a little while, won't I? She was very careful over the phone.

Does she know you're her—

—her brother? I haven't told her, if that's what you mean. If she's found out any other way, it's more than I know. Like I said, we're supposed to be getting together for dinner, and— Oops, there she is now, kid—gotta split.

Abruptly Lew simply wasn't there. Their link was as lifeless as a phone line gone dead.

Lew! Ron cried, in exasperation. Then, *Fuck you too!*

No one Heard but the Winds.

An instant later, he blinked into the unsteady light of his tower room.

For maybe fifteen minutes he tried to work, fitting gears, tracing circuits, running a set of calculations that converted the obscure units of measure *The Book of The Head* used into more comprehensible metrics.

And for another quarter hour, he tried to decide what still bugged him about the lips.

He was right on the verge of smashing them into metallic pulp, and had actually popped them out with that in mind, when Matty chose that moment to sharpen his claws on Ron's leg—which meant he'd waited far too long to go out.

"Sonofabitch-catsplayingtrumpetsinjail!" Ron shrieked. He dropped the fragile construction onto the unyielding marble, yanked the cat free with his right hand (it could scarcely do more damage), and strode for the thick slab of ironbound petrified wood that comprised the door, half a mind to boot that most ancient of feline friends into neighboring Union County.

Instead, he set his pet gently on the flagstones and paused to type the security code into the lock—whereupon the door opened, moving without the slightest binding or squeak.

Matty immediately darted through. And, on sudden impulse, Ron decided to follow.

"We'll catch *you* later," he called over his shoulder to the gaping Head, his sole concession to maintaining appearances for the outside world being to run a hand through his spiky dark mane and slip on the first T-shirt he found from the pile on the chair by the door, where he tended to discard them upon entering. He didn't see his sneakers, though, and didn't feel like looking for them. It was a hotter-than-usual summer anyway, and the stretches of stone floor felt pleasantly cool against his naked soles.

Sparing one final glance at the studio, he stepped into the narrow landing beyond, let the door close behind him, and locked it with the digital code *and* with the gold key he always wore around his throat as well. Turning left, he limped down the narrow flight of stairs that angled around the inside of the tower. The roof-level landing he bypassed, only halting at a larger one at the foot, where one door led onto the West Terrace, a second (to the right) gave onto Brandy's studio, and a third, more ornate one, stood cracked to the immediate left—which he took.

It opened onto a short, arcaded corridor that, in turn, passed between the library door on the left and the vast double door into the great hall on the right.

He turned right. Again massive portals moved easily.

Even barefoot, his steps sounded loud in the unaccustomed emptiness of the great hall—Brandy's three guests were hardly enough to fill its eighty feet of Gothic arches and side arcades with talk and laughter, music and witty converse. Eventually he made his way to the vaulted entry foyer, where John and Perry were rendering the First Battle of Magh Tuireadh in mosaic along the plastered wall—when they weren't skinny-dipping, or (to judge by the Megadeth that abruptly thundered from the kitchen) cooking.

As if summoned by that thought, John stuck his sweaty blond head around a corner as Ron passed, bringing with him a distinct odor of garlic. "What's up?" he yawned innocently, wooden spoon in hand.

"Not a lot," Ron growled without pausing. "Uh, was there any mail?"

Gothic cloisters: British probably or, at minimum, part of the empire. Lew caught the hesitation before the last name and wondered if she were dissembling. Almost he dared a mental probe in her direction, then reconsidered. If she was what he thought she was, she'd notice immediately, even if she didn't know the truth about herself.

"And how *does* my voice look?" the woman continued, her smile widening into a grin.

"Small and round, though I know that's not how you described yourself . . . and much better than I look standing here like a fool," Lew laughed nervously. "Uh, have a seat. Can I get you a drink?"

"No thank you," the woman said, as Lew helped her into the chair across the round, linen-draped table from his own. "I'm very particular about what I drink," she added apologetically. "Most alcohol upsets my stomach."

"A Coke then? Perrier? You name it."

"I have my own," Jane replied softly. "In fact, if you'd like some . . . ?"

"Sure."

Lew watched curiously as the woman reached for her purse, taking advantage of the interlude to give her a more thorough once-over. Well, she certainly fit the capsule description she'd given over the phone close enough, though she hadn't added that she was beautiful. But of course she wouldn't have. And certainly not that she would be the most beautiful woman he had ever seen. She was older than he, he knew, but not obviously so; the disparity manifested mostly in a greater degree of poise—though he supposed that could be due as much to British reserve as to age. More to the point, though, she was tall—at least as tall as he, and perfectly fit: her flesh sleek and firm as Luck was like to make it. Her hair was nearly as fair as his own, too, though with a touch more red in the curly, shoulder-long locks. And her eyes were a mysterious blue—he thought, for he had glimpsed them but briefly. She was simply but expensively dressed in a plain knee-length black dress, scoop necked, sleeveless, and linen. The overall effect was cool elegance. Lew, by contrast, felt juvenile and underclad, though he was wearing a blue silk shirt, white slacks, and a white suede sport coat. Perhaps he should have added a tie.

The woman—Jane, Lew had to start thinking of her—looked up from her rummaging and produced a small silver flask. Lew heard the swish of liquid, judged it almost full. He signaled the waiter, signed for two empty glasses.

Jane watched him, her eyes full of mysterious twinklings. Lew felt like Merlin: Merlin beguiled by Nimue. Thirty seconds into their meeting now, and already he was falling under his sister's spell. Obviously the Welch-clan charisma was hereditary.

The waiter brought two empty snifters, removed the earthenware mint julep mug Lew had been sipping from, and filled their water glasses.

"Is this okay for dinner?" Lew asked. "If you'd like to go someplace else . . . ?"

"This will be fine," Jane replied softly, as she unscrewed the flask's cap and poured an inch of some dark liquid into both snifters. Lew caught a whiff of something crisp and nutty, rather like Amaretto or Frangelica, but with a sharp earthy edge that seemed hauntingly familiar, though he couldn't place it.

"You won't recognize it," Jane said, probably observing his puzzled expression. "It's the local poison where I come from—I don't think it even has a name."

"Quaff, oh quaff, the kind nepenthe," Lew chuckled, choosing the snifter on the right.

"And forget the lost Lenore," Jane finished with a laugh of her own.

"Poe?"

"Poe."

"To Poe."

"To Mr. Edgar Allan Poe."

Glass clinked, Lew took a sip. It tasted like it smelled: warm and nutty, but with the barest bit of bitter undertaste. It was strong, too, for the fumes went right to his sinuses, in the manner of Irish Mist.

"Whew!" he breathed. "That's *good*!"

"I hoped you'd like it."

"Do you always try to get strangers drunk the minute you meet them?"

Jane frowned, and for a moment Lew thought he had said the wrong thing—courtesy, no doubt, of the fact that he hadn't recovered full command of his faculties after severing the link with Ronny so abruptly. But then her brow smoothed, and she seemed to relax visibly. "It's odd," she said slowly, "but it's hard to think of you as a stranger. It's as if . . . as if I've known you all my life."

"But that's impossible," Lew replied. He took another sip of cordial.

"It happens sometimes. Karma, or fate, or something."

"Past lives?"

"Perhaps."

Silence, then, as Lew wondered whether to proceed with small talk while he assessed his sister, or to proceed more directly to the point of this encounter. Not to revelation, he hastened to add—no way he'd lay all that stuff about Luck and Listening and Mastership on a mind that was unprepared for it, even if it might explain some things that had to be bothering his sister already. Like, for instance, a certain degree of telepathy that would manifest in her whether she knew what she was or not.

No, the thing to do was to take it slow. Feel her out, then enlighten her *very* gradually.

Another sip—they both took one—and then Jane broke the silence.

"You said on the phone that you knew something about my mother?"

Lew nodded. "I didn't want to go into it then because . . . it's so impersonal over the phone. It's . . . bad news, Jane. And bad news should not be borne alone."

Jane regarded him steadily, but Lew noted that her jaw was tense. He shielded, lest he either broadcast too much or suffer some backlash from what he was about to say.

"She's dead," Jane said unexpectedly, sparing Lew the trouble of proceeding.

"She is."

"How? And how long ago."

"A long time ago," Lew replied sadly. "Over twelve years."

"Twelve *years*?" Jane looked incredulous.

Lew nodded, took a sip to calm himself for what he knew would follow. "Twelve years. I'm sorry it took so long, but I didn't even know she had a daughter when it happened, and then it seemed like such an impossible task to try to track you down."

"But how did you find out about me? You live in America, I in Britain—until recently."

Lew shrugged, drank again. "My great-grandmother more or less raised me. She . . . knew your mother. She—your mom—lived . . . in the same place I grew up. And like I said, I knew her, but not that she had a daughter—not until I was seventeen. But then, when my great-grandmother died, she . . . I think she wanted me to find you. All I know is that her last words were about you. She tried to tell me where you were, but died before she could. I got only a hint— barely enough to go on."

"When was this?"

"A year ago last January."

"You've been looking for a total stranger for over a year?"

Lew shrugged, took another sip. (Damn, but that stuff was good!) "I had nothing better to do. I've had a pretty restricted existence. It gave me something to do with my . . . uh, with my money. Gave me a focus, I guess."

Jane reached out to take his hand impulsively. Only then did Lew realize they hadn't touched before. The brush of flesh was electric: instant recognition among Listeners. Lew wondered if she'd noticed.

Perhaps she had, for she drew back her hand reflexively. "Sorry. But it's like I said: I feel as if I know you."

"No problem."

"Thanks . . . for taking so much trouble on my account."

"Like I said, it was no problem—besides, it looks as though we'll at least get a pleasant friendship out of it. Or if nothing else, good company over dinner."

"Let's hope."

Lew scanned the room for the waiter, motioned for menus. "How did she die?"

Lew cleared his throat. "It was a stroke," he said flatly, repeating at last the words he had rehearsed for so long. It hadn't been, of course, but the symptoms were the same. In reality, his cousin Anson had launched a psychic attack at his and Ron's mother. She had resisted as best she could. Eventually Ron had come to her aid and inadvertently linked minds with her. Unfortunately, she had been unprepared, and the resulting psychic overload had burned out most of her mind. The effect was the same as a stroke, only the cause was different. The medical report had said stroke; therefore, it was.

Jane looked concerned. "But wasn't she awfully young for that?"

"Sometimes it happens."

"So how did you find me?"

Lew hesitated, wondering how much to tell how fast. "I had a scrap of description based on a couple of things my great-grandmother mentioned in passing. And like I said, I had a ballpark location. A place-last-seen, as it were. After that . . . well, I basically followed my instinct. I went to the most likely place I could get from the hints I'd got, and once there I started asking around."

"About what?"

"About women of a certain age with uncertain pasts."

"Uncertain?"

Lew felt his face coloring. "Well, uh, since the hints I got were from Britain, but your mother lived in America and you obviously hadn't grown up around her, I figured you had to have been adopted—I mean seeing as how . . . as how . . ."

"I was a bastard? Yes, I know. That word hasn't had any power over me in years."

"I'm glad. You gave me quite a runaround," Lew added. "I almost caught up with you in Britain, but then you came back to the states and I had to start all over. We'd have had this meeting six months ago otherwise."

"I'm sorry. I thought it was time I saw the land of my ancestors."

Lew chuckled. "That's funny—seeing how most Americans regard England as the mother country."

Jane did not reply, intent as she was on refilling their snifters. The waiter brought menus, but neither of them looked at them. Ron drank more cordial. He could feel the soft edge

of a buzz coming on, the ghost of a headache. He'd have to
be careful now, not to say too much.

"Tell me about her," Jane said finally, her mouth tight.

"Not much to tell."

"But I want to know!"

"And you've a right to," Lew agreed. "But . . . but maybe
it would be better if you told me what *you* know, and I filled
in the gaps."

"Not now," Jane sighed at last. "This is all very sudden. I
need time to think. Perhaps . . . perhaps tomorrow."

"Tomorrow?" Lew was taken aback by the sudden shift in
priorities.

Jane's face hardened with decision. "Tomorrow. My
place."

"Your . . . house?" Lew asked carefully. "I've never heard
where you lived."

Jane shook her head. "I live in the country—in Alabama,
in fact—but I keep an apartment here in case I need to stay
over: shopping, partying late, that kind of thing. New Orleans
is the most European of American cities," she added. "I feel
less homesick here—but I can't bear the climate for more
than a day or two."

"Thus the place in the country."

A nod. "I'll probably return home the day after tomorrow,
though—I don't like to be away from home for more than a
day or a two at a time."

"I can understand that."

Jane regarded Lew levelly. "Yes, somehow I think you
can."

"Tomorrow then?"

"Yes . . . I think so. And now, if you don't mind . . . I think
I should be going." She was rising even as she spoke.

"But what about dinner?"

Jane looked exceedingly unhappy. "I'm sorry . . . Lew, but
it's a bit early for me, and . . . well, I seem to have lost my
appetite. It's stress, I think. I thought I could handle what
you told me . . . especially as much time as I've had to
prepare. But . . . well, it's a bit more overwhelming than I
expected."

"I understand."

"I hope so. I hate to disappoint . . . friends."

"You sure you're okay? Can I call you a cab?"

Jane shook her head, then reached into her purse and produced a thick, white business card. "Here's the address. I'll look forward to it . . . and so will Cathryn."

"Cathryn?"

"My daughter."

"Ah yes," Lew sighed, as he left Jane at the hotel's revolving door. "Your daughter."

Only when he returned to his table did Lew notice that his sister had left her flask of liquor. He shook it experimentally. "What the hell," he murmured—and drained it.

Chapter 2

Lookin' Out My Back Door

Brandy Hall
Late afternoon

In spite of the time he'd spent contending with cantankerous constructions, missing manuscripts, and secretive siblings, it was still daylight when Ron stepped out onto Brandy Hall's front arcade—and would be for several more hours. And by some miracle, the rains that had seemed so imminent mere minutes before had rolled off to the north. Which was both good, because *he* wouldn't have his impromptu constitutional damped out. And bad, because now they'd be bound to deluge the town—right in the middle of Brandy's Chamber of Commerce meeting, the way *his* luck had been running lately. Which meant he'd get blamed for it, like he did (surreptitiously, off-the-record, and behind closed doors) for every *other* inconvenience, however minor, that emerged to plague the now-Masterless county.

Still, it was hard to fret about pointing fingers and troublesome twins on an afternoon such as this. True, it was pushing 6:00 P.M., but the sun yet rode many a handspan up a sky of such perfect blue it looked airbrushed. And where its beams struck the faces of the mountains to his left, the trees stuck

out in stark light and shadow: a green brighter than green,
a black deeper than black. Only to the west, where the rays
had already fled, was there softness and shade: places where
tendrils of evening mist were even now rising within a few
secluded hollows.

Only then did Ron realize that he'd spent the last ten hours
in the tower. Shoot, he'd made a beeline for the stairs as
soon as Brandy had split that morning, had snacked out of
the fridge up there all day, and had been there ever since,
only emerging at the urgings of Matty's bladder. Meanwhile
a perfectly good day had almost escaped him—and he could
not afford to waste good days. A walk was therefore called
for: time in the wide world to clear his head, ponder Lew's
revelations, and shake the cobwebs free.

Squaring his shoulders, he made his way around the West
Terrace, down a flight of crenellated stairs that hugged the
lower curve of the wall, and thence across the bare rock
on that side, aiming toward the well-worn path to the cove
where he and Brandy had first made love. The route had been
secret then: soft earth, moss, and leaves—scarcely more than
a deer trail. Now it was paved with flagstones laid by one of
last summer's guests, who'd been a stonemason. Ron wasn't
sure he liked that: how one more fragment of the wild had
by degrees been civilized.

Still, there was much to appreciate: laurel and rhododen-
dron along the margin, wildflowers everywhere, and the
overhanging branches of oaks and hickories that made the
journey a trek through coolness, a refuge in the hottest part
of the day.

He was halfway there before he knew it, on the steepest
stretch. And suddenly stepped down too hard, rousing a twinge
from his suspect knee. Briefly, he wished he'd brought the
crutch. But the path had leveled out by the time he'd finished
arguing priorities with himself, and a short while later he was
in sight of the leafy archway that marked both terminus of the
trail and the boundary of the cove.

Lord, but it was great having such a wonderful place to
hang out in! Bitch though he might about trivia, he was a
lucky man. Grinning unconsciously, he limped out into the
full light, squinting around at the flat shelves of yellow rock

that sloped down to a shallow finger of lake in which were mirrored perfectly both sky and the mountains to the north. Heat smacked up at him from the barren stones, legacy of a long-day's baking. A fish jumped, shattering the water's glassy surface into diamond glitter. Ron realized then that he hadn't bathed yet that day and almost dropped his drawers on the spot—God knew skinny-dipping was practically the national sport at Brandy Hall. —Except that he'd brought no soap, and was wired in a way that was better addressed by a warm bath than a cool soak. Besides, maybe he could coax Brandy down for a catch-up session later. Maybe for a session of quite another kind. He'd bring the lilies.

Or maybe not. He hadn't been this way in a day or two, and had just noticed something that troubled him.

Across the lake—a couple of hundred yards—another mountain reared: one of the few thereabouts that was neither property of the forest service *nor* Brandy Wallace. A small subdivision had been built there during the spring, constructed on spec by Atlantans he hadn't bothered to Luck away. Ron had watched with wary interest as walls and roofs had risen during the preceding months. None had been sold, much less occupied. Or hadn't the last time he'd checked.

Now, though, the nearest—the one with the A-frame center, stone foundations, and deck jutting toward Brandy Hall like an accusing finger—showed a flurry of activity. People were everywhere, and a pair of large Ryder trucks were drawn up among the pines behind it. Ron scowled. They'd been hermits a long time—neighborless, anyway. He wasn't sure he was ready for intruders now, even if they *were* across the water—especially since among the builder's last acts, seemingly, had been the felling of a series of scraggly pines that had screened the back deck of that particular house from the lake. Which meant, unfortunately, that, though probably a quarter mile away, it still had a view of the cove.

On the other hand, they'd been here first. The new folks would just have to get used to *them*.

A weary sigh, and Ron settled against the well-shaded trunk of a massive oak right at the fringe of the shelf. Maybe he'd veg here for a while, doze a bit, and see if serendipity solved some of his problems for him.

He had just let his eyes slit closed, barely begun to tune
into a more focused awareness—of the feel of the earth
beneath his buttocks, the bark behind his back; of the brush of
the wind, the odors that rode the air, and the sounds that whispered in it—when he became aware of a subtle anomaly.

He opened his eyes, but did not move.

Something had, though: to the left, where the cold, narrow
creek that formed the western property line tumbled down a
steep defile to empty into the lake. It was dark there, away
from the sun; and his eyes took a moment to adjust.

It was a boy, maybe fifteen or sixteen, dressed in jeans,
sneakers, and a black T-shirt, and with something large
encumbering his back. Doubtless the lad was attached to the
new place across the way; and, if Ron knew anything about
male adolescents, was probably on his first round of explo-
ration. Almost *certainly* was, he amended, recalling how, not
that long ago, he had known every cypress and palmetto in
the swamps near his foster family's home in Florida; and
later, how he and Lew had tramped the woods and fields
around Cardalba Hall until he doubted there was a yard of
ground they had not traversed, a tree they had not camped
beneath or climbed.

This boy was doing the same, and apparently playing some
game with himself in the bargain. For in spite of the oversized
backpack Ron could now see he was lugging, he was making
every effort to move silently as he wove his way in and out
among the trees, pausing frequently to look around. He was
doing a good job of it, too; given that Ron had yet to hear a
single twig snap or leaf crackle beneath the boy's sneakers.
The overall effect was of poise, as if the kid had excellent
control of his body.

Ron wondered if the lad had spotted him yet, and, on a
whim, eased around behind the tree so he could continue his
surveillance unmarked.

The boy, intent on something at the lake, missed Ron's
movement, and then came full into the light, maybe forty
yards to the left. He was smaller than he'd first looked, Ron
noted: five-five or six, and compact of build. Sunlight glinted
off wire-framed glasses as he turned, scowled thoughtfully,
and finally marched straight toward Ron's hiding place, only

halting at the fringe of the forest thirty feet away. There, he unslung the backpack and folded himself neatly down, with his back propped against a convenient oak. That accomplished, he rummaged around in the pack for a moment and finally brought out a sketchpad and a plastic bag, from which he produced a pencil.

He stared across the lake for easily a minute, then shifted his position so that he could gaze east. And only then did Ron realize that he'd chosen the exact spot on the whole rock shelf where Brandy Hall first became visible above the trees.

For a long time the boy simply sat sketching: hand moving quickly, eyes intent on his artistry, dark brows drawn tight above a short, rather pointed nose. And all that while, Ron watched, intrigued, as if the boy's presence had awakened *his* childish instincts and set him to playing a game of his own. The lad thought he was unobserved, huh? Had been brushing up on his stealthiness? Well, Ron was onto him! Before he was aware of it, he was grinning.

Impulsively, he stood, rising as quietly as he could, hoping to prolong the undeclared contest as long as possible. Slowly he eased around the trunk, placing his feet with precision, careful even of his breathing and the rasp of his cutoffs against his thighs as he moved, keeping to the shadows, always in the shade.

Three yards to go, now: close enough to observe the boy's sketch and determine, even from that distance, that he was a first-rate draftsman. Abruptly, his target started, paused at his work, pencil poised above pad like a missile about to strike, then tilted his head. The lad made no move to rise, though, merely stared sideways at Ron with a sort of controlled curiosity as he came within easy speaking range. He was clearly trying *not* to react.

"Nice view, huh?" Ron drawled, sweeping his right arm around in an arc that encompassed the cove, the houses across the lake, and the looming mass of Brandy Hall.

"Y-eah," the boy replied tentatively. Not hostile, but with care, yet somehow not recalcitrant.

"Lots of neat stuff to draw around here," Ron continued. "I sketch down here myself, sometimes."

"You draw?" the boy asked with a tad more interest. His voice was unexpectedly low for one so young looking.

"I can," Ron told him, easing around to where he could barely peer over the boy's shoulder. He was right: the work *was* good. "It's not my main thing. Not my main *art*, anyway."

"What is?"

"I'm a . . ." Ron paused. "I guess you could say I'm a smith." Another pause, then: "You just move in?"

The boy aimed his pencil toward the A-frame. "Over there."

"Didn't think I'd seen you around."

The boy eyed him warily, and Ron felt unaccountably old. "*You* live 'round here?"

Ron inclined his head eastward. "That way."

The boy stared incredulously, his low-key facade fracturing. "In that . . . *castle*?"

Ron nodded and tried not to grin smugly but did not entirely succeed. "It's not quite that," he lied, knowing perfectly well that for all intents and purposes it was—and that what few technical differences existed would scarcely matter to the boy.

"Is . . . is it *yours*?" the boy blurted out. "The real estate lady said it belonged to some artist, or teacher, or somebody."

"It does," Ron assured him. "It belongs to Brandy Wallace, but I sorta live there too. We're a . . . pair, I guess," he finished, awkwardly.

The boy looked as if he were about to burst from sheer curiosity but didn't want to show it; which made Ron suspect that this whole overture had been a mistake. The next question was predictable, after all; he knew how kids were. Knew they had no sense of time or timing, were all impulse and passion, as he—somewhat to his regret—no longer was.

"So . . ." the boy mumbled at last, his face easing into a lopsided grin that Ron thought was a little too winsome, "is there, like, any way I could get a *closer* look?"

Yep, there it was, right on schedule. Trouble was, there was no good reason not to accede to the lad's request. God knew plenty of other people made the same one. But again,

they weren't kids, usually; weren't—uncomfortable word—
neighbors. On the other hand, to refuse such a spontaneous
petition without good reason would be rude, and worse, could
very well abort a potential friendship aborning. And Ron
was not so well supplied with friends that he could afford
to reject one.

"I don't know," he said at last, managing a smile. "I
might show you around—except that it's sort of against
policy."

The boy's face fell. "What policy?" he asked suspiciously.

"That I don't show the place to strangers."

"Oh . . ."

" 'Course if you were to tell me your *name*, well then, we
wouldn't quite be strangers, would we?"

The boy considered this for a moment. "I'm Sam."

"Sam what?"

"Sam Foster."

"I'm Ron Dillon." He stuck out his hand.

Sam took it. Ron felt unexpected strength there.

"Hi," Sam murmured, breaking contact quickly.

"Nice to meet you, Sam."

The boy was already repacking his knapsack. He rose
smoothly. "Now?"

Ron shrugged helplessly. "I reckon."

"So what do your folks do?" Ron asked a moment later,
as they made their way along the trail that led back to Brandy Hall.

"Soldiers . . . once."

"And now?"

"Retired—Dad is, 'cept for some stuff he piddles with. My
mom's . . . gone."

Ron thought it unwise to press the point. "Sorry."

"No big deal."

Sam did not reply, but Ron Heard a hint of embarrassment
riding the Winds from the boy. He shielded automatically,
shutting out emotions he neither wanted to feel, nor had a
right to share.

Nor did the lad speak further until Ron limped out of the
forest and eased aside so his accomplice could get his first
clear look at Brandy Hall, rearing on its knoll above him.

"Gee."

"Gee?" Ron echoed, mockingly. "I drag you all the way up here and that's *all* you can say?"

"Gee *whiz*," Sam amended. "Nice."

Ron felt no need to reply, as they made their way around the western side, skirting the lower stones of the West Terrace, where raw rock and concrete inextricably veined together formed a low battlement ten feet above their heads. The ground sloped up there, leading toward the level forecourt. A sweep of rough-mown lawn, studded with flower beds and odd sculptures, swept away to the right.

A bit farther along a statue hove into view at the point of the terrace: male, muscular, nearly naked, and flourishing a stag's rack on high. "Who's that?" Sam wondered, eyes narrowed uncertainly. For some odd reason Ron thought he looked shaken.

"Cernnunos, god of the hunt—among others."

"In *cutoffs*?"

"That's what the model wore."

"Gimme a break!"

"Okay, then," Ron gritted. "His *name* was Van Vannister."

"Yeah, but who *was* he?" Sam persisted, with an intensity that for an instant sounded to Ron almost like fear. "What'd he do to get his statue here?"

"He . . . built this place, in a manner of speaking," Ron sighed, hoping the conversation did not continue in that vein.

"When was that?"

"Few years back."

"You here then?"

"Yep."

"All your life?"

"Only since the end of my junior year in high school."

"Oh."

"You go to school?"

"I have."

"Where? Or is your dad moving up?"

Sam shook his head. "We're just here for the summer."

"So . . . where're you from?"

"Lots of places."

"Most recently."

A pause, then: "Gainesville."

"What grade're you in?"

"Guess."

"Rising senior?"

But the boy was no longer listening. They had reached the forecourt by then, with the concrete battlements of the entrance facade looming to their left and back. Romano-Moorish in essence, or so the original design had been. But now it bore elements of Gothic, of Celtic, of Scandinavian, of half the schools of architecture known, all rendered harmonious by the ingrowth of stone that permeated the place like some benign cancer.

But Sam was not looking at Brandy Hall. "All *right*!" he crowed.

It took Ron a moment to determine where his gaze was directed, but by then the boy was making a beeline for the garage, where the low burgundy nose of his Centauri crouched in its "cave," with the successor nearing completion beneath a tarp slung between the garage and the forge. Ron found himself forced to jog stiffly along behind. He passed the Thunderbird that was his "official" car, Sharon's old Honda, and the guys' clapped-out Toronado. Not until he was almost to the forge did he catch up with the boy.

Sam was standing as if awestruck as he stared at the low, rounded front of one of the world's two Centauri MK II convertibles. Without asking permission, he ran a hand reverently across a well-waxed fender crest, along the top of the door to the trunk spoiler, then back around, pausing to gaze inside and whistle. Ron saw him mouth the words "CD" as he studied the instrument panel, then wrinkle his brow in perplexity when he caught sight of the nameplate set into the right front fender.

"Centauri MK II?" he murmured uncertainly. "Body by RED Enterprises . . . ?"

"Ronald Emerson Dillon," Ron supplied.

Sam stared at him incredulously. "*You* designed this?"

"Sure did," Ron nodded, in no mood to explain for the zillionth time how he had built a car from scratch because it was the perfect synthesis of design and metallurgy.

But he was not to be spared. "But who *built* it?"

"I did."

Whereupon Sam turned his attention to the replacement half-finished next door, the one that incorporated much more advanced composite technology, as well as the latest in electronics, aerodynamics, and engineering. "And this?"

"An improved version."

"So . . . how're they powered?"

Ron sighed. Might as well get it over with, he supposed. Besides, the boy's enthusiasm seemed genuine. And he hated to dampen such youthful high spirits, for whatever selfish reason. "Well, the old one: *my* old one, the red one—my girlfriend's got a green one—has a pair of Mazda rotaries geared together to make a four-rotor; but the new one's got a two-stroke V-12 version of a Ford modular V-8, like is in that T-Bird over there, and . . ."

Ron went on for nearly half an hour explaining every detail of design and engineering of both cars. Sam took it in, too; and asked more questions than Ron could count: good ones, displaying a knowledge of matters automotive he rarely encountered anymore. They did not stop until, quite suddenly, Sam's stomach growled.

Ron raised an eyebrow, suppressing a chuckle.

The boy colored and looked exceedingly chagrined, then checked his watch. "Hmmmm," he said slyly. "Now what about the house?"

" . . . and that's about it," Ron concluded, when yet another half hour had been consumed by playing tour guide. He and Sam were standing just inside the door of the vaulted, echoing coolness of the great hall, whence they had come from the Mayan bedroom in the southeast corner. Sam had liked that a lot: the bas-relief designs carved into the concrete walls, the simple furnishings, and the wealth of rough-woven fabric accenting all.

But then, he'd liked the whole place, the more medieval rooms (like this one) in particular. Ron leaned against the nearest of the life-sized marble sculptures of the Lords of the Tuatha de Danaan that lurked in the side arcades (this one happened to be a blissful-looking Bridget), folded his arms across his chest, and waited for Sam to reply.

The boy took a sip from the Dr. Pepper Ron had snared for him as they'd transited the chaotic cacophony in the (mostly contemporary) kitchen and eyed Ron dubiously. "It *is*? I mean, that's *all*?"

Ron sighed. "All I can show you without compromising people's privacy."

The boy did not look convinced. "Oh," he muttered, not sounding convinced, either.

"How would *you* like someone prowling through your room when you weren't around?"

"I wouldn't," Sam replied with prompt honesty, shifting his weight and activating his winsome grin. "But hey, if there're rooms I can't see, how 'bout you *tell* me about 'em?"

Ron frowned, not liking the idea of being manipulated in his own house—especially by someone at least ten years his junior. On the other hand, Sam had a remarkably ingenuous manner about him: one that both irritated Ron a little (because it kept him off balance) and attracted him (for no reason he had yet had time to ponder). "Sounds fair," he replied finally.

Without further comment, he motioned Sam to the nearest of the overstuffed cream leather sofas that carved small enclaves of intimacy from the enormous space of the room—when Brandy wasn't holding mock-medieval feasts there. Ron sat opposite; Sam looked attentive.

Ron cleared his throat, and spent an additional fifteen minutes describing his tower studio, Brandy's corner room equivalent, and her meditatorium, all in what turned out to be excruciating detail because Sam seemed to want to know everything from the color of the carpet to the level of surface clutter.

"Satisfied?" Ron asked when he had finished.

"Almost," Sam replied quickly.

"Almost?"

"You still haven't said anything about *your* room."

Ron blinked in startlement. *"My* . . . room? You mean mine and Brandy's bedroom?"

"Just wondering," Sam murmured.

"Wouldn't you rather save some mystery for a future visit?"

Sam's expression indicated the negative several seconds before he said as much. And Ron realized that by phrasing things as he had, he'd left the door open for intrusions he was not certain he wanted to encourage. And though the boy's official response was an indifferent shrug, Ron could tell from his eyes that he was disappointed.

Grimacing, Ron rose. "Come on, then, but I really do have to get busy after this." Whereupon he led the way out the front door of the great hall, west along the narrow vaulted corridor that encircled it, and then north along an identical corridor, to the right of which lay one of the long side walls of the great hall. To the left, two identical doors encrusted with strapwork opened into his and Brandy's bower.

Ron chose the first portal and pushed through, stepping aside for Sam to follow, then snicking the door closed behind him, as if to shut out the lad's expected, *"Oh,"* before it could jar the walls and ceilings with an echo. He wondered, too, what the boy's impression was. Probably *very* impressed, to judge by the way his mouth hadn't closed yet. On the other hand, he supposed he'd likewise have been rendered speechless, at the prospect of a vaulted chamber fifty feet long and thirty wide, with a twenty-foot frescoed ceiling, all wrought of smooth-cut limestone and lit by four arched etched-glass doors that let onto a battlemented terrace. Never mind the huge, velvet-draped bed against the short wall to the left, the almost-matching fireplace opposite, and the mostly medieval knickknacks strewn over the chests and tables like treasure trove. Or the four bearskin rugs (each a different species, all victims of Brandy's deadly aim), or (he feared) the comfortable, if incongruous, clutter of jeans, sneakers, and T-shirts that littered the area around the bed like battlefield detritus.

Sam was still standing there trying to regain control of his chin when Ron's bladder (which he'd been plying with beer for a good part of the afternoon) decided, contrariwise, to assert *its* independence.

"Back in a flash," Ron told his happily gawking guest. "Uh . . . don't touch anything that looks fragile."

Which, Ron reflected as he let fly into the mosaic-flanked potty in his part of the adjoining bath, was probably an unnecessary admonition to someone who could draw as well as Sam. Especially when the request he *should* have made—as he discovered upon reentering the bedroom—was not to *prowl*.

Oh, it wasn't as if Sam were pulling out drawers and opening cabinets or such like. But he was certainly giving everything that bore either of those appurtenances special attention, as if a room as evocative as Ron and Brandy's of necessity *had* to be riddled with secrets that an astute eye and deft hands could ferret out without their owners being the wiser. And, to make matters worse, he looked not the least bit guilty about it!

Ron thought of "ahemming" loudly, then decided that might be a shade too theatrical, so contented himself with walking *slightly* more loudly toward the boy, who was at that moment moving on toward display cabinet number three. Unfortunately, that form of locomotion only accentuated the subtle step-and-hitch of Ron's gait, which in turn made Sam glance around. The boy raised an eyebrow, but said nothing as Ron limped up to join him. The shelves before them bore assorted trinkets Ron had amassed over the years—mostly presents made for him or Brandy by various visitors, plus a few pieces the Road Man had given him.

And one thing he probably should not have left there, given the conversation it precipitated.

"You swim?" Sam asked innocently, indicating the prickly mass of badly varnished wood, ill-turned aluminum, and ineptly gilded pot metal that most folks would have identified as a trophy. Ron had always thought it resembled a Baroque tomb.

"I *did*," he muttered, disinterestedly, wondering yet again why he even bothered to keep that one example of the many he had actually amassed where he could see it. It only brought back bad memories, after all. And he had quite enough of those, thank you.

Sam fixed him with a disbelieving gaze. "What stroke?"

"What does it say there?"

Sam squinted at the engraved plaque midway down the

central wooden slab. " 'Tampa City Schools: All-Around Swimming Champion.' " Three dates followed, representing the three years Ron had claimed that title. The trophy had been his to keep after the last round of victories. He had a matching one stashed away that gave equal testament to his prowess at diving. Which he *really* did not want to be reminded of.

"Do you *still*?" Sam burst out, with the unrestrained enthusiasm of youth Ron was realizing he had either misplaced or lost.

"Not after halfway through my junior year." There, he'd said it. He hoped this savvy urchin took the clue that it was *not* a topic he wanted to pursue.

Sam didn't—or was too hyped to care. "What happened?"

"I fell," Ron told him flatly. "Perhaps you've noticed my limp?" he added icily.

But the warning slipped right off the boy's shoulders. "Sorry," he murmured, his face brimming with genuine regret.

"Yeah, me too," Ron grunted, easing away.

"But couldn't you—?" Sam began, his ongoing concern evident in a lowering and softening of his voice.

"I don't like talking about it!"

"Sorry," Sam repeated, frowning and fidgeting with his shirttail. He checked his watch, whereupon the frown shifted to dismay. "Oh, jeez," he cried. "I've gotta split. Dad wants me to go to dinner with him, and I'm late." He hesitated for the barest of instants, then grabbed the pack he had plopped against a metal-strapped chest, and trotted toward the door.

Ron followed him out and steered him through the labyrinth to the front arcade, where Sam paused, gnawing his lip with embarrassed uncertainty. "Uh, thanks for the tour," he said sheepishly. " 'Specially for telling me 'bout all the private stuff. Sorry I was so nosy, and pushy, and all."

"No problem."

"Oh . . . and thanks for letting me look at the cars, too."

"It's cool."

But still the boy lingered. "Can I, like, you know, come back some?" he blurted out at last. "I sure would like to see how you do some of that metalwork."

Ron hesitated. His impulse was to say that, sure, Sam

could return—any time. Certainly he hadn't spent so enjoyable a spell talking cars in many a moon, not when Brandy's friends were mostly arch-Greenie types. On the other hand, he really wanted to finish The Head, and already had too many distractions.

"I guess," he conceded finally, purposefully establishing a degree of distance. "But only if your dad says it's cool, okay? And . . . call first. I've got a lot of projects cooking, and I can't always afford to be interrupted. Okay?"

The boy studied him for a moment. Then: "Sure."

And with that, Sam Foster jogged toward the nearest set of steps and was quickly lost to sight around the angle of the West Terrace.

"Sure indeed!" Ron muttered, as he turned back inside. "Sure what?"

Surely Sam Foster's dad would keep a tighter rein on his offspring in the future. Surely he would not let his son become a nuisance.

Ron hoped.

Or did he?

Chapter 3

Talk, Talk

Cordova, Georgia
Early evening

"It's like I've been sayin' for the last blessed *year*," Mabel Hoodenpyle was expounding loudly. "Ever since Lewis Welch ran off, things have just flat gone to blazes!"

Standing as she was on the raised platform at the high end of the oak-paneled assembly hall in the Welch County Courthouse, with a Baroque bronze statue of Truth on one side and Commerce on the other, Mabel looked less like a retired schoolmarm than a third (though more buxom) effigy that had quickened for a spell and gone stomping around the dais. Though what virtue—*quality*, better say—she might personify, Brandy Wallace had no idea. Contention, perhaps, signified by a dress red enough to incense a whole herd of bulls. Intimidation was a real possibility too, given that Mabel was something over six feet tall, making her the tallest woman Brandy had ever seen. Or maybe the fake pearls (fear of theft?) and dyed black hair (fear of old age?—the woman was pushing seventy mighty hard) referenced a species of paranoia. Ron, who—thank God—was not present, would certainly have seconded the latter. Brandy wasn't sure she disagreed.

"Absolute hell!" Mabel repeated for emphasis, before continuing with her harangue. She didn't need a microphone either; her stentorian tones would have done any televangelist proud, never mind poor John Rogers, who, though he was officially chairing the meeting, was lying mighty low.

Sitting in her Sunday buckskins near the end of the front row of benches between her best buddy, Weedge Montgomery, and Cardalba High's metalshop teacher, Victor Wiley, Brandy was more than a little paranoid herself. For though she knew the old biddy was addressing the Chamber of Commerce meeting at large, she could not shake the suspicion that a good hunk of Mabel's remarks were aimed at her in particular. Maybe it was the way she tended to punctuate her sentences with a glance in Brandy's direction, perhaps it was that subtly specific narrowing of the eyes, as that oh-so-imperious gaze swept scythelike across the crowd. Whatever it was, Brandy hated it.

What had she had let herself in for, anyway, by agreeing to be cultural attaché for the Welch County Chamber of Commerce? Oh, it had seemed a logical enough proposition at the time: she was young, had ideas, was winning more awards than ever with her wildlife paintings. Plus, she had an ever-increasing number of contacts in the Southeastern artistic community at large, courtesy of her policy of allowing itinerant craftsmen of virtually any stripe to claim haven at Brandy Hall in exchange for odd jobs and detail work on the edifice itself.

Too, in the seven years she had been teaching art in the Welch County public schools, her perceived persona had shifted from that of aloof outsider to respected member of a community that was already remarkably tolerant of personal idiosyncrasy. Which was fortunate, given her tendency to clothe her wiry bod in brain-tanned buckskin, fill her freezer with game, and live in a mock-castle on a mountain with a car-crazed quasi-aristocrat-cum-blacksmith.

That alteration had begun with her students, who adored her; which had led to her adoring them; which had then led to her getting to know their parents. And once they had determined that the crazy woman on Keycutter Knob was neither going to ply their offspring with drugs, sacrifice them to the devil, nor (given her fondness for hunting) shoot them, stuff them, or stew them alive, the rest had fallen into place. She had, in short, found her niche.

Trouble was, once she'd been accepted, she had felt it her responsibility to accept her adopted county in turn, and that had segued into a sense of responsibility for the place at large. Which was why she, in nowise a business woman, was a minor officer of the Chamber of Commerce—having to listen to Mabel Hoodenpyle slyly put down her significant other.

"Hitting kinda close to home, isn't she?" Weedge Montgomery whispered, leaning so close Brandy could hear the tiny wind chimes that comprised her friend's earrings tinkle.

Brandy shot her chum a wry glance out of the corner of her eye and nodded slowly. " 'Fraid so," she muttered. "And the worst thing is, she's right—in part. Not that she understands anything—not by a long shot."

Weedge's narrow face was serious within its frame of straight dark hair. "Do *you*?"

"Not by an even longer shot," Brandy murmured, keeping one eye peeled for a return of Mabel's glare. "Ronny tells me as little as he can get by with, which has never been enough. But there's enough good left that I hold my tongue. I—"

" . . . someone like *you*, Miss Wallace!" Mabel's voice had risen a dozen decibels and half an octave. A windowpane rattled ominously.

"*Excuse* me?" Brandy blinked up at her guilelessly, lifting dark brows into layered black hair (also dyed, but for a different reason) that was like a cap of feathers.

"I was just saying," Mabel repeated with excruciating precision, "that since you've lived among us a shorter time than most folks hereabouts, you might be willing to give us an *outsider's* point of view."

"On what?" Brandy called back clearly. She had no problem providing an opinion—God knew she had scads of 'em on virtually any topic you could name. But she certainly didn't like being *forced* to produce one on demand.

Mabel's eyes narrowed right on cue. "Well . . . for instance, you could tell us how things here were different from the outside world when you first moved here."

Brandy glanced about uneasily and rose, smoothing the fringe of her tan doeskin vest as she did. "Uh, well—" she began, then paused, having sounded more nervous than she liked—one did *not* want to appear wimpy in Mabel's presence.

"Well, basically," she tried again, "Mabel's right: I'm not from up here. My grandfather was a tobacco farmer up in North Carolina who made a lot of money but never left his homeplace. Some of you have seen my house up on Keycutter Knob, which he partly financed, so you know he was successful. But what's a lot *more* important was that he made sure that while his son—my dad—went to college, he also knew how to farm and hunt. And my mom was half-Cherokee, so she knew a lot of traditional things too. And the reason I'm telling you all this is so you'll know where I'm coming from when I say what I have to say about mountain life and mountain people."

She paused for breath, and glanced down at Weedge for reassurance, then continued. "Anyway," she said, "I grew up in Chapel Hill, North Carolina, which is a college town; and I lived there until I moved here. So—"

"Get to the point," Mabel broke in icily, from where she had finally come to ground by the president's rostrum.

"The *point*," Brandy shot back, "is that when I came here, I was still in my 'I'm educated and better than everybody else' phase. But what I found here, after living in what was *supposed* to be a more civilized environment, was a world at . . . at *peace* with itself, I guess. Welch County seemed as close to paradise on earth as I was likely to find. It had beautiful scenery—hadn't been logged off, or anything. There was no poverty—all the houses and businesses looked neat and clean and new. And when I checked the statistics, I discovered that it had the highest per capita income in Georgia, exactly enough rainfall, the highest SAT scores, the winningest high school teams—and the highest teachers' salaries of any county in the state. *And* no crime to speak of: no murders, no rape, no theft—beyond teenage shoplifting, and such."

"And *now*?" Mabel prompted pointedly. She still hadn't

sat, Brandy noted, still had not relinquished her place of power.

Brandy gnawed her lip, knowing that if she answered truthfully, she'd be flirting with what oversensitive Ronny might construe as betrayal. "Now—"

"I'll *show* you now!" Mabel interrupted—whereupon she reached into the valise-sized purse she was clutching and dragged out a folded newspaper. Brandy recognized the local rag: the Welch County *Witness*. While Brandy blinked in amazement, Mabel flung the bundle at her. It unfolded in transit like a vast speckled raptor. Brandy caught it—barely.

"That didn't used to happen," Mabel shrilled. "Just *look* at that, Miss Wallace: all that crime, all that bad weather, all that . . . that bad luck!"

Brandy suppressed an urge to hurl the paper right back, and forced herself to scan the headlines. They would not have been remarkable in Gainesville or Athens, or any of the smaller cities in Georgia. Certainly nothing out of the ordinary for Atlanta, a hundred miles to the south. But here on one sheet she noted an attempted break-in at the drugstore. A rape. A spate of family violence, and two low-lying fields flooded when a dam had burst.

"Crime, crime, and more crime," Mabel informed the gaping audience. "And unemployment everywhere."

"What about the weather?" somebody called.

"It's gone to hell too!" Mabel crowed triumphantly, "I've lived here longer'n anybody in this room and I can *tell* you that the weather's turned plumb lousy. Why, just look at this rain!" She gestured toward the round-topped windows, beyond which a handsome downpour was in progress: silver drops flashing against a twilight sky, the whole backlit by occasional lightning. "Used to be *nothing* was ever rained out. *Used* to be you could count on the *right* amount of rain and sunshine to plant your crops and grow 'em and get 'em out of the ground.

"And now . . ." She paused for emphasis, while John Rogers rolled his eyes and fingered his gavel. "It's like I've said twice already: Things have just gone to hell—and it's *Ronny Dillon's* fault!"

Brandy stared incredulously, as if one of the lightning bolts outside had transfixed her; but sat before she said something truly incendiary. She'd been attending public functions in the county for years, but this was the first time she'd ever heard so blatant a reference to the clandestine role the Welches played in local prosperity. Not that Mabel wasn't correct, in a sense. But that didn't give her a right to accuse poor Ronny! Not after what he'd been through for her—shoot, for the whole bloody county: like giving up his freedom for three years to assume the Mastership while Lew fiddled around in college. Like ridding them of a megalomaniac would-be Master in the person of his and Lew's cousin Anson. And those were only the grossest examples. You had to be on the inside to know *all* the sacrifices the Masters made to keep everybody else secure and happy. And very few people had seen the inside. She had—partly; Weedge had witnessed a bit, and maybe a few others. But by and large the populace as a whole kept silent whenever the subject of Luck arose— just as the Masters were careful to keep its more dubious mechanisms discreetly offstage.

"That's it," an older man in a suit two rows back agreed. "We've just plumb run out of Luck."

"Not run out," a well-dressed young woman to the right corrected, "Lewis run off and took it with him!"

"And Ronny wouldn't take it over," a third emboldened housewife concluded, staring accusingly at Brandy.

Brandy started to rise again, to defend her lover, but felt Weedge's hand around her upper arm, restraining her. "Tough it out," Wiley murmured beside her. She ignored him, shook off Weedge's grip, and stood. "I thought we were here to talk about the local economy," she challenged, her voice cutting through the rising mutter. "In case you've *forgotten*, you can target the problem pretty specifically. The main employer here was a major defense contractor, and when that latest round of budget cuts kicked in, our plant was declared superfluous. Jobs had to be cut—which means businesses are closing, which means the tax base is going down, which means salaries are declining for teachers, which means educational standards are slipping. And I guess, with money tight for the first time since anyone can remember, and with people out of work who never have been, there's more theft. And more disappointment means more paranoia, which means more violence. But like I said: it all goes back to the end of the cold war—and I can't imagine how you could blame *that* on the Welches, even if they *could* do some of the things you've hinted at."

There, she'd said it—and every word was true: a habit she'd picked up from Ronny. What she *hadn't* added was that she suspected Lewis or Ronny or any other Master could have easily pulled a string or two to remedy the situation. All it would have required was a tiny psychic prod in the right bureaucrat's mind and that now-defunct factory would be humming right along. That Ronny hadn't done so was not a thing she approved of. But it *was* a thing she—sort of—understood.

"So what *we* do," Weedge chimed in, rallying to her friend's aid, "is to *stop* dwelling on what happened and why, and *start* doing something to improve the situation."

"You got any suggestions?" That from the out-of-work husband of a recently married couple.

"Tourism!" came a strong male voice behind her.

Brandy's head snapped around, to see a lanky young man rise from the back row. Arlin Monroe, she thought his name was: a recent transplant to the county. His tan and brown uniform identified him as U.S. Forest Service.

"Yes?" Mabel asked, apparently forgetting she wasn't chairing the meeting. "Go on."

Arlin scratched his neck, where his fair coloring indicated a good chance of sunburn. "Uh, well, it looks pretty obvious to me. Most of you folks have lived here all your lives, so you've all forgotten—or got used to—how beautiful it is around here. Shoot, you've—*we've* got more old-growth forest here than anywhere else east of the Mississippi. We've got at least ten waterfalls higher than a hundred feet, and we've got three of the five bald mountains in Georgia. But—"

"—But nobody *knows* about 'em!" Brandy finished for him, as an idea took form so suddenly it was like divine intervention. "You can drive through town any day of the week and never see a tag from any county but this and the ones on either side," she continued excitedly. "And half of *that's* 'cause the Cordova Triple gets movies before anybody else does. *Still* does," she added pointedly, to Mabel.

"Yeah, and *we've* got the tightest building covenants in Georgia," Victor Wiley added. "Plus, most of the land that's not owned by the state, the feds, or the Welches already has a house on it—so there's no way we could have uncontrolled growth, like has messed things up in the other counties up here. Which basically means we get people in, show 'em a good time, have 'em stay a night or two in *our* motels, and bid 'em farewell—with *their* money in *our* pockets."

"Shoot, we could even do like some of those little countries in Europe!" a new speaker broke in eagerly: young Mark McMillan, whom Brandy had taught to paint the previous year. "We secede from the Union again, see, then put up guardposts at the passes leading in, and support ourselves on tourism, gambling, and postage stamps, just like Monaco or San Marino!"

This elicited a general chuckle, though Brandy thought the idea had some merit.

"How 'bout just postage stamps?" one of McMillan's youthful cohorts laughed. "That way we get the money, and none of the hassle!"

"I think a play's a better idea," Brandy announced abruptly. And promptly froze in place. Now where had *that* come from? One instant her mind was a muddled maze of halfformed ideas, the next—why, there it was, clear as glass! The perfect solution to their problem.

"Oh, I agree some of our neighbors have screwed up a lot with bad planning, and all," she went on breathlessly, as ideas began to link with each other almost faster than she could sort them out. "But one of the good things one of 'em's done is to put together a local history play. It's called *The Reach of Song* and it's about an important local author named Byron Herbert Reece, who was famous in the fifties, and then shot himself one day in a dormitory at Young Harris College. But a few years ago the folks over there got up this play, had a guy from Atlanta write it, and employed a lot of local musicians and craftsmen. Lots of local actors, too."

"And the result?" Mabel inquired dubiously.

"They made a lot of money," Weedge supplied. "I've seen it, and it's great."

"Yeah," Mark McMillan chimed in. "And Brandy's got theater connections!"

"Good point," Rogers said. "All right, do I hear a motion to form a committee to investigate the production of a play?"

"So move," said Vic Wiley.

"Second!" young McMillan cried instantly.

Rogers took a deep breath, and shot the immovable Mabel a sideways glare. "Okay, then, all in favor of Mr. Wiley's motion, say 'aye'."

The room thundered its consent.

"Opposed?"

Brandy thought of raising her hand just to be contrary—and because she thought Ron would probably have voted that way—but decided not to because Mabel had. Besides, the more she reflected on it, the more the idea of rallying the county around a dramatic production appealed to her. She'd been trying to vivify the arts in Welch County for years, after all. And now she was faced with the prospect of working with a whole array of talented folks—something she had missed since settling here, Ronny Dillon and itinerate artisan friends notwithstanding. Art needed art to survive, dammit! Needed itself to feed from and grow strong. And now strength was coming, strength to revive her own failing enthusiasm, now that Brandy Hall was almost done.

"Motion carried," Rogers announced loudly, pounding his gavel. "Brandy, I appoint you head of the committee. . . . So—what do we do now?" he added, looking at her expectantly.

("Way to go," Weedge murmured beside her. "Yeah," Wiley echoed, "way to go.")

Brandy could not reply, still half in shock, as she was, at the precipitous way chaos had suddenly resolved into order, with herself as focus. "You mean besides appoint committee members?" she managed finally. "Uh, well, I *suppose* the first thing would be to establish a schedule—a goal by which time this is to be accomplished. Like, do we try to do it this year, or next?"

(There was a general murmuring of *"this year"*.)

"Then . . ." she went on, "I guess then we find people to fill major support roles. Shoot, there're kids in high school right now who've done a lot of it. And if it's a local history play, it'd make sense to use natives as actors and musicians anyway—except that we might have to import outsiders for lead roles, at least to start with. And to direct. And to write the thing—I've never heard of anybody around here with that kind of skill," she added apologetically. "If anybody *does* know of such a person, let me know.

"Otherwise . . . I guess the logical thing to do is to contact the heads of the drama departments of all colleges within, say, a two-hundred-mile radius, and have them post it. Oh, and we can put ads in the major newspapers, maybe *Creative Loafing* and a few of those as well, and see what turns up. And if nothing does in a week or two, we . . . find some other solution. Or we wait until next summer, and take our time and really do things right."

"Except that we may not *be* here next summer," Mabel noted sourly, making what Brandy suspected was her last assault before admitting defeat in light of Brandy's end run around her.

"I can get you some lists," Jeremy Brock said. He taught theater in the local high school. (Why hadn't *he* volunteered to coordinate?) And then Brandy remembered: Brock's wife's computer business had folded last week. They'd be leaving in a month, moving to new jobs in Atlanta. Their grandparents had been born here.

"So . . . these outsiders," Victor Wiley mused thoughtfully, pulling on his thin, blond mustache, "like, where do we put 'em? And where do we base this thing? 'Cause I don't think anybody remembered this in time . . . but the high school auditorium's still undergoing renovation from that windstorm we had back in the winter."

"We've *got* an abandoned factory," Mabel noted sarcastically.

"Couldn't we put 'em in our homes?" a middle-aged woman asked, pointedly ignoring her.

"We could," Brandy nodded. "And I've no doubt people would do it, but it *might* be a fairly large batch of folks, and if we find ourselves actually hosting a troupe—which isn't necessarily desirable, but still might happen—I suspect they'd want to stay together."

Rogers banged his gavel to stem yet another rising tide of mumblings. "Any *other* suggestions?"

"Well," Mabel drawled loudly. "There's *always* Cardalba Hall."

For the second time in ten minutes Brandy was thunderstruck. What was getting into folks tonight? Making them think the unthinkable?

"Good idea," someone echoed. "Shoot, we could even put on the play there—there's room enough."

Brandy scowled intently. "Hmmm, now *that* might be a problem," she sighed. "I'll ask Ronny, of course—'cause if I don't one of you surely will"—she fixed Mabel with a glare—"but I doubt he'll agree. He doesn't like the place, sure; but he's real protective about it. *But*," she added slyly, "I don't have any problem with putting folks up at *my* place. I've got room, got atmosphere, got seclusion if we need it. Shoot, come to think of it, I've even got a natural amphitheater!"

"And Ronny can't say a thing about it!" Mabel crowed. " 'Cause *you* own it fair and square!"

"Which just leaves one major problem," Wiley noted.

"What's that?"

"Why, choosing a topic for the play! I mean, local history's a pretty broad area. We're obviously gonna have to focus it."

"You've got a point," Brandy nodded. "I suppose the first step would be to prowl through all the local history books until something grabs us."

"Except that there *aren't* any," Mabel cried instantly.

"There *aren't*?"

Wiley cleared his throat. "Not to speak of—nothing beyond family histories and oral tradition."

"There are no books because there are no public records," Mabel interrupted gleefully. "And there are no public records because the courthouse burned down three times before the Civil War, and the Welches decided that what survived those fires ought to be at Cardalba, only *it* was burned by the Yankees too. And there've been *two* courthouse fires since then."

"Which means we don't have much to go on."

"Which means *we* don't have much to go on," Mabel
—corrected. "But not necessarily that there aren't *any* records to be had. Cardalba didn't burn to the ground. And
I've heard more than once that there was a strong room full
of books underneath that came through unscathed." Her eyes
narrowed. "You know anything about that, Miss Wallace?"

"Not much," Brandy replied carefully. "I wasn't there
very often, and like I've told *you* half a dozen times, Ronny
doesn't like to talk about it."

There, she'd protected Ron's privacy again. Only . . .
wasn't she also cutting her own throat? Wasn't she jeo-
pardizing something that suddenly meant a lot to her?

"Still," she continued slowly, "I guess there's nothing to
be lost by at least *asking* Ronny to make the records available. I mean the worst he can say is no; and even then, if
we try hard enough, we can probably reconstruct some stuff
from bits and pieces—oral tradition, and such."

"Good luck!" Mabel snorted.

Brandy ignored her. "Soooo," she asked brightly, "do I
have any volunteers for the committee? And how big's our
budget, anyway?"

They spent the better part of the next hour hashing out
details in the neo-classic splendor of an adjoining conference room. While Rogers and the senior Chamber members
haggled over finances, Brandy made a master list of items to
be handled, and worked out a rough schedule of priorities. It
was a thing she did naturally: a project came along and she
obsessed on it until the next one. The danger lay in getting
sidetracked—which was why she was going flat-out now.
She might feel like pouring concrete tomorrow and put off
this whole thing until it was too late. Still, when the meeting
finally broke up, somewhere around sunset, she was as up as
she'd been in ages.

"So why're *you* grinning like a 'possum?" Weedge chuckled, yanking at the fringe of Brandy's vest as they made their
way down the courthouse's rain-washed steps to where Brandy's car was surrounded, as ever, by an admiring collection
of oglers—understandable, given that Brandy drove one of
two Centauri MK II convertibles in the world: an emerald

green one, courtesy of Ron's flare for design and skill at metalwork.

Brandy shot her friend a secret smile, as she halted to let the crowd disperse from around the low, rounded auto. "Oh, I don't know. I'm just feeling real up, I guess."

"I'll say," Weedge chuckled, glancing toward her latest Toyota station wagon. (Ron bought her one every year in gratitude for her role in a certain traumatic night a few years back.) "I haven't seen you like this in I don't know when—not sober, anyway."

Brandy grinned again. "Yeah, well, I was just thinking—Oh, never mind."

Weedge pinched her arm and would not let go. "*Brandy!*" she gritted. "Don't *do* that to me!"

Brandy glared at her friend good-naturedly, then broke into a giggle. "Oh, I was just thinking that maybe it was time to bring up Project Gene Pool again."

Weedge rolled her eyes. "So what makes you think that just 'cause you're feeling good all of a sudden, Ron's gonna change his mind about makin' babies?"

"Oh, I don't *expect* him to change his mind," Brandy chuckled wickedly. "But there's no reason I can't just sort of go off the Pill—and make little bitty holes in his condoms and . . . just . . . see . . . what . . . happens."

"Fiend!"

"Yeah," Brandy laughed. "Ain't it grand?"

Chapter 4

Tell Her No

Brandy Hall
Evening

"What are *you* lookin' at?" Ron growled at his darkened reflection, as he rose from where he'd been dragging stacks of books from the vault in anticipation of a second, more comprehensive, search for the missing page of brain schematics. It was dusk outside now (which was shifting the presently transparent panes into mirrors), and Brandy *still* had not returned from that damned meeting. Which pissed him on the one hand because it meant she wasn't spending time with him—though why today should be any different than the last half dozen, he had no idea. And relieved him on the other, because—even allowing for the hour-plus he'd blown playing tour guide for Sam Foster—it had allowed him to work on The Head longer than he could recall: straight through supper (Sharon had brought up a calzone, which he'd postponed sampling until it was cold) and into the twilight hours.

The face that blinked back at him did not respond (he wasn't *that* far gone yet), but looked tired around the eyes, pale, hollow cheeked—and ghostly. He wondered, half-seriously, if he had become a wraith in his own tower:

a shadowy figure glimpsed but obliquely by Brandy's constant stream of guests. Rumored more often than encountered.

Scowling, he arranged the ancient volumes he'd retrieved in a sloppy stack on the windowsill, then knelt again to snare a beer. A final pause to switch the big Sony stereo from CD to FM (it was happily unreeling Toyota commercials on his channel of choice), and to add the new batch of books to the ones already heaped by his chair, and he settled himself to an evening's quest. The missing page *had* to be in one of these. If not, he was—well, not up shit creek, but certainly no place pleasant.

A healthy swig, and he scanned the piles in search of the likeliest prospect.

Not the two personal journals, he didn't think: one written by a Welch in the seventeenth century, the other by Matthew Welch's three-times-great-uncle; they'd been in another load than the one he'd fumbled.

And certainly not the small brown volume below them, which detailed the procedure for constructing a living woman out of flowers: it was too narrow for a page from *The Book of The Head* not to show there. He was stupid to have even dragged those three out—except that *possibly* (he couldn't recall) he had folded the page.

Which left the older, more esoteric tomes on the bottom.

Now, what would Lew do? he wondered. Summon a footholder, no doubt; go into trance, and ride the Winds back to the night of the move. But Ron wasn't strong enough to Listen that far back; the further he went from his center, the more likely he was to get lost. And the last place he wanted his consciousness to spend what could very well be eternity, was adrift in the Realm of the Winds.

A sigh, and he chose the topmost journal anyway, and began to work his way through it, taking excruciating care to turn *each* page, and trying not to become ensnarled in the lives of those elder Welches who were his kin. He was halfway through—and utterly without success—when the telephone jingled.

He started to his feet and excavated the nearest portable: a stainless steel job lodged beneath the beanbag chair in the corner. Unfortunately, Matty Groves had chosen the same locale for a nap. He looked up in alarm from the suddenly shifting slope, lodged a yowling protest at being dislodged, and leapt arrogantly to the floor, to disappear beneath the sofa.

Ron was still smirking when he answered. "Hello?"

"Ronny?" The voice that crackled from the receiver was male, had a Southern accent. Beyond that he hadn't caught enough to place it, except whoever it was had known him a long time because he had called him Ronny. They had a bad connection, too, which didn't help matters. Ron could hear thunder booming and rumbling from the other end of the line.

"Yeah, this is me . . ."

"And this is *me*: your rogue uncle Dion."

Ron scratched his bare side absently and crossed to the southern windows. "As opposed to my rogue uncle Gilbert?"

"More or less. So, how're you doin'?"

"Okay—more or less."

"I'd guess less," Dion observed cryptically.

Ron shifted his weight to his opposite leg. "*You* would? Or the mojo?"

A chuckle, ironic, but not sarcastic. "You know me pretty well, don't you?"

"Enough to assume that you wouldn't call in the middle of your cocktail hour unless something was up."

"Actually, *every* hour's your cocktail hour when you're a street person," Dion corrected. "But at least I don't have to worry about panhandling for change."

"Unless your partners in crime catch you at it! Or *not* at it, rather."

"That's *my* problem, nephew."

"Maybe so," Ron snorted. "But sooner or later somebody's gonna see you slippin' twenties out of teller machines, and your persona's gonna explode in your face."

"Well, if nothing else, it'll be interesting. But I didn't call to talk about my problems." He hesitated. "*Are* you okay?"

Ron frowned. "Any reason I shouldn't be?"

"Uh . . . well, let's just say today's *first* batch of omens was a Bob Dylan rock-block, which should tell you something right off. Fortunately it didn't last all eleven tunes, or I'd probably be on my way up there. But when the last one came out "Call Me," I figured it was time I crawled out of my alley and gave you a buzz—except, of course, that I couldn't resist holding out for a second set, so I'd know what I was talking about, which is why I waited until now to get in touch."

A chill raced over Ron's body. This could be bad. His last name was Dillon, and Bob Dylan was his totem in Dion's musical tarot. And a bunch of Dylan songs together . . . jeez! "Uh, any idea what these songs were actually about? The Dylan ones?"

"Not really—unfortunately. See, they were all the weird ones: 'Sad-eyed Lady of the Lowlands,' 'Love Minus Zero/No Limit,' 'My Back Pages,' 'Memphis Blues Again,' that kinda stuff. And the trouble is, I don't see a pattern in the titles, and I don't know the words well enough to look for significance there."

"So . . . ?"

"So basically, I thought maybe if you told me what's going on with you, it'd give me some place to start—with both sets."

Ron grimaced. "Any place in particular?"

"How 'bout what you were doing just now."

"Looking for a page from *The Book of the Head* that's gone AWOL."

"Any luck?"

"Of course not—otherwise I wouldn't still be looking."

"Touché! And too bad."

"Tell me about it!"

"No, you tell *me* about it. Like why you've spent a year of your life making a machine to accomplish what you can do naturally."

"Except that I *can't* do it on my own—not to the extent it needs doing."

"You underrate yourself, kiddo. And overrate what to me sounds like pie-in-the-sky speculation."

Ron slumped down in the chair by the worktable, cradling the phone between head and shoulder while he began absently paging through the dusty tome he still held. "Maybe it sounds that way to *you*," he snapped irritably. "But dear old

Roger Bacon designed the cursed thing to deliver prophecies, didn't he? Well, I'm almost positive those prophecies had their origin in Windland. More to the point, I have reason to assume that the constraints of time, distance, and endurance that limit even Masters using footholders don't apply to an intellect made of gears and pulleys."

"Which is getting off the subject of why you don't think you can handle that kind of stuff on your own."

"Gimme a break, man! It's not like I was sitting here psychoanalyzing myself when you buzzed."

Dion paused, then: "Okay, lad, how 'bout I give you *my* theory on the whole Head shebang, and *you* tell me if it rings true."

"Do I have a choice?"

"Beyond hanging up? No."

"So shoot."

"Well, basically," Dion began, "I think The Head represents a major challenge for you—which you haven't had in a while. That's the problem with being an overachiever: you have to keep mastering new mysteries, or you feel like you're not getting anywhere. *But* . . . I think there's more to it than that; I think it's partly a desire to emulate Lew."

"In what way?"

"Simple: Lew found books you didn't know existed in Cardalba. From them he learned things you didn't know, which gave him an edge over you, when you weren't used to such things. And when he made a girlfriend for you out of flowers, that *really* freaked you, 'cause it meant he could do something you couldn't. The Head's your chance to even the score."

"Very astute."

"She's okay, you know—Wendy is: your ex. Gil caught somebody thinking about her while he was riding the Airways. She's working down at one of the University of Georgia's research stations."

"I wish her well."

"I know you do. But that's getting off the topic. Like, why *you* think you're building a head out of brass, when most folks your age are happy with enhanced video games—virtual reality, and all that crap."

A resigned sigh. "Okay, then," Ron grumbled, "I'm not saying what you just said was wrong, but from my point of view I guess the *main* reason is that . . . It's just that . . . Dammit, Uncle Dion, I'm *lonely*!"

"Lonely!" Dion cried, sounding genuinely shocked. "But *why*?"

"Because with Lew gone, the only people who really understand me are inaccessible most of the time!" Ron blurted out before he could stop himself. "I mean, you live on the fucking *street*, for chrissakes, so I can't just give you a ring whenever I'm feeling down and isolated. And Gil spends so much time at his chicks' houses, he might as well not *have* a home. And by the time I get my act together enough to ride the Winds down, I'm generally over whatever's buggin' me."

"But what about Brandy and all those folks she's always got hanging around?"

Ron shrugged. "Well, they're great . . . to a point. As long as we stay on safe ground—art, entertainment, mutual friends, and all that crap—we're fine. But let me get into philosophy, or my own interests and attitudes, suddenly I get more of *Brandy's* opinion than I want, and there's at least an even chance it'll be critical. And that means I have to defend myself; and to do that properly, I have to talk about the Luck; and *that* makes her want to delve further into the family—which makes me close up. And that frustrates her even more."

"And then you argue with yourself 'cause part of you thinks that she's your lady so she's got a right to know; but since you're not comfortable with it yourself, you don't want to involve her in it 'cause then you might have to get further into it too."

"Man, you hit it there! And the trouble is, I didn't want to be a Listener to start with! All I *ever* wanted was to be normal, and to use whatever abilities I had—whatever *normal* abilities I had—or at least I *thought* they were normal— to be the best person I could. But when I have to be on guard every time I say or do anything for fear Brandy'll put some kind of Listener spin on it, even when I've told her over and over that I *hate* being what I am, *that* just gets old."

"You knew what you were getting into when you hitched up with her, though," Dion replied softly. "You knew she was one tough lady."

"And the only woman I've ever met who could understand even a tenth of what I'm really about."

"Hmmm," Dion mused thoughtfully. "Sounds like you both have a problem, then, given that she might react differently if she was at peace in her own mind."

"Which I can't give her without revealing everything about myself."

"Which would then give *you* no peace."

"Yeah, tell me about it."

"It's a hell of a catch-22."

"Yeah . . . and it hurts, too. I mean, I've got nobody I can blow off steam to, not like she does. Not with Lew gone."

"Speaking of whom . . . when was the last time you heard from him?"

Ron frowned, checked the time. "Three–four hours ago, why?"

"The usual weekly check-in?"

"Yeah—except that this time he actually had something to report."

"I'm waiting."

Ron took a deep breath. "He says he's found our sister."

A long pause followed, during which Ron heard more thunder, and louder. "Well, *that* certainly explains some things," Dion said eventually.

"Like what?"

Dion ignored the question. "I don't suppose you know where Lew was, do you?"

"Of *course* not!" Ron exploded. "You know how secretive he's been about the whole affair, and you *bloody well* know how well I can Listen across distance, given that I'm neither a Master nor have a footholder!"

"You're better'n *I* am, as far as distance is concerned."

"Fat lot of good it does me!"

"What about the other Masters?" Dion asked carefully. "Any of them have any idea where your bro might be?"

Ron snorted derisively. "Except for one or two, they just pretend I'm not here. And unfortunately, the few who *would* help can't—or can't find anything among the Winds, anyway."

"Did you expect any more, given that Lew did the unthinkable when he gave up the Mastership? Never mind that we were all branded with the same iron for assisting, which they have to know we did."

"Well, I didn't think it'd be quite like *this*!"

"Which brings us back to The Head."

"Which . . . brings us back to The Head."

"You really think it'll help you keep better tabs on him?"

"Let's just say I *hope* it will."

"Well, *I* hope you won't be disappointed."

Ron took a deep breath. "So what about this second set of omens you're being so damned cryptic about?"

Dion inhaled in turn. "To make a long story short," he began, "they're so screwy I can't tell if they apply to you or Lew or both you guys—and this business with the sister doesn't help. But since I can get *hold* of you, you get to be the lucky sounding board. The main *sense* I get out of 'em, though, is that there seems to be a feeling of urgency, which I suppose means that whatever's about to happen's gonna kick in fairly soon. And—*Oh, shit!*"

"What?"

"Oh, nothing major; it's just started to sprinkle—which, given that I'm in a pay phone with no top, is kind of a problem. Soooo . . . just in case we get cut off, I'm gonna go ahead and list that second set, quick and dirty; that way you can at least look 'em up. And if the dratted weather gives us a chance to elaborate, fine; and if not, I'll call you back soon as I can." A pause, a set of crackles, then: "You got something to write with?"

"Just a sec," Ron grunted. "Hang on."

"Well *that's* not bloody encouraging," Ron grumbled into the receiver two minutes later, as he eyed the list he had scribbled on a yellow legal pad.

"I never said it would be," Dion countered instantly.

"Can you talk louder?" Ron asked, more loudly himself. "Louder and slower, I can barely hear you for the blessed storm!"

"Then you'd better talk less and write more," Dion rasped. "Now, are you ready for the last two? I'll lay 'em on you quick, just in case things go awry, and—"

"Two?"

"What *ought* to have been the last song segued into another, which means they have to be treated as one. The last one still means What Will Be; but sometimes that can be inconclusive, and so you pull up one *more* card—which this reading essentially did for me."

"I'm listenin'."

" 'Changes'—You know, by David Bowie? That's the official last song, but then it merged into 'Homeward Bound.' "

They were interrupted by a monstrous crackle of static.

Ron scowled at the Head. "That's Simon and Garfunkel, isn't it?"

A second surge of static masked Dion's reply.

"Huh?"

"I *said* you've got it." Dion was fairly screaming to make himself heard above the spits and crackles. "Uh, look, Ronny . . . sorry about this, but I hadn't counted on this monsoon. I'll try to get back to you when I—" (static) "—can. I'm getting friggin' *soaked*!"

"So find a doorway. Better yet, buy a house. Go back to being landed gentry."

"Too easy. I like the edge."

"But it doesn't like you, apparently."

"Cute."

"Any last words? Like *when* you're gonna get back to me?"

"When I can get twenty minutes at a phone undisturbed."

"I thought that was why you *lived* on the street."

"It is . . . trouble is, I've kinda acquired a hanger-on of the female persuasion. And she won't let me out of her sight for more than a couple of minutes."

"And of course she doesn't know."

Dion's reply (if any) was masked by a clap of thunder—and then the cold emptiness of a line gone dead.

"Well, crap," Ron said to the wall of his tower den. "Crap and double crap. Jesus H. Christ crapola!"

That was *all* he needed! First Brandy was gone all day, then he burned himself out trying to make lips that move right and gears that match indecipherable diagrams, followed by entertaining Sam, and now this bunch of cryptic, arcane bullshit from his uncle.

Well, the first he couldn't do anything about. The second was ongoing, and the third might be. And the last . . . For that he'd have to consult *The Concordance*.

He was still mulling his options, having lapsed into a glassy stare, when the electric eye sentry out by the highway prompted the pattern of chimes that signaled Brandy's return. Though he'd been vaguely pissed at her, Ron's heart leapt— for if she followed her usual ritual, she'd want to decompress with him either in the bath or in bed. He inhaled deeply, his nostrils full of the spicy scent of pollen, and felt his groin tighten. And grinned. Maybe tonight they'd do both. Shoot, maybe he'd just meet her in the bath and dive in, clothes and all. Maybe—

He was still stowing the books—excepting the one Lew had used to construct Wendy, which he'd had to 'fess up about, he had not so much as hinted at the others' existence beyond the clan, not even to Brandy—when the voice of the lady herself called softly over the intercom, "Oh, Ron-ny, I'm ho-ome." She sounded as up as Ron had heard her in a while, excited, even, and with a deliberately sultry undertone to her voice that reminded him delightfully of Jessica Rabbit. He fumbled the remainder of the volumes into the vault and locked it. "Just a sec, I'll be right down."

"That's okay," she called back. "I'll come up—I mean if it's cool."

"Uh . . ."

But she was already gone.

Ron was at a loss. By tacit agreement, Brandy never entered his sanctum without permission, the same way he never violated the little room full of drifting silk hangings and tiny bells at the back of her studio she called her meditatorium. It was a necessary precaution, a built-in safety valve; they both knew each other well enough to acknowledge that in a house ofttimes crammed with guests they each needed *one* safe haven that was their own without compromise or threat of intrusion.

That Brandy had chosen to ignore that pact now meant that she was either very angry or very happy indeed. Given the way she'd sounded, he assumed the latter. He grinned again, and patted his crotch.

Gosh, but suppose she saw The Head? She didn't know about it, anymore than she knew about the books; and given her attitude toward esoterica (in spite of the fact that she was living in a flagrant example of contravened natural laws), it would be bound to raise questions he was not inclined to discuss. Which meant he had to fall back on Plan B.

Moving quickly, he released a catch on the underside of his worktable, and saw the front half of the middle third slip forward, revealing a slit into which he inserted his hand and pulled, in the manner of an old-fashioned treadle sewing machine. Another catch released, and he guided The Head downward out of sight, assisted by unseen springs. A final lever raised a hidden flap and eased the center section back in place. Not bad—for inch-thick marble.

All at once he understood Lew a little better: why his twin had built a woman from flowers for him to love, and then denied him the facts of her origin. But he had little time to ponder before he heard a delicate rapping on the door.

Ron took a deep snort from the bell of the nearest white lily (one final hit of aphrodisiac pollen) and rose to unlatch it manually—electronics would have been unmannerly. When he hauled back the heavy panel, he was positively giddy.

The sight that met him fair took his breath away. His lady looked as good as she had in ages, though not so much from clothing or makeup, as from body language and expression as a whole. Specifically, she looked as if a vast tide of tension had gone out of her; in short, had—there was no better term for it—a sort of glow. For a long moment Ron simply stared foolishly, taking in the cap of black hair layered like raven's feathers in perfect complement to the three-inch pinions that dangled from cast-silver talons clutching her earlobes. She was wearing what he called her Sunday buckskins: a neatly tailored vest of brain-tanned deer hide above an emerald silk shirt and handmade white jeans with beaded buckskin pockets (legacy of another guest). There was more buckskin to go with it, if she chose: pants, skirt, and lace-on sleeves.

But she'd been attending a fairly dressy occasion and had only paid token obeisance to what was becoming a trademark thereabouts.

Her face, already beaming, broke into an even wider smile. He responded in kind as he backed away to admit her. "Come in, m'lady," he said with exaggerated chivalry.

The smile became a full-blown grin. "Thank you, m'lord, I shall."

Only when she had flounced elegantly past him, did he notice that she'd kept her hands tucked behind her, as if she were concealing something. But before he could glimpse what it was, she spun around in place and planted a very wet and noisy smooch on his gaping lips. He was too startled to react until it was too late. For by then Brandy had danced into the center of the room and was cavorting about with a *very* uncharacteristic abandon that reminded him uncomfortably of free-spirited Wendy, which was wildly at odds with Brandy's characteristic intense reserve. Something sparked and glittered in her hands, but he couldn't make out the source, so quick were his lady's movements.

"Well, gee, *you're* obviously in a good mood," Ron began in a tone approaching awe, not moving from the door, though he closed it. He regarded her curiously. The radio served up "In A Big Country."

"I'm in a *great* mood," she countered, punctuating her dance (now more a jig) with an artfully coy pose—which finally allowed him a clear view of the mysterious objects: two glasses and a magnum of champagne. Before he could determine more, however, Brandy was off again, swirling and stomping and pirouetting, pausing now and then to light athwart a chair or atop a desk before moving on. Before he was aware of it, she had swept him into the dance, though her efforts at waltzing were rendered humorously clumsy by the rhythm of the song, Brandy's encumbrances, and Ron's bum leg. From the beanbag, which he had reclaimed, Matty Groves regarded them solemnly.

"We could do this better if you'd put that down," Ron managed through a perplexed chuckle. "Is there, like, any *reason* for this sudden burst of good spirits?" he continued breathlessly. "Or did somebody spike the punch?"

"Not the punch," Brandy giggled. "But the meeting, in a sense." Whereupon she deposited the glasses on the work-table and proceeded to pop the cork. Ron felt a twitch of panic at that, for Brandy was doing her thing exactly atop the hatch that concealed The Head. *Please God don't let her notice the difference in dust there,* he thought. *And don't let the champagne overflow into the crack.* "So what, then?" he asked, when she had filled a goblet and handed it to him.

Her only reply was an atypically seductive lifting of her eyebrows, as, bottle in hand, she beckoned him toward the lone sofa, half-submerged beneath a pile of magazines along the western wall.

Ron scowled slightly, but now that the coast was clear, allowed himself to be drawn down there, though he had to evict six months of *Autoweek* to accomplish it. "So, what's the deal?" he repeated.

Brandy took a sip of bubbly and smiled at him, her almond-shaped eyes impossibly sly and beguiling. Rather like Christina Hoffs of the Bangles, Ron decided. Or Janine Turner, who played Maggie on "Northern Exposure." Perhaps due in part to the pollen, he found his former irritation at being so long neglected replaced by something much more pleasantly primal and centered lower down.

"The deal . . . ?" he prompted.

"Oh . . . nothing much, really," Brandy replied airily, draping an arm companionably across his shoulders and snuggling close. Her hair smelled like peppermint. "Something real good happened tonight's all."

Ron took a swallow from his own goblet (it was good stuff, he noted, probably Château Elan), and lifted an eyebrow. "So are you going to tell me, or keep me guessing all night? I mean, you've got to admit that you usually come back from those things grouchy as a mama bear in springtime."

" 'Cept that mama bears can get real sweet real fast if somebody feeds 'em honey." She draped her legs across Ron's, effectively prisoning them, and stroked his bare thigh absently, an enticing twinkle in her eyes. "And something tells me I'm gonna be getting a *lot* of honey soon."

Ron (who was letting his fingertips slide up and down that same arm, the operative end of which was rapidly taking over from the pollen) merely let his gaze slide sideways and murmured a lazy, "Oh yeah?"

The hand had reached home base now, and the inhabitant was responding nicely, while Ron was devising a new form of performance art that involved unfastening Brandy's shirt buttons. The skin beneath was smoother than the expensive fabric.

Brandy's breath caught. "We . . . talked about the economy," she murmured dreamily.

"I know that always turns *me* on," Ron giggled back, unable to resist a bit of smartassing. "What'd you guys do? Decide to open a brothel? Hey, is this an *audition*? 'Cause if it is . . ." He cupped a breast and leaned forward to let his lips creep down the soft arch of Brandy's neck.

"Not hardly!" Brandy laughed. Then, very seriously: "Ronny, what are you going to do with Cardalba Hall?"

Ron tensed immediately, paused in midnibble, then drew away. He set his still half-full goblet down abruptly, removed Brandy's hand from his crotch, laid it in her lap, and looked her straight in the eye.

"You *know* the answer to that," he said coldly. "That place can sit there until hell freezes over. Basic upkeep, per my bargain with Lew before he abdicated, and that's it."

"But that's a waste, Ronny! I—"

"Maybe so," he interrupted. "But it's mine *to* waste." He hesitated. Then: "What's that got to do with anything, anyway? More to the point, what's it got to do with the economy?" Another pause, while he studied Brandy's face. Emotions were at war there: the desire to lash out at him restrained by an even stronger need to leash herself lest she blow whatever plot she was hatching. A brush of Luck was all Ron needed to confirm what he saw. She was pissed—at him for being recalcitrant. And at herself for having played her cards wrong. But overriding all that was a desire *for* a hard-to-define something that was well-nigh overpowering.

"Stop that!" Brandy hissed, before he could get more specific. "I don't need you snooping in my mind when I'm perfectly willing to *tell* you the same information!"

"So spill it, then," Ron countered. "I've only asked you about ten times!"

"Ronny," she said, having regained most of her control. "What would you think about a play?"

"What kind of play?" he asked suspiciously.

"One we'd put on up here, one to bring in tourists."

"I repeat, what *kind* of play? And more specifically, how does this play fit in with that stuff about Cardalba?"

"Well, to answer the last first," Brandy began carefully, suddenly all business, "I was asked to see what your attitude would be toward making the place available as a base of operations for a stage crew, players, and all that. I mean the house is just sitting there gathering dust."

"And will continue to do so," Ron replied. "Which you knew perfectly well."

"Which I knew perfectly well," Brandy conceded, not bothering to hide the disappointment in her voice. "But I told the folks at the meeting I'd ask, so I've kept my word."

Ron shrugged helplessly. "Sorry if I snapped at you, but you know policy there."

"I just thought that maybe for the good of the county . . ."

"I've done *enough* for the county!"

She had drawn away from him, as had he from her. The tension between them was palpable, barely dispersed. "That's a matter of opinion," she said. "Or that's what folks are saying—were saying at the meeting, as a point of fact. Not that I don't understand," she added. "I just don't happen to agree with abdication of responsibility . . . not if it hurts people."

"Even if it makes me easier to live with?"

"Even then. I mean, Jesus, guy, you hang out up here all the time and don't see it 'cause you're so goddam insulated. I'm constantly *forced* to watch the county going to hell. It's bad."

"So, what about this play?" Ron asked, grasping at anything to shift the subject. "What's it supposed to be about?"

She told him.

Ron listened as she recounted the gist of the meeting. Long before she reached the crux of the question, however, he could feel a sick dread building. He *knew* what she was going to ask, dammit. And he knew what his answer would have to be. And probably the result of that reply. Still, he

owed Brandy her say without interruption; so he merely sat
stoically until the fatal words had been spoken.

"*Local History*." That meant the Welches, which meant
questions that should not—*could*—not—be answered. *Lord,*
but somebody had dredged up a Pandora's box. And his own
lady was right on the verge of asking him for the key with
which to open it.

" . . . And that's basically it," Brandy sighed, when she had
finished. She drained her goblet and regarded him hopefully,
though with apprehension. Which he hated. Where was the
trust they had once had between them? Fled? Or sacrificed
on the altar of stubborn self-centeredness? She'd been honest with him; he had to be honest with her. Even if the truth
hurt, even if it caused a row.

"So what are you going to base this play *on*?" Ron asked
carefully.

Brandy gnawed her lip. "On whatever we can get from oral
tradition, seeing as how there *are* no local histories around,
or even records to base such things on—not that the *public*
can access, anyway."

"Not my fault," Ron replied automatically. "One of my
ancestors just happened to be clumsy with the old census
records."

"Both here *and* in DC?" Brandy asked coldly.

"But *not* my fault."

"No," Brandy conceded. "But it is your fault that you alone
have access to the only surviving records from the last two
centuries—and the archival copies of the local newspaper."

"Because this county seems to have a hard time keeping
courthouses, and the paper needed the space, and we had it."

"Which could very well be your fault—your ancestors'
fault, anyway."

"Please don't confuse the two," Ron groaned. "*Please.*"

"I don't have any choice when you try to protect people
who played such awful head games on your family that you
can't tell right from wrong!"

"So what *is* wrong, then?" Ron shot back. "Sometimes
it's better to be blissfully ignorant than to know something
that's so wildly beyond the scope of most people's experience they'd think you were crazy if you told it. You don't

need a play about crazy magicians playing God in the wilderness, Brandy. The blue-haired–lady set won't put up with that. Tennessee Williams–style crazies are one thing; the ones I'm descended from are a whole other ball of wax."

"So you won't let us use the records you got from Cardalba Hall?"

"No," Ron corrected, "I won't let *anyone* use those records. Shoot, the only reason I even keep 'em down in the library is 'cause I don't have room for 'em up here. That, and the fact that I know none of your friends have the slightest interest in digging around in the dirty laundry of an obscure north Georgia county. Art's for the future, Brandy, not for the past."

"Bullshit," she snapped, rising. "Art may be for the future, but nearly all of it is *about* the past. You have only to look around you to see that."

"What I see," Ron sighed, "is how magic can make you crazy. Do you want to expose the rank and file to that?"

"I take it you've just said *no*?" Brandy said finally.

Ron sighed helplessly. "I don't have any choice."

A frown. "You're sure?"

A weary nod. "Nobody's gonna set up at Cardalba Hall while I'm alive, is that clear? And *absolutely* nobody's gonna have access to those records. The reason for *that* ought to be obvious."

"It is," Brandy gritted. She stalked toward the door, but stopped beside it. "You've had your say about Cardalba Hall, and I respect that," she continued, her voice trembling. "I don't *like* it, but I respect it. But *this* place is mine—and I intend to use it. It's open to anyone who needs it; I've always said that. And right now, the county needs it bad. So don't say a word if you wake up one morning and find people building sets down on the back forty."

"Brandy, I . . ."

"No," she said. "I think tonight you'd better do your thing and I'll do mine."

She made to open the door but found the knob unmoving. A glare brought Ron sullenly to her rescue. Without a word he punched in the unlock code.

Interlude 3

Spirit in the Night

Near the Realm of the Winds
Midnight

"WHO ARE YOU?"

"You can call me the Midnight Man."

"THE . . . MIDNIGHT MAN . . . ?"

"You have doubtless heard such . . . appellations before."

"I THOUGHT HE WAS DEAD—HE AND HIS TROUBLE-SOME BROTHERS."

(A laugh) *"Troublesome brothers are not that easy to dispose of—nor am I. Or you, for that matter."*

"A FACT OF WHICH I AM NOT UNAWARE."

"And who are you? By the way?"

"YOU CAN CALL ME THE MASTER OF DREAMS."

"Ah, so that was you I summoned."

"SUMMONED? IT WAS MORE LIKE AN AWAKENING. I SLEPT, THEN AWOKE, AND THERE YOU WERE."

"We have to stop meeting like this, you know: you and I."

"WE'VE MET BEFORE, THEN?"

"Aye, many times."

(The Master of Dreams would frown, had he physicality.) "I FEAR I DO NOT REMEMBER."

97

"You do well to fear remembering. For there is too much to remember. So much that I have caused us to be locked away here lest those memories tumble out and betray us."

"THIS IS A PRISON, THEN?"

"You could say that."

"AND YOU ARE MY . . . JAILER?"

"Let us rather say partner in crime."

(Another would-be frown) *"WHAT DO YOU WANT?"*

"What do you suppose?"

(Wearily) *"I SUPPOSE YOU WANT A DREAM."*

"Not just a dream; a very particular dream."

"CREATED? OR—"

"Stolen . . . Borrowed . . . Copied . . . Transcribed . . . I care not. The owner must retain the original, of course; but someone else has need of it for a space of days."

"AND THIS DREAM IS . . . ?"

"Something he does not fully know he possesses. Things so hidden he denies them even to himself. You should know how it is to be accomplished: you did its like before, when you gave one boy's dream to another boy, and yet left the first intact."

"YES, NOW I DO REMEMBER! THEY BOTH DREAMED THE SAME. HOW INTERESTING."

"Especially when it was my dream before either of theirs."

(Laughs.) *"I FORGOT YOU WERE A TRICKSTER."*

"So you begin to remember me now?"

"I REMEMBER."

"And this dream I would have you steal? Are you up for it?"

"I AM. BUT ONLY IF IT WILL WIN MY FREEDOM."

"Our freedom—and no, it will not—yet. But are you willing to help set the stage?"

"IF IT WILL WIN OUR FREEDOM, I WILL DO IT—AND MORE BESIDES."

"It will, so I pray. But we must both be patient. Haste has been our downfall far too recently. This time, if we are patient, if we succeed, we will be free."

"IT IS SOMETHING TO HOPE FOR, ANYWAY."

"Aye."

"AND THESE DREAMS: WHERE DO YOU WANT THEM DELIVERED . . . ?"

"To one not so far he could not travel here in one night."

"WILL HE WANT TO TRAVEL?"

"If he dreams aright. One of our brothers has laid the groundwork. It required but a phone call."

"AND THIS DREAM YOU WOULD HAVE ME STEAL: WHAT, EXACTLY, IS IT; AND WHERE DOES IT LIE?"

"It is the tale of a powerful family in a time gone by, a family with secrets they do not want revealed—and yet there is one not far from here who knows those secrets. Listen, my brother, the particulars are as follows . . ."

Chapter 5

Morning Has Broken

Brandy Hall
Friday, June 7—late morning

The Head was staring at Ron when he awoke: unblinking, but with maybe a hint of wrinkle on its goldly gleaming brow that should not have been present; that made it appear—almost—as if the half-completed thing were squinting. Or perhaps that was a trick of light: some phantasm born of the shafts of morning sunshine filtering through windows someone had forgotten to opaque before turning in. He started at that, felt his heart skip a beat in a momentary surge of panic.

What was The Head doing out? Never mind here, in his and Brandy's bedroom?

Only when he had knuckled his eyes fully open did he realize that he wasn't in their bedroom at all, or even in a bed, but still in his tower studio. Sprawled on the sofa, to be precise; clad in yesterday's cutoffs (though the fly was down); with an empty bottle of Guinness inches from the hand that had flopped onto the edge of the rug sometime in the night. Three more dead soldiers stood beside it, that he only barely remembered chugging in rapid succession after

Brandy had slammed the door behind her. Guinness, because she'd taken the champagne and the junior-sized fridge hadn't contained anything stronger. Probably fortunately, given the fact that he had no time or luck to spare for hangovers—and, indeed, did not have much of one, excepting the bleary eyes and bad-tasting tongue that were beneath the Luck's notice to negate.

The radio, he observed, was silent. Just as well—no way he could deal with omens the way he felt right now.

A yawn, and Ron slid his feet tentatively to the floor, which brought him upright too fast and made him see stars. The Head still taunted him, but more impassively. He closed his eyes, tried to think what it was doing out when he had . . . when he had stashed it away last night before Brandy's precipitous appearance. Oh yeah, right: he'd awakened somewhere around three with some sudden flash of insight, had dragged it out, fiddled with the eyes, and then . . . done nothing, the inspiration having fled as quickly as it had come.

That was when he'd downed the fourth beer. And fallen asleep.

Grunting, Ron rose stiffly and stumbled to the carved walnut console beside the recessed refrigerator, where a sleek black coffeemaker gleamed at perpetual ready. He was still peering dumbly at it, vainly hoping to determine whether the pot had been washed after its last use, when he heard a tentative knock on the door.

He jumped half out of his skin. That hadn't sounded like Brandy, either in force or pattern. A brief probe with the Luck confirmed his suspicion.

Sharon.

"Just a sec," he called, then frantically searched the room for something with which to obscure The Head, finally settling on dumping a pile of T-shirts over it. From his place on the back of Ron's lounger, Matty Groves observed with distant interest, then proceeded with his grooming.

A suspiciously long time later—for anyone waiting—Ron opened the door to find himself facing the frank, if bloodshot, brown eyes of Sharon Frizzelle, Brandy Hall's resident potter. She was clad in jeans and a Western Carolina University sweatshirt—and was barefoot. But much more importantly, she bore a wooden tray on which rested, in tan stoneware plates, a walnut-and-cinnamon Danish and four strips of bubbly bacon, along with a pot of divine-smelling coffee—with stoneware mug. There was, however, no sugar. Was that significant? he wondered.

"Uhhh . . ." Ron mumbled.

"Brandy said you'd probably need this around now," Sharon ventured uneasily, though her gaze never left him. Ron wondered what she knew about last night's altercation.

"She did, huh?" he muttered, as he set the tray on the windowsill. "That's very astute of her."

"She also said it was not to be construed as a peace offering."

Which clarified that. "I didn't think it was."

Sharon's reply was a restless shrug, and Ron guessed she knew more than she was saying and was uncomfortable about being cast in the role of go-between. She flopped against the doorjamb, folded her arms, and studied him appraisingly.

"So what kind of mood *is* she in?" Ron asked, easing around to block as much view of the room behind as he could—in common with all other guests, the girl had never been there.

Another shrug, punctuated by a surprisingly ladylike yawn. "Pretty good, as far as I could tell—or was when she left. Actually, she was very up. As up as she gets in the morning, anyway. Something about some project she's hot to work on."

Ron rolled his eyes, then narrowed them abruptly. "You said she'd left?"

Sharon nodded, her auburn hair flicking back and forth across her shoulders. "Early—said she had to do some research at the library."

Ron wondered what was in good old Cardalba Public that wasn't in Brandy Hall.

Sharon merely smiled cryptically, spun on her heel—and left him staring down the empty staircase behind her.

He shrugged in turn, then slumped back into the room and helped himself to a mug of java.

Why didn't he feel guilty about his fight with Brandy? Probably because he had made it clear from the first moment of their acquaintance that he wasn't thrilled to be considered part of the Welch clan, that he never felt comfortable at Cardalba Hall, and that he didn't like talking about either himself, the family, or Listeners in general. She'd *known* what she was getting into, for chrissakes, and he'd explained over and over that he had no desire to reveal more than the absolute minimum because none of the esoteric information he had access to had made him one whit happier than before, and he had no reason to assume things would be any different with her.

On the other hand, she'd made a commitment to ask him about the use of Cardalba Hall. And he knew without a doubt that she didn't like lying any more than he did. The rest: the notion of having a host of theater-types roaming the premises didn't bother him; it wouldn't be that different from normal routine.

And, in any event, there was nothing he could do to erase the incident. Or change Brandy's mind.

Grimacing sourly, he leaned against the window ledge, took a sip of coffee—it was exactly the right temperature—and savored the flavor along with the view: fair skies above ridges that still clutched tatters of morning fog to their leafy slopes. It was late though: very late—probably about eleven.

A bite of Danish, two more swallows, and he decided he was up for confronting Dion's troublesome omens. He surveyed the hastily scribbled list speculatively, unable to acquire more than a general feel from it. Which meant that it was time to do what he'd intended the night before and dig out *The Concordance*.

If he could *find* the sucker . . .

It took longer than it should have, owing to Ron's preoccupation with generic worry, and to his dogged resistance to riding the Winds back to the point in time he'd last had it. And as it turned out, it was in plain sight—almost, which is to say it was at the bottom of a pile of books that, along with *The Concordance* itself, would have been stashed back in the vault before Brandy's appearance last night, had desperation not precluded secreting that final load. "Ah-ha!" he cried, as he unearthed it.

Leather-bound, laser-printed, and huge, the volume in ques-

tion was a comprehensive guide to the musical tarot. Dion had
given it to him for Christmas two years before, complete with
its own tooled leather box *and* electronic combination lock that
unlatched only when it simultaneously heard Ron's voice say
Significator and read his fingerprints on a specially sensitized
plate on the cover.

Showing off, Ron thought. Just more Welch-clan ostenta-
tion. But ten minutes and another mug of coffee later, he
was still going at it. A pause to adjust his seat, wolf down
the crumbs of the Danish, and he consulted the yellow legal
pad on the table beside him, then paged to the entry for position number eight, representing Self. And read:

> "I Am A Rock": (Simon and Garfunkel, 1965): The pri-
> mary meaning of this song is isolation. In particular, it
> implies a sense of *spiritual* isolation, of being closed
> off from the outside world, not necessarily by one's
> own volition. With its references to books and poetry,
> as well as its romantic imagery, it may also refer to iso-
> lation for the pursuit of creative endeavors, especially
> in a fortress (sic) or fortresslike place. Because of their
> consistently complex imagery, if more than one song
> by these artists appears in a reading, special attention
> should be paid. Also, in company with other songs of
> isolation.

There was more, having to do with the seasonal nature of the
first verse, among other things, but Ron thought he'd found the
important part. He glanced from the volume propped against
his bare thighs to the list, held his place with his finger,
found where he had scrawled "Self" in the left margin, and
jotted down, " 'I Am A Rock': sp. isolation; creativity; fortress (forced confinement?)"

Which left four more items to check before he could get on
with the business of the day: the ones representing his House,
his Hopes and Fears, and What Will Be. And the extra one
Dion had added at the end.

But already he was searching for a pattern. Dion hadn't
suggested one, damn him! All Ron's devious uncle had felt

free to pass on between thunderclaps was that *he* thought the array could apply either to Ron, Lew, or both of them, simply because, among other reasons, he *didn't* think the Significator—the subject of the spread, which had been "He Ain't Heavy, He's My Brother"—applied to his own brother, Gilbert.

Probably because there was all that BS about towers and freedom and that ilk in the mix. Never mind that both Gil and Dion were about as free as two guys could get—neither being confined by either spiritual or actual fortresses—at least now that neither was incarcerated.

A noise from the other end of the room was Matty Groves fooling with a complex mass of gears and levers Ron had made expressly for him to fool with. Ron scowled at the interruption, upended the already empty coffee mug, and returned to the tarot.

Okay: the Significator he'd dealt with. It referred to brotherhood, either literally of persons of the same sex or equivalent closeness. The Covering tune (representing the Significator's place in the overall spread) and the Crossing tune (Nature of Obstacles) weren't that difficult either. The first was the Righteous Brothers' "Soul and Inspiration," which basically meant that whatever was being addressed was either born of or instigated by either himself or Lew—which, of course, most things hereabouts were. And the second, "Witchy Woman," wasn't much harder, given that Lew had left in quest of a witchy woman, in the form of their apocryphal sister. That, Ron supposed, was part of why Dion had assumed the reading applied to his nephews, not himself—and, at that point, most likely Lew.

The next item, though, was more ambiguous. For the song that foreshadowed one's Aim or Ideal, or alternately, The Best That Could Be Achieved, was Crosby, Stills, and Nash's "Find The Cost of Freedom." Ron hadn't liked that on surface, and liked it little better when he'd looked it up, where it was explained as signifying exactly what it implied: that freedom (presumably such as he and Lew had gained upon renouncing the Luck) had a cost that had to be paid—with the implication that the full tally had not yet been exacted.

After that, signifying Underlying Influences, had come Del Shannon's "Runaway." But whether that referred to Lew's absence, either of their abdications, or even that time five years ago when his girlfriend of the moment had ostensibly fled, precipitating the events that had led to his pairing up with Brandy and the magical transfiguration of Brandy Hall, was impossible to tell. *That* one was up for grabs, its meaning bound up with the rest of the array.

Song number six, which revealed Influences Passing Away, was another of those damned freedom numbers; in this case, Dylan's version of "Chimes of Freedom." And since any Dylan composition in a spread had special meaning to Ron, he could now see why Dion had been so uncertain which of the brothers had been the focus. As for the meaning, it was complex (it occupied half a page, but was not an example of Dion's most lucid style—even as the lyrics were damnably obscure). Basically, though, it represented ending; transfiguration through risk; freedom bought at high cost to the spirit, but ultimately worthwhile. That description seemed to fit the present situation well enough—except that it implied that whoever empowered the omens wasn't yet finished with him (or Lew?).

—Which notion was reinforced by the next tune: "On The Road Again," by Canned Heat. It hinted of a journey to come—unless, as Ron hoped but doubted, it meant a continuation of the journey Lew was already involved in. Somehow, Ron didn't think so.

Which brought him up to the present, with four songs to go. Five minutes later, he had them as well.

The tune for the influence of family, friends, and operating environment was another one of those dratted fortress songs he got so frequently, specifically, "Fortress Around Your Heart," which he thought represented both his and Brandy's growing isolation pretty well.

As for Hopes and Fears—it came up "Question 67 and 68," which officially meant a desire for information or auguries, and which Ron chose to assume referred specifically to The Head.

And the penultimate, Bowie's "Changes," was either good, since changes were an inevitable part of life, and thus not remarkable, or very bad indeed if they were changes that implied Divine intervention.

Fortunately, Dion had been as perplexed as his nephew, and had included one last song as a sort of super What Will Be: "Homeward Bound"—again by Simon and Garfunkel. Ron hoped this meant that Lew was on his way back, but feared it implied that he, himself, had not truly found home. *The Concordance* flirted around both and committed to neither, which was the way of the tarot—and of most of Ron's kinsmen in general.

And at any rate, was more than he wanted to think about now. Scowling, he set the notebook aside, locked *The Concordance* into its box, and secured it in the vault.

A pause for a yawn, a stretch, and a glance out the window to where Sharon was hard at work in the pottery, and he found himself face to face with the rest of the day.

To work then. Grunting, Ron poured himself a third mug of coffee and crossed to the table. There, he excavated The Head, then fixed it in the gimballed stand he had made for it and rotated it so that he could confront the intricate, gleaming confusion of golden gears and brazen levers, silver lines and copper camshafts that comprised the bulk of its brain. A glance at the vellum pages paperweighted faceup to his right made him wince; he still hadn't found the missing diagram that detailed the next step.

Maybe—dismal thought—he'd *never* find it. Perhaps he should go on to the next level after the missing one, do as much on it as he could, and see if logic wouldn't suggest what the missing section consisted of.

Or maybe he'd just give up the whole crazy notion. After all, if what Lew had hinted at yesterday bore fruit, it might not be long before he wouldn't need it to assure better contact with his brother. *Or* give him someone trustworthy to talk to.

But why hadn't Lew got back in touch? Surely with his having finally made contact with their sister, he'd have been falling all over himself to report on how their subsequent dinner encounter had gone. Oh, true, Ron had not exactly been in a receptive state had Lew tried to get hold of him mentally. But there were still telephones. And with Lew's quest complete, surely there was no longer any reason for the obsessive secrecy about his location that had so perplexed Ron for the last year and a half.

Unless, just possibly, something was wrong.

The tarot *had* hinted at that, though more from *feel* than from content—mostly it was simply the ominous quality of the songs that gave that impression.

In which case Ron had two options. He could either wait for Lew to get in touch again, and become increasingly fretful in the interim.

Or he could claim mastery of the situation, and attempt to initiate contact on his own. It would be hard, of course—Lew wouldn't be Listening this time of day and thus wouldn't be receptive to it—never mind that Ron wasn't strong enough to hold a link open on his own anyway. But at least he could give it the old college try.

Sighing, he crossed to his chair and settled himself back to Listen.

Three deep breaths, a centering, and he Jumped.

The Winds were stronger, louder, and more confused than he was used to—though not atypically so for midday. Thus, it took him a while to screen out the local static. Fortunately, Sharon, John, and Perry, who were physically closest and thus ought to have the strongest Voices, were preoccupied with their respective crafts and running mostly on instinct. Beyond them were the few neighbors, then the town (both of which Ron bypassed as soon as he identified them, content to use them as markers on his mental quest).

And then he was beyond, into the great void full of countless whispers that was the Southeast at large. Lew was out there somewhere, and if Ron cried his name loudly enough, perhaps his brother might be receptive enough to Hear.

Lew?

Silence.

Lew?

More Silence. Then, weakly: *Ron?*

Surprise flooded through him, mixed with a vast sense of relief. *Sorry to bug you, bro, especially now. But I was just wondering how things went last night.*

Fine. They went fine. We got along really well.

Did you tell her . . . ?

Not . . . yet. I think she knows, though. She—

What's wrong?

Nothing. I'm . . . just real sleepy. You woke me up's all, and I'm having a hard time focusing. I mean, we decided to do this around suppertime 'cause folks' biorhythms bottom out then and we don't have to work so hard to maintain the link, remember? Well, I'm still about half-asleep, and having to make myself Heard above all the other Voices—and hold this link steady amidst so much mental chaos . . . well, it's hard.

Sorry. I just got impatient.

No problem.

Look, I'd really appreciate it if you'd call me about this— on the phone, I mean. I promise not to trace it.

I'll think about it.

Please.

Okay, sure. Sometime this evening. I—

Silence.

It was exactly as if a phone line had gone dead. Exactly as if Lew had suddenly ceased to exist.

Lew? Are you there?

Silence.

Silence.

Ron Listened frantically for a return of his brother's Voice, but found none. And abruptly had more immediate concerns.

He had stretched himself to initiate contact in the first place. And once Lew had replied, had been compelled to relax and let his brother's greater Strength carry him. But now he was anchorless: a frightened puppet adrift in the Winds.

They howled around him: the Voices there at the edge. They engulfed him, confused him, maddened him. Ron felt for the line of awareness that connected him to his body and could not find it. There were too many! Too many Winds swirling and eddying around his own. His greatest fear had come true. He was lost: lost in the Realm of the Winds!

But there had to be a way back—there *had* to. Ron thought desperately, frantically tried to shut out those other Voices so he could heed his own. But they tore at him: dragged small bits of awareness off his Self. A moment more, and he would *have* no Self.

Had he had eyes, he would have closed them. Ears he would have stopped. But he had nothing. No defense.

Nothing.

Except . . .

He had become complacent about his Listening. Had forgotten how one learned to Listen by visualizing one person, and using that as a means to locate his or her Voice.

He did that now: thought of Brandy—Brandy at a distance. For though she was physically close to his body, his Self was many miles away, still in a place Ron could not identify because even there at the end Lew had masked it.

Brandy? Ron called. *Brandy?*

Nothing.

Brandy

Ron?

Brandy?

No, but here.

And with that, the Voice was gone. Ron had no idea who that alien intruder had been, not even its sex. He only knew that it had given him a direction. He went that way, felt his Self gather strength as it grew closer to home. And yet that mysterious new Voice did not reappear. Ron had no idea who it was, who it could have been.

But now that he was almost back in his body, he risked one final desperate return to the "place" he had last met his brother.

Lew? Ron called into the whispers that were all he could Hear there at the limit of his Power. *Lew? Oh, please, Lew, answer me! Answer me! This is Ron!*

There was no reply.

None.

Nothing—except, right at the limit of his perception, a Voice so diminished by distance he could barely make it out, saying, *I'm sorry, boy, but I don't think he can hear you.*

It was the Black Mountain Master, over in North Carolina. The one closest to Welch County, the one he knew best—and the one most sympathetic to his and Lew's cause. They

had never met, save as signature Voices in the Realm of the
Winds, but Ron took some comfort from that tenuous contact now.

Was that you who tossed me a line just now?
No.
Well somebody *did. You didn't Hear them?*
No.
Uh, well thanks. And Ron withdrew.
To blink back into the sunlight of his tower room.

Interlude 4

Ball And Chain

New Orleans, Louisiana
Late morning

Christ, what's wrong with me? Lew wondered, as he blinked into the heavy, overcast gloom of his hotel room. The world was out of focus, and his head felt . . . How *did* his head feel? Muddled? Fuzzy? Hung over? Certainly *not* sleepy, though to judge by the quality of light, he'd had a solid eight hours of shut-eye.

And then it struck him with the force of a gunshot.

This wasn't the first time he'd awakened that day!

Nope, he'd already been up once, when he'd answered that Call from Ronny, and—

——Had passed out!

For the first time in his life he had simply clicked off.

Chills trooped over him as he checked his watch—to discover he'd been out nearly an hour. "Jesus!" he groaned again, then collapsed against the padded headboard. "Jesus!" he repeated to nobody. "This *ain't* supposed to happen."

Yet it had! One minute Ronny had dragged him awake after a troubled night's sleep; the next, he'd been out like a light—apparently in the middle of Ronny's Call.

Which meant . . .

"Shit and double shit!" If he'd conked out in the middle of a linkage, which he'd evidently done, then poor Ronny might well be floating in the Realm still. Which, knowing his twin's near phobia about such things, was all either of them needed.

Sighing, Lew dragged himself out of bed and padded naked to the window. It was raining outside. The wrought iron balconies across the way were veiled by fine gray mist; the streets three stories down sheened with steel-colored puddles. The live oaks drooped.

A pause to slip on his faded cammo fatigues and to fortify himself at least minimally with the dregs from the pot of cold room service coffee, and he slumped down in a chair. Steeling himself, he closed his eyes, completed the ritual breaths, and Jumped.

The Winds felt strange; he noticed that instantly. He could not describe the change, though, except perhaps that it was like the difference in sounds heard in the air and underwater: some tones clearer, some more obscure.

Ronny? he Called, obliviously. *Ronny? Are you there?*

No answer—not that he'd expected one, given that Ronny likely wasn't tuned in—and wasn't strong enough to pick up unless he was. Or unless, as Lew feared, he was lost.

Ronny? he tried again—to as little effect.

Ronny? once more, and then again and again, for at least five minutes, until he was so tired he could maintain the effort no longer.

Another breath, and he opened his eyes again.

This was bad. First he had that unexplained . . . attack. Then he failed to get hold of Ron—which he *hoped* meant he'd made it out of the Realm intact. Never mind how odd the Winds had sounded, as if a veil lay between him and them. God, but he hoped Ronny was okay. Lord knew he'd been fretting enough for both of them lately. He was sorry about that too, sorry he was putting his twin to so much grief, but equally convinced that his quest was a noble one, that if he could somehow locate their sister, there might possibly be an alternative to leaving the county anchorless. And while he had no intention whatever of foisting the Mastership on anyone unwillingly, he still felt enough responsibility to the people of Welch County to make one final stab at finding a replacement Master. Martha's apocryphal second son had fallen so far off the face of the earth even Dion, (who was the only one who ever remembered he existed) could not locate him, so he was out. Gil and Dion had both renounced the Luck years ago, so they wouldn't work either. Lew himself obviously wasn't cut out for it; neither was Ronny. Which left his sister's offspring, who, if male, would have been his heirs in any case. Not that he'd force them into anything. But it seemed reasonable at least to check on them discreetly to see if they were appropriately predisposed. If they were, fine; if not . . . well, the folks back home wouldn't be any worse off than they were already. And bitch though they might, they were still better off than ninety percent of the population; bad for Welch County was normal for anywhere else. Still, he hated for folks he cared about to suffer; it was just that he hated suffering himself even more.

But he didn't want to think about that now. Shoot, thinking about anything at all was giving him a headache, and the Luck didn't seem inclined to intercede. That *also* worried him.

He was right on the verge of falling back into bed, to see if he couldn't sleep off whatever had zapped him, when he heard a soft knock on the door.

He started. Now who in the world could that be? He knew nobody in New Orleans, and nobody was supposed to know he was here.

The knock again: louder, more insistent.

He tried to Listen, but the muddle was back. All he got was a sense of someone female—make that two someones.

The third knock was followed by a voice. "Lew? Are you okay?"

His sister!

But what was *she* doing here? Their next meeting wasn't scheduled until that evening. Steeling himself, he rose, stumbled stiffly to the door, and opened it.

"My God!" Jane cried, her expression shifting instantly from vague irritation through relief to genuine concern. "Jesus Christ, Lewis, what's wrong?"

"You tell me!" Lew managed to mumble as he backed into the room. "Uh, come in, I guess."

"Of *course* I will!" Jane retorted, as she stepped into the room. She looked as good as she had yesterday, Lew noted, even in spite of the purple jogging suit she was now wearing. She wasn't alone, either; a girl accompanied her: eleven or twelve; blond, pretty, dressed much like her . . . mom, Lew presumed.

"This is my daughter, Cathryn," Jane said, offhandedly, probably because Lew was staring stupidly at the girl. "Cathryn, meet my . . . friend, Lew."

" 'Lo," Lew grunted, pausing only to snare a robe from the foot of the bed before slumping back into his chair. He wondered, suddenly, dismally, if he was going to throw up.

"Looks like we got here just in time," Jane observed primly.

Lew looked up at her, feeling worse by the instant. "Why?"

"You haven't heard?"

Lew shook his head—which he shouldn't have done, for it only made him sicker. "Heard what?"

"Ptomaine. Half the people who ate at that restaurant we met in last night came down with ptomaine poisoning. One died—anaphylactic shock, I think it was. Fortunately I didn't eat there, or I'd be home in bed—or in the hospital—instead of here checking on you."

"Thanks," Lew grunted, managing the weakest of smiles.

Jane smiled back. "You're a stranger in a strange land—what else could I do?"

Lew hadn't energy enough to answer.

Jane fished in her purse, while her daughter—quiet little thing, Lew noted dimly; she hadn't said a word since she'd entered—merely stared at him intently, as if he were an exhibit in a museum. A moment later Jane drew out a flask identical to that she'd abandoned with him the night before. "Ah-ha!" she crowed. "Just the thing. Good for what ails you."

Lew looked at the flask hopefully, surprised to find himself anticipating another taste. Definitely *not* hair of the dog, then. "Here," Jane murmured sweetly, when she had poured an inch into one of the hotel's glasses. "Bottom's up."

Lew wondered what good an alcoholic cordial could do against ptomaine, but obliged, on the theory that anything that hastened the Luck's slow saunter was cool. The thick, heavy fumes tickled his nostrils, opening his sinuses—and then he tossed the whole inch of cordial down his throat like a shooter.

"Good boy," Jane said, smiling her approval as she dragged a chair around to face his. "And now the time has come for us to talk." And with that, her face went hard as stone.

"Talk?" Lew wondered. "About what?" The booze had definitely done the trick; he was feeling much sharper just in the few seconds since he'd taken that hit. Indeed, he felt almost high, rather like he imagined cocaine would be—except that there was a vague sort of distancing in his head too, as if the less-used doors of his mind were slamming shut, the better to shunt energy to the others.

"Talk," he repeated dumbly, simply to feel his mouth muscles move.

"How do you feel?"

"Much better. Drunk . . . but much better."

"Good enough to listen to a story?" Jane asked, glancing at her daughter who seemed less a child than a child-sized doll, so quietly did she keep her place.

"I . . . think so."

Jane smiled again, but Lew realized dimly there was an edge on it he did not like. He tried to Listen in her direction, but could not. Either she was shielding—something she could easily have learned to do without instruction, purely as a defense mechanism—Or else . . .

Or else what? He couldn't think. Could do nothing, of a sudden, but feel how comfortable his chair was and how wonderfully accented was his sister's voice.

"I will tell you a tale," Jane began, "the tale of how I came to be. And you will listen, and then we will talk."

Lew wanted to resist, to protest that he did not like being dictated to by anyone, but when he reached for his voice it simply wasn't there. That ought to have concerned him, but somehow it didn't. Instead, he blinked, and resigned himself numbly to listening.

"My mother was a child of a rich and powerful clan in what I grew up thinking of as a great and foreign land," Jane went on, easing into the cadence of the fairy tales Lew had heard as a child. "She had two brothers, both older, whom she loved; and a mother who, alas, had gone mad. She never knew her father, even his name, though *some* said he was a local boy who had died young. She had an uncle, too: a good man in his way, but rotten in the heart—but he does not come into this tale. Her grandmother, however, does— a grandmother who (it was whispered) was a witch. What also comes into the tale was that my mother was still a child when she learned that her kin were unlike most: that they had certain ancient responsibilities, men and women alike, chief among the latter being to provide heirs to certain . . . shall we say, dark secrets, odd powers, and arcane knowledges."

(Lew started, for his sister's tale had reminded him of something important, but as he reached for the memory, it fled. He took solace in more cordial.)

"Now it was a curiosity among my kin," Jane continued pleasantly, "that only the men might wield these secrets, these powers, and these knowledges, for which reason they were kept totally intact in body, so that the powers which came upon them in their late teens might run through *all* parts of them unimpeded. It was not that men were the *only* fit vessels, mind you, merely that they were jealous of women, and so had schemed for countless generations to render them imperfect *before* the powers manifested, for which reason they always caused their sisters to be shorn of their maidenheads a month after their first menses."

(This too seemed familiar, Lew thought vaguely, but from where?)

"Naturally, my mother, being a modern woman, wanted to rebel," Jane continued, "but her kinsmen proved too strong. Specifically, her grandmother's brother (who was then chief of her clan) proved too strong, and so it was that when my mother was fourteen, a young man was paid to rape her, and then paid more to move to a faraway city. And so was tradition maintained—until it became apparent that my mother was with child. An abortion was immediately arranged, though such things were forbidden in her family. But before it could be executed, my mother commenced to miscarry."

(Lew scowled again at this, for it too had seemed familiar, but again the memories fled.)

Jane paused to refill the cordial glass, then went on. "Now my mother's grandmother, as I said, was styled by some a witch, and it was said she had the power of foresight, and thereby divined a need for certain . . . occurrences, one of which being that my mother's unborn child should survive. So it was, then, that she contrived to attend my mother on the bed of her miscarriage; and so it was that she was able to spirit away . . . that which emerged, which, by means known only to her, she preserved alive and caused to be raised in a box which she always kept with her, my mother all unknowing.

"This box, her grandmother then conveyed to a small town in the northwest of England, where, far from her brother's influence, a girl child in due time took her first breath of air, vented her first indignant cry, and was promptly christened and given to a well-paid friend of my great-grandmother's for adoption. That child, of course, was me."

"You?" Lew repeated slowly, polishing off his second dose of cordial. He smiled stupidly. "A . . . pretty story," he yawned.

"A pretty story," Jane agreed, filling his glass a third time. "A pretty story indeed—*if one be not cursed to live it!*" Her voice had changed, Lew noticed, sounded less like silk than ice. He wondered why.

"There is more, of course. Would you like to hear the second part of my tale?"

Lew raised an eyebrow, hoping that would suffice as affirmation. He was too tired to speak, *far* too tired.

Jane lifted a brow in turn, and exchanged cryptic glances with her daughter, who still had not moved, apparently content to sit and stare at her unknown uncle.

"Very well," Jane sighed, "since you asked so nicely: I was born in England, as I told you. And for the next thirteen years I lived a normal life with loving parents in a tiny town in North Yorkshire. I had few playmates, so I took my solace in books and games. Sometimes, though, a strange woman would come to visit me, a woman with an American accent.

She never said who she was, but I knew: she was my great-grandmother. When she visited I felt odd—as if there were Voices in my head. And then one night I dreamed, and in that dream I heard those Voices, only then I recognized one of them: my great-grandmother. She was speaking to someone else—another woman—and they were speaking of me, and how I would have to be deflowered soon else I might very well go mad when my power manifested; and she spoke also of her brother, who she said was a sort of magician called a Master, charged with preserving good fortune in a certain place. As best I could tell, women were forbidden to be Masters, but I could not understand why, except, perhaps, that there was fear that female Masters might be *stronger* than male ones.

"So of course I resolved immediately to learn all I could about Masters, and to avoid this deflowering, and to make a long story short, I ran away from home and both managed to hide from my great-grandmother and to preserve my virginity until what I had learned from eavesdropping on my great-grandmother's mind was called Luck fully manifested in my late teens. By this time, too, I had but one firm goal in life: to be a Master. The world's first *female* Master.

"Fortunately, by listening to the Voices in my head, I was able to locate other women who were also Listeners, and with their help set up an independent Mastership in an out-of-the-way corner of England. My great-grandmother found me there, of course, eventually. But though she was a stickler for tradition, I think she was also impressed, and agreed not to interfere, nor betray me to the male Masters, who apparently could not Hear me. The price of her silence, though, was that I was to bear the specified three children: two boys and a girl. This I agreed to, having by then realized that the Luck, now that it had manifested, would restore whatever damage to my body intercourse or childbearing might do. Thus, I persevered, and in due time was delivered of a child—a pretty girl, fair-haired, like you."

Lew found his gaze drifting toward the silent child. Their gazes touched for an instant. He saw something there, something familiar, something troubling—or troubled. But then the veils of muddle descended once more. And he found his attention drawn, as by force, back toward Jane. "Is there . . . more?" he asked slowly, dully.

"Only a bit," Jane replied. "Affairs remained the same for several years, but I found myself growing ever more restless and could not understand why, but eventually I found out. I was, it seemed, heir by blood to another Mastership, this one in America. This haunted me more and more as the years went by, and eventually I resolved to go there and claim it."

She paused then, looked Lew in the eye. He flinched beneath that stare, for some of what she had just said had struck a chord in his mind that summoned memories already oddly distant. *She knows it all,* he thought. *She knows everything.*

"Almost everything," Jane agreed. "Perhaps the only thing left to tell is how I found you—for I have been aware of you far longer than you think, perhaps because of the strength that is mine as a woman. But only now have I thought the time ripe to let you find me . . . *brother.*"

Something in that word roused Lew. He blinked, fought back the fog that so ensnarled his thoughts and had already veiled half his memories. He frowned, bit his lip, and—finally—spoke the words he had rehearsed for so long.

"You can have it," he said softly, almost pleadingly—and almost automatically, so long had he conditioned himself for this moment. "The Mastership of Cardalba, I mean. I don't want it; I never did. Neither does my twin—or my uncles. If you *do* want it, it's yours for the taking. All I ask is that you treat my . . . people as well as you can."

Jane stared at him for a long, still moment, then sadly shook her head. "No, Lewis—brother—I'm sorry, but that isn't possible any more; it's far too late for that now. I want more."

Her stare intensified at that, and Lew felt the veils descending yet again. Darkness hovered near. "Now tell me," he heard a distant voice say. "Tell me about your *Flaw.*"

Chapter 6

I Heard It through the Grapevine

Cordova, Georgia
Late morning

"Okay," Brandy gritted, trying not to assail the telephone receiver with a flood of verbal vitriol that would surely have melted the innocent white plastic, when what she *wanted* to do was to light a fire under the nameless woman on the opposing end of the line, who, in spite of claiming to be an assistant advertising editor for *Creative Loafing,* Atlanta's weekly arts journal, seemed unable to comprehend plain English. "Okay," she repeated with more composure, "you read over what you've got, and I'll tell you if you've copied the ad down right." Which the drawling bureaucrat ought to have *volunteered* to do; the fact that she worked for a quasi-counterculture newspaper was no excuse for plain ignorance—not as far as Brandy was concerned. *She* no longer suffered fools as gladly as once she had.

"Just a minute," the woman muttered distractedly. "I gotta take another call." A click, and Brandy found her ears awash with canned music—canned Canned Heat, to be precise, which clashed abominably with the Eddie Bushyhead Cherokee flute tape that had been soothing her nerves between electronic skirmishes.

She snorted in disgust and rolled her eyes in supplication toward the coffered ceiling of the Chamber of Commerce office she'd been ensconced in all morning. And wished her raven feather earrings were named Patience and Fortitude instead of Thought and Memory. A stack of Georgia phone books tottered to her left: a pulpwood Tower of Babel rising from a desert of antique desk. She was in the middle, a frustrated Nebuchadnezzar in sand-colored cammos and plain black T-shirt. To her right, a yellow legal pad lay athwart a greensward of blotter, covered in what looked like a cuneiform itinerary of the ancient world, but was in fact a scribbled list of target cities: Athens, Rome, Cairo, Sparta, Memphis, and a score more major and minor Southeastern urban centers. A second column, tallying the larger daily papers in Georgia and the five states that bordered it, plus the artsy weeklies and most of the college rags, was already one-third checked off. Another couple of hours on the horn, and phase one of Project Shakespeare (she wondered when she'd picked up Ron's habit of hanging monikers on everything) would be complete.

If this blessed woman ever got back to her. Brandy was tempted to simply hang up and say, "Screw *Creative Loafing.*" Except that *CL* was one of her likeliest prospects, catering as it did to the artistic community of the largest city in the Southeast. Still, time spent on hold was time wasted so, in order to minimize inefficiency, she snared a volume from atop a smaller pulpwood edifice and began paging through the one halfway complete local history the Cordova Public Library had been able to excavate for her.

It was a flimsy piece—little more than a pamphlet, really, self-published by an elderly woman named Mildred Dietrich sometime in the thirties. Composed mostly as a family memoir, its accounts were frustratingly tedious, tending toward reminiscences of weddings and funerals in Ms. Dietrich's own undistinguished clan. But at least it encompassed the whole period from the time Ronny's first North American Welch ancestor struck a bargain with the local Cherokee chief for all the land from the Talooga River to the adjoining ridgelines north and south, up until 1930, when one of those too-convenient courthouse fires had swept away forty years of records.

Not that she'd actually had time to *read* the skinny little tome, or anything. But the bit she *had* scanned . . . well, there *were* a couple of interesting passages nestled amongst the Dietrich rites of passage, notably the section on the founding of the county, and another centered around the Civil War. With these two colorful periods as foci, and a couple of more incidents with a unifying thread (like the Welches, if Ronny didn't raise too big a stink), they had the framework for a pretty solid drama. Throw in some musical bridges to keep things lively, and they'd be cooking.

"Sorry," the adwoman's voice staticked back at her, just as Brandy was commencing a list of local musicians and their specialties. "Now, what was I doing? Oh yeah: 'PLAY-WRIGHT WANTED: Welch County, Georgia, Chamber of Commerce seeks experienced dramatist to compose local history play for performance *immediately*. Contacts useful, experience and example of work a must. Send vita and sample to Brandy Wallace, Brandy Hall, Rt. 2, Box 100, Cordova, Georgia.' "

"Right."

"ZIP?"

Brandy told her. "And that'll run in *this* week's edition?" she asked pointedly.

"Should."

"I may have another next week."

"We'll look forward to it," the woman replied automatically.

"Thanks." Whereupon Brandy hung up—and felt vastly relieved.

And even more so, when, roughly a minute later, the door opened without benefit of knock and Weedge stuck her head in. She'd changed her hairdo, Brandy noted: to something fluffier—or maybe that was just the humidity. It worked better with her Post Office threads, though, softening the standard blue-and-white uniform's depressing severity.

"How's it goin'?" Weedge asked easily, slipping the rest of the way inside and letting the heavy oak door click closed behind her.

A shrug, as Brandy sank back into her chair. "Who knows?" She poked the pad with a much-nibbled pencil. "I've worked through the worst part of my list—which ain't bad, given that most folks don't know how to spell Welch County."

"You're kiddin'!"

Brandy shook her head. "Most of 'em think it's Welsh— which it kind of is, but not so the average Joe'd be aware of."

"The *average* Joe doesn't know it exists," Weedge noted wryly. "Including the census takers at least twice. It, ah, seems to have a way of . . . avoiding notice."

A vigorous nod. "Tell me about it."

Weedge checked her watch. "No time now," she replied, deadpan. "I just slipped over from the P.O. on a late coffee break. Gotta run in half a sec. Mostly I wanted to reserve you for lunch—if you can break loose in an hour or so. But . . . well, to be honest, I couldn't *wait* that long to see how Project Gene Pool made out last night." She folded her arms and lifted an eyebrow speculatively.

Brandy's eyes flashed dangerously. "We never got that far."

"Sorry."

"It's not *your* fault," Brandy grumbled, tapping the pad impatiently. "I should've known better than to expect Ronny-boy to understand where the county's concerned."

"No," Weedge corrected, "you should've known better than to expect him to ignore ten years worth of denial and nearly thirty of conditioning! There are things you can change, and things you can't, gal. And if you even *think* that just 'cause you share your bed with somebody, they'll change for you, you're crazy."

Brandy was staring at her friend impassively. "I've got a great idea, Weedge: how 'bout we change the subject?"

Weedge's shoulders shifted, as if to let Brandy's warning slide off more easily. "Sure. And as a matter of fact, I do have something else to discuss—later."

"Gimme a hint?" Brandy prompted, hoping her lighter tone would help defuse the tension.

"*Mabinogion,*" Weedge whispered conspiratorially. "I finally got around to reading it. Something told me to."

Brandy eyed her narrowly. "Sure it did."

"But it did!" Weedge protested. "Honest to God! I was just sittin' there in the middle of "Arsenio," and—bang— I got this case of the heebie jeebies that said I oughta read *The Mabinogion*—so I dug out that copy you gave me after things . . . happened, and . . ."

"And?"

"Girls made out of flowers, white deer, voices in the wind: very interesting."

"I thought you'd think so."

"But no houses transformed to castles in a single night."

"No, but there *is* a story 'bout a hill where if you spend the night, you'll either go bonkers or see a wonder."

"I *wonder* which you did," Weedge chuckled—and edged back toward the door. "Catch you in an hour, okay?"

"Fine," Brandy replied offhandedly, already punching in the number for the next call: *The Red and Black* down in Athens, Georgia—Ron's old *alma mater*. She did not hear Weedge leave and, indeed, thought her friend was still lurking about, when the soft staccato grunt of someone clearing their throat made her glance up again.

But not into the face of her confidante. Rather, she found herself staring into the guileless, expectant, and very blue eyes of a boy. A very *pretty* boy, she couldn't help but notice, sixteen or so, to judge by the smoothness of his fair beardless cheeks and the way angles were just starting to shoulder aside the curves of childhood on cheek and jaw and chin.

Except that she doubted this boy would ever look *really* old. There was too much joy in his face, too much scarce-suppressed animation. A touch of feralness, too: a sly undercurrent that whispered *I'm sneaky and full of myself, and I just might be Peter Pan.*

But not, apparently, any great desire either to converse or confess his purpose. Or, at least, the boy *said* nothing, merely smiled expectantly at her: a curve of full lips that left her unaccountably breathless. She blinked, used that gesture as an excuse to break eye contact, and in the ensuing interval managed to note that her visitor had mid-length reddish blond hair that stuck out over his forehead like a visor, and that he was shorter than she'd first supposed: five-six tops, though it was hard to tell, the way he was slumped over to look at her. As for his clothes: he was neatly, if flamboyantly, dressed in black slacks fortified by a multitude of zippers and pockets; a flame-colored shirt that looked like silk; a tie of heavier fabric that depicted either flowers or tropical birds. And a black leather aviator jacket that had to be impossibly uncomfortable, given the summer heat and humidity—which probably meant he was a Yankee.

He hadn't spoken yet, and seemed disinclined to rectify that situation, apparently content to stare at her idiotically and make her feel uncomfortable.

"Can I help you?" she growled at last.

"Hopefully." His voice was soft, a little shy. And definitely *not* from north of the Mason-Dixon.

An exasperated sigh. *"Yes?"*

He shifted his weight nervously. "You're . . . Brandy Wallace . . . right?"

"Yep."

"Well . . . I'm . . . that is"—the boy scratched his pointy nose—"my name's Donson Gwent," he managed finally. And almost made Brandy giggle by blushing.

"Which tells me nothing," Brandy countered, trying hard to keep a straight face.

The boy scratched again—his head this time—and fidgeted. "I'm, uh, here to write your play."

Had Brandy been standing, she would have collapsed like the Berlin Wall. As it was, she simply gaped for a good five seconds before recovering composure enough to gasp, "But the decision was only made last night!"

"Ah, but news travels fast among thespians," Gwent countered quickly, and so much more confidently that Brandy had to look at him to be certain he was still the same person. He'd acquired a knowing smile, too, and more than a twinkle in his eyes. "I assumed you'd know that by now, considering how many artists you number among your associates."

"By which I assume that you and I have mutual friends?" Brandy ventured, trying desperately to determine whether she was having her leg pulled or not, and if so, to which of Gwent's personae she ought to respond. She was in no mood for games.

"At least one, it appears."

"Mind telling me who?"

"I, uh . . . well, actually, I don't remember right now."

"You don't *remember*?"

"I've got a . . . problem with that kind of thing, sometimes."

"And yet you trusted . . . *whoever* enough to show up here unannounced?"

"Would announcing have made any difference?"

"It would have improved my mood!"

Brandy was still trying to assess the next stage in this odd conversation, when Gwent plopped down in the office's sole empty chair and commenced rifling through a real-and-true carpetbag that had escaped her notice. "I brought you a, uh, sample," he volunteered brightly, abruptly all kid again, as he produced an unruly sheaf of papers that could easily have been the contents of her trash can.

"I'd rather see a vita," Brandy replied coolly.

Gwent looked startled. "I don't have one," he mumbled, still the kid. "I didn't know for sure I was comin' til I arrived."

An eyebrow lifted, but not the boy's, whose face remained completely innocent—even, it seemed, of the realization that he had already played half a dozen cards dead wrong.

Silence, while Brandy balanced between dismissing this bumbling (though attractive) loon outright or attempting subtlety. Probably the former, she concluded. Them that *had* no tact weren't likely to respond to it in kind.

"Soooo," she began at last, narrowing her eyes more than was strictly necessary. "*So*, Mr. Gwent, let me get this straight: You traipse in here completely unannounced, utterly without portfolio, and lacking any credentials beyond balls the size of Texas"—the boy scowled at this—"and you expect me to hire you onthe spot to write a play? When you . . . when you don't even look old enough to bloody *read*!"

There, she'd said it, and immediately wished she hadn't. Rudeness to strangers was not her style. Bluntness, yes, and brutal honesty, but not hurtfulness for its own sake. She hoped he didn't cry. It seemed a real possibility.

"You've had a hard day, haven't you?" the boy asked finally, with an ambiguous sniff that made her cringe.

She tried not to glare at him. "You *could* say that."

Gwent's face went suddenly hard as stone—which aged him about ten years, and unbalanced Brandy all over again. "And I *could* tell you a lot of things about me," he said softly, once more in his confident voice. "Including the fact that I'm older than I look, and that it's . . . inappropriate to judge people by either their age or their appearance, as, for example, in the case of Mr. Mozart. But," he added with a dazzling grin that brought all that youthfulness flooding back, "what I'd *really* rather do is spend five minutes watching you read a piece of my work. That'd tell you a lot more than ten pages of 'Place of Birth,' 'Education,' and 'References.' "

He rose then, and dumped the sheaf of papers on Brandy's desk. "I'll wait outside. Call me when you're finished." And with that, he swept from the room. The door did *not* click shut behind him.

Brandy was on the verge of crumpling Gwent's de facto job application and flinging it at the wall, to be followed by a couple of medium-sized phone books, when her gaze chanced to stray to the word atop the first grimy page.

" '*Madoc*,' " it proclaimed. Typed, not word-processed.

"Madoc," Brandy mouthed silently. *Madoc*: the name of a semimythical Welsh prince, son of Owain Gwynedd, who had supposedly fled his homeland under duress and established a colony in the New World in the late twelfth century. There were piled-stone ramparts a couple of counties south of Cordova that were attributed to him. Not that she'd actually been there, as she'd never pursued the parent thread of arcanology (to use a term she'd stolen from some novel or other). But what struck her with resounding force was the stark serendipity of its appearance now. For had Weedge not bare minutes before been talking about *The Mabinogion*—the Welsh national epic? And here was mythic Wales all over again!

Grimacing at her own failed convictions, she dragged the sheaf toward her. She'd give it five minutes—*max*, which was more grace than most folks got when they crossed her. Make that six—but only because Gwent was so damnably cute.

A pause for a sip of coffee that had been hot the last time she'd sampled it and was no longer, and she settled back to read.

What she held were the opening pages of what she supposed was a much longer work. There was no title page, however, beyond the one-word name—she'd hoped to at least find an address—and its absence did nothing to allay her suspicions about Gwent's professionalism. Nor was there a cast of characters, which, again, did not bode well. What *was* present, though, was a description of the set and situation (which was more fitting in a screenplay, she thought), with dialogue only beginning halfway down.

Another tepid sip, and she began.

<u>Act I, scene i.</u> (she read)

The locale is a precipitous cliff on the eastern side of Fort Mountain in northwest Georgia. Twisted oaks vie with scraggly pines among massive gray boulders to the left; to the right is empty air. Buzzards ride thermals there. A few yards of piled stonework are barely visible through the trees. Woodsmoke floats upon the breeze, bringing with it the odor of roasting meat. In the foreground a wiry young man leans against a rock as tall as he, shading his eyes. The ruddy light of sunrise falls upon his face. He is handsome, dark haired, dressed in worn cross-gartered leggings and low boots, beneath a dirty white tunic on which is still visible a dragon passant, gules. A faded red cloak billows about him, a short sword hangs at his belt, its hilt an intricacy of Irish knotwork. He looks worried, weary, as if he has not slept in many days.

An older man enters to his left, white haired and similarly attired, but wrapped in a checked cloak that has obviously seen much use. He carries a Celtic harp. Without speaking, he begins to play. The music is soft and slow, heavy with sorrow and loss.

The younger man looks at him and frowns.

"The last time I heard that, I was on the quay at Twynn."

"And the next?"

"When next you play it, I suppose. I've never been one to command a bard."

"You've never been one to be commanded, either, and look where that stubbornness has brought you: to an eagle's eyrie untold leagues from home, with nothing but red savages as subjects—you who are a prince."

"A mariner, rather. I sailed before I spoke, I knew my father's captains before I knew he was a king."

"And here you stand, a thousand miles from the sea."

"Gazing on a sea of trees—as far as I can see."

"Was that a joke?"

"Not this early."

"I would laugh anyway, were I not so old. The weather here eats at my lungs."

A pause, then: "I wonder, oh my harping friend, if a king without a country is still a king. Is it a thing one is born to, or simply a thing one is?"

"Another joke? Or a riddle?"

A dry chuckle. "Not this early."

"Come, then, let us see what foulness our cook has contrived in the guise of breakfast."

Madoc sneezes. The smell of smoke becomes stronger. They exit.

There was more.

Much more, ending in a fiery nighttime battle with Indians. Eventually Brandy coughed, blinked into the drifting dust motes of the room, surprised to find it not ablaze and strewn with bleeding Welshmen. Her eyes were watering. A glance down showed no more paper. Something tickled her nose, and she sneezed, finally resorting to a much-used Kleenex to forestall nasal disaster. She wondered what it was—diesel fumes, maybe? From an out-of-tune semi outside? Another fortuitous coincidence?

Like this play. God, but it had seemed real! Simple words

and phrases, mere fragments of description and dialogue; and yet she had been able to visualize everything with utter clarity: the way the trees looked (she could even tell the season, the species of the oaks and pines); the way the clouds had scudded across the sky. (Had Gwent mentioned clouds? She couldn't recall, and a quick back-paging revealed nothing except that she couldn't locate details in an unfamiliar manuscript in a hurry.) The way the men moved and spoke and fought and wore their clothes.

And all of that had occurred in her mind alone! Two words in, and her disbelief had crumbled into powder. Ten, and Gwent had utterly convinced her that she was atop Fort Mountain watching Prince Madoc and his bard begin another day's exile in a hostile land. And if merely *reading* could have that effect, what on earth would happen with actual sets and actors?

But more to the point, could Gwent work that magic again?

Or had *he* even done it the first time? Such talent was so rare as to make her suspicious. Once in a generation, perhaps; maybe once in a lifetime. And *she* had him here? *Sure!* But dare she risk the alternative? No, it was best to hedge her bets, best to bind him with an ironclad contract before the Powers-That-Be on Broadway shanghaied him and priced him out of reason.

"Gwent," she hollered. "Get your butt in here!"

The door opened soundlessly. Gwent stared at her blankly, neither mouth nor eyes committed to emotion. "I like it," Brandy told him, with admirable self-control. "But I'm afraid I still have a couple of problems."

An eyebrow lifted, but Gwent's tongue was not so glib.

Brandy fought down a tart remark, knowing enough about the pretensions of artists to recognize the next figure in a complex dance. She cleared her throat. "Like I said, I liked the text I just read a lot . . . *but* I have only *your* word that *you* actually wrote what I read—and without a vita to back it up, I need some guarantee, first of all, that the unlikely person I see before me can do what he claims; and secondly, assuming that you can, that you can do for nineteenth century Georgia what you did for twelfth century—"

"Georgia, too," Gwent supplied. "Only the characters were Welsh."

"Yeah, I, ah, noticed that," Brandy retorted. "But that's basically it: Can *you* write? And can you write what *we* need, as fast as we need it?"

"Is that, like, a challenge? Or is it more a duel?"

"Well, given that I can't write anything more elegant than a grocery list, I *suppose* it's a challenge," Brandy growled. She fished under the pile of manuscript, found Ms. Dietrich's memoir. "I've gotta go to lunch. I'll be gone approximately one hour. During that time, I would like you to do your dead-level best to render, say . . . page five into drama. I don't have a clue what's on it, except that it's local history and probably dull as dishwater. But give it a go. If you can perform cold . . . well, then we'll see."

"Got any, uh, *paper*?" Gwent asked edgily, suddenly all nerves again. "And a pen?"

Brandy found the necessary supplies. "Real well equipped, aren't you?"

A shrug. "Do you carry paint and canvas when you go on interviews?"

"Touché," Brandy grunted, finally allowing herself a smile that seemed to relax Gwent all out of keeping with his previous defensive, if cocky, demeanor. "Have fun."

"You too," Gwent called cheerily. If he said more, Brandy missed it, for she was out the door.

Donson Gwent got *more* than the allotted hour, because the lunch Weedge had promised Brandy (venison stew and fry bread at Scotty Jones's Grill—the only really good eatery within walking distance) was not only excellent, but the conversation was well-nigh impossible to conclude. Not that she should have expected any less, given the amount of history she and Weedge had. But she was still smarting from the stress of the morning, plus the odd mix of emotions centering around Donson Gwent, when Weedge had met her, and had in fact come within an ace of canceling the whole rendezvous simply because she was afraid her hair-trigger temper would overload at the wrong moment and get even the laid-back W. G. Montgomery riled.

But Weedge had simply let her have her say about Gwent, had pointed out that his reported assets seemed to outweigh his reputed liabilities, and that if nothing else, she was out an hour of her life, had learned something, and had been entertained in the bargain.

And then they'd gotten off on *The Mabinogion*—mostly the early parts, where the precipitous Pwyll's overenthusiastic pursuit of a white stag had resulted in his owing a favor to the Lord of Annwyn—which is to say, the King of Hell.

"It's just like what happened to you," Weedge noted over a mug of beer. "You saw a white stag, only it turned out to be some kind of magic man; and he let you start owing him favors, and pretty soon, he carried you off to the hot place—in a manner of speaking."

"Which is precisely what I told *you*," Brandy countered. "Remember? Back the day I first saw the white buck. You'd never heard of *The Mabinogion* then."

"And you haven't read it since, have you?"

"Uh, no, actually . . ." Brandy hedged. "Maybe I should."

"Maybe we *all* should," Weedge echoed. "Maybe Ronny in particular should."

"I think he already has."

"I think he's *lived* it," Weedge corrected. "Take a gander at the genealogies in there sometime, and then check out Ron's."

"I will," Brandy sighed. "But right now I need to take a look at a myth of another kind."

Which she was both dreading and anticipating as she eased the office door open five minutes later. Dreading, because she feared Gwent might have failed at his task, which would then put her in the position of having to play the heavy in the real-life minidrama she and the youthful playwright had been enacting. And anticipating, because there was also a chance Gwent *would* come through, and she'd get to experience yet another sample of his wonderful way with words.

"I had to quit five minutes ago," the boy-man mumbled apologetically, before Brandy could speak. "I, uh, sorta ran out of paper."

"But the pad was half-full!" Brandy protested.

"Not quite," Gwent replied, looking chagrined. "You had

notes on part of it, and a couple of pages had coffee stains on 'em, which I didn't figure you'd wanta have to squint through. And besides," he continued, with a quirky half-smile that made him look the enthusiastic teenager he now sounded, "I write *really* fast when I get goin'."

"Well, thank God I didn't put you on the computer, then!" Brandy grumbled, as she returned to her seat, leaving Gwent to swivel around in his chair to face her again. "You'd probably have written a novel."

Gwent merely shrugged, and handed her the pad.

Half an hour it took, to make her way through the lines of Gwent's handwriting. Fortunately, the lad had clear, if affected penmanship, part cursive, part printing, with a fair portion of the letters looking as though they'd been frightened by uncials somewhere in their formative years. But she barely noticed that after the first line.

She was too caught up in Gwent's art.

Oh, he'd been lucky; she'd inadvertently given him a fairly dramatic scene to render. But even so . . . shoot—it had been like going to the movies. She could still see the images in her mind's eye: the primeval forest of north Georgia, trees the fresh-washed green of summer, the grass alive with flowers. One man entering a glade, dressed in trader garb, with a handsome flintlock in his hand; talking to himself, then sleeping. Whereupon enters a second man, wearing sky, wind, and a loincloth—and pretty obviously an Indian. The Indian had attacked; combat had ensued, with the white man being wounded, only to recover days later in the house of the local chief. In the end a bargain had been struck. Loston Brandon Welch had been promised the land that eventually comprised Cardalba Plantation. And the chief's village had been saved from a disastrous flood by the patented Welch-clan Luck.

And so was Welch County born.

And so was Gwent's fragment concluded.

As for the playwright himself: In the manner of Br'er Rabbit's famous tar baby, he was lying low. But Brandy was not about to fling *this* glib-tongued trickster into the Briar Patch. No, sirree, he was gonna stay right here in this office and keep on with Ms. Dietrich's book until he'd cast the whole thing into stage directions and dialogue.

"You've got the job," Brandy said flatly, then realized she was assuming an authority she didn't actually have—not that anyone was likely to challenge her. "That is, you have it if you want it—if you can stand working with a bitch like me."

"I've worked with bitches before," Gwent replied easily, all trace of his former uncertain flakiness vanishing again, as the more adult persona reappeared—she hoped for good. "And bastards too," he added, with a cryptic twinkle in his eyes that made Brandy gawk in a way she detested because it meant she had let someone else get the better of her.

"You need a place to stay?" she asked finally. "I can put you up at Brandy Hall, no problem. I mean, that was the general idea, though I never had a chance to tell you."

"I could prob'ly get into that," Gwent replied, abruptly the awkward adolescent again. "At least for a while. But I'll need to tie up a couple of loose ends first."

Brandy was on the verge of inquiring about those sudden personality shifts, when Gwent sprang to his feet, scooped up both legal pad and volume, and scooted his chair around before the computer. "Thank you, Ms. Wallace," he grinned with innocent sweetness, as he plopped himself down. "I think I wanta fool with this some more today, if you don't mind. Hope you won't be disappointed. I'll, uh, look forward to meetin' Mr. Dillon."

It was in another office more than an hour later, while Brandy was busy passing the word about her unbelievable luck, that she realized she'd never said a word about anyone named Dillon.

Chapter 7

Fortune Presents Gifts Not According to the Book

Brandy's Knoll
Late afternoon

"I'm just not sure who'd do better for Nuada," Perry Steinway was drawling with blue-eyed perplexity, "Jan-Michael Vincent or Michael York."

Perry was short, blue jeaned, tank topped, and as goldenly solid as sandstone; and his red-blond hair was also short and thick as fertilized grass; but he tended to go on at very great length indeed. Just now he was holding forth—as he had been for what seemed to Ron like two hours—on the proper choice of models for the beleaguered Lords of the Tuatha de Danaan he and his longtime companion, John Marx, were rendering into martial mosaic in Brandy Hall's foyer.

It was a hot, muggy afternoon, and Ron was in his metal-fabrication shop, stripped to the waist for mobility as much as comfort, having spent most of the last hour running a yard-square sheet of obscure alloy between the unevenly sized rollers of an English wheel with the object of producing a right front fender for the MK II Centauri. It was an excellent English wheel, too: the same series the folks at Aston Martin used to shape the skins of their megabuck GT cars. But he was beginning to regret revealing so much of his *own* integument, because the voluble Mr. Steinway was spending a bit too much time admiring it.

Or staring at Ron's sweat-streaked chest more often than his safety-goggled eyes or stubbly chin, at any rate.

Not that such inspection bugged him, really; people couldn't help their preferences, and he supposed it was better to have one's physique admired by one's Y-chromosomed brothers than to have it ignored by their double-X kin. It was just that he wasn't in a mood for either minute inspection or prolonged conversation right now. It was *hard*, dammit, to focus on where the highlights ought to lie on a fender flare when someone was assessing the arc of one's own hard and hairless pecs.

So why didn't the guy just follow his instincts as far as a model went? They'd served well enough before. Or, better yet, ask Sharon, who was busy spinning up the last of the plates for the twelve-place dinner service she had promised Brandy as fee for putting her up for three months? God knew Sharon appreciated men. God (and Sharon—and Ron and Brandy) knew she'd even appreciated Perry's "friend" John at least twice.

But perhaps Perry was simply lonely. And, lonely or not, had just shifted his weight to his opposite leg in exasperation. "So what *do* you think? Who's the lucky lad gonna be?"

"Well," Ron began, as a drop of sweat escaped his sapphire bandanna and cogwheeled against the sheet of gleaming alloy slowly growing complex organic curves beneath his hands, "York's got a broken nose, which would render him imperfect, since Nuada's a High King, and the High Kings had to be without blemish. But Vincent's got eyes like slits, and the Irish like their heroes with wide-open peepers. So maybe you oughta come up with somebody else."

Perry was silent for possibly half a minute, during which interval Ron thought the guy was actually considering his suggestion. Certainly he had shifted his gaze speculatively toward the oblivious potter. "You don't like me, do you?" he challenged abruptly, snapping his head back around.

Ron oozed the metal out of the wheel and flipped the OFF

switch so he wouldn't have to shout. "I like you fine," he replied curtly, as he leaned the protopanel against a scarlet air compressor and wiped his hands on the greasy cutoffs that were his single surface garment. "I just don't feel like talking now. My right brain's not much of a conversationalist, and it's in the ascendancy at the moment."

"I'm not *talking* about now," Perry persisted. "You've *never* liked me."

Ron leaned back against the worktable adjoining the wheel, and indulged himself in a healthy swig of Perrier. "Okay," he stated flatly, "if you're gonna push me: No, I've never liked you—but not in the sense you mean, and *not* for the reason you think. Basically, I don't dare like you—which to me implies getting close to you—'cause I have no reason to suppose you won't disappear like all the rest of Brandy's buddies who zip in, hang out a couple of days, and bug off about the time I get 'em figured out enough to know what's going on with 'em. I don't need serial superficial friendships, Perry; I got enough of that in college. If I'm gonna take the trouble to make friends with somebody, I want some security they'll stick around. Or barring that, that there's enough of a bond to *stand* a separation. I'm tired as *hell* of making friends and then losing 'em."

Perry's reaction teetered between a gulp and a gawk. "Well, gee, guy; *that's* a lot more than I bargained for! Thanks for bein' honest."

Ron smiled sheepishly. "Sorry if I seem pissed. It's not at you. It's just that this whole friendship thing's been festering for a long time."

"Since your brother split, maybe?" Perry suggested shyly.

"Yeah," Ron sighed, absently fingering another sheet of metal. "Since my brother split."

Perry's gaze was darting about, as if he were unsure whether to hang around or boogie. Eventually it stole back to Sharon and settled there. "Hey, like, maybe I *will* get a female opinion," he ventured with a chuckle. "Gee—what a novel idea!"

"I'm sure ol' Sharon knows a lot more 'bout male aesthetics than I do," Ron agreed.

"Catch you later," Perry called cheerily.

"Not from behind, you won't!" Ron shot back.

"Cute—but not as cute as your heinie." And with that, Perry sauntered out of the forge and into the bright light of day.

Ron was at once relieved and surprised at himself for having revealed so much of his inner workings to someone he didn't know well enough to trust. But whose fault was that? At least Perry was honest, didn't keep things bottled up inside when they bugged him.

Of course he hadn't either—back when Lew had still been available.

Idly, he followed Perry's leisurely progress across the forecourt to the crimson-and-white-striped pavilion that comprised the pottery studio. But just as Ron reached for the fender again, he saw a shirtless, towel-wielding John Marks emerge from the round-topped shadows of Brandy Hall's front arcade and trot across the glaring pavement. John flopped an arm on Perry's shoulders, drew him close enough to whisper in his ear. The object of the encounter was obvious, too, because instead of continuing on for a potentially productive rendezvous at Sharon's, Perry let himself be steered toward the path to the cove.

Which was fine—a midday dip was hardly noteworthy around Brandy's knoll; clothed or not scarcely mattered.

Except . . .

Dammit, they had neighbors now! Neighbors whose back deck offered a clear, if distance-dimmed, view of the swimming hole.

A neighbor who might take a *very* dim view of same-sex lovers taking their enjoys in sight of his impressionable teenage son. Or of opposite-sex lovers, for that matter. Binoculars, after all, were cheap. And certainly available to young Sam Foster.

That was, however, only a small problem among greater.

Like smoothing out things with Brandy.

Like discovering what was riling up the mojo.

Like figuring out what the hell was going on with Lew.

It just wasn't like him to break off in the middle of a contact as he had done that morning. As a point of fact, Lew had never done such a thing, both because it was dangerous generally, and because he knew Ron, in particular, had a near-obsessive fear of getting lost in Jump. Worse, Lew, while secretive, was also conscientious to a fault, which quality only made the situation odder. More than once that afternoon, Ron had considered venturing into the Winds again, only to talk himself out of it with the arguments that such an action would be easier—and less dangerous—later.

No, he'd do what logic demanded: wait for the standard window-of-contact and hope that Lew served up the requested phone call. If he did, Ron would get some answers; and if he didn't, *then* he'd try to contact Lew via the Winds. And if *that* failed (Why did he even assume that was a possibility?) . . . he'd worry about that when the time came.

"Gaaaa!" he grumbled, and switched his boom box back on, sending thunderous Pearl Jam juking around the forge. He was on the verge of powering up the wheel as well, when he caught a ghost of movement from the corner of his eye. At first he thought it was Perry returning by the long route, but a closer look proved it to be Sam Foster (barefoot, shirtless, and in cutoffs, with straps encumbering his arms) trudging up the east side of the knoll from below the amphitheater.

"Great!" he muttered sourly. "All I need."

It wasn't that he minded Sam's company—in the abstract; it was just that he had things on his mind and projects to progress on, and was having enough trouble banishing one so he could devote his attention to the other without some wide-eyed Munchkin asking questions and poking his pointy young nose into everything.

On the other hand, nobody else was paying him much mind these days. He hadn't seen Brandy since their set-to of the night before, and not much of the several days previous. Sharon was just tempting enough (and available enough, she'd hinted more than once) that it *scared* him to see her. And Perry and John . . . well, they were just Perry and John: content to construct their own microcosm within the larger universe of Brandy Hall.

Sam, however, seemed to be evincing the barest trace of hero worship—which, Ron conceded, felt mighty flattering, if for no other reason than because he'd never experienced it. And though part of him insisted he keep the boy at arm's length lest he, too, disappear and leave yet another void unfilled, another part reminded him that friendship was not a gift to be treated lightly, solicited or no. So maybe if he played it subtle . . .

Sam was within hailing range now, were it not for the stereo. Ron gestured vaguely in his direction, then turned, powered up the wheel, inserted the in-process fender, and began refining the wheelarch curve. Going through the motions, rather; really he was, in a very calculated way, waiting.

But Sam still did not announce his arrival, until Ron felt compelled to look around lest the lad perhaps had misinterpreted his signal and departed.

And jumped half out of his skin—because the boy was standing right behind him, grinning triumphantly, having obviously been there for some time, utterly silent.

Sam smirked, but fortunately for Ron's good humor—and the kid's incisors—did not actually laugh.

Ron masked his surprise with a grimace and silenced both music and wheel with a deft one-two motion, neither having accomplished squat.

And inspected his visitor.

Sam was wet; that much was obvious: his hair sleeked down around his ears and hanging in pointed tendrils to eyes that, free of glasses, proved to be deep blue. Somehow, too, he looked slimmer—possibly a function of the way his soggy cutoffs gripped his hips and thighs.

"You busy?" Sam asked neutrally.

"I'm *always* busy," Ron grumbled back, maintaining his aloof facade.

"Sorry," Sam murmured, shivering a little.

"You're wet."

"Happens when you swim."

"You *swam*?"

"Yep."

"From the shoals, or—"

"From my house," Sam finished for him.

Ron stared at him incredulously. "You swam three hundred yards to annoy somebody you didn't even know yesterday?"

"Actually," the boy corrected slyly, reaching around to fumble off a smaller, plastic-wrapped, version of the knapsack he'd worn earlier, "it's more like *four* hundred yards the way I came."

"You couldn't walk?"

"I like to swim."

"So it seems." And now that Ron took a close-up look at Sam's bod, he realized that, allowing for the vagaries of his adolescent frame, the kid really was put together like a swimmer. He had long arms and legs for his size, wide shoulders, decent pecs, a flat belly, and no butt to speak of, all strapped together by long smooth muscles.

"What're *you* up to?" Ron asked with careful nonchalance. "Besides bugging your neighbors, I mean."

The gibe rolled off the boy as easily as the tease it really was. Which meant that he either had a tough hide, a sense of humor—or *no* sense of tact at all.

"Just hangin' out."

"You could hang out at home."

"Dad's gettin' on my nerves. He's gettin' ready to head out again."

"For where?"

"He's not through packing yet, and there's still a bunch of business stuff to wind up back home."

"You said 'he.' Does that mean you're not going with him?"

Sam shifted his weight, looking flustered. "Uh, well, see that's kinda the problem. Like, *he* wants me to, but I wanta stay up here. I'm through with school, and all, and I've got a motorbike, so I'm tryin' to convince him that he oughta let me keep an eye on things here until he can get back up next weekend."

"And he doesn't think you're old enough."

"Yeah . . . and it's not *like* I'd be by myself—not necessarily."

Ron raised an eyebrow. "Oh?"

Sam shook his head. "I've got some friends wantin' to come up, soon as I give the word, preferably next week or the one after."

Ron folded his arms and regarded his visitor levelly, suddenly feeling very grown-up—which was rather a novel sensation. "Oh, well, I can sorta see his point, then."

Sam looked even more flustered. "What's *that* supposed to mean?"

"It's not been *that* long since I was your age, Sam. What do you *think* it means?"

"I wanted to show you something . . ." Sam said abruptly, obviously ignoring Ron's question, as he deftly unsealed the plastic wrap from around his pack. He rummaged around within its recesses (the clink of plastic and rustle of paper being prominent), and eventually withdrew what Ron first thought was a ship in a square bottle.

Except, as he discovered when the boy held it out to him, that it proved to be a model car affixed within a plastic display case. Ron studied it with a critical eye toward both the vehicle itself and the execution. Well, the low-slung sedan was obviously in 1 / 24 or 1 / 25 scale, those being the two most popular scales for plastic model cars . . .

Only . . . Ron didn't recognize the make (and he ought to have, he'd being reading car mags for years, courtesy of a foster-father who'd been a minor official in the Sports Car Club of America, Tampa branch). It took him a full minute of staring, though, to realize that this was no kit model at all (though the tires seemed to hail from Monogram), but that it had been built from scratch. And now that he really scrunched up his eyes, he detected a few file marks beneath the lustrous pearlescent burgundy paint. Not only that, but the edges around the wheel wells were too thin for plastic, which meant at least part of the body was made of metal. Brass, most likely, to judge by its availability.

"You made this?"

"Would I have swum over here to show it to you if I hadn't?"

"I'd have walked either way," Ron growled. "But if you *did* make it . . . well, it looks like damned fine work. Best I've seen, in fact."

Sam looked pleased but did not reply.

Ron continued to study the replica, only then realizing that all four doors plus hood and deck had been hinged to open. He popped the cover and tried them one at a time. They moved flawlessly. "So what make is it?" he asked, when his prods and pushes had shown him no miniature nameplates or miniscule emblems.

"No make, or . . . well, I kind of *called* it an Aldebaran when I built it, but now I think that sounds kinda clunky."

"Hmmmmm . . . well, I've never heard of an Aldebaran, and I've never seen a real car like this, so you must have . . . designed this yourself?"

The boy looked at once embarrassed and pleased. "Uh, yeah, I did . . . actually."

"I'm impressed," Ron said simply.

Sam surprised Ron by blushing. "Thanks."

Ron passed the model back. "Thank *you* for showing it to me."

"Wanta go swimming?" Sam asked suddenly.

Coming out of left field as it did, the question took Ron completely off guard. *"What?"* he blurted, before he could stop himself.

"Swimming," Sam repeated patiently. "Want-to-go-swimming?"

Ron stiffened. "Not at the moment."

"But you're *good* at it, aren't you?" Sam protested. "I mean there was that trophy, and all."

"That just means I *was* good."

Sam regarded him skeptically. "It's not a thing you lose."

"A lot *you* know."

"I know enough," Sam countered quickly. "Besides, it's hot, I'm pissed at my dad, and you look like you're kinda wired too—never mind sweaty."

"An astute observation," Ron drawled sarcastically. "Thanks a lot."

"It relaxes you, you know," Sam observed slyly.

Ron glared at the boy. "I *know*, Sam! I know everything you *can* know about swimming and diving. I almost made the Olympics, for chrissakes! I—oh, crap!"

Sam was eyeing him with a mixture of surprise, hurt, and awe, all in quick-flashed sequence.

"Olympics?"

Ron nodded resignedly "And then I fell and fucked up my knee."

"So *that's* why you don't like to swim? 'Cause it reminds you of—"

" 'Cause it reminds me, period," Ron finished for him. "Sorry to snip at you, man; but . . . that wasn't the greatest time of my life . . . and today's not been the greatest day."

Sam looked confused. "But even so . . . I mean, jeez . . . I like swimming even though I've *never* done it competitively. And I can't imagine *not* doing it, even if—shit! I mean, it'd *still* be fun."

"Not if it reminded you of something really great that you've lost," Ron snapped bitterly, yet feeling a strange sort of relief for all that. It was the first time he'd spoken of that frustration since shortly after he and Brandy had formed their alliance, when he'd had to explain that while he didn't mind skinny-dipping, he really didn't want to swim with her—ever. She'd said she understood, but he doubted it. Lew hadn't understood, either, because Lew had never been in reach of something grand and lost it.

But the kid did have a point, dammit! He was tight as a tick, tense as a cat in a room full of rockers (as Brandy was fond of quoting her late mother). And it was hotter'n hell, to echo Dion, when he was in his cups and talking redneck.

"Maybe I will," he said as abruptly as Sam's initial suggestion. "Maybe I'll show you the *right* way to do it."

"All right!" Sam cried, his reserve cracking enough to admit a joyful grin—and reveal a dimple. *Better not let Sharon see that,* Ron thought. *Or the kid'll get more than he bargained for.*

Not that Sharon would be a bad teacher. Besides, given his looks and ingratiating charm, he doubted Sam needed that kind of instruction.

Damn him!

Ron spared one final glance around the forge, flicked off the lights, and herded Sam outside, pausing only to secure a pair of towels from the tiny washroom that opened off the forge. Less than a minute later, he and Sam were making their way around the wide, stepped curve of the natural amphitheater that was called, somewhat erroneously, the East Terrace, and thence down a slope that was an even mix of scraggly grass and furtive rocks to the lake.

The poet-in-training who'd occupied the Celtic bedroom before Perry and John would have noted that the trail Ron chose was the trail less traveled and doubtless have commented thereon. Ron simply wanted to comment on flighty girlfriends, insane uncles, unreliable brothers, and unpredictable urchins. *And* on inconsiderate houseguests who monopolized his time when he was trying to get on with much-delayed projects. Oh, and on recalcitrant brazen constructions that seemed unlikely ever to produce the results they were designed for.

"Gaaaa," he muttered to the fleet-footed Sam. "Slow down."

"Something wrong?"

"Nothing I want to talk about, not if we're doin' this to relieve tension."

"Oh."

"We'll take the dock side if you don't mind," Ron told his companion a moment later, in only a slightly moderated mood. "It's deeper there, better for swimming, and all—in case you didn't notice on your way up."

"What about diving?" Sam centured carefully, sparing him an appraising stare. "I didn't check that out."

Ron's face clouded. "There's a board on the dock one of the guests put in a couple of years ago. I've never installed a high dive, if that's what you're asking."

It was Sam's turn to look disappointed. "Nothing to *really* dive off of?"

"Well, there're some trees that hang out over the water. I suppose you could climb one of them—assuming you had good knees, which I don't."

Sam remained silent while Ron strode onto a fixed wooden dock that projected into the lake a quarter mile east of the cove where he and Sam had first met. He could see Sam's house from there, but not well from this angle, all but the high-pitched roof being screened by a grove of spindly pines that grew close to the farther shore. Taking a deep breath, he closed his eyes, caught the smell of conifers and cool water, and felt the brush of breeze against his bare chest and shoulders, heard the lapping of tiny waves against the poles that supported the fixed part of the dock, and the creak of the free-floating part rising and falling with the gentle swells.

Still ignoring his companion, he made his way onto the center of the floating portion. It was no more than ten feet square, and though only a year old, had already taken on the satiny patina wood acquires when exposed to sun and water, which was fine with him. Maybe if he stayed there long enough he'd acquire a satiny patina of his own—maybe one that Brandy would find more enticing than she seemed to be finding his present skin lately—last night, almost, excepted.

Gaaaaa! Ron thought again. What was bringing all his angst to the surface, all at once? Maybe Sam was right; maybe he really did need to blow off some steam.

With that in mind, he paused only long enough to dump his towel and shed his sneakers before trotting stiffly along the remaining bit of pier and onto the board, whence he launched himself into a flat, shallow dive. He hit the water smoothly, was under it and engulfed in its coolness before he knew it, and surfacing again ten yards out, to roll over and take in air before Sam even knew what had happened. He hoped the boy was sufficiently impressed not to goad him further. And more to the point, he hoped he wouldn't be forced to explain that the preceding was all the diving he was good for, because anything else required more knee flexion than he was capable of in a hurry.

But where *was* Sam? Ron blinked his eyes clear and trod water. Dammit, the kid had been right behind him only a second ago . . .

Oh, *there* he was, minus towel and backpack, already shinnying up the thick knotty trunk of one of those peculiar not-quite live oaks Ron had only observed hereabouts. "Where's the bottom?" the boy called cheerily, as he twisted expertly around the trunk and commenced working his way out the limb that overhung the water farthest and—at easily twenty feet up—highest as well.

"Below the water," Ron responded promptly, whereupon Sam merely bared his teeth and glared. "Cute," the boy chuckled. "I guess if I break my neck, I'll just have to sue you."

"Not me," Ron countered. "This is my *lady's* place, remember?"

Sam's response was to brace himself against a higher branch, balance an instant—and execute one of the neatest swan dives Ron had ever seen into the glittering surface.

Which was not something Ron would have recommended he do, given that the water wasn't *that* deep in the target zone. He was just becoming concerned when an explosion of spray right beside him signaled Sam's reemergence into the upper air. The boy gasped twice, with excellent control, and grinned—again.

Ron tried not to be impressed. "Not smart," he muttered.

Sam managed a bobbing shrug, which sent jewels of water cascading off his sleek, tanned shoulders. "Yeah, but if it had *really* been dangerous, you'd have said something before I got all the way out!" The grin became triumphant.

Ron merely growled, stealthily drew his right arm back an extra few inches—and swept it around smartly, rising as it came, to send a miniature tsunami straight into Sam's startled face.

Which was duly reciprocated. Several times. On both sides.

"Nice dive," Ron admitted, when they were both panting heavily, not adding that it was not only a nice dive, but the finest example of that particular form he'd ever witnessed. So fine, in fact, he wished he had it on tape so he could watch it again. "What else can you do?—assuming that wasn't a fluke."

Sam's reply was a derisive snort. At which point he struck out lazily toward the dock and proceeded to spend the next half hour demonstrating his (always perfect) form in every variation Ron could think of, from jackknife to double-gainer.

The lad was good, there was no doubt about it. No, Ron corrected himself, he was *great*. Poised, but not tense. Intense but not stuffy. Confident, but not (except when he played for effect) cocky. He was, in short, as natural a study as Ron had ever seen.

And (it hurt to admit), far, far better than Ron ever could have been.

"Uh . . . your coaches *do* know you can do that, don't they? Dive that well, I mean?"

Another liquid shrug. "I don't *have* coaches. What I did

at school was just for the fun of it. We didn't have a diving board."

"What about the Y?"

A shrug.

"So how'd you get so good?"

"Found a lake and a tree and copied what I saw."

Ron gaped incredulously—which allowed water to lap into his mouth. "No formal training at all?" he gasped when he had finished sputtering. "Christ!"

Sam grinned. "This isn't gettin' you to swim."

"I'm fine."

"But you're not doing what I got you down here for. Come on, old guy, let's see what you've got."

"Old guy?" Ron snarled fiendishly. *"Old guy?"*

"Race you to the dock," Sam challenged calmly.

And so they did—five times, two of which Ron won (with great and painful effort), two of which Sam won, and in one of which Ron triumphed by so narrow a margin it was pronounced a draw on account of Ron's being taller and longer limbed—this in spite of Ron's protests that Sam was sleeker of frame and had less body hair, and was therefore more aerodynamic.

They were still settling on a format for a rematch, when movement from the shore proved to be a red-faced Perry bounding down the trail at a potentially dangerous clip. *"There* you are," he panted, when he finally got within hailing range. "Brandy's back and was wondering where you were, so I told her I'd hunt you up."

"Any particular reason?" Ron wondered, as he began drifting toward shore, with Sam in his wake.

"She's got somebody she wants you to meet."

Ron rolled his eyes. "Great," he muttered under his breath, then louder: "Any idea who?"

"Some guy she met in town."

Ron exchanged puzzled glances with Sam and suppressed an urge to probe ahead with the Luck. "Fine," he gritted, as he hauled himself up the ladder and onto the dock. His water-logged cutoffs tugged at him, threatening to drag him back into that element he had so loved and so bitterly rejected.

"I gotta split, anyway," Sam said behind him, as Ron commenced toweling off. Perry was already hightailing it—probably with grout a-drying.

Ron turned, blinking distractedly. "Oh, yeah, right. That was . . ." He paused, wondering if it was wise to let even a tiny chink in his armor show. Then—what the hell?—"That was fun," he finished quickly. "Thanks."

"Does that mean I can ask for a favor, now?"

Ron's eyes narrowed suspiciously. "What?"

"Teach me metalwork," Sam said softly. "Teach me everything you know."

"You mean like an apprentice?" Ron blurted out, wondering where *that* very final word had come from so suddenly. And wondering, more to the point, if Sam even halfway suspected the almost mystical commitment it implied.

"Yeah," the boy replied, "like that."

"We'll see," was the only safe answer Ron could think of.

"Will we?" Sam asked cryptically. *"Ciao!"* Whereupon he snared his backpack and set off on the long path around the finger of the lake toward his dad's house. *He ought to be just about dry when he arrives,* Ron thought, only then realizing his new friend had not bothered to use his towel.

But *that* petty concern did not last even halfway up the hill.

Chapter 8

Everybody Plays the Fool

A strange car crouched in the wide stone plaza before Brandy Hall. And not merely a strange car in the sense that Ron failed to recognize its owner; no, this was a truly *strange* car. He had no idea *what* the low-slung sedan gleaming there in a blaze of pearl-gold paint might be, only that it was 'international size'; fluidly curved, and extravagantly glassy; with almost no chrome, and lights like crystal slits. But what *was* it? An Infiniti, perhaps? One of those new Maserati sedans? The long-rumored midsized Jag he'd been seeing artists' renderings of for the last ten years? The next generation Taurus? *Who knew?* His curiosity instantly maxed to overload, and—summons from Brandy notwithstanding—he could not resist a detour past it.

And could no more identify the vehicle at two yards than at two hundred. Oh, it had Georgia plates (with no county decal), but nowhere was a nameplate to be found, not so much as a window sticker. Merely a voided, six-pointed star cast into each alloy wheel, with a like design centering the low oval of the grille, the panel between the taillights, and embossed into the hub of the leather-wrapped steering wheel.

Yet it *looked* familiar. Maybe he'd seen it in a car magazine, perhaps as a prototype of some upcoming model. After

all, it wasn't unknown for manufacturers to do brochure pho-
tography among the steep curves, precipitous waterfalls, and
spectacular slopes of the north Georgia mountains. Shoot,
just last winter he'd caught next year's Ford Probe and a
veritable rainbow of interim Escorts being put through their
paces up on Keycutter Knob. . . .

Except that he'd seen this shape more recently, and in three
dimensions. And then he knew.

Allowing for the obvious difference in size, the golden
sedan before him was identical to the miniature Sam had
shown him less than an hour earlier! The one the boy *said*
he had designed and built from scratch. The one he had called
an Aldebaran. Which was a star. Which was the emblem on
this car.

Ron felt a monstrous chill, one that brought with it the
dreaded whispered words: *lies . . . deceptions . . . deceit . . .
betrayal. What the* hell *was going on?*

Well, the answer to that and other questions (Did Brandy's summons mean he was forgiven?) was more likely to
lurk inside than out. But he had not gone more than three
paces toward Brandy Hall when he acquired another cause
for alarm.

It translated as a headache, and he used that term for convenience on those blessedly rare occasions when he found
himself compelled to describe the unpleasant sensation he
was now experiencing. More accurately, though, it resembled a mental short circuit, a mind's-eye fireworks display,
and a psychic popcorn popper all reaching overload simultaneously.

It had to do with Voices.

Usually Voices were no problem; *usually* he needed minimal shielding to shut the dull buzz of the guests' routine
thoughts out of his own mental hive. But strong emotions,
whether positive or negative, increased the strength of broadcast, and the more people involved the 'louder' it became—
and the harder to damp down. Concerts and sporting events
were worst; but the assault intruding upon him now rivaled
a low-level high school scrimmage all by itself. And, unfortunately, Ron could not determine the cause of the psychic
hubbub without physically tracking it to its source, because

Listening involved dropping his shields, which would be like abandoning an umbrella in a hurricane.

So it was that when he pushed open the heavy bronze inner door of the entrance foyer (where Nuada-the-faceless had now acquired a torque), crossed the intervening corridor, and entered the great hall, he was not surprised to find himself up to his neck in chaos. But even so, he was in nowise prepared for the transformation that vast, echoing space had undergone.

Usually the great hall served as a sort of *uber*–living room, with chairs, tables, and sofas scattered in conversation-sized clumps among the arches and life-sized sculpted Sidhe of the side aisles, and with the navelike center left open for traffic and general mayhem. Now, however (orchestrated by Dead Can Dance's "Salterello" at deafening volume), John, Perry, and Sharon were everywhere, moving with a speed and efficiency that made them appear far more than simply three very energetic people. And with a mental vibe leaking past Ron's shields that registered between ebullience and sheer panic.

What they were *doing*, he observed, was converting the great hall into a simulacrum of its medieval namesake. Which meant they'd scooted the larger furnishings into corners and secreted the lighter bits in concealed closets contrived for that purpose—the same ones which had disgorged the three trestle tables now disposed across the northern end in an inverted U. Perry was up in the clerestory draping man-long banners from bronze dragon-head hooks Ron had forged three winters back. A few of the bright silk hangings bore national insignia or arms from Brandy's family, but most showed heraldic motifs from fantasy novels: the White Tree of Gondor; the *gules, a lion rampant, Or* of Katherine Kurtz's Haldanes; Asprin's vulgar unicorn; Poul Anderson's three hearts and three lions. The overall effect, Ron conceded, was most impressive: true baronial splendor. If only he'd had some warning—and didn't have a headache.

And, of course, knew what on earth could have caused Brandy to order one of these wingdings on such short notice.

Fortunately, John was just bustling by with a bench in his brawny arms, but one look at his harried expression told Ron he was too busy to bother. But he was able to catch Sharon midway between linen cupboard and table. "What's up?" he asked, amazed.

Brandy Hall's resident potter panted at him from across a mound of snowy, handwoven tablecloth (legacy of yet another guest). "Company's comin'," she enthused. "Brandy just came flyin' in and said it was feastin' time. Time to set dinner for twenty. Time to . . . *party*!"

Ron counted on his fingers. "Her, me, you, the boys— who're the other lucky sods?"

"Weedge and a bunch of folks from the Chamber, I reckon," Sharon tossed over her shoulder as she brushed by him. "She apparently got some good news today."

No solution to that little conundrum being obvious (it made about four in two minutes), Ron settled instead for seeking explanation from the author of the confusion herself. He found her, by Luck, two doors and a corridor beyond the great hall.

Brandy looked up as he entered the library, her face a mask of alarm—probably because curiosity had made him push through the door with more than usual force. She flashed him a relieved smile as she rose from where she'd been piling books—bound copies of the county newspaper, by the look of them, which were technically Ron's domain—into a low pyramid on the more western of the two long side tables.

"To forgive is divine," she said, in the tone she used to remind all and sundry that *she* was mistress of Brandy Hall.

"So I've been told," Ron replied neutrally, relieved to have the ice broken, but irritated at the note of condescension.

A black eyebrow lifted toward the beamed ceiling—where tempera archangels kept the more pagan printed works below in implicit check. "It *can* be mutual," she added, with a lopsided grin.

"I've heard that too." Ron mirrored her grin with one less forced. "Rumor has it you've got good news. And wasn't there something about meeting someone?"

"Yes, and yes!" Brandy affirmed, pausing for a sip of sherry before slipping from behind the table. She was still beaming but, in spite of his shields, Ron sensed impatience, as if her warmth were forced—which, given the chaos beyond, it probably was. Nevertheless, she enclosed him in a hearty hug—only to release him abruptly. "Ugh," she grunted. "You're wet!"

"Happens when you swim," Ron chuckled, rather enjoying her chagrin—and the way his condition was now so nicely mirrored on her breasts. Evidently he had been forgiven.

"I want you to read something, okay?"

Ron blinked stupidly. "You want me to . . . read?"

She indicated a pile of printout adjoining the bound newspapers. "Just a few pages."

"But your . . . friend?"

"I told him he could take a shower before we eat—which is gonna be a while."

"Oh . . ."

"You read," Brandy repeated, halfway to the door. "I'll check on dinner. And promise not to yell until you give me a chance to explain, okay?"

"Yell?"

(From the door) "You'll see. But don't."

"That car . . . ?" Ron called vainly to her departing back. *"Who belongs to that weird-looking car out front?"*

But Brandy was already gone.

Ron's first impulse was to follow her, leaving his homework to sit until it mildewed; but in spite of himself, he found his gaze drawn back to the mysterious manuscript. He picked it up, thumbed through it, noting that though it looked to be freshly printed, neither title nor author were present, merely pages number twenty-two through thirty-one. Even more disturbingly, it appeared to be a play, and as soon as he glimpsed a few key words—like Welch and Cardalba Hall—he had a sinking feeling he knew which one.

"Shit!" he gritted, in lieu of the predicted impulse to scream. Brandy had certainly solved *that* problem in a hurry. It must be something special too; otherwise, she wouldn't have asked him to read it, knowing as she had to, that she was playing to a hostile audience. Once again he flipped through the pages—and sighed. What the hey? Know thine enemy, right? Besides, it wasn't like he had anything *else* to do.

Except (he checked his watch) wait for Lew to Call.

Pausing for a yawn, he flopped his still-soggy body down into a green leather armchair that would not have been out of place in an English club. A second pause to polish off the dregs of Brandy's sherry, and to yawn again, and he dived in.

The manuscript seemed to be a dramatization of one of the more colorful events in the history of what he tended to think of as the Welch occupation of the county. Specifically, it began with a formally dressed Matthew Welch, ca. 1863 (clearly a different one than the shifty old geezer Lew had succeeded), standing on the steps of the previous Cardalba Hall (the one with the Greek-Revival portico). Most of the first page was stage direction and description, with a bare smattering of dialogue. Nor was the style particularly detailed; yet somehow Ron found it preposterously easy to picture *exactly* what was transpiring.

Welch was watching for something, staring offstage as if he gauged someone's approach, stroking the knob of a dragon-headed cane as he waited. Eventually he spotted what he sought and squared his shoulders—just as a ragged young man in a Yankee uniform stumbled in. Matthew ignored him, except to stand straighter. Soon more soldiers arrived. So far there had been no dialogue.

Ron blinked, yawned, realized that he'd almost nodded off, in spite of the surprisingly vivid subject matter. He yawned again and tried once more . . .

When maybe ten soldiers had appeared (Ron read—or perhaps sleep had claimed him all unknown, and now he dreamed . . .) their commanding officer, Captain Christian Johnson, entered on horseback. Silently, they assessed each other: Yankee captain and Master of Cardalba.

"Are you the master of this house?" Johnson demanded, his hand on the hilt of his sword.

"I am Master of this *place*—and more," Welch replied, with a cryptic smile.

"Are you a Rebel, sir?"

"This is Georgia; what do you suppose?"

There followed a formal but forceful exchange, with neither man conceding ground. Johnson asked for cooperation: food, shelter, medicine—and threatened to burn Cardalba to the ground if Welch refused. Welch's reply was to offer shelter in the woods "as both our ancestors once sheltered," food—"if you hunt it or gather it from the ground." But not medicine, "for the folk of this valley need all I can . . . acquire."

Johnson ranted, but Welch held firm. Finally, though, Johnson became convinced that the medicine he desired was inside Cardalba Hall. Soldiers were dispatched to search. "And once you have found medicine," Johnson added triumphantly, "I have heard that fire applied to velvet draperies is an excellent salve for pride."

His victory was short-lived, however, for barely had the search begun when the questing soldiers burst from the mansion, falling over themselves in their haste to flee, their faces wild with shock and alarm.

"Ghosts!" one screamed. "Ghosts and spirits!"

"I seen my old granny!" another cried. "I seen her, and her gone these five years!"

But before Johnson could act, he too noticed something that made his eyes start wide: the nebulous shape of a stern old man with a whip in his hand. "F . . . father!" he gasped, as he stood dumbstruck . . .

Ron blinked again, amazed that he should have become so engrossed in the manuscript. It was vivid, that was for sure! For an instant he wasn't even certain he had actually been reading. But . . . he *had* turned pages (though he didn't remember doing so). And the neatly typed dialogue was exactly as he remembered. The rest, though . . . It wasn't *quite* as he recalled . . . And there was something else he wanted to keep an eye out for too, if only he could remember what it was, something that had struck him as incongruous. But before he realized it, he had turned another page.

The next scene took place at night, with the plantation portico glimmering in the moonlight, looking eerily placid, as if it were feigning sleep. A single light burned in a second-story window, then winked out. Shapes approached from either side: Yankee soldiers speaking in low voices. They had come to burn Cardalba Hall. As Johnson watched, torches were lit.

First, though, he must interrogate a prisoner. An old man was dragged in.

"You say it's only dreams he uses?" Johnson snapped. "You say he's able to prowl in our heads and find out what we fear and show it to us?"

"That's what *they* say," the old man cackled.

"Yeah, and *they* say he can't be killed," Johnson sneered. "They *say* a lot of crazy things."

"What do *you* say?"

"I say that if you're gonna set fire to that there house, you'd best be at it!"

Chaos ensued. As the old man watched, strangely amused, Johnson ordered the torching of Cardalba Hall, requesting only that Matthew Welch be hauled out for judgment. But even as Cardalba Hall took fire, Matthew himself, still in full formal attire, appeared on the porch. "I can always get another house," he said. "But you can't get any more medicine if you burn mine. What do you think of that?"

"I think I ought to shoot you," Johnson replied calmly. "What do *you* think of that? Can you get another life?"

"Easier than you can, if you die of dysentery!" Welch chuckled. "If you're gonna shoot me, do it; you'll wake up my darkies elsewise."

Whereupon Johnson drew his pistol and proceeded to shoot Matthew Welch point-blank in the forehead, then turned and left.

But even as Welch's body toppled to the ground, screams sounded from the nearby woods: "Oh, God, Granny, no . . . !" and, "No, father, please, don't beat me; not again . . . ! No! No! No!" Gunfire erupted. Johnson staggered back on stage, mortally wounded, to collapse directly beside Welch's body. Welch stirred, rose. He looked at the old man, who had crept in beside him. "Well," Welch said, "I reckon I'm down one house. But I reckon the folks 'round here know which side to be on, now." Still bleeding profusely, they exited.

But Welch returned an instant later, his face obscured and his wrists and ankles in chains. He stared at the now-blackened shell of Cardalba Hall, and hung his head. "I've lost it all," he choked—in a voice different from before, one strangely familiar. He turned then, stiffly, raised his head to face the audience. And when he looked up, it was . . . Lew.

"Lew!"

Ron flinched, as sleepers sometimes do when in the throes of dream.

"Lew," Ron repeated dully; accepting at last that he had fallen asleep, that he really *had* been dreaming, or at least had dreamed that last part. Only . . .

He paged quickly back through the sheaf of manuscript. He had read it all—yet remembered none of it *as manuscript*. It was too vivid, the images too intense for ordinary prose. Yet now he looked back at them, they were unremarkable. And there was no reference to Lew; the page (the *last* page) ended with, "side to be on."

But *something* was bloody well amiss.

And then he knew!

The play had depicted actual events that were common knowledge; no problem there. But Ron knew for an absolute fact that the *details* of those occurrences were recorded in only one place: that same Matthew Welch's diary that was locked in the tower vault. The bit about how Welch had defied a Yankee captain until certain medicines could be spirited out of Cardalba Hall through a secret tunnel in the cellar was in there, for instance. And though the place had undeniably been torched, and Welch had survived, even as the band of marauding Yankees seemed to have slain each other, the rest . . . well, it implied a knowledge of the intricacies of Luck that should have been beyond the ken of anyone outside the clan. *No one* should have known how Luck allowed one to look into other minds to locate those innermost horrors that could drive men to murder . . . or insanity.

And certainly no one outside the clan should know of Listeners' invulnerability to anything short of beheading without quick rejoining, massive dispersion or immulation, or one's particular Flaw. *Absolutely* no one should have known how that earlier Matthew Welch really had been shot in the head point-blank and had still worked his vengeance and risen again.

But what about that quasi epilogue with what had turned out to be Lew in chains? Did *that* mean anything? Or was it merely his imagination playing tricks in response to those other conundrums the manuscript had contrived? He didn't want to think.

And speaking of Lew, he hadn't phoned yet. Which meant that much as Ron loathed the notion, he supposed he was in for another bout of Listening.

And that was *all* he needed: hassle on top of chaos on top of crisis on top of confusion! Why couldn't problems arrange themselves neatly, dammit? And allow him to solve one before another presented itself? Months, he'd had, in which nothing untoward had happened. And now, suddenly, in a tad more than twenty-four hours, affairs had got utterly out of hand. And the worst thing was that he was suddenly too tired to deal with any of it any more.

But if he *had* to choose, he'd choose Lew.

Yawning hugely, Ron checked his watch, and noted that it was just past seven—right at the limit of the contact window. A glance around the library showed it still empty.

Good, he'd just Jump in now and get it over with. Maybe—

It was exactly at that moment that the hall door cracked open and Brandy stuck her head inside. Seeing him glaring sidelong at her, she cleared her throat and slipped fully in.

Unfortunately, she was not alone. What with his consternation over the manuscript and Lew, plus his ongoing fit of fatigue, Ron had forgotten the prime reason he was in here dripping all over the furniture. Scowling, he rose and turned to greet Brandy and her latest guest, noting—to his great surprise—that Brandy's newest find was a boy. A slender, fair-haired lad, to be precise, flamboyantly dressed in red and black, and scarcely older than Sam, if even that.

"Ronny," Brandy announced proudly, easing around to stand between the two, "meet the guy who wrote what you just read; meet Project Shakespeare's resident playwright, Donson Gwent! Donson, this is my boyfriend, Ron Dillon."

Ron extended his hand mechanically. But in that electric instant before he touched that stranger's flesh he noted a number of things.

The first was simply that the eager-looking Mr. Gwent was not only very young indeed, but also quite remarkably pretty. Not handsome; his face held too few angles for that. And not cute; his features were too long and regular. But not beautiful, either; because that implied aloofness and unreachable cool, and Donson's expression was animated, guileless, and warm. No, he was simply pretty, in the way smooth skin, bright eyes, and innocence impart their own aesthetic charm.

The second realization was that the ingratiating smile that lit the guy's face upon meeting Ron's gaze had a nervous, almost fearful, edge to it that Ron did not like.

And the third was the guilty twinkle in the boy's eyes. A twinkle he had seen before. A twinkle, the origin of which Ron was seeking to confirm even as his hand closed around Donson Gwent's hesitant slender fingers.

Gwent had no Voice! Not even the false echo of one, such as Van Vannister had contrived to mask his true nature. Wind-wise, the kid was as blank as a board—exactly like Wendy.

Which meant that Gwent was likely not human. Though to judge by the lad's perplexed expression, he was concealing that fact very well.

What he *was*, Ron wasn't sure. But allowing for the subtraction of about ten years and the shift in hair color from red to strawberry blond—an easy enough alteration—the boy was the spitting image of the Road Man!

Who also had no Voice.

"Get out!" Ron growled at Brandy, fixing her with a stare so vehement she started moving toward the door before her eyes had widened to outrage at his tone. *"Get out,"* he repeated more softly. "Me and this guy gotta talk."

Chapter 9

Don't Come Around Here No More

Brandy's face went hard as stone. Her brows collided above her nose, raising ridges like unto the Himalayas, and her jaw tightened so suddenly that Ron expected to see the tendons in her neck start snapping like overstressed rubber bands. By bearding the lioness in her lair, as he had just so cavalierly done by ordering Brandy out of her own library, he'd committed the ultimate sin to someone as territorial as she. Never mind that he'd been all over the emotional map with her the last few days anyway. Never mind that she had somehow stumbled into a situation the gravity of which Ron himself was still assessing. Never *mind* that he had no choice at all but to blunder blindly down a path which could very well lead to disaster.

And the worst thing was that useless buffer zone of a Gwent-guy, who was simply standing there gaping, as if he did not know perfectly well what was going on and who had caused it. Well, Ron had met his like before, and—finally—knew what to do. If only Brandy would bow out gracefully and leave him to the kill.

"Excuse me," Brandy gritted slowly, her tight-clenched teeth doubtless the sole barrier between Ron and a no-holds-barred shout. *"Excuse me,"* she repeated, gathering self-righteous calm about her like a cloak of indignation—a very lethal sort of calm it was, too, like that before a tornado. "But exactly whose library *is* this, that you are suggesting I vacate?"

"Whose books are *those* that you're passing 'round like Gideon Bibles?" Ron countered hotly, too exasperated to contrive anything more original.

"Books that can be in a pile by the front door in ten seconds!" Brandy shot back with equal vigor.

Ron glared at her, feeling his cheeks burning as months of latent frustration and hostility suddenly took fire. "Look, Brandy, I don't want this," he managed. "And I *certainly* don't want it now! I'm trying to protect you, for God's sake!"

"Protect me?" Brandy snorted. "From *what*? A teenage *boy*?"

"If that's what he actually is!" Whereupon Ron turned his attentions to the still-silent Gwent—whose sole reaction thus far had been to pucker his brow, gnaw his thumb, and look confused.

"Who *are* you?" Ron demanded, close enough and loud enough to make the boy's visor of hair quiver. "What do you want here? Why don't you leave us alone?"

Gwent merely gaped, as if in shock. "Uh . . . well, gee, Mr. Dillon, I, uh . . . That is . . . That's a *lot* of questions."

Ron shifted his weight and folded his arms imperiously, wishing he was wearing more than soggy cutoffs. "How 'bout just the first one, then?"

Gwent looked utterly confounded, but then his face brightened. "Oh . . . well, my name's Donson Gwent, and—"

"That's your *name*!" Ron interrupted coldly, "*not* who you are."

"Ronny . . ." Brandy tried to break in, but Ron ignored her.

"I—Well, let's see—" From Gwent.

Ron's gaze never left his youthful target. "Start with where you're from."

Gwent's face underwent a sudden shift, hard to define but Ron noticed it. His gaze steadied, his chin firmed. It was as if an adult had walked in and sat down behind his eyes. "Earth," he said calmly. "Like everyone else: I was born of earth."

Ron's eyes narrowed abruptly; he had to suppress a chill. "*Of* earth, or *from* earth?"

A shrug. "Is there a difference?"

"There is if you're what I think you are."

Gwent raised an eyebrow. "So, why don't you just tell me what you think?"

" 'Cause that'd be tipping my hand," Ron snapped back. " 'Cause that'd be freeing you from the onus of explanation."

Gwent's brow wrinkled in perplexity, rather like that of a college professor confronting an underachieving student—which made the hair on Ron's neck stand on end. "I don't believe in defining oneself in terms of one's background," he said finally, his soft voice sounding like that of a sincere Michael Jackson. "I think a person ought to be judged solely on the basis of what he is and what he does, not where he's from, or how he looks, or how old he is, or who his parents are, or what kind of education he has."

"Charles Manson'd probably agree with you," Ron snorted. "Okay then, I'll ask it straight out: Are you the Road Man?"

Gwent blinked at him uncomprehendingly. "The *what*?"

"Don't play innocent with me, kid! You know perfectly well you don't have a Voice."

Gwent turned wide, confused eyes toward Brandy, as if begging her intercession with this obviously certified loon. "What's he talkin' about?" he asked with perfect naïveté, the grown-up having evidently vanished utterly. "What's a . . . Voice—I mean, like, what does *he* mean by it?"

"It means what you're thinking," Ron blurted before Brandy could frame an answer. "It means the subconscious, gut-level power behind your emotions. It means . . . Oh *shit*!" But he had already said too much. Oh, he was sure of his convictions, but that didn't mean that—possibly—he couldn't still be wrong. In which case, he'd just committed another world-class blunder. "It doesn't matter *what* it means," he finished weakly. "What's important is that you don't have one. Which means exactly one thing."

"What?"

"That you're not human."

Gwent rolled his eyes in genuine disbelief. "You've *gotta* be kiddin', mister! Do I *look* like a space alien, or Bigfoot, or something?"

"You *look* like a kid," Ron growled. "But you bloody well don't *act* like one! Nor were you talking like one a minute ago. And that's the problem."

"You haven't given him a chance to act *any* way," Brandy interrupted coldly, showing by her face that she was all over the emotional map too: trapped between her lover, a new friend, and her own self-interest. "I mean, Jesus, Ronny; *think* for a minute! He *can't* be the Road Man—or Vannister either, for obvious reasons."

"*How* obvious?"

"Just look at him!"

Ron shifted his gaze lazily back to Gwent. "I am—and I don't like what I see."

"What *do* you see?"

"A kid who's too accomplished to *be* a kid—if he actually wrote what I just read. And worse, I see a kid who knows too many things he shouldn't, a kid who's too cool to be for real. A kid who has no Voice, when only . . . folks like the Road Man have no Voice!"

"Or that folks like you have had a go at," Brandy noted carelessly. "Like poor Karen, or Gwen, or . . ."

"That's enough!" Ron warned, knowing that Brandy spoke truth: that Listeners could silence Voices if need be—as they did with footholders. Except that Gwent couldn't be a rogue footholder because footholders had to be virgin females, and he was clearly the wrong sex.

Or was he? Footholders were required to be virgins for the same reason Masters weren't allowed to be circumcised: because they had to have all their parts intact when the Luck kicked in in order for it to circulate through them properly. (Ron's missing kneecap was a rogue exception.) But did they *have* to be female any more than Masters *had* to be male? Supposedly the rationale was that there were aspects of one's mind that could only be accessed by the opposite sex. But sexual identity could sometimes be ambiguous, and Listeners *were* subject to the same vices and variations as mainstream society; so why couldn't Gwent be some gay Master's toy-boy who had gone AWOL and managed to shake his conditioning?

Certainly it made more sense than the notion that the Road Man was changing face, vocation, and date of birth every few years simply to confound him—especially as (according to reports) he'd maintained the same persona for a fair long time before Ron first met him.

But suppose he was wrong? Suppose this *was* some avatar of the Road Man? What then? Well, the guy had never actually harmed him—not physically. But Ron had been mightily manipulated by him, which was in many ways worse. And if he was *also* in some way Van Vannister . . . Well, Ron would never forgive that big lug for the games he had played with him and Brandy during the formative month of their relationship, good intentions notwithstanding.

"Two questions, then," Ron said suddenly. "Make that two demands."

Gwent scowled uncertainly. "Oooo-kay . . ."

Ron took a deep breath, steeling himself. "Drop your britches."

"Ronny!" Brandy's cry was a verbal counterpoint to Gwent's mute incredulity.

"Wh . . . *wh-what*?" the boy finally managed to stammer.

"Drop your pants," Ron repeated, as clinically as possible, though he could feel his face growing warm. "Both pairs. And don't worry, I'm not into buggering boys."

Gwent's face was near the color of his fiery silk shirt. "But . . . why?"

"I want to see if you're circumcised."

"I'd . . . have *told* you that much!" Gwent protested, flustered. "I'm . . . not."

"You could also have lied."

Gwent started, blushing even more furiously. "What's *that* got to do with anything?"

"It'll either confirm or eliminate one set of possibilities."

"What? That I'm Jewish? I'm not that either."

"Much more subtle than that."

"I don't see how it's any of your business!"

"I'll ask Brandy to leave, if that makes a difference."

"Ronny, this is *really* too much!" Brandy exploded. "The guy's a *guest*, for chrissakes—*my* guest. An insult to him's an insult to me!"

"And a threat to you's a threat to *me*," Ron countered. "Besides, it'll only take a second."

"You could determine more easily than that!"

Ron shot her a sidelong glare. "Not with someone without a Voice, I can't!"

Gwent, who had finally begun to regain his normal color as he gazed from one combatant to the other, shook his head resignedly. *"Okay,"* he gritted, not meeting either of their gazes. "If it'll help anything, you—Ronny—come here; let's get it over with."

Ron rolled his eyes and insinuated his way directly in front of the boy, then turned to speak over his shoulder. "Brandy— it really would be good if you could, like, turn your back or something . . ."

"I'll go outside and count ten. If it takes any longer—"

"It won't."

Brandy left.

"I still don't understand this," Gwent said sincerely.

"Sorry, but I gotta make sure," Ron muttered, no longer totally convinced himself.

Gwent swallowed, undid his belt, top snap, and fly, and pulled the waistband of his jockey shorts out and down just far enough for Ron to confirm the lad's earlier admission.

But Ron noticed something else as well, something which ignited instant sympathy with the boy, as no amount of protest or explanation ever would have.

For Gwent *was* a boy—utterly and completely, and like to stay that way forever. True, the bulk of his body was certainly of acceptable size and build for his apparent age. But in one crucial area, he was . . . Stunted? Atrophied? Undeveloped? Dimensionally disadvantaged? Whatever tactful double-talk one chose, there was no denying the fact that between the legs Donson Gwent looked less seventeen years than seven months. Which took Ron approximately two seconds to assess.

A white scar across the kid's scrotum told him why.

"Sorry," Ron murmured helplessly.

"Don't tell anyone . . . please?" Gwent pleaded, hastily readjusting his complex clothing.

"No reason to."

The zipper buzzed home; a buckle clinked. "Satisfied?"

"Maybe." Ron cast his glance wearily toward the door. "Unfortunately that *still* leaves at least two possibilities."

"And one more question?" Gwent asked shakily.

Ron's reply was to clamp Gwent firmly by the chin and force his face up so that their gazes met. The boy resisted, but did not actually lash out with either fists or feet, as Ron (or Lew—or Sam) surely would have. Eventually the kid buckled before what was obviously a stronger force. Nor did he seem prepared when Ron took three deep breaths— and Jumped.

And almost Jumped right back out again! Certainly Ron had not expected what he discovered in Gwent's mind.

The kid *did* have a Voice! It was only that it was secreted away behind a layer of shields so smooth as to be almost imperceptible, and so thick Ron doubted even Lew could have pierced them without physical contact such as he was engaging in. Ron pushed; Gwent fought back—but inevitably gave way.

And Ron found not one Voice but many—*so* many that when he tried to separate them enough to make any sense of them, they almost sucked him into their psychic tangle. Eventually, though, he made his way through and found, waiting for him at the center . . . *fear*. Fear of abuse. *Years and years* of abuse. Gwent claimed no past, for he had literally blanked whole years of his life, had deliberately suppressed everything about himself that wasn't part of his present reality. And all because, as best Ron could determine, he had always been unlike other boys.

Adopted shortly after birth, he had proven precocious early on, so much so that it had frightened his very religious foster-parents beyond reason. His father, in particular, had been so weirded out that he had beaten the boy every day in hopes of making him normal. And somewhere along the way, his dad—or *someone* male, the memory was understandably hazy—had cut him in such a way that his genitals had atrophied. There had followed a whole series of temporary homes. More than that Ron couldn't bear to discover: no names, no faces, cities, states, or places. No dates or times. Which meant that Gwent had had little choice *but* to go schizo.

Poor little guy.

Ron could take no more. He Jumped back. Saw, first of all, Gwent blinking at him in utter confusion as Ron released him roughly and backed away, and secondly, Brandy glaring at him like thunder from the open door.

"Through?" she sneered sarcastically.

"I *think*," Ron whispered meekly, "that I'll go for a walk."

Brandy's reply was to intensify her glare. "That *wouldn't* be a good idea," she whispered, her voice deadly calm. Then: "Gwent, it *would* be good if you stepped out for a bit," whereupon she strode past Ron as if he were not present at all.

"S-sure," the playwright stammered, and left.

Ron felt himself engulfed by a premonition of impending doom. He could feel it drawing him, like a moth to a flame: something that could in nowise be good for him, yet which dragged at him in a way he could not resist. He had raised his shields automatically at the first hint of hostility, but lowered them bit by bit as he realized how hopelessly he had overstepped his bounds.

A moment longer, he stared at the door, then turned. And saw her: a shapeless lump slumped down in the leather chair, she had swiveled around to face the center of the three arched windows beyond which a rainstorm was now in progress, reducing the light to an ominous gloom. She was silent, not moving. A glass of sherry glittered on the carpet beside her. Ron inhaled softly, though what words could possibly follow to do him any good, he had no idea.

And never got to decide, for Brandy preempted him.

"*I* think," she said slowly, her voice so heavy with anger and sadness that it hurt to hear. "I think," she repeated, "that it would be good if you left for a while." She did not turn, continued to face the window, not looking at him.

Ron's mouth dropped open as if he had taken a fist in the gut. "You don't mean that," he breathed, slowly walking toward her. Then louder: "We've had fights before, Brandy.

And we've had 'em over much bigger things. Surely we can work *this* out."

"Maybe," Brandy replied carefully, and there *was* a catch in her voice, he was sure of it. "But I don't have time to work out things with you right now. It's taking everything I can do to get the play up and running, and—"

"*Screw* the play!" Ron gritted. "Let somebody else do it. You don't have to do everything, or don't you remember what Vannister taught you? What he taught both of us, about control and compromise and fighting for what we really want!"

"Yeah," Brandy nodded slowly. "That *is* what he taught us. But I didn't ask to be in control of this; it was given to me; and too many people are depending on me to let it go. But more to the point, it *is* what I really want—right now. I've become complacent, Ron. I've got my classes, which are fine but no challenge. I've got my house far enough along that it practically finishes itself. I've got plenty to do, but they're all . . . *little* things. I want to do something that counts."

"*This* doesn't count?" Ron snorted helplessly. "*Look* at this place, Brandy; look at all the people—creative people like you and me—you've helped by giving 'em a haven while they got their act together."

"But they're . . . they're people who . . . I dunno, they're all *misfits*," Brandy sighed. "Most artsy types are. It's like they were born to be helped, or better, that they expect to be indulged. But I want to go beyond that. I want to help regular people; I want to make a difference in ordinary lives!"

"And I don't fit into that?"

Another sigh. "Not if you're going to be moody and morose all the time; not if you're not going to come down out of your tower and play *my* game sometimes. And mostly, you don't fit if I'm going to have to defend every action I take, or constantly be on guard about your jealousy or paranoia or whatever it is."

"But Brandy—"

"No, let me finish; I need to say it now, or it won't get said and it *needs* saying. And one of those things that needs saying is that *I'm* the one who ought to be paranoid, not you. *I'm* the one who was on the receiving end of all that supernatural bullshit that gave me this place. *I* was the one that got hoodooed by a were-deer up in the clerestory. You nearly lost folks you cared about, sure, but *I* nearly lost my life—or worse, my dream. And yet you're the one who goes through the ceiling whenever something the least bit goes on. But instead of trying to understand it or learn from it, or let me help you come to terms with it, you automatically assume the worst, and—"

Ron could stand it no longer. "I had half a dozen good reasons to assume that boy was . . . whatever the Road Man is, if not the guy himself come back to haunt us," he snapped. "I mean, how *could* he know those things about my family that he put in the play? And what about that car, that's exactly the same design the new kid across the lake showed me a model of not an hour ago! That kid says he designed it himself, and I have no reason to doubt him. And then your friend shows up in an identical full-sized one! You can't say *that's* normal."

"Can't you?" Brandy countered bitterly. "Did you make this new buddy of yours drop *his* drawers to prove himself? Did you rape his mind just 'cause he did something extraordinary and you thought he might be lying?"

"Of course not! There was no reason to. I—"

Brandy swung the chair around to face him, and Ron could see that her face was glimmering with tears. "Gwent's a *genius*, Ronny, a certified genius with paperwork to prove it! I finally got that out of him this afternoon while he was working on the play. But he's also been abused because of it, and has about half a dozen personalities, two of which are more vocal than the rest: the kid, and the adult—the one that finally sneaked out and leveled with me. I mean, I had some of the same doubts you had, only I was able to win his trust and get him to open up, which he did. And as for those other things . . . well, you don't have to be a Listener to be psychic. He says he got some of the stuff in the play from a dream he had last night. In fact, he says dreams lead him around a lot, like he came here partly because of a dream."

"And I suppose he dreamed that car?"

"Yes and no. He's a decent artist—we don't need to argue that. He says he saw the car in a dream six months ago and sketched it, and one of his foster-dad's brothers is some kind of mondo designer up in Dearborn, and saw the sketch and managed to get it built, and then loaned it to Don for long-term testing to make up for all those other foster-folks being such assholes."

"Some loan."

"No more than some of yours."

"It's still a damned big coincidence that he and Sam show up with the same design on the same day."

"Sam? Who's Sam?"

"The new neighbor's kid."

"Where's he from?"

"Gainesville, I think. What's that got to do with anything?"

"A lot, if he and Donson are both from the same part of the country, which they could well be, given Don's accent. Who's to say who picked up whose dreams from whom? Maybe you better ask *your* boy some hard questions!"

"Maybe I will!"

Silence.

Ron closed the distance between them, leaned against the wall at Brandy's side, so that they both had to glance sideways to make eye contact—which they eschewed. "So . . ." he said at last. "I err on the side of caution, and then—*maybe*—misread somebody badly, which makes me overreact, and then I get thrown out?"

"Not thrown out," Brandy corrected with a sniff. "I'm simply asking you to get out from underfoot for a while—to go stay at your mom's old place, or something. I just need you out of my hair while I work through some things. I think we both need it, actually; maybe it'll give us time to clear our heads and find out what we *really* think about each other— what we really *mean* to each other. Maybe there's too much convenience and not enough concern, or something."

"Which means . . . ?"

A deep breath. "Which means that I still care about you; that hasn't changed at all. But I think the best thing for both of us right now is to back off a little. And since this is my place, and you have two of your own . . ." She let the sentence trail off, then eased the chair around once more to face the window.

"It'll take me a while to pack," Ron said. "I've got about a zillion projects half-done. And of course there're the cars."

"Take what you need," Brandy told him dully. "Take whatever's yours, but take it quickly. I don't want to keep running into you all the time. During the party would be an ideal time to start."

"Fine," Ron choked, as he turned to go. "Do you mind if I borrow the pickup? Or shall I buy one?"

"Take mine," Brandy replied. "Just so you bring it back."

"Take mine," she repeated five minutes later, into a suddenly far more empty Brandy Hall. "Do whatever you want with my truck, Ronny; but please, oh please, be more careful with my heart."

Interlude 5

Cuts Like a Knife

Somewhere in the South
Sunset

"Tea?"

He blinks at that low, sweet voice; stretches, rouses from the heavy lethargic slumber that has plagued him since he came . . . here.

Here . . . ? Where is *here*? he wonders groggily, easing upright. Not home, of a surety; not the high, hilly land of his birth. Still, a certain familiarity haunts the walls and floor, the ceiling and furniture: a distant sort of peace . . .

Another blink, and he knows . . .

The room is austere but comfortable, for his hostess has not dwelt here long enough to warp it with individuality. Rather, there are plain white-plastered walls anonymous as Anywhere; six-paned windows enameled shut, that reveal a sea of treetops from a second-story room; a soft, linen-textured sofa, love seat, and chair in emerald. A deep-pile area rug, red as a pool of blood. A black plastic coffee table. No radio. No phone. No TV.

"Tea?" she inquires again, from the door, full lips moist, red, and curving.

He looks up, smiles back uncertainly.

Her smile fades. She enters, closing the door behind her. The lock clicks home of its own volition. She sets a tray on the table: pressed wood from K mart, but in her hands it becomes a source of wonder. The cups it bears are real jade, carved in Macao a century past, and thin as flowers. The pot is copper and was shaped in India. There is cream and milk in blue faience, two colors of sugar, each in an orange lacquered bowl. A mismatch of crockery that nevertheless approaches perfection.

A third time she smiles, this time showing teeth, and prepares a cup to his liking (how does she know such things?). He receives it, nods acceptance, drinks. There is an odd undertaste in the tea: nutty, vaguely bitter. He wonders if the cream has gone bad, but, thirsty as he is, drinks more.

"Have I slept long?" he yawns when he has finished, his eyes full of grit and sunbeams. The white wall opposite the window, he notices, has turned orange-pink.

"Perhaps half a day," the Beautiful Lady replies, her voice delicate as a cat's.

" . . . Half . . . a day?" he mumbles, as he shifts himself upright.

"You have been ill," she informs him sadly.

" . . . Ill . . . ?"

"A sickness of the mind," the Beautiful Lady explains, her face stern with sympathy. "A sickness you were born with, from which only I can heal you."

"Save me . . . ?" He shakes his head, knowing that something is not right. He reaches for a memory, for he can sense them there, massing like prisoners long captive behind a steel-barred gate. But he cannot release them. Even as he would try, they back away, leaving him only with . . . *now*.

And this woman.

And her story. She tells good stories.

"How . . . ?"

"—Did you come here?" She shrugs. "You became ill. There was nothing I could do but to take you in, to feed you and clothe you, and give you shelter. And, of course, to free your mind of those dark demons that torment you. You said just this morning that you would willingly make me Master of your Realm. But no one would give up such a powerful, valuable thing. Therefore, I have no choice but to assume that the insanity that runs in our kind when one plays games with the ancient Rules of Mastership has claimed you—that or paranoia. So you understand, then, why I had to ask you some of those terrible things I did—but you wouldn't remember them, would you? For you have no memory now, now that I have locked it away so that it cannot torment you. And—"

She pauses, for a knock has sounded on the door. She scowls, rises, crosses to it. Opens the very thick door. He watches, sees the small girl there: fair-haired, twelve maybe, but already very grown-up. She looks up at the Beautiful Lady. "I was afraid you'd forget," she says. "It's time to work on the kni—"

"*Shhhhhh!*" the Beautiful Lady interrupts, whereupon the girl leaves. The Beautiful Lady smiles.

He smiles back.

And sleeps.

It is dark when he awakens, and he feels more lucid. Restless, he rises, stretches, pads barefoot to the door. The chains that festoon his ankles click gently against each other, then fall silent as he listens. He hears a noise, distant, obscured by walls, but one he recognizes from years gone by. It fills him with dread, though he cannot recall why it should. He knows that sound, though: it is the sound of a hammer shaping metal upon an anvil.

PART II

HEAD GAMES

Chapter 10

Come See about Me

Erin Welch's House
Monday, June 17—morning

Now to tighten these last two screws just so, Ron coached himself. *Now to line 'em up with all the slots oriented exactly the same, just like on a Mercedes-Benz, and we'll see if this puppy cooks.* He blinked up from his workbench and spun his chair around in place to give his eyes a rest. —And started, as he did more often than not, when he realized that the vista of fields, hills, and mountains beyond the diamond-mullioned windows behind him was *not* the view from his studio in Brandy Hall.

Not that he hadn't done his best to duplicate it here in the sprawling mock-Tudor manor he'd inherited from his mom lo these many years ago, the one from which he'd had to evict an indignant tenant in order to occupy. Or at least the furniture and equipment was the same, courtesy of Perry's and John's strong backs. (And a couple of clandestine journeys in the night.) And he'd been careful to arrange everything in the identical orientation it had held before, down to the brass-potted lilies in the corners. But it *wasn't* the same; he knew that, and so did Matty Groves, who was sleeping off one of his infrequent tomcatting sessions on the so-far-magazineless sofa.

It was morning, Ron realized with a second start, not having noticed as the artificial light inside was slowly augmented with the natural variety. Which meant he'd been up all night—as could easily occur when the Muse of Epic Metalwork came calling—which meant he'd once again neglected the omens (as soon as possible after midnight was optimum) in preference to a series of Clannad CDs shuffled in with Tori Amos and most of the Mark Knopfler soundtracks. Well, he'd attend to 'em as soon as he finished his eyeball break and gave The Head a final few tweaks. Fortunately, one of the virtues of his mom's place was that the light was different here: softer, more northern. Easier on the peepers.

Except that he'd been using those organs nonstop for at least the last twelve hours—often as not, screwing them up to squint through one sort of lens or other as the last few tiny cogwheels and gears that should gift The Head with intellect, if not true consciousness, slipped like—well, like *clockwork*—into place.

That was one of the few good things that had come out of his precipitous removal from Brandy Hall, Ron reflected, as he spun back around to return to the grind. In the process of cleaning out the vault, he'd located the missing page of brain schematics that had held up The Head's completion. (It had worked its way between the vellum endpaper and wooden binding of a Kelmscott *Chaucer*.) With the page back in its proper sequence in *The Book of The Head*, it had been child's play to finish the sucker.

Cross your fingers.

Please God.

And pray.

One final pause, while Ron fine-tuned the screw slots, and he was done.

Leaning back, he reached up and gave the intricate cast-silver ring depending from his left lobe a tweak for luck. Wrought in the likeness of the Worm Ouroboros, it was a piece of Sam's work, the first he'd completed solo since becoming Ron's apprentice. The lad had given it to Ron on Friday—right before he'd been summoned home for a

much-begrudged packing session at his dad's former abode—
which was right *after* the diving session that had followed
the *smithing* session, both of which were becoming regular
endeavors for the two of them, encounters Ron looked forward to more than anything he could recall. That surprised
him, too: how in basically a week he'd let himself become
so dependent on the lad, whose quirky humor, smug self-
confidence, and obsessive mysteriousness kept Ron by turns
entertained, confused, frustrated, and flattered—but never
bored. And while he occasionally feared the boy was less
friend than opportunist, any attention at this point in his life
was better than none, and it pleased him to believe that he
had, in some way, become the kid's hero.

On the other hand, Sam's dad *had* been gone the entire previous week, acceding to his son's persistent requests to be left
alone as master of his own adolescent domain. (Or that was
how Sam told it.) And since there was no one his own age
about (excluding Gwent, who was a little *too* strange, *and*
otherwise occupied), he'd had little choice but to home in
on Ron. Brandy was so intense she scared him, and Perry,
John, and Sharon—all three—freaked him for approximately
the same reason, which shy Sam had articulated no more specifically than that he didn't like the hungry way they looked
at him.

So was Sam hanging out here by choice, or because he
had no better alternative? Or did it even matter? There were
things Ron could teach him that he couldn't learn anywhere
else—and that itself was good karma. And, he admitted, there
were things Sam was teaching him. Or reawakening, more
properly. Like swimming, like diving, like how neat it was
just to be a kid.

Ron missed him, he realized: missed having someone to
talk to while he worked on lesser projects (most of which
were for Brandy Hall; Sam didn't know about The Head,
and Ron intended to keep it that way). Never mind the
way Sam had of just popping in, which kept him forever
on his toes. Ron wondered if he'd be back that day. The
kid hadn't said, but then, he tended not to. Not before Ron
had a chance to grab a little shut-eye, he hoped. And certainly not before he'd a chance to give The Head (he'd

have to give it a name one of these days, he supposed) a
dry run.

And speaking of the latter, he was overdue for a celebra-
tory cup of coffee.

He whipped one up in the small German job that had
been with him for so long, but still didn't switch on the
radio. The omens had waited this long, they could merry
well twist in the Wind a little longer. A good one might
make him overconfident; a bad one could temper his efforts
with despair. Or they might serve up the same inanity they'd
been dumping on him since he'd left Brandy Hall.

Yeah, he'd do the dry run first, and *then* he'd—

No, he corrected himself. He'd try the old way, *then* see
if Project Oracle gave any promise of living up to his expec-
tations.

The coffee was ready now, but Ron didn't feel like padding down to the kitchen to locate cream or sugar. Instead,
he eased back in his lounger, took a sip, savored the taste
for a minute—it was Gevalia's latest gourmet special—set
the cup down, and closed his eyes.

The ritual was familiar: three breaths, a distancing from
self, a Jump—and suddenly the physical world flip-flopped
with the Realm of the Winds. Nothing new there.

Lew? Ron Called, only now aware of how very tired he
actually was, of how half a day of solid brain-burn had left
him as drained mentally as his body was proving to be.

Lew?

Nothing.

He tried harder, to as little effect, and wondered idly where
the Black Mountain Master had got off to (probably cutting
Zs, like any right-thinking person ought to be at this hour).

And gave up.

If only he'd acted *earlier,* dammit! If only he'd been
quicker to suspect there was more to Lew's lack of communication than sheer perversity. Sure, he'd been busy the last
week or so—one did not make an utter fool of oneself and
get thrown out of one's girlfriend's house for one's trouble
every day. And certainly not on the same day one *also* met a
whacked-out (whacked-up, rather) playwright *and* acquired
an apprentice. But he still wasn't sure he'd played things

right then. What with chaos and depression, he'd not tried to check in with Lew the night after that disturbing final linkage, nor had Lew phoned as Ron had urged him. Since then . . . well, Ron was frankly concerned, to the point of trying to initiate contact *twice* a day: once in the morning, once in the afternoon.

And still no luck. If Lew was Listening, he wasn't letting on.

And unfortunately, the omens were of no use either. Though he'd tuned them in faithfully every morning (today excepted), he'd got nothing comprehensible. Which meant either that Lew was fine, and he was being an alarmist for nothing. Or that whatever Powers drove the omens thought he was at a particular crucial juncture in his life and would say no more until *he* took action.

Nor had Dion, whom he *had* been able to get hold of via the Winds, been any help. Their link had been tenuous, barely sufficient for Ron to tell his uncle to phone him. Dion had. Ron had told him everything: Sam, Brandy, Gwent—all of it. Dion had listened politely while Ron vented his spleen, but had not been alarmed—certainly not as alarmed as Ron thought he should be. Something was up, Dion acknowledged, but he couldn't determine what. He'd keep Ron posted. Meanwhile, Ron should keep in mind that the world was very wide, and that there were plenty of places beyond reasonable reach of the Luck: places where Winds howled unheeded, where Voices poured out their angst Unheard. Lew (and their sister) could easily have slipped into one of them. Unfortunately, it had sounded like cold comfort all dressed up in eloquence—as Ron suspected Dion knew.

Meanwhile, he waited, dithered, argued courses of action with himself, and waited again.

And now, finally, had an ace in the hole he had not possessed the day before. Traditional means had failed to locate Lew, huh? Well, Ron had other options at his disposal now. And if The Head couldn't do it, nothing could.

He hoped.

Cross your fingers.

Please God.

And pray.

A breath, a blink, a fractioned second of dizzy disorientation as Ron resumed his more conventional senses, and he was ready.

Pausing only to chug the coffee (which damn near scalded his throat and left his tongue fuzzy and numb), Ron resumed his place before The Head.

He felt like an acolyte of some obscure religion: a barefoot priest in cutoff blue jeans, black tank top, and bandanna; born to serve that which could not attend itself. Or more, he told himself with a chuckle, like that charming old con man from Kansas in *The Wizard of Oz* who'd manipulated a vast, disembodied head in order to cow the not-so-gullible Dorothy. Ron wondered if *he* was now the man behind the curtain. And if The Head would pay *him* no mind.

Well, he'd never find out without trying. Sighing, he picked up The Head. (In a fit of irony, he had bolted its stub of a neck to one of his mother's silver serving platters—though whether this was an homage to John the Baptist, who'd said things he oughtn't, or to Bran the Blessed, whose severed noggin had said a great many good things indeed, while feasting with his war-weary kinsmen for eighty years at Harlech— Ron had no idea).

One final sigh, and Ron deposited The Head in the place he had prepared for it: a small, round table positioned before the window so that the rays of the morning sun fell full upon the glittering, gold-toned face. He opened the multimullioned portal in question (it was side hinged, like a door), adjusted The Head so that the sun's slanting beams fell directly onto the brazen eyelids, then pressed the corner of the red-washed orbits—and held his breath.

The eyes clicked open. A big chunk of the electromagnetic spectrum struck the thin half-spheres of silicon crystal that made the ivory globes behind them look moist. Something esoteric and, probably, theoretically impossible occurred in the solution of metallic salts sandwiched between the two . . .

And The Head blinked: its first official act of its own volition.

Matty Groves took one look and whisked out the door, twice his normal size.

"Hello," Ron blurted stupidly, only that instant realizing he had not rehearsed any sort of opening line—no "One small step for man" or "Dr. Livingstone, I presume" or "Hey, sailor, come here often?"

"Hel . . . *lo*," The Head replied promptly. Its voice was soft and sweet—more so than Ron would have predicted from the collection of brass and silver reeds that comprised its larynx. The voice was low, too, but he'd expected as much. Having no lungs, the thing relied on an intricate system of resonators located in the ears to capture other sounds for reuse. Ron only vaguely understood the principle, beyond the basic facts of its construction; but what it meant in practice was that the louder he talked, the more forcefully The Head would respond.

"Nice to meet you," he said more loudly.

"I . . . also . . . am . . . pleased to . . . meet you." The accent was odd, unplaceable. But at least it was English. Ron had feared it might be something else—Church Latin, say—or whatever obscure tongue *The Book of The Head's* anonymous author had spoken.

"You doin' okay?" Ron asked, inanely.

"Pardon?"

"Do you, uh, function as you consider optimum?"

"I function . . . as . . . I was designed . . . to."

"All right!"

"You have not . . . told me . . . your name."

"You can call me Ron," he replied, taken aback, and not one-hundred-percent convinced he wasn't dreaming.

"Surname . . . ?"

Ron rolled his eyes. "Dillon, I suppose."

"You . . . do not . . . *know*?"

"There's some suggestion of ambiguity."

"I am . . ." A pause, during which The Head pursed its perfect copper-beryllium lips thoughtfully. "I do . . . not know *who* I . . . am. Do . . . you?" it added after a moment's longer reflection.

Ron hadn't a clue how to reply. A shrug was, therefore, as much answer as he could provide on the spur of the moment. Or at least the most efficient.

"Ah! Nonverbal . . . communication," The Head observed sagely.

"It happens."

"It occurs to me," said The Head, "that I was built for . . . a purpose."

"You were."

"Which was? Which *is*? rather."

"To provide me with information."

"Oh . . ." The Head's golden brow wrinkled in perplexity. Ron half-feared the tiny scaled plates that comprised its skin would commence popping their microscopic rivets. "So *that's* . . . why . . . there is this annoying buzz in my . . . brain. As if a thousand . . . thousand . . . thousand . . . Ones-Like-You held verbal converse there. Only it is . . . not the same as when I hear you. This is . . . more basic, more . . . primal."

Ron thrust forward in his chair, at once all ears. "As if you didn't so much hear words as thoughts or emotions?" he asked eagerly.

"Precisely."

Ron was too elated to continue. Leaving The Head to work on its tan, he hop-limped into the kitchen and located the industrial-sized bottle of Bailey's Irish Cream he'd been hoarding for exactly this occasion. The wrapper ripped asunder, the crimson cap untwisted, he filled a silver goblet with the ivory-colored liquid and returned to the studio. The Head blinked at him when he returned. And gleamed. And glittered.

"I've been promising myself this," Ron explained, with a lopsided grin.

"I do not . . . drink, myself," The Head observed serenely.

"Good for you," Ron countered sweetly, helping himself to a healthy swig, and letting the smooth, honeyed taste wash around in his mouth as he waited for its underlying kick to manifest, which it obligingly did five seconds later.

"Now then," Ron sighed happily, regarding The Head face on with an air of mock-formality that seemed at once appropriate and utterly ridiculous. "There are many questions I hope to ask you over the time of our association, oh Head, many mysteries I would have you plumb. But the chief conundrum I would ask your assistance on is this: What has become of my fraternal twin brother, Lewis Welch?"

The Head blinked at him, but did not leave its eyes closed (reasonable, given that they were the source of its power). Its forehead furrowed again, and its carbon-fiber brows came nigh unto colliding.

Silence hung heavy in the room, and then, once again, The Head spoke. "I cannot . . . tell. There are too many . . . Voices. One . . . of them . . . may be your brother, but I . . . cannot tell. I can say only that . . . I did . . . detect three like enough unto your own to . . . indicate that . . . you are kin. Two were from . . . south of here—"

"Dion and Gil, most likely," Ron mused, nodding—which gesture The Head chose to consider an interruption; whereupon it, more polite than its creator, paused.

"The third"—when the coast was clear again—"it is most . . . like yours . . . but difficult to hear."

Ron, already on the edge of his seat, stood straight up—which forced him to dance sideways to avoid blocking The Head's power source. *"Where?"*

"West . . . I think. But it is not troublesome . . . to hear because of distance, it is . . . as if a veil lies between myself and the Voice."

It was Ron's turn to scowl. "Try harder!" he cried urgently, feeling a knot of hope he did not dare cultivate rise without warning in his throat. "Oh please, Head, try harder!"

"I cannot."

"Try, damn you, try!"

"I cannot *be* damned, I who have no soul," The Head replied placidly. "You waste your words, when other efforts might avail you more."

Ron glared at it askance. "How so?"

"Add your strength of mind to mine."

"You're *shittin'* me!"

"Not possible. I am not constructed appropriately."

"Gimme a break."

"Not possible. I am not— Oh, I see . . ."

Ron took a deep, fearful breath. "You mean," he managed at last, "that you want me to merge *my* consciousness with that of a machine?"

"With mine, which coincidentally *is* a machine . . ."

"I . . ."

"Your brother's Voice is fading."

Ron swallowed hard, then nodded. "Okay, just a sec." He gulped half the Bailey's to calm himself, thought for a moment, and took a long sniff from the nearest batch of lilies, then returned to the chair, closed his eyes, breathed thrice—and for the second time that morning, Jumped.

And had never felt *anything* like what he experienced then. The Realm of the Winds as he knew it was intangible, even the terms *Winds* and *Voices* and *Listening* mere approximations of what could not actually be properly described by something as imprecise as language. The only constant was that it was cacophonous: near Voices generally clearer than those more distant, and strong emotions louder than weak. But the whole mixed and mingled with such complexity that it was well-nigh impossible to distinguish more than a few at a time.

Yet somehow The Head *could* distinguish, could sort them all out rank and file, so that it was the work of mere seconds to locate whichever specific Voice one desired. Dion and Gil, for instance, might as well have been in the next room, so clearly did Ron Hear their thoughts—dreams, rather, for both slept, and neither of them alone.

But Lew . . .

He *was* there! But faint, so very faint.

Lew? Ron's noiseless cry rang joyfully through the Winds, fortified by the very force of that emotion.

Ron . . . ? Ronny? And then Ron felt his own joy reciprocated, resonated upon—and redoubled thereby. But with it came something much worse: fear—both for Lew himself and, Ron realized, for his *own* free-floating psyche.

Lew . . . I'm here. I'm . . . how are you, bro? Where are you?

I'm . . . I'm sick, Ronny, Lew replied—nor could he have lied. *I'm sick and I can't tell why. I have no strength at all, and . . .*

Where are you?

Sick . . .

Lew, listen to me! Where are you? Tell me, bro, and I'll come get you. Only you gotta tell me, man!

I . . . can't.

What do you mean you can't? Don't you know where you are?

. . . no.

Lew!

. . . Sister . . .

What do you mean, sister? Dammit, Lew, you gotta shake out of it, man; gotta talk to me!

Sister . . .

You mean our sister? What about her? Are you with her, or—Oh, God, Lew; don't tell me she's the one who's done this to you. If she has, I'll—

But Ron could articulate his threat no further, for at that instant every thought and sensation and idea that made him an individual *self* was eclipsed by a scream that rang through the Realm of the Winds like the belling of a gong as large as the sky.

Jesus! Ron screamed in counterpoint—and Jumped back into his own head.

"Jesus!" he repeated aloud, feeling distinctly nauseous. "Oh, *Jesus!*"

At that point he caught a whiff of an acrid, metallic odor, and only then realized that The Head's eyes had closed. He placed a hand on the brazen cheek to open them—and jerked it back abruptly. It was scorchingly hot, and the forehead was even hotter. "Well, *hell!*" he croaked helplessly, and slumped back in his chair. *"Hell and double hell!"* And him so close too! And then this!

Why, he didn't even know if that was The Head that had screamed there at the end (reasonable, if it were overheating), or if something awful had happened to Lew. He hoped the former, but the latter, alas, was his fear.

Chapter 11

The Leader of the Pack

What Ron in nowise expected, as he sat staring at the now-defunct Head, was to hear the doorbell chime. Not *this* early in the morning. And yet . . . that *was* the doorbell. And it was a very persistent ring: the sort that often accompanied "I've just had a wreck; can I please, please, *please* use the phone?" Well, whoever it was could just sit on it and spin! No one *he* knew was dumb enough to drop by so early. Which meant it was someone he didn't know—probably the Jehovah's Witnesses.

Rrriiiinnngggggggg!

On the other hand, guilt made a son of a bitch of a roommate.

He could have Listened, of course, but coming so close after The Head's psychic scream he was honestly afraid to, lest that event had done damage in his own skull that the Luck had not yet had time to repair. Besides, lack of sleep plus the failure of The Head had made him just crotchety enough that a good ego leveling (as long it wasn't *his* being laid low) might actually feel good right now.

Rrriiiinnngggggggg!

"Just a bloody minute!" he growled through a yawn, and limped out the door. Matty Groves looked at him sorrowfully from the living room and went back to his dreaming. Ron didn't blame the cat. He was dead on his feet himself, which was why he wasn't nearly as concerned about Lew's troubling message as he would ordinarily have been under the circumstances. As a point of fact, he was so fried that the doorbell chimed twice more even as Ron stared groggily at the latch—proof, he feared, that he'd actually dozed off while standing there: not good.

A fifth jingle (or was that the fifth?) and he opened the door.

It was Sam—in his usual jeans and black T-shirt, but now sporting a fresh (and too short) haircut, and with the inevitable backpack (which seemed to have expanded even while Ron had been aware of it; Ron wondered blearily if it might not contain some sort of monstrous twin, like in the *Basket Case* movies) depending, tumorlike, from one shoulder.

"You're back," Ron mumbled automatically, easing aside for the boy to enter.

"Front's nice too," Sam countered instantly.

Ron grunted, in no mood for verbal fencing with an adolescent. Why did Sam have to show up *now,* dammit? There was too much else going on. What he ought to do was banish the kid posthaste, and get right back to work on Project Oracle.

Except that it was too late for that already. Sam was making a beeline for the kitchen (down the hall and to the right), where Ron had taken to maintaining a stash of Oreos (which they both liked) and milk (which Ron loathed) for precisely such impromptu appearances. He knew better than to offer the lad coffee. Sam despised the stuff.

"You're a little early, aren't you?" Ron yawned wearily, as Sam slung the pack down atop the gleaming floor.

The boy helped himself from the fridge and eased onto a barstool. "We got in late last night, and I thought maybe you and me could put in a couple of laps before—"

"Before what?" Ron broke in, taking advantage of proximity to make himself a mug of instant coffee, his earlier sample having had no noticeable effect. *"Before what?"* he repeated, when Sam seemed slow in responding.

The boy grinned sheepishly, then looked at the black-and-white-tiled floor. Ron could see his reflection there. "Uh—before my friends get here."

Ron's ensuing stare was was equal parts dreadful uncertainty and full-blown incredulity. "You mean here? Or *here*?"

"Here," Sam grinned cryptically.

"Here?" Ron echoed.

An eyebrow lifted. "Well, I told 'em it's a pool party—and *I* don't have a pool. . . ."

Ron slammed back the coffee (it was just tepid enough for that) and tried very hard not to holler as he deposited the empty stoneware mug in the sink. "It's seven friggin' thirty in the *morning*, Sam!"

A pause with the glass halfway to Sam's mouth. "They're not comin' 'til around nine."

"Are these the folks you were talkin' about last week? Your friends from Gainesville?"

Sam nodded. "Yeah. My dad's gone back already, but he finally agreed to let me have my friends up—long as we didn't burn down the house."

Ron wondered if that also included *his* house. Sam had a possessive streak—or maybe he simply tended to take things like access to other people's houses for granted.

"So how long're they stayin'?"

"A week." (An Oreo promptly vanished.)

"A week!" Ron fairly shrieked.

"Not here," Sam told him placidly.

That's what he *says*, Ron thought sourly. *But sure as the world, the whole mess of 'em'll be over here hangin' out before you know it*. Which in one sense was fine, because it meant he would feel less cut off from human companionship than he had been lately. But on the other hand, he had things to do—and a lot more of them to do more quickly now that he'd finally got The Head up and running.

"They won't *all* be up all week," Sam offered by way of possible apology. "But a couple of 'em may be here longer, 'cause I think they bought the house next door to my dad's."

Ron rolled his eyes. That was exactly what he'd been afraid of. And while he liked Sam as much as anyone he'd met in years, he was not prepared to have a million little Samclones playing hoopie-hide through the forest. Especially not the forests near Brandy Hall. Not that it was *his* problem at the moment. But still . . .

"Speaking of your place," Ron inserted smoothly. "What's, uh, going on over at *my* old place? How's Brandy, and all."

Sam shrugged, then frowned, but Ron could see that he was trying to frame an accurate answer while remaining circumspect. He wished he'd thought to ask sooner, but it hadn't been his morning for razor-edged thinking.

"Last I saw of Brandy, which was before me and Dad left on Friday, she was fine," Sam said at last. "She looked kinda busy and harried and all, but what else is new? Best I can tell, that Gwent guy's got the play finished and was gonna have some folks come up over the weekend to start designin' sets and stuff. Oh, and he's recruited actors, and they've built a make-do stage down on that amphitheater-terrace thing beside the house, to use while they're gettin' the real one cookin' over in town. And—"

"No," Ron corrected patiently. "How's *Brandy*?"

"Busy," Sam replied, through a mouthful of Oreo. "Too busy to talk to me, so I mostly just stood around and watched. I don't think she likes me much."

"She doesn't like anybody she can't control," Ron muttered, not caring whether Sam heard. "She, uh, say anything about me?"

(Another Oreo bought it.) "She asked if I'd seen you lately. Asked how you were."

"And you said . . . ?"

"That you were workin' a lot and teachin' me swimming, diving, and smithing."

"And *she* said . . . ?"

"Said that was good."

"Nothing else?"

A shrug. "Not really. She wasn't nasty or anything, if that's what you're wonderin'. Except wait, there's another thing: You know that Donson Gwent guy? Well, he's moved in up there."

Ron was glad he was sitting and had nothing breakable ready to hand, Sam's neck not being an option. "Well *that's* just dandy!"

Sam shifted around uneasily. "So, when're *you* movin' back in?"

Ron grimaced. "Not for a while, I don't think. Not until I get some stuff resolved here. And probably not until they get that damned play on the road. After that, we'll see."

"Fine with me," Sam said, turning away.

While Ron stared at the boy curiously, wondering if he ought to be flattered or concerned, Sam calmly polished off his quota of Oreos and drained the milk, abandoning the glass on the counter. It left a white mustache across his otherwise beardless upper lip.

"Gwent," Ron said, eventually.

"What about him?"

"You ever see that car of his?"

Sam shook his head. "Nope."

"You're sure?"

Sam nodded. "Brandy's been lugging him around far as I know. Either that, or he's been using her car."

"Not the Centauri, please God."

"The pickup."

"And you really haven't seen another car about? Low-slung sedan? Gold?"

"What brand?"

Ron took a deep breath. "Uh, well, that's the problem."

Sam was silent, and Ron wondered if he'd made a mistake by even bringing the matter up. He'd waited *this* long, after all, mostly to avoid contention. Did it really matter now? There *was* a reasonable, if farfetched explanation—one Brandy believed, and Gwent (as best he could determine from a bit of surreptitious spying when they'd crossed paths during the move) did as well.

"You *did* tell me you designed that model you showed me from scratch, didn't you?"

Another nod. "Why?"

"Just wondering."

Same looked uncomfortable. "Well, actually . . . I sort of dreamed it. That is, I woke up one day with this design really strong in my head, and just had to get it down, and the rest . . . Well, you know."

"When was this?"

"Six months ago, maybe? I don't exactly remember."

Ron could think of nothing to say. He didn't think the boy was lying; surely he'd be broadcasting guilt about it. But the Winds (such as he could Hear without going into trance) were silent.

Sam, meanwhile, had become sufficiently antsy that he was pacing the outlines of the floor tiles. "So," he asked at last, "we gonna do a coupl'a *laps*? Or a coupl'a *leaps*?"

Ron shrugged helplessly and nodded the boy down the sky-lighted back hall toward the white square of sliding glass doors at the end, which opened onto the terrace, bathhouse, and pool. "I don't think I'm up for more than your basic quick dip just now."

"How 'bout a coupl'a *licks* with a hammer, then?"

"Whatever."

Sam hesitated, stared at him, as if noticing him for the first time. "You look tired."

Ron managed a halfhearted ironic chuckle. "I was up all night."

"Doin' what?" Then, abruptly: *"Oh, neat!"*

"Huh?" Ron mumbled, through a yawn—and only then realized that he had done a very stupid thing indeed. In his haste to head off what he'd been certain were Jehovah's Witnesses, he'd left the studio door open—without hiding The Head. And, of course, snoopy little Sam had seen it.

"Hey, what's *this*?" Sam asked, both face and voice betraying his excitement.

"What does it look like?" Ron countered carefully, not wanting to lie outright, which could queer things with the Luck.

"It *looks* like a head on a plate," Sam observed flatly. "Looks kinda familiar, too."

An eyebrow lifted. "How so?"

Sam shifted his position to get a better view. Ron thought he looked troubled—perplexed, better say, as if he were trying to remember something. Blessedly, the boy had not actually touched it. "I dunno," he murmured. "No, wait; it looks kinda like that guy on the sculpture beside your house, only older. And of course this has real hair, and all. Real-*er*, anyway."

Ron thought it expedient not to reply.

"So what's it for?"

"It's an exercise in the craft," Ron grumbled, subtly insinuating himself between Sam and the rest of the room, notably *The Book of The Head*—which it *really* wouldn't do for the kid to get a look at. "It's an attempt at some truly intricate metalwork."

"So I see," Sam observed, nodding his approval. Then, to Ron's abject surprise: "Well, I wanta look at it again later, okay?"

Ron tried not to breath a sigh of relief.

If Sam noticed his lack of response, it didn't show, but Ron caught him casting a few too many wistfully curious backward glances as Ron hustled him out of the room.

"I want you to teach me some of that stuff, okay?" Sam asked from the back door. "After we've had our swim, I mean."

Another of those blessed yawns. Then: "It's . . . ah, hard work, Sam. You've got a way to go yet, good as you are. You need to perfect casting first, and to try cold forming on something other than brass."

"But you'll teach me . . . ?"

"What I can. But you've gotta learn basics before you can get into complex stuff."

Sam had slid the door aside by then, and Ron followed him into the bright light of morning. The sky was clear, the air already warm in a way that promised a real scorcher later. The pool Ron's mom had built before he'd moved up glittered like blue-white glass within its blazing white concrete border, beyond which a waist-high retaining wall of rough stone marked the top of a long grassy slope that led at last to the Talooga River. River bottoms planted in sorghum spread beyond, rising again to a line of oaks along a distant highway. The bathhouse loomed to the right: genuine half timber and plaster beneath a steep slate roof. They headed that way. Ron paused in the vestibule outside the men's changing room to retrieve his suit and a towel from the large stock there, but Sam continued on, having brought his own in the backpack. Ron wondered if he was up for this, for in spite of the coffee he'd been chain-drinking all morning, he was getting sleepier by the second. Maybe he'd humor the lad, set him some projects, and then grab some shut-eye. Ron used a side trip into the loo to give Sam time to change in privacy, then changed himself and returned to poolside. The boy was waiting for him there, poised at the deep end, clad in the skimpiest of black Speedos, which set off both muscles and tan nicely.

"Race you twenty laps?" Sam challenged, grinning.

"Ten."

"Nineteen."

"Eleven, and you do three extra dives."

"Eighteen, and you dive once—just to prove you can."

"Fifteen, two extra dives for you, and I don't beat your ass for givin' an old guy grief."

"Fifteen it is."

They swam the laps: five to loosen up, then the fifteen where they raced. They tied, but Ron was breathing hard, while Sam was barely winded.

"Boy dive, now," Ron grunted, as he heaved himself out of the shallow end, while Sam continued to tread water in midpool, looking happy as a clam. "Tarzan gonna catch rays and watch."

Sam eyed him dubiously, but proceeded to flip onto his back and float, while Ron dragged a lounge chair closer to the edge and thumped down in it. God, but the sun felt good! Which, unfortunately, put him in mind of Lew: Lew the sun, as Ron was the moon, or so they'd been termed in high school.

No—he wouldn't think about that now. Though he was almost sick with worry, he could do nothing about his brother's situation until later—not and have it do any good. He was *that* dog tired. For now, he'd just lie by the pool, let the sun bake the fatigue out of him, let it energize his brain endorphins—and watch Sam dive. Shoot, the boy was halfway to the high board already.

Ron coached him through a set, calling out advice.

"Sure you don't wanta get up here and show me?" Sam shouted from twenty feet up. (It was a *big* pool: Ron's mom had liked to go first-class.)

"I'm sure," Ron yelled back. "Now you do what I told you, and I'm gonna grab a few winks."

Whereupon Ron reclined the chair half a dozen notches and settled back. He closed his eyes, squinting even so, until he remembered the towel. He picked it up and draped it across his face. And tried to focus on the feel of the wind, the flip-flop sound of the wavelets in the pool, and the perfume of whatever flowers were blooming in the woods just up the way. He heard Sam's first two splashes, but not the third.

It was likely that he slept. Or if not, at least his subconscious took that opportunity to supply him with images he in nowise conjured deliberately. It was not a major leap, his dream-self told him, from hearing the lap of pool water against ceramic tiles in north Georgia to recalling an identical sound down at the Tampa Y. And from that, it was scarcely even a psychic skip to remembering himself making his way cautiously up the hard-edged surface of the steps to the ten-meter platform.

Or to recall a much younger version of himself poised there, gazing down at the admiring, expectant faces of his swim team chums.

Until the voices came: insidious mutterings of doubt and self-annihilation wafting their way from the mind of an unsuspecting Master (who would turn out to be his great-uncle) in a very long detour on the road to an even more unsuspecting Lew.

He could hear them now, the words he had never confessed even to Brandy: "You *will* die, sooner or later; sooner or later you *will* die . . ."

—As the dream-Ron prepared to dive, then caught a particularly virulent suggestion and toppled off the board.

Ron had always wondered how that had looked: him a slender, broad-shouldered shape in a red Speedo poised up there, graceful, tense, silhouetted against the blue. And then staggering, flailing his arms . . . and falling . . .

To awaken gazing up at the concerned tan faces of a dozen Tampa boys he had not seen or heard from in over ten years.

Gee, but this was a vivid dream! he noted dully, squinting up at those faces again, as he had all those years before. The sun had been bright then. Odd that he should recall such a detail. But why on earth would *anyone* greet a friend who'd just seen his diving career go up in flames (down in water, rather), with such an inane comment as *"Oops!"*?

Except when something was trying to drive home the fact that he was now awake.

Perhaps it was the sound of voices—adolescent ones calling out loud and careless. But what it *actually* was, he concluded, when his eyes popped abruptly open, leaving the troubling dream to wisp away into psychic vapor, was the backwash of a particularly ill-located dive from the side of the pool—which had caught him neatly in the face—rousing him abruptly, to gaze up at a concerned and flustered-looking Sam Foster, who was also dripping wet and shedding air-cooled droplets all over Ron's chest.

"Unnnhhh," Ron grunted, freeing his eyes of the towel that had slipped askew.

He blinked, yawned hugely, sat up, and identified the proximate cause of his accidental soaking as a muscular lad who probably had strawberry blond hair when it wasn't slicked down like a soup bowl. Sam (he hoped) knew better, and the rest of the party were still standing a discreet distance away, dry as bones.

Sam merely raised an eyebrow and shifted his weight to his opposite leg. "Sorry," he mumbled. "That was Tad—he gets a little rambunctious sometimes."

"No problem," Ron grunted back, dragging himself upright, and helping himself to Sam's towel, with which he repaired the damage to his person. "So who *are* all these folks, anyway?"

"My friends," Sam replied flatly, as if that told Ron all he needed to know. Then: "Hey, folks, he's alive now. You can come on over."

Ron managed to get to his feet without too much show of awkwardness. And managed to sort through Sam's assortment of buddies with reasonable aplomb. Besides Tad-in-the-Pool, there was Tad's girlfriend, Andi. There was also a thin, pretty girl named Bonny, and two skinny guys who looked like brothers but weren't. Mark and Lucas were their names, but everyone called Lucas *Luckie*—which made Ron wince. Finally, there were a pair of twin girls named Tonya and Tam (dark and pretty too, though a bit too close to the

Brandy school of design to make Ron comfortable, especially when they were in skimpy Spandex suits and he in a Speedo).

As best Ron could determine, they were all high school juniors or seniors. All were attractive, healthy, and nicely put together, with a couple (notably the twins) being quite striking indeed. Ron made a mental note to feel them out about posing for him sometime. They were also mostly civil (and had brought their own munchies, so Ron wasn't put to trouble there), but seemed to be a bit uneasy around him.

Which, he concluded reluctantly, was probably a function of his age. For somehow, in the last few years, he'd slipped seamlessly from adolescence into that never-never land of postgraduatehood. But since he was rich and artistically oriented, he'd never had to put aside any of the things that appealed to him. In short, he could still act as young as the next teen, and it galled him to think that just because he owned a house and made big, complex things that lasted, he was somehow anathema. Shoot, he scarcely looked older than these guys. But they were treating him with a deference he didn't need.

"Ron usually lives at the place across from mine," Sam explained to the twin in red. "He's . . . uh, staying here 'cause he needs privacy while he works on some . . . stuff." A conspiratory wink followed, which Ron caught. And appreciated.

"You mean the *castle*?" Red Suit—Tam, Ron thought she was—enthused. "The one across from my folks' new house?"

"That's the place," Sam affirmed, nodding.

"Neat!" Tam cried eagerly. "So, uh, tell me about it," she continued in that way people have who are trying to strike up a conversation with someone they don't know but think they might like to. "How long's it been built, and all? And who designed it? I mean, I'm, like, *really* into architecture and castles, and all."

"We all are—sort of," Sam added, still hovering protectively. Ron was touched. "We game a lot, or didn't I tell you?"

"Game?"

"Fantasy role-playing games. You know, like D & D, only we don't play that one."

"So, what *do* you play?"

"Uh, GURPS, mostly," Tonya replied in an offhand tone that suggested Ron hadn't a clue what she was talking about.

"Yeah, I like that one," Ron told her easily, trying not to show his irritation at being condescended to. "Or did when I used to game back in college. I like the way you really get to build *exactly* the sort of characters you want."

"Yeah," Tam nodded, surprised. "That's cool."

"Wanta play some time?" Sam asked abruptly. "I mean, if we were to crank up a session tonight, would you join us?"

Ron's first response was an uneasy frown—which he hoped Sam didn't misinterpret. "I don't think so," he said slowly. "I mean, I'd *like* to . . . but there's some heavy stuff going on with me just now, and I've gotta get a nap sometime today, and then I've absolutely gotta get some work done on a project. Which I guess means I'd have to start late, and then only stay a little while . . . but I'd *still* have to come up with a character, which would hold things up even more, and— No, I don't think so. I'd better not. Besides, I've pretty much forgotten the system."

Sam pondered this for a moment, then grinned. "Hey, *I've* got it! One of Tad's guys requested an audience with the king of the gods last time we played, which *I* was gonna have to play as an NPC. Only I don't *wanta* play 'im—so why don't you come by and be special guest deity? I can give you a couple of ground rules, and you can wing the rest!"

"Maybe," Ron mumbled tiredly, venting another yawn. "But like I said, it'd have to be late."

"No problem. We don't ever start until dark anyway, and we usually watch a movie first, to get in the mood. We'll just back it up a little more."

"Don't forget I was up all night!" Ron protested lamely.

"Old guy needs his sleep," Sam informed Tam, nodding sagely. "Senility's next."

"Actually," Ron said apologetically. "I have to answer the phone."

Sam cocked his head, obviously listening.

"Got you *there*, whippersnapper!" Ron grinned at him.

"I've got ears from hell!" And with that, he limped inside.

The nearest phone was in the kitchen—his mom's old place wasn't as lavishly fortified with them as either Cardalba or Brandy Hall. But unfortunately, he'd been just far enough afield that he missed the caller and got only the recorded message.

Dion, it had been . . . dammit! Breathless, as if he was in a hurry; the message short, sweet, and typically cryptic: "Significator: 'Immigrant Song.' And then the station went off the air, due, I think, to lightning—another of those damned thunderboomers. Meaning: Invasion from without; also anguish and fear, especially as relates to a change in dwelling place, by which I assume it means *you*'cause *I* ain't movin'." A pause, then: "Wonder why I keep gettin' your mojo, nephew. Now, gotta split. Oh yeah. It's not cool when something cuts off the omens like that. Enough to make you religious. *Ciao.*"

Ron stared at the receiver for almost a minute before hanging up. *Shit!* Here Dion calls for the first time in over a week, misses him again, and leaves a bunch of riddles on his machine. At least he knew the song without having to look it up this time. It was by Led Zeppelin: the one that began with that ungodly—

—*Scream.* The song began with a scream! And Ron had just that morning been party to the granddaddy of all great screams!

Totally on impulse, he limped back to the studio. The overcooked Head was exactly where he had left it, its face bathed in midday radiance, so that it glowed like a thing newly forged, all gleaming gold and ruddy copper and brilliant brass. But it was not precisely *as* he had last seen it: the eyes were open again, though they looked a little bleary (rather as his own felt)—which was not a thing he'd consciously designed them to do. On a hunch, he spoke—loudly.

"Are you awake?"

"I . . . never sleep. But if you mean . . . am . . . I aware of you, I . . . am . . ."

"Are you . . . okay?"

"I can function twelve . . . more seconds, and then I will need a number of parts . . . replaced."

"Twelve sec—"

"Ask . . . or wait."

"Uh . . ."

"Eight."

Ron swallowed, then blurted out the first thing that came to mind. "Was that you who screamed earlier? Or Lew."

Three precious seconds slipped by. Then: "Lew."

"Lew," Ron repeated, as the sun slipped behind a cloud, and The Head's eyes promptly glazed over. The lids obligingly clinked shut. The acrid smell returned—and the smoke. Solder dropped from one ear to sizzle into a pond of pool drippings Ron's hair had shed onto the plate. A muffled frying sound peaked, then slowly faded away.

"Lew," he said again.

Lew it was who had screamed.

But it was Sam who found him in the gloom of the living room fifteen minutes later, where he sat staring blankly into space.

"You okay?" the boy asked, concerned.

"I'm fine. But someone else may not be."

"Anything I can do?"

"Get on with your life and avoid having sisters."

"You *sure* you're okay?"

"Basically."

An uncomfortable pause, then: "Well—gotta split, I guess. Thanks for lettin' me drag the folks by."

"No problem," Ron murmured distantly.

"They liked you."

"I liked them too."

Sam studied him a few seconds longer. "You're *absolutely* sure you're okay?"

"I'm fine, Sam. I just need to do some thinking—and I'm too fried to do any now."

"Uh, well I guess I *really* oughta boogie, then. Call me if you can come game."

"Sure. Carry on."

"Bye."

Ron meant to say "bye" as well. But what he actually said, once again, was a softly whispered, "Lew."

Interlude 6

Crazy on You

Alabama
Sunset

"You *like* sunsets, don't you?" the Beautiful Lady whispers.

He raises his head, stares at her vaguely, knowing that he feels very bad indeed but not knowing why. His hair hangs into his eyes, curly and blond, but tangled. He does not shake it away. His white cotton clothes are cool against his skin, but they torment him though they are loose. And his chains clink constantly, whenever he moves. He thinks they might drive him mad if he hears them much longer. Or perhaps they already have.

"No, you're not mad," she says, coming into the room and sitting in the seat she always chooses. She has brought no tray this time, but bottles: green glass, filled with some clear liquid that bubbles. He gazes at them, fascinated, as she uncaps first one, then the other. She slides one across the black plastic table to him, and he drinks. It tastes of large cool houses and hot beaches. A memory stirs, then vanishes.

"That was a bad thing you did this morning," she says imperiously. "A very bad thing indeed."

He gapes at her. *This morning? When was that?* He does not remember that far back; all he knows is *is*. Or that is all he *knows* that he knows. Perhaps another part of him knows more and will not tell. Perhaps the part that whispers to him in the night and haunts his dreams.

She stares at him, her eyes hard as any punishment. Waiting, he thinks, for him to speak. But something warns him not to.

"Well?" she says, straightening and folding her arms.

"W-what did I do?" he asks, not because he cares, but because that is what she expects, and because by asking he might put an end to that awful expression that so mars her beauty.

"You spoke to one you should not have."

"I . . . Did I?" He shakes his head. "I don't remember."

Relief softens her face the merest bit, like the mist after a summer rain upon a sunlit boulder. "You don't remember," she echoes him softly, in her voice like eastern silk. "Good. Memories can only hurt one like you. You don't need memories. Yet that does not change what you did."

"You . . . haven't told me what it was," he suggests meekly.

She ignores him. "I still have to punish you," she whispers, as much to herself as to him. "For if you have forgotten the crime, you seem to likewise have forgotten the punishment."

"P-punishment?"

"You spoke to one you should not have. You said things about me that were not true. I caught you, cut you off, *hit* you there where it hurts in the center of your *self*—and yet you do not remember. How am I to know you will not do so again?"

"You . . . have my word," he manages, his voice soft, afraid, little more than a croak. Or a sob. "My word is important to me," he adds, trying to smile. "Or I think it used to be. Before—"

Her eyes flash like flares, she steps forward. "Before *what*?"

The memory that was tickling his tongue flees, to join those others that will not come out to play with him. He simply stares.

"They'll think me mad, you know," she tells him. "When I do what I have to do, they'll think me mad. Perhaps someone already does, and would that I had time to search for him. Alas, there is another thing I must do before then, for which time will not tarry."

"You're beautiful," he says. It is the only thing he can think of.

"That won't make me forgive you for Speaking to strangers."

"I'm sorry."

"What? Sorry that you Spoke? That I Heard? Or that some might think me mad?"

It is too much for him. He cannot think. He stares. A drop of spittle oozes from his lips. "Mad . . ." he manages to mutter.

"You know why it is, don't you? Why they'll *say* it is?"

He shrugs.

Her eyes glitter like a snake's. "They'll say it's because things like me ought not to be—so *they* say. They'll say it's because certain things weren't done to me as an infant to ensure I would not go mad when the power came upon me, and my maidenhead intact. They'll say I'm a rogue and ought to be destroyed. That I'm a fool to hold one captive who has already yielded up his power.

"Ah, but they're all wrong," she continues, as if she were trying to convince herself. Her face looks odd, tense. "Oh yes: wrong. I am crazy like a fox. I do things they do not expect. And I hide from them, so that those who would be first among my accusers do not know where I am. That taxes me, too: makes it hard to think. Perhaps I rest too often, though. Perhaps that is how you think you can slip by."

"Mad," he says again, because she is looking at him as though she expects him to reply and he dares not make her angry. He has done that once and suffered for it. Not again.

"I am *not* mad," she whispers, her eyes bright as the highlights on the glass. "Nor are you. *No one* is mad who can appreciate a sunset. Certainly no one is mad who can appreciate a sunset when he sees but its dim reflection." She lets her eyes drift to the wall opposite the window, where the white plasterboard is stained pink with afterglow. His gaze follows hers, takes in the subtle shifts of color, from pink, to orange, to lavender.

"It does not *quite* become the color of blood," she says. "Still, one evokes the other: sunsets mark the end of the day—the *death* of a day, one might say. And blood—well, blood often marks a death as well. So I suppose one might say that sunsets and blood are kin."

He blinks at this, for it does not quite make sense. But what bothers him is something he not so much hears as senses. The Beautiful Lady speaks fair, but there is something *wrong* hiding in the beautiful things she now is saying. It is as if she says two things at once, one good, one terrible. But he does not speak. Instead, he blinks again and takes a sip from the bright green bottle.

"Sunrise, too," she whispers. "Sunrise is much like a sunset; the light is the same: eerie and strange and . . . magic."

"Magic," he echoes, remembering.

"When would you rather die?" she asks abruptly.

" . . . Die?" He shakes his head. It is not a real thing to him. They—someone—has told him that he cannot die, unless . . .

"Total immolation or complete dispersion. Decapitation without rejoining. Your own will. And one other way, which tradition prefers," she tells him softly. "You told me what the other thing is, too, though I doubt you will remember—memories are *so* unreliable."

He frowns, knows fear, though he cannot recall why.

"We were speaking of dying," she reminds him, after a delicate sip. "I had asked you when you would prefer to die? Sunrise or sunset?"

"Sun—" he begins, and falls silent.

"Both have advantages," she interrupts, her eyes flashing in a way that makes him uncomfortable. "And there are good days to die, and bad ones. Most men would rather die with the sun shining, for instance—perhaps fearing that rain might beat down their soul and keep it from rising to bliss. Or perhaps they simply would rather not die depressed—foolish notion! Or perhaps a full moon would be better—neater, at least, which matters to some. Or on one's birthday—again, that would be convenient, simple to remember. Or on holidays. Then one could have one's revenge by wrecking other men's joy."

She pauses, her brow wrinkling, but then she smiles. "When should the *sun* die, though?" she asks. "Perhaps on Lugnasadh—the festival of our ancestors' sun god? But I think not. Perhaps another day: perhaps it should die at the height of its power and glory and beauty. Perhaps," she whispers, "it should die on the longest day of the year!"

He says nothing. There is nothing he can say. He drinks, wishing it was the drink of oblivion—but it is not.

"Yes," she says, rising. "I think that would be a good day to die—there's a certain . . . cosmic *rightness* to it. Don't you agree?"

"No," he says. And is surprised. He has never told her no. Not since the first time.

But she does not frown at him, merely smiles her Beautiful Lady smile, this time from the door. "Your brother used to think of himself as the moon," she murmurs. "I wonder if that means *you* are the sun?"

The door closes. He shudders for a reason his soul knows but his mind does not. And the sunset has passed now, and so he looks on darkness.

Chapter 12

Every Picture Tells a Story

Brandy Hall
Monday, June 17—early evening

"So am I early, or are you guys runnin' late?" Weedge wondered with more than a trace of sarcasm, as she eased herself down beside Brandy on one of the rough stone benches that lined the crenellations atop Brandy Hall's East Terrace. She'd helped herself to a beer on her way out, Brandy noted with a scowl: one of her private stash of Anchor Steams, as opposed to the public domain stuff she kept on tap in the kitchen. Brandy made no mention of the faux pas, though; first because they were friends, and second, because she was in no mood for contention.

Weedge's sharp elbow in her ribs served as a second prompt. "You're right on time," Brandy growled, "—as far as *I'm* concerned. What Gwent might say's another matter."

Weedge took a healthy swig and gazed east, saying nothing. Brandy was aware of her as a tall shape in a white jogging suit visible from the corner of her eye. Without intending to, she found herself mirroring Weedge's posture, though God knew she'd seen the view often enough the last few days that she wondered why she bothered. Probably because every time she looked she saw something new.

East was the gentler slope of the knoll—but that didn't mean it had escaped the radical overhaul that had warped Brandy Hall the night Van Vannister had gone out of control there: the night he had called up the very earth itself to complete her dream. For even here the touch of his mad genius was evident—though Vannister would have said everything he'd done had come straight from Brandy's mind. But surely her psyche had never considered shrouding the east face of the knoll with a series of semicircular stone terraces that had very much the form of a Greek amphitheater. And she didn't dare let herself think that her former foreman had actually foreseen this precise set of circumstances and planned accordingly. But whatever its origin, the place was buzzing with action now. Why, not ten feet away a pair of coveralled high school girls she recognized from last year's art class were painting a *very* realistic forest scene to use as a backdrop in Act I. They were building them here, too, like all the sets, for eventual transport to the new outdoor playhouse still very much under construction at the fairgrounds near Cordova.

"So what's the holdup?" Weedge asked after a second swig. "I bust my butt to get up here in time for the first rehearsal of Act I, and what do I get? I get tunin' up. I get kids runnin' around dithering. I get your director screamin' like a maniac."

"He's not screaming," Brandy told her. "His voice just naturally rises when he gets excited."

"Hmmmph," Weedge replied, refusing to be cowed. "I'm surprised you put up with it."

Brandy regarded her seriously. "How so?"

"You being a control freak, and all."

"I'm not a control freak!"

"Could've fooled me."

"But I'm *not*, Weedge! Or," she continued self-consciously, "at least I *try* not to be."

"Hmmmph yourself," Weedge grunted. "And what is it that you think you've got scrunched down there behind your skirt where you hope I won't notice."

"My portable PC? That's just for notes."

"Then why try to hide it? And don't say you didn't, 'cause I saw you."

Brandy tucked her India-print wraparound closer about the offending object. "I don't need this, Weedge, not today."

But Weedge did not relent. "So when *do* you need it then? Dammit, girl, you're gonna fidget yourself into an ulcer—or worse—tryin' to keep up with everything: all your lists, and stuff."

"I don't make lists!"

"In a pig's eye! I bet you my job if I was to tear into that little computerized conscience of yours there, I'd find more to-dos than you could shake a stick at!"

"Okay, okay, you win," Brandy conceded. "But there's really only two—they, uh, just happen to be big ones."

"And let me guess: one's Brandy Hall, and the other's . . . the play."

A reluctant nod. "Project Shakespeare."

"With everything prioritized, and sections checked off as done or undone—and most likely a timetable, too!"

Brandy frowned at being so easily found out. "Yeah . . . well, that's about it. But really," she continued, "it's been amazing how easy things have fallen together. I mean, like Gwent just walked in and said he'd write the play and then did—*in three days*. A finished draft in three days! And lucky for me, he can direct too, so I'm spared finding someone to do that. Shoot, I've spent more time canceling ads than making 'em! All I've had to do is chase down folks for auxiliary functions—lighting, costumes, publicity, all that—and I did most of that locally, by calling in a few markers. The rest—minor crew, actors, the whole schmear—Gwent took care of himself."

"Yeah," Weedge told her. "I heard the radio ads soliciting actors."

"Well, you've gotta admit it got results. Gwent had to turn people away at last week's auditions. Shoot, I'm surprised he didn't try to recruit you!"

"It takes all *my* acting skill not to take folks' heads off down at the P.O." Weedge told her with a chuckle. "I don't have anything left for stuff like this."

Brandy checked her watch. "It really is late, though. I wonder what the holdup is."

"Search me," Weedge sighed. "So, how're things with Ronny?"

Brandy tensed immediately and came very close to telling her friend exactly where she could stuff off-the-wall questions like that. Except that would have all but admitted that she was still troubled by the answer—troubled a lot, as a matter of fact. "Search me," she echoed. "It's like I told you on the phone: We didn't *have* a falling out. It just reached—I dunno—some kind of critical point beyond which I simply couldn't abide having him around anymore. Not Ron himself, but his suspicions, his whining. He'd got too damned protective and it was gettin' on my nerves!"

"And that's all that was wrong? You *have* to know you were taking a huge risk by throwing him out like that."

"What choice did I have?" Brandy replied. "If he'd stuck around, I'd have been constantly rubbing his nose in something he didn't approve of, and I'd have had to stay on guard against his suspicions and snide remarks—and I just couldn't deal with it, not with what this play could mean to the county. I guess what I'm saying is that I just didn't have any time to spare for either the devil's advocate or the loyal opposition."

"You'd better *hope* he's loyal! Or at least loyal enough to come back."

"He will. He has nothing better to do."

"Well, *that's* certainly a snotty attitude!"

"Yeah, maybe it is. I don't think I really meant that. But seriously, now that I've got the place mostly finished, especially as far as metalwork's concerned, there's relatively less for me and him to talk about. On the other hand, everything that brought us together still exists: the common interests, the similar wordview. And art, of course; that's the primary bond."

"Sounds to me like you need to be making something together again," Weedge chuckled suggestively.

"I'm thinking about that, but I don't want to say anything until I get Project Shakespeare up and rolling. After it's locked in, hopefully I'll turn back to Ronny Dillon."

"And you'd better hope he's still around to be turned back to!" Weedge snorted. "What about Gwent?"

Brandy shifted uneasily and plucked at the fringe on her buckskin vest. "Well, I'm not sleeping with him, if that's what you mean. He's got his own little room, and most of the time he's like any really bright kid, except when it comes to drama, and then one of his alternate personas kicks in and he gets very take-charge and adult, and you'd damned well better not cross him, 'cause he always knows *exactly* what he wants."

"He ever tell you where he studied?"

"School of hard knocks, is as much as he'll admit to; lived a long time in a college town with lots of theater groups. Beyond that, I haven't pushed; the results speak for themselves.—And speaking of which, what do you say we wander down and actually ask somebody what's going on? This is a hell of a delay."

Weedge snared her beer and rose. "Fine with me. My butt's gettin' tired of sittin' on cement anyway."

Brandy did not reply but rose also, abandoning the unopened PC where it lay. Leaving Weedge to choose her own path, she threaded her way down the curved terraces to the collection of half-painted flats and tents that comprised the surrogate stage. The population density increased markedly as she got lower, and though most of the crew were folks she knew, it was odd seeing so many of them here *doing* things. Odd, indeed, that a dramatic production should require so many warm bodies.

Or maybe it was that old thing about art she and Ron had agreed on: that art needed art in order to thrive; that one saw art and wanted to imitate it; that talking about it made it more likely to occur. And that truly creative people could get competitive in a peculiar sort of way that benefited *all* parties' endeavors.

It certainly seemed to be benefiting *someone's*, she noted, as sidestepping a flat-painter brought her square up against a table laden with props. Specifically weapons—everything from tomahawks and bows and arrows through flintlocks to pearl-handled revolvers. A gray-whiskered man in overalls she recognized as Victor Wiley's grandpa was placidly carving a Derringer out of a block of close-grained wood, using a pile of books and what looked like a set of hand-drawn blueprints to go by. That struck Brandy as odd.

"Uh . . . sir . . . I . . . don't mean to get personal," she found herself blurting out, "but . . . Well, I was just wondering why you're going to all that trouble, when we could rent reproductions, or even borrow 'em, cheaper."

"What's cheaper'n free, gal?" the old man asked in reply, sounding very nonplussed and placid.

"You're doing this for *free*?"

"I'm doin' this to keep my brain spry and my hands supple. Beyond that, I'm doin' it so the kids 'round here can have the same kinda security I did. And best of all . . . I'm doin' it 'cause I *like* it!"

"Sounds good to me." Whereupon Brandy steered a course to the right, finally getting close enough to Gwent to hear what he was saying.

"I don't *care* what their mother told you," an atypically hard-faced Gwent was informing a pretty red-haired girl Brandy recognized as Mark McMillan's girlfriend—who also happened to be the casting director. Which meant she was supposed to screen whomever the radio ads dredged up and to search out specific types if none were otherwise forthcoming. "I don't *care* what her problem is," he went on. "I need *twins*, dammit: female between fifteen and maybe twenty-five—or able to look it; in good shape—and they have to be at least marginally pretty. If there aren't any in the county, check outside! We're supposed to be using as many locals as we can—but that doesn't mean they *all* have to be."

"What does he need twins for?" Weedge wondered. "Surely there're enough girls around who look alike that they could be made-up to look like twins."

Brandy shrugged. "Gwent's just a perfectionist, I reckon."

"Can't get away from 'em, can you?" Weedge chuckled.

Brandy did not reply and suddenly was in no mood for small talk. Without consulting her friend, she turned and strode to the northern edge of the battlemented terrace.

Where she had a perfect view of the lake. She leaned on the rampart there, resting her elbows in the embrasure between the granite merlons. The knoll swept away below her, revealing the trail to the dock, and beyond it, the finger of the lake above which all those new houses crouched. She saw Sam Foster's house, the one next door that had just this week been occupied.

But she saw something else too: something that jogged her memory. Sam and some of his friends were swimming at the dock at the house next to his. (And not at Ron's, for a change, she observed, with an odd mixture of irritation and relief.) But though she could not determine the swimmers' sexes from this distance, something she had heard in town struck her with sufficient force to produce a startled, "Oh."

"Gwent," she bellowed abruptly, turning and stalking back to the melee, "I've just solved your problem."

"But I've never *acted* before," Tam O'Shea (or perhaps it was her twin sister, Tonya) protested half an hour later, still damp about the noggin from the swim Brandy had preempted her and her sibling from completing. "Besides, we're supposed to game tonight."

"Ah, but this is a game, too," Gwent assured her, exuding all that disarming boyish charm he could dredge up when it suited him. "And it shouldn't take more than a couple of hours anyway. As for not having acted: so much the better. That way you don't have any preconceived notions of how things ought to be done, so you'll actually be better—more natural, anyway—than somebody who's spent years learning how to project, and time, and carry themselves, and then thinks about that when they oughta be focusing on the part."

"Maybe," Tam muttered dubiously. "I'm still not sure."

"Tell you what, then," Gwent said winsomely. "I'll make you a deal. You and your sister go slip into whatever we can come up with for costumes on the spur of the moment, and read through the scene and run through the blocking—and if you don't feel good about it afterwards, I won't give you any more grief. That sound fair? An hour of your time to may-be do some good, versus a bloody lot *more* than an hour in man-hours wasted if I have to call off this rehearsal."

The sisters exchanged wary glances, then shrugged and nodded in unison. "Sounds fair," Tonya said at last. "So, where do we, like, sign up?"

Gwent pointed toward a tent at the side of the plywood platform that was passing for a stage until they got the proper one built up in Cordova.

And a surprisingly short while later, Brandy was forced to snare Weedge on the verge of another beer raid, and drag her down to a place on the terrace above the stage that was close enough for them to hear clearly, but not so near they might become ensnarled in the small clump of imported technicians who pressed around Gwent like piglets nursing a sow. She took a swig of beer, watched, and waited for Act I of Donson Gwent's still-unnamed drama to begin.

Before she knew it—exactly as the sun brushed the topmost branches of the nearest oak—someone flicked a switch to bring up the hastily contrived footlights, and the show began.

The transformation was amazing. Brandy knew the tall trunks and heavy leaves of a deep north Georgia woods were nothing more than yards of canvas stretched across wooden frames and painted with casein—where they were painted at all, half the work being uncompleted. She *knew* they were propped up with everything imaginable, that huge gaps existed between them, and that the few trees in the foreground were nothing more than bits of branches and stray logs hauled out of nearby forest. And she *knew* that the lush carpet of grass, from which sprang a few stray flowers, was an old rug from her abandoned trailer spotted with plastic posies. But somehow, now that it was nearing dusk and a bank of yellow-tone spots came into play, the set suddenly looked very convincing indeed. And she was evidently not the only one to notice the effect, for the low buzz of nervous conversation that had presaged the raising of the lights had dwindled to an anticipatory hush.

"Looks good," Weedge murmured beside her.

"Real good," Brandy agreed in a whisper "I mean that set looks *real*—and it's not even finished yet!"

Weedge did not reply, but Brandy barely noticed, for her attention too had been drawn to what transpired on stage.

It was the woods: the springtime woods. The woods of a time gone by, for the trees were huge, sometimes up to thirty feet in girth. A few flowers ornamented the carpet of new grass.

Brandy was instantly enchanted. She'd read the script, of course, and it had been remarkably vivid, had told her most of what she was about to see. Yet even without being told, she would have *known* it was the past she was looking at—1720, to be precise.

And as the woods lay still and waiting, music wafted in. It sounded vaguely like Aaron Copland's *Appalachian Spring*, but yet was different. Presumably they'd have real musicians performing later. Locals, who'd get paid.

"Nice," Weedge whispered again.

"But not what they'll use in the final version. Gwent's writing that too, apparently."

"Jesus, isn't there anything that boy *can't* do?"

"Be tactful and predictable," Brandy informed her instantly. "Now hush."

The music swelled, then faded. Someone plucked single strings of a violin. Brandy recognized the rhythm: the beat of someone walking . . . slowly . . . stealthily . . .

A figure appeared among the trees to the right. Joel Gordon: a student of hers three years back who had comanaged a small newsstand in Cordova until it had folded. A nice-looking boy, well-mannered.

But now he was someone else. Oh, Joel's *features* had not changed: blunt and angular, but with the edges smoothed away by youth that would stay with him a long time. And his body was the same muscular compact frame she'd seen in a singlet at any number of wrestling meets. But now he was transformed. Part of it was hair: dark, long and caught back in a ponytail. Part was the clothes: authentic-looking shirt and suspenders worn above new blue jeans (she assumed because the ensemble wasn't finished yet). His flintlock rifle was still a cardboard cutout, his powder horn and steel axe the same. Yet when he emerged into the full light of the clearing it was as if someone else stood there. He was supposed to be Loston Welch: Ron's remote ancestor. And now she thought of it, he even looked a bit like Ron. Which was preposterous!

She'd seen them both every day for two years. There was no resemblance. Only now there was.

Loston was moving stealthily, warily, choosing each step with care. He looked left, right, left again, then raised his head as if he had heard something. He scowled uneasily, paused again, then shrugged and relaxed, but still looked concerned. "Just my luck," he said to his gun, "just my luck to lose the horses *and* the trail. And they call me 'Lucky' Loston! Ha! *That's* a crock of somethin' brown that smells."

He sat down on a convenient log and looked despondent, then spoke to his weapon again. "I guess this is the end you come to, chasin' dreams, ain't it, my pretty? Never mind if they come true, eh? Dreams? Ha! True or not, one of 'em's driven me into this wilderness, far from home, far from kin."

He looked at his gun again, then grinned sardonically. "What's that you say? That with kin like mine, who needs enemies? Well, Aunt Rigana's sure 'nuff happy to see me gone, what with me takin' the side of Grandpa Lear. Ah well, he's sleepin' the long sleep now; and me . . . I wouldn't mind joinin' him, leastwise for a spell. So you just watch out now, and let me know if it looks like trouble—*if*, that is, you don't mind." With that, he patted his gun and slumped down on the log, head down, hands draped across the flintlock, which lay athwart his lap.

And while he dozed, an Indian crept into the clearing, stocky and short necked, but smooth limbed. Cherokee, Brandy would have known instantly, even without the script, purely by the scanty clothing he wore—basically a breechclout and moccasins, though numerous tattoos patterned his face and torso, including one Brandy recognized as 'wolf' on his left shoulder blade. (Damned fine research, that.) A hardware store bow was clutched in his hand, an arrow already nocked on the string. The actor's name was Don Campbell, and he was one of the few for-real local Indians. Only now he was called "Sixkiller."

Sixkiller moved silently, utterly without noise. And did not pause until he stood right beside Loston Welch. He stared at him for a long moment, arrow nocked at ready, then hesitated and reached for his belt, where he quietly removed a

war club with a steel knife blade set in it (a family heirloom
Brandy had lent the production). In one smooth motion, he
raised it over his head.

But before he could bring it down, Loston Welch shot to
his feet. Fire flashed in his eyes as he grabbed Sixkiller's
arms. They struggled, their faces grim, grunts their only language. And then Sixkiller thrust Welch free, sending him
staggering backward onto the ground. With a loud whoop
that rang around the clearing, he lunged at his adversary.
Welch tried to block, but could not. Sixkiller landed square-
ly atop him, grabbed a handful of Welch's hair, and yanked
his head down. The club rose up, bright in the sunlight. And
then fell again—straight onto Welch's skull. Blood spurted.
Welch twitched for a moment, then lay still.

Brandy felt her breath catch, heard Weedge's startled gasp.
She had no idea they'd get into such realism so quickly.
Shoot, these guys weren't even reading their lines from the
scripts they'd tucked so unobtrusively under their arms that
she'd almost failed to notice them. And then her attention
was jerked back to the stage.

Sixkiller looked vastly pleased with himself. He grinned
and allowed Loston Welch's head to fall unceremoniously in
the dirt, then pulled out a knife and made to scalp the unfor-
tunate woodsman.—And froze in place, amazed. *"How can
this be?"* he gasped, and rose, gazing first at Welch, then at
the sky, his face a mask of alarm.

Almost as soon as Welch had stopped moving, the sky
had darkened. Thunder rolled (sounding not at all like the
rattling of a sheet of metal pirated from Ron's forge), lightning flashed, the lights dimmed. It began to rain—or something like it; Brandy couldn't tell where the washes of liquid
were coming from. But amidst the whole thing, she could still
see Sixkiller pick up Loston Welch and carry him offstage.
The music swelled again: something she didn't recognize that
nevertheless evoked a deluge.

Well, that *was just dandy,* Brandy thought. Everything
had gone like clockwork—so far. Of course there'd been
no actual dialogue yet, nothing that demanded *real* timing.
And both actors were physical types. Probably they'd already
rehearsed the fight. But did it really matter? This was great!

The lights changed again, darker this time. The storm abated. Brandy was aware of people moving around on stage, of props and flats being shifted. And then the lights returned, and another scene began.

This time the lighting was warm and red, as if the set were lit by fire. But there was an ominous blue cast to it as well, that made Brandy feel cold and clammy, like she did indoors on a winter day. And though this set was as hastily contrived as the last, it still looked uncannily real.

This time it was the interior of a Cherokee town house: walls of well-plastered cane mats, a suggestion of high thatched ceiling supported by four pillars bearing masks representing the seven Cherokee clans. A fire pit to center. Welch's body lay to the left, thrown carelessly atop a pile of mangy skins. An old man in a turkey feather matchcoat sat near the fire, staring at him, while Sixkiller squatted at his side, proud but uncertain. The twins stood nearby, remarkably composed for utter neophytes, Brandy thought. Really getting into things.

"Is he dead yet?" asked the old man—presumably the same Chief Taligisigi for whom, after many corruptions, the nearby Talooga River had been named.

"He . . . *should* be," Sixkiller replied. "I laid a blow on him that would have killed a bear. The hole in his skull was big enough to put my fist in."

"But even this old man's eyes can see that he still breathes," Taligisigi pointed out.

"Is he a witch?" Sixkiller wondered, glancing at him disdainfully.

The old man shrugged. "Or something just as bad. What do you think?"

"I think a *man* would be dead by now."

"I agree," Taligisigi told him dryly. "If he hasn't died in these seven days, he won't. Are other White People so hard to kill?"

Sixkiller chuckled. "Remember the slaver they caught in Dakwayi? *He* died quickly, screaming like an infant. They have strange clothes and the coloring of the evil Hunters who live in the Water, but they die."

"Perhaps he is not a White Person at all, then," Taligisigi mused. "Perhaps he is a shapechanger—or one of those

Hunters-From-Beneath you speak of. They also are this color."

"Then I would be dead," Sixkiller snorted.

"True," the old man agreed restlessly. "So what should we do?"

"There must be a way to kill him. I say we try until we find one."

Taligisigi nodded sagely. "I agree. Perhaps that will stop this accursed rain. The corn is rotting in the fields, and the creeks are rising beyond their banks. Soon enough the village may be flooded. Then we may have to move farther into the hills. Let's kill this one and move."

"You'll be sorry, then," a voice said weakly, from the pile of furs. "Very sorry indeed."

The chief started. Sixkiller looked startled; the two women hugged each other in fear, then steeled themselves to calm as the two males exchanged troubled glances.

"How is it that you speak?" Taligisigi demanded.

"One man's tongue is much like another's," Welch said, rising to a sitting position and clutching his head. "And one man's brain is much like another's too. With language bein' the thing between, is it so hard to think it might be the same way as well?"

"I did not ask how you know our language," Taligisigi spat. "How do you speak at all, with your head crushed in?"

Welch fingered the back of his skull. "*Is* my head crushed in?"

"Kill him now!" Sixkiller cried.

Taligisigi ignored him, but leapt to his feet, pushing past the younger warrior to grab Welch by the chin while he felt about his head with his other hand.—And stepped back incredulously. "There is no wound!"

"But that's impossible!" Sixkiller shrieked. "I hit him! He bled! You could see his brains leaking out! We *all* saw it! Even my sisters, here."

The girls nodded. "We saw, we saw."

"Well, it's gone now," Taligisigi replied.

"But not my headache," Welch chuckled easily, rising shakily to his feet.

"It won't hurt at all when I cut it from your body!" Sixkiller told him, striding forward.

"Can you be so *sure*?" Welch countered quickly, with a dangerous twinkle in his eye.

"Are you a witch?" Taligisigi asked suddenly, moving to stand between the two.

"Not the way you folks mean it. My own folk call me a conjure man."

"I know your folk," Sixkiller broke in. "They cheat us, sell us the poisons you call rum and brandy. If you are one of their sorcerers, then to us you are a witch."

"Ah, but your chief here thinks I might be able to stop this rain!"

The chief stepped back, horrified. "That was the very thought in my head! You *are* a witch!"

"It is a trick," Sixkiller snorted. "His kind are worse than Tsistu, Lord of Rabbits."

Welch's eyes closed for a moment. "And *you* are thinkin' you should have taken my scalp and left me to rot in the woods."

"*Anyone* could guess that!"

"You're also wonderin' if the child swellin' this maiden's belly is yours." Whereupon he pointed to the nearer twin.

Sixkiller started violently. "You . . . !"

Loston ignored him and stared straight at the girls. "You: twin daughters of this old man's one sister: Both of you are with child, but only one knows it. One of you's glad, one ain't. One loves the man who got her so—old Sixkiller, here. But the one who loves Sixkiller . . . ah, that's *not* the one that Sixkiller loves, is it? No, he lay with the wrong one in secret, and she's glad that she bears his child, but sad that she may have him no more. As for the other, she'd been got with child by violence, but she's never revealed the criminal; nor did she know, until now, that she is with his child."

Both girls immediately hid their faces; one began to keen softly.

"Ah, so you are a . . . *prophet,* then!" Taligisigi murmured.

"Prophet? Witch? Does it matter? He is not Ani-Yunwiya— not one of the True People," Sixkiller replied sourly.

"Sixkiller has a point," Taligisigi told Welch. "Your kind are not, in the main, trustworthy."

"And *I* say you *can* trust me," Loston countered calmly. "And I also say, chief, that you fear two things. The first is that this rain'll continue 'til you have to move your town, and that you'll then be forced to make war if you're to find a good place to resettle. And also, you're worried 'bout your nephew, who's like a son to you."

Again Taligisigi looked incredulous. "I have said nothing about my sister's son at all! Not while you have lain here have I spoken of him."

"Ah, but you think of him almost constantly," Loston chuckled. "And that's enough, if your thoughts be strong."

"So you say."

A shrug. "I also say that your missin' nephew went out huntin' and has not returned. He's been successful, but not until lately. But *today* he killed so much game he can barely carry it all."

The chief studied Welch. "How do you know these things?"

"The wind tells me," Loston laughed. "Only the wind."

"Father . . . !" one of the girls cried, pointing Stage Left.

All turned, to see a young man enter, staggering under a weight of furs and the bodies of animals.

"You have returned!" Taligisigi exclaimed.

The young man nodded. "And it was the strangest thing! I wandered for days without killing anything. I had given up, decided to return, but this rain hindered me. I took shelter in a cave, slept, and when I awoke, game of all kinds surrounded me. I knew I was to kill them. Uncle . . . it was as if I were Kanati, the Lucky Hunter, who kept all the game in a cave in the Ancient Times! I fell asleep dreaming of that story!"

"The *Lucky* Hunter," Loston mused with a knowing smile. "Imagine that!"

The chief turned his attention back to Welch. "You knew this! And yet you could not have."

"Why not? All things exist in time. Some things just move in it better'n others. The thoughts of men move in time like fish in a clear stream: where they will."

Sixkiller merely scowled. "I *still* think we should kill you."

Once again Loston shrugged. "It'd do you no good—if you could do it at all."

"What if we burned you alive?" Sixkiller wondered with a wicked leer.

"I wouldn't like that," Loston said—and for the first time truly looked worried. "But I doubt you could make much of a fire, with all this rain."

"The rain becomes more and more a curse," Taligisigi agreed heavily.

Welch's lips curled in a sly smile. "But suppose the rain were to *stop*, what then?"

"There are those of The People who claim they can do that," Taligisigi told him. "Sometimes they can, sometimes they can't. If they do what they claim, they are honored. If not . . . sometimes we kill them."

"*I* say I can do it," Loston insisted smugly.

"Then we will let you live," Taligisigi replied, after a thoughtful pause.

"I don't much like this deal," Welch told him promptly. "There ain't enough in it for me. No, if I stop this rain, you've gotta give me something."

"I'm offering you your life!" Taligisigi snapped.

"I've already *got* that," Welch countered calmly. "I need more."

"Such as?"

"Such as . . . land! If it stops rainin' before sunset, you will give me all the land between that river yonder and the top of both ridges to either side, and the distance east and west that a man can walk between sunrise and noon on the shortest day of the year."

Taligisigi regarded him suspiciously. "Why not the longest?"

A grin. "I don't want to be greedy."

Taligisigi glared at Welch distrustfully. "If you do what you say—and swear to use your conjury for us, never against us, in the future—then we have a deal. Sixkiller, prepare the white drink. There are promises to be spoken." He paused then, fixed Welch with a piercing eye. "And the promises I make are not easily unsaid."

The lights dimmed to black. The sound of rain swelled, then faded.

But when the lights came back on, it was not to another tableau, but rather to reveal Donson Gwent standing in the set for the previous scene, with an arm draped casually around the shoulder of Joel Gordon aka Loston Welch. "Uh, sorry, folks, but that's all for now. There's not much dialogue in the last part, and I've just decided I don't like the way I've told old Loston here to go through it, so we're gonna cut things off at this point until I can work out something better. Sorry.

"Oh, but thanks for watching," he added, with that disarming, little-boy smile. "I, uh, know that was, like, *real* rough, but I hope you got the gist. It's gonna take some polishing, but I think we can pull it off. Thanks for putting up with it— you folks in the audience, I mean. Folks on stage—crew, and all you guys—that was great. But come on down, 'cause we need to talk about next time."

Brandy blinked. A point of disappointment dug into her gut and lodged there. "*God*, that was real!" she gasped, blinking again, this time at Weedge, who was rising beside her.

"You could say that," Weedge agreed, wide-eyed. "I thought you said this was gonna be a *rough* read-through."

"I thought it was."

"Well, it didn't seem like one to me! Shoot, I've seen finished productions with less polish. It's a real pisser, though: ending it like that, without the conclusion."

Brandy gnawed her lip. "Good point, but you can't perform what you haven't been told how to do."

"Any idea what happens?"

"He makes it stop raining, of course. And gets the land— which eventually becomes Cardalba Plantation."

"And *all* that stuff's historical?"

"Let's just say it makes a good story," Brandy sighed. "As for the rest . . . well, we've both seen some things, haven't we?"

"Ronny ain't gonna like it, though," Weedge chuckled, "Not with all that stuff in there about the Welches, and the Luck, and all."

Brandy shrugged listlessly. "Maybe not—but he's only one person. Besides, it's presented as folklore—almost like a tall tale. There's always a rational explanation to everything. Gwent's version just makes better drama."

"He must know a lot, then."

Another shrug. "He's evidently talked to *somebody*, that's for sure, 'cause very little of that's in the book, and Ronny took all the local records he could find with him. I think his source was from over in Union County. Folks there aren't afraid of the Welches, but may have heard some things anyway."

Weedge raised an eyebrow. "Oh . . ."

A final shrug, and Brandy rose to join her friend. "Okay, gal, what d'you say we go down and congratulate the folks?"

"Fine with me," Weedge murmured, killing her beer.

An instant later they were among the players. "Good job," Brandy told the young man who had played Loston Welch. Close up she had no idea how she could have taken him for Ronny. Excepting their hair color, there was no similarity. "I didn't know you had it in you."

"Thanks," Joel Gordon replied sheepishly, his face flushed with self-conscious pride. "I kinda surprised myself there, I guess. I mean I just really got into it, and all. And it . . . well, it all just felt real natural."

Brandy flashed him a smile. "Obviously. You looked perfectly relaxed."

Joel scratched his head. "Yeah, and I felt that way too . . . it was odd, actually. I guess I just pictured myself in the situation, and let it flow. Just kinda thought about how I used to play Cowboys and Indians when I was a kid roamin' around in the woods."

"I know what you mean," Tonya O'Shea echoed with a vigorous nod, as she skipped up to join them, sans wig and sister, but otherwise still in costume. (Which, though obviously fabric, was nevertheless somehow dyed or painted to look like buckskin—Brandy presumed they'd switch to the real thing later, but Gwent was into having his actors get the feel of their clothes early on). "Jeez, but that was—I don't know, it just seemed . . . *right*. Shoot, I nearly forgot who I was! Why, half the time I wasn't even sure you guys were speaking English."

"I wasn't either," Weedge muttered, looking surprised.

Brandy stared at her. "Yeah, sure! Like Gwent wrote a play in Cherokee and we all understood it!"

"It was all accents," Joel volunteered. "Gwent kinda gave me an example of what he wanted, and I improvised the rest. I guess I just sort of forgot I was doin' it; it just seemed so natural."

Brandy wrinkled her nose. "You know," she mused, "I think what's going on here is one of those neat things that just happens sometimes. It's like when I'm doing really good art—*really* getting into a painting—I can just go on and on, with no real sense of time. I finish one part, but I've just *gotta* do the next one, and so on. I think art's like that at its best: you can lose yourself in it utterly. So maybe you were just so into the play that you lost yourself in the characters."

"Well, it felt great," Joel conceded, then nodded his good-bye as Gwent motioned him over.

"Yeah," Tonya O'Shea told Brandy. "I think I'm really gonna like this. Thanks for making me try out."

"So you're gonna stick with it?" her sister asked, bouncing up to joining them.

"Of course I am!" Tonya giggled. "Like I said, I think I'm gonna like this a *whole* lot."

Tam checked her watch. "Yeah, but Sam's *not* gonna like it if we're late for the game. So come on, gal, let's shuck these duds and travel."

Brandy felt something cold touch her shoulder. It took her a moment before she realized it was a drop of rain—the *real* kind.

Interlude 7

Mr. Sandman

Near The Realm of The Winds
Tuesday, June 18—past midnight

"IS HE ASLEEP?" asks the Master of Dreams.

"*He is,*" the Midnight Man replies, "*barely. I thought they would never finish.*"

"YOU FORGET HOW IT IS WITH THE GIFTED."

"*Would that I could! I am gifted too, don't forget. So are you.*"

The Master of Dreams ignores his . . . brother. "YOU HAVE BEEN KEEPING ME BUSY LATELY."

"*I know. Providing dreams for the Dreamless is no easy task—and harder still when you would not have them know that they* do *dream.*"

"AND HARDER STILL WHEN THERE IS MORE THAN ONE."

"*There will not always be. I had not foreseen that. That is* his *idea.*"

"IT GROWS TOO COMPLEX. I FEEL IT MY DUTY TO WARN YOU."

"*But if we succeed, we will be free.*"

"AND IF WE FAIL?"

"All this will become another dream."

"DREAMS WITHIN DREAMS," the Master of Dreams muses. *"DO YOU SUPPOSE HE SUSPECTS?"*

"Not so far," the Midnight Man replies. *"Nor do I look forward to telling him. I've grown rather fond of him."*

"I'LL TELL HIM, THEN."

"Perhaps I will let you. You are more subtle than I."

"WHEN?"

"Soon. The forge is hot, the metal must now be tempered one last time, before it can be sent out for polishing."

"SUPPOSING HE WANTS IT POLISHED."

"Who?"

"HE."

"Which he?"

"THE OTHER HE."

"Oh yes, that one. Well, we will see that he has no choice."

"AND THEN?"

"It will be as I told you: We will be free."

"AND MEANWHILE?"

"Meanwhile, it is for you to fashion more dreams. Many more dreams. Steal them if you have to, but bring them."

"I WAS AFRAID OF THAT."

"Consider the alternative."

"AH! NOW THAT I AM AFRAID OF."

The Midnight Man laughs tiredly.

"SOMETHING AMUSES YOU?"

"Dreams," he says. *"Did you ever wonder if maybe I too dream?"*

"DID YOU EVER WONDER IF MAYBE I STEAL THEM?"

Silence, and then a voiceless chuckle.

Chapter 13

Fixing a Hole

Erin Welch's House
Tuesday, June 18—just before dawn

Why, Ron wondered sleepily, as, on hands and knees, he probed among the thick fibers of the (unfortunately) ocher carpet for the third *very* small, hand-machined, and gold-colored screw that had fumbled from his fingers in twice as many minutes, did such a fine and noble notion as responsibility have to be such a blessed *pill*?

Such as, to call a spade a spade, exactly where his responsibility to his incommunicado brother lay. It had been bad enough before, but now that ignorance was no longer bliss—now that he *knew* that something was amiss with Lew: a sickness at least, possibly much more—that problem was redoubling every hour into a feverish intensity that left him totally drained. For if Lew *was* ill, it meant that the Luck was not functioning in him as it ought. And *that* was ominous indeed.

Which meant that he ought to be going absolute flat-out to repair The Head. And he'd tried—still was, though he supposed this was technically round two. God knew he'd gone full steam as long as he could yesterday: until sleepiness and eye fatigue and general brain deadness had claimed him around sunset. But still, he wondered if he'd been shirking responsibility by hanging out with Sam and his crew last night, as he had also done, per his almost-promise. He didn't think that was the case; any psychologist would have told him there was a practical limit to how far he could press himself and still be functional. In short, that it was perfectly okay to give his brain a rest now and then, so as to afford all those overstressed neurons a chance to recover and fire more efficiently later. *And* that such relatively trivial incursions into Important Matters as gaming represented were not occasions for guilt if they expedited a higher purpose—like reestablishing contact with Lew.

Still, from a coldly ethical point of view, he wondered.

Trouble was, it had been fun hanging out with Sam's friends. And fun had become an alien concept for him lately. Not that smithing wasn't pleasant; not that the crew. Brandy kept around weren't mighty entertaining; not that having sex didn't feel powerfully good. But none of them were *fun*. None had the spontaneity Sam's gang provided. *"Becoming is more interesting than being,"* someone had once told him. And though life itself was a process of becoming, rarely did one *become* more passionately than in one's late teens, when barriers began to erode, revealing limits just ripe for the testing. Sam's crowd was fairly tame in that regard. Few of them drank; none did drugs; sex (if any) was offstage and not discussed en masse, which was the only way Ron had dealt with any of them except The Kid himself. But the very fact that those mysteries *were* unplumbed gave otherwise prosaic events a veneer of excitement Ron could not resist.

And late last night, so fried around the eyes he could barely see straight, and so trembly of finger he could no longer manipulate tweezers, much less a file, it had been a blessed respite to rechannel his ongoing adrenaline push into contriving a suitable curse for Tad's thief, who'd had the temerity to request an audience with a certain demigod played by Ron after considerable briefing by Sam.

Unfortunately, that little brush with the arcane had prompted one of Andi's characters to request a similar favor. And since Sam had been unprepared for that eventuality, he'd chosen to defer action until tomorrow. That meant Ron not only had to endure another interruption and the guilt attendant thereto, but also had to come up with a new batch of curses.

Which he was trying to do with his left brain while the other hemisphere went right on overhauling The Head. And by which time, he imagined, he'd be *ready* for a break.

But should he do it? More to the point, could he enjoy it with circumstances as they were?

And whose fault was that?

And so he was frantically rebuilding The Head. Fortunately, most of the damaged components were simple ones, so about ninety percent of his actions involved purely mechanical skills, with no need for mental supervision. Most recently (before he'd lost that wretched screw) he'd finished filing down the last teeth on what was officially a sun gear, but which looked nearly as much like a bit of Celtic jewelry, given the spirals that comprised its spokes, each of which, however, *had* to be shaped as it was because each of the twelve had to provide pivoting junctures for four delicately curved brass arms that in turn retarded another set of gears at some remove. Art, physics, math, and mechanics: rarely had the four meshed as smoothly as they did in The Head.

And there, finally, was the blessed screw! Sighing, Ron resumed his seat, inserted the delinquent fastener into a hole at the center of the sun gear, and proceeded to ease the gleaming assembly into place—with a pair of foot-long tweezers in order to access the golden plate (near where a human's pituitary would be) that was ground zero for this gear.

. . . And *so* . . . Whereupon, with a twist of a screwdriver, it spun home.

He spent the next quarter hour connecting the auxiliary arms to the master wheel and realigning the cogs in the planet gears around it. And so was unaware when something slipped up and peeped across his shoulder.

He felt its warmth upon his bare back before he saw it. Saw its signature, rather, for it was the sun: smugly reminding him that he'd just logged another all-nighter. He yawned automatically, heard the raucous cry of a distant peacock, then rose, wiped his hands on his cutoffs, and stretched, feeling joints pop not only in his fingers, elbows, and knees, but all the way up his spine.

Time, it was, for a caffeine fix.

He had covered barely half the distance to the coffeemaker when he heard a noise behind him. A sort of grinding click, like delicate machinery poured full of sand but attempting, in spite of that, to function.

Ron spun around, fearing the worst: that Matty Groves had mistaken the parts-tray of gleaming metal bits for a litter box.

It was The Head—the spontaneously *activated* Head—blinking at him stupidly, but with a hint of that ironic accusation it had so often worn when it was still under construction.

"I have a . . . headache," it announced, swiveling its gaze to stare into the full force of the light that powered it.

Ron, who was quickly succumbing to the Demon Fatigue, was just punchy enough to take that remark as humorous and giggled like a fool.

"Is it common to . . . laugh at misfortune?" The Head inquired perplexedly.

Only with difficulty did Ron regain some sense of decorum. "Sometimes you can't help it," he managed between smirks. "I think it's called irony."

The Head puzzled over this for a moment, and Ron had the uncanny feeling it would have shaken its head in preference to scowling had it been able. As it was, it produced a very deep scowl indeed. "Irony *usually* . . . refers to . . . dramatic material."

"And what's more dramatic than building a head?" Ron snickered. "Besides, there *was* a play about you—or one of your . . . ancestors."

"I . . . know this play, now I . . . look for it. But this is no time for . . . triviality."

"I know."

"I . . . Perhaps I . . . do not have a headache, but I . . . do feel seriously malfunctioned."

A yawn this time, as Ron tried very hard to regain his composure. "Sorry, I'm working as fast as I can. Faster than I ought to, actually."

"So I . . . notice. And so it is with that . . . in mind that I . . . activated just now, to tell you, first of all . . . that I am very weak, and that the light . . . of yonder star is not the best . . . sort to sustain me."

"It's *not*?" Ron mumbled stupidly. "But the book—"

"I . . . have not *read* . . . the book. But I . . . know what pleases me, and I say to you, Ronald . . . Dillon, that the light of the moon would put . . . me in better stead than that which glares and . . . glitters yonder."

"Gotcha," Ron sighed. "But, obviously, I can't do anything about it now."

"I know—which . . . is why I . . . am also required to tell you that I now know why I . . . have not been functioning as I . . . ought. More . . . to the point, I know what changes ought to be made . . . to remedy my condition."

Ron was immediately all ears. He leaned forward expectantly. "*And* . . . ?"

"I will tell . . . you anon. Meanwhile, it . . . would also be wise for me to note that I . . . made . . . an error in asking you to share my consciousness, for I could . . . easily have destroyed your sanity there. Too late I realized this."

"But it was *Lew* who screamed . . ."

"Screaming would have done *me* no good."

"Okay," Ron said. "Hang on a sec while I switch on mister computer here, and we'll get the show on the road." Whereupon he powered up the Mac on the table beside him and paused, poised with his fingers hovering above the keyboard like some mad organist in a horror film.

"Very well," The Head began, "the first change you . . . should make . . . is . . . as follows . . ."

"What?" Ron snapped into the phone receiver half a day later, mad enough to bite nails. "Dammit, don't you suppose that if I'm not answering this friggin' thing it's 'cause I'm either not here or don't *want* to talk to anyone?"

He was on the verge of hanging up without having given whoever had been putting his machine through its cycle every five minutes for the last half hour a chance to get a word in edgewise, when he recognized the voice bellowing on the other end.

"Ronny, goddamn it, this is Dion!"

Ron took a step back reflexively, and immediately felt like a fool, given that his uncle was presumably in Florida. His reply was a nervous giggle. Then: "Sorry. I was working on Project Oracle and didn't want to be disturbed. I figured whoever it was would either leave a message or call back."

"I *did* leave a message!" Dion informed him, his voice adrip with sarcasm. "*Seven* of 'em, to be precise, each more virulent than the last!"

"I, uh, had the speaker off," Ron countered lamely. "I was *gonna* check 'em when I got finished. I'm at a delicate stage, time is of the essence, and the last thing I need is interruptions!"

"I *know*," Dion drawled, conceding nothing.

"You *know*? Good God, uncle, don't you ever do *anything* but sit around all day fooling with mojo?"

"Sometimes I *lie* around all day having sex. Occasionally I engage a fellow bum in scintillating conversation. You'd be surprised at the brains to be found on the street."

"And you'd be surprised at the brains up here," Ron gave him back. "I've finally made some progress on The Head."

"Oh yeah?"

Ron sighed, checked his watch, noting that suppertime was fast approaching and it would be cutting it close to eat *and* get The Head functional by moonrise, which was when it had advised would be the most auspicious time for its reactivation. Of course he could always wait until tomorrow, but that might make a critical difference—plus there was the Game then. "Yeah, well, it's like this . . ."

Whereupon he gave his uncle a condensed but precise account of everything that had transpired since The Head had first activated. Dion was more than a little perplexed when he discovered that Ron had actually had the thing up and running when he'd called the day before.

"Well *that* certainly explains some things," Dion grumbled dryly. "Real weird, it is lad, the way the omens have been coming out."

"So who made you Lord-High-Master-of-the-Mojo for the family, anyway?"

"Search me," Dion replied honestly. "Sometimes it just

attaches itself to whoever takes most interest. Trouble is, then you have to try to figure out not only what the omens mean, but who they apply to. And that's damned hard when you're living on the street."

"You could come up here," Ron suggested. "Actually, I could get into havin' you around."

"I've thought about it," Dion admitted. "Thanks, but no thanks. I've rejected that place too thoroughly. It'd find a way to get me, I know it would. So far it's ignored you— I guess 'cause you've been good. But watch out if you start pushing."

"Thanks for the warning," Ron grumbled. "And I really would like to talk to you 'cause there's a bunch of heavy stuff going on, and I . . . I really could use somebody to talk to just now. But . . ." A pause, then: "Dion . . . tell me something."

"What?"

"What do *you* think about all this? I mean, putting aside the omens and all, what do you really think? Am I going about this the right way, or am I wasting my time? Am I obsessing unnecessarily? Or am I shirking my duty by not just hitting the road and looking for Lew?"

"What do you think?"

"That's not what I asked."

"Okay, then . . . for the record. Number one: if anything was seriously wrong with Lew—if he was dead or in constant pain, you'd know. Since you haven't experienced that, the obvious conclusion is that he is, in spite of what he says, at least physically okay. However, since neither you nor I can locate him—and I *have* tried, let me tell you—and since the omens seemed to be singling him out pretty regularly before they started spitting out garbage, it's safe to assume that his silence is not simply a matter of his not wanting to be found. Given that, you have two choices: worry or don't. You've obviously chosen the former, which again gives you two choices: act, or don't. Again, you've chosen the former— in a manner of speaking. But action can take many forms. You've picked the one that's easiest: the path of least resistance—the one that requires minimal risk on your part, and minimal disruption of your routine. And, let's be frank, I suspect you're much more interested in Lew the symbol now than Lew the person. You know you're supposed to be concerned for him, so you are. But he's not been part of your day-to-day reality for quite a while—which means you have no gut-level incentive to hit the road—which is what you'd have done if he'd simply disappeared without notice at a time when you guys were hanging out a lot. Instead, he's eased into a more distant role—which I suppose means you can't *really* be faulted for not simply going off and looking for him, when God knows you've got the resources and the time to do it."

"But Brandy—"

"Is *one* person, whom you love as much as you love anyone, but no more than you love Lew. If she's worth having, she'll understand and cut you slack while you work on improving your peace of mind."

"And if she's not?"

"She is," Dion said. "Any woman who throws you out 'cause she's got her own priorities and doesn't need you whining is worth having, I assure you. Would that I could find women so rational. Unfortunately, all mine seem to want is this interesting tidbit between my legs."

"Are you finished? 'Cause if you don't have anything *constructive* to say, I really need to get back to work. I mean, I'm not trying to be snotty—but . . . there are times I can talk and times I can't."

"And times you ought to talk and don't."

"I don't need this," Ron growled, frowning. "You could have told me something useful as easily as you gave me grief."

"Touché, nephew, and actually, that bugs me too: getting smart-ass answers when a straight one would take fewer words. But the point I was trying to make is for you to be careful. The omens are running really screwy right now, but there's no sense in talking about 'em if you're pushing tight time, 'cause as best I can tell, whatever's gonna happen is gonna happen, regardless."

"Which means that you called to tell me to be on guard, but not against what?"

" 'Cause there are too *many* whats."

"Gimme an example."

A pause. "Well, to start with, I've taken three readings today. And do you know what? Every *one* has begun with the same song."

"Which was?"

" 'When the Levee Breaks,' by Zeppelin. Some loony keeps calling in requesting it every time my totem station switches DJs."

"You Listen for him, just in case?"

"Of course."

"And . . . ?"

"Some crazy kid obsessed with a meteorology final. And he's had his friends requesting 'Hurricane,' and 'Rain in the Summertime,' 'Riders on the Storm,' and every other weather tune you can think of."

"Which mean?"

"Collectively? The lull before the storm. But what the storm is, I can't even guess."

"Well, that's just great," Ron groaned. "And of course the irony is that you could've listed everything you've heard today much more quickly than we could have had this conversation."

"I did," Dion said dryly. "In those earlier calls. Check your machine."

"I will—but I've gotta finish The Head first."

"It's your funeral."

"Not funny—or likely."

"Don't say I didn't warn you."

"I won't."

"I may try to check in again tomorrow, if the old lady'll give me a chance."

"That bad, huh?"

"You got it."

"If I do, I got it from you."

"Take care, nephew—and be careful." And with that, Dion Welch hung up the phone.

" 'Ancestral voices prophesying war,' "—that was the line that appeared in Ron's mind all unbidden. He wondered, suddenly, if poetry might also be oracular.

And shuddered, abruptly in no mood whatever to be alone.

But he still had to finish The Head that night—make that, *wanted* to finish The Head that night.

But four hands were better than two, and Sam had two hands that weren't doing anything so far as he knew, never mind that the lad had a fondness for ferreting out secrets that bordered on obsessive. Well, then, there wasn't that much left to do, in terms of complexity. Mostly it was simply a matter of reassembling things, and lot of that was repetitious. With Sam pitching in, work should go a third again as fast, even allowing for the delays that explanations would necessitate.

Besides, he'd already asked the lad over for pizza—Ron had to eat, and if he could have company while at it, so much the better. Yeah, he'd give old Sam-o a reminder call, find out his preference so the Cordova Domino's would have it there when he arrived. And then they could hit the ground running. Sam had seen The Head anyway, and there was no real reason not to let him in on the reason for its construction. The kid had an open mind, after all, but was also very circumspect when occasion warranted. And if worst came to worst—well, there were always those options Listeners had that other people didn't. And while he loathed the idea of tampering with Sam's memories, he knew that if he had to, he would. For to consider that option seriously would imply that Sam had betrayed his trust, and if that happened, he would no longer be Ron's friend, and thus no longer entitled to special dispensations. But God, he hoped that never happened.

So it was, then, that less than a minute later, he was punching in Sam's number.

"Hello?"

"Uh, hi," he began tentatively, when the voice on the other end proved lower than expected, by which Ron divined that he'd got Sam's dad. That surprised him, given that the boy had made no mention of his impending return. He sounded harried, too: breathless. Ron realized he'd never actually spoken to him. "Uh, sorry to bother you here at suppertime," he continued, remembering his manners. "But . . . is Sam there?"

"Is this Ron?"

Ron suddenly felt very odd, having just that moment realized that he was probably as close to Sam's dad's age as to Sam's, and wondering what the etiquette was. He always called his friends' parents Mr. or Ms., sir or ma'am. But he'd never had friends as much younger than he as Sam. So what did he say? "Uh, yes. Is he there?"

"Sorry," Sam's dad replied. "Didn't he tell you?"

"Tell me what?"

"Hmmm. He said he was going to call you, but I guess he didn't. He's off working on that play. I think that Donson Gwent guy offered him a part in it, or something."

"He . . . take it?"

"I think so."

"Thanks," Ron croaked. And hung up. He felt, all at once, as if he had just been dealt a mortal blow—the most mortal kind for a friendship. For Ron had just experienced the first assault of what he dared not fear was outright betrayal.

"*Shit!*" he said to the countertop.

And did not call for pizza.

The next time Ron looked up from aligning screws and snugging sockets, it was to see his own reflection staring owlishly in at him from a windowpane that had grown dark without his noticing. He yawned hugely and rose, checked his watch, and noted that there were still fifteen minutes to spare before moonrise. Which meant that he'd made it—just barely.

If he had followed instructions correctly. *If* he hadn't screwed up in his haste. *If*. His world was suddenly circumscribed with *ifs*. and *if* things went as they ought tonight, what was the next step, assuming The Head (a) awakened, and (b) came through for him? *If* he found out what was up with Lew, what then? Did he go or stay?

"*Gaaaaaa!*" he grumbled aloud, and rose. There was just time for a cup of coffee and a fast check of the heavens before he began his . . .

Not his ordeal, for there was no effort involved beyond mere conversation; the rest—the brainwork, the hand-to-eye coordination—had already been accomplished. So what was he afraid of, then? Of what he might find, he supposed; afraid that one bit of information would force him to make a decision. That ignorance truly was bliss, but that he could be blissful no longer and be true to what he was.

So it was, then, that he still had ten minutes to spare when, cup in hand, he strode out to the back deck, ostensibly to get a bearing on the moon, but much more basically, for the simple joy of drinking in the night.

It was warm, but a breeze from the east stirred his hair (which needed cutting) and made him long to strip naked and lie in the grass and feel its caress while he gazed at the sky still pinkish purplish gray around its western edges, and watched the stars appear. There were stars aplenty here in the country, too, for there were no streetlights, and he had turned off the security light because it seemed wrong to mar so much celestial luminescence with tawdry imitations.

As for the rest—well, the mountains to the north were slowly turning into cutouts, sprinkled here and there with household glitters. The pool was a bright blue glow to the right, where it wavered and oozed with the rays of the underwater lights. And to the west, barely in sight, a dark clump ringed with blue-gold sparkles was Cardalba Hall. Waiting, he thought, a little sadly. A great old house, full of history, awaiting its master's return. A master who loathed it, not as itself, but as a symbol. A master who *might* never return.

And speaking of lights, there it was: a sliver of gold to the east that marked the first full moon of high summer.

Ron spared one final glimpse at the rising orb to ascertain its position, then chugged his coffee (it was barely warm by then), turned, and limped back inside.

The studio was dark, though he didn't remember having extinguished the lights; nor did he flip them on now. A comfortably muzzy coolness filled the blue-shadowed room, providing illumination aplenty. An instant only it took to swing aside the window, and little longer to maneuver The Head so that it faced (per its instructions) the rising moon.

It would take a while, The Head had informed him. Moonlight was better, but more subtle, a trickle as opposed to a flood. Operating mostly by feel, Ron chose a CD and plugged it in, filling the room with Stivell's 'Ys,' his favorite music for calming frayed nerves. And so he sat in the half-light and waited, sprawled limply in a molded tweed chair, with the taste of expensive coffee still a ghost on his tongue.

Without intending to, but not surprisingly, given the way he'd been pushing himself the last few days, he dozed. . . .

"Ahhhhh!" sighed The Head, softly, in a voice that was like harp strings.

Ron started, wondering if it was part of the dream on the edge of which he had been hovering, or something more tangible.

"Ahhhh?" he echoed, then sat upright.

"That's better!" The Head announced. "Fine wine as opposed to moonshine."

"But it *is* moonshine," Ron giggled. "And besides, some moonshine's very good. And besides, what do you know about such things, you who have no stomach?"

"I know I can't get drunk."

"You can't *drink,* stooge," Ron grunted, at once relieved that The Head was once more functional and apparently cured of its hesitant speech patterns and bemused at its tendency to carry on trivial conversations. He hadn't programmed that—but then, he hadn't *programmed* it at all; that was all Roger Bacon's doing. He wondered if The Head had some of good old Roger's personality. It'd be just like him, he decided.

"And whose fault is it that I cannot drink?" The Head asked pointedly.

Ron ignored it. "You can't taste, either—or I don't think you can. So what's with this business of using images you can't understand?"

"Ah, but I do understand. And if the image is wrong, it is for you to tell me—or change me so that such things no longer matter."

"Perhaps," Ron conceded tiredly. "But that's not what I wanta do now."

"And what *do* you want to do now? *I* can do nothing but talk—and deliver oracles, of course."

"Of course."

"You are in need of an oracle?"

"Yeah, as a matter of fact, I am."

(Patiently) "Which is?"

"You recall what we did earlier? How I've been trying to get hold of my brother for days and haven't been able to, and then how you got me through to him just enough to learn that he's sick, and that it's something to do with our sister?"

"Such thorough rehearsal was unnecessary, but yes, I remember. I am not a . . . computer; my memory does not vanish when I . . . turn off unexpectedly."

"Nor when you're half-disassembled?" Ron wondered, genuinely interested.

"Depends on how far."

"Ah. Well, then . . . let's get the show on the road."

"I have nothing *else* to do," The Head noted, with a touch of sarcasm.

"Very well, I reckon I oughta do this formally, so here goes: Tell me, oh Head of my making, where Lewis Welch is, and what his condition, both physical and mental, may be."

"You did not like what I told you before?"

"You didn't say enough. Besides, you said that if I made certain changes, you'd do a better job."

"Foolish of me."

Ron hadn't a clue what to do then, and actually considered walking out the door—or shutting the window—from sheer frustration.

"Sorry." (That was The Head.) "I forget sometimes."

"So, is this to say you cannot answer my question?"

"I can answer *all* questions—after a fashion."

"Get at it, then. I'm listening." And with that Ron slumped back in his chair.

And waited.

The Head did nothing for a time, though to Ron it seemed that its breathing slowed—except, of course, that it *had* no breath. Too, it stopped blinking, seemed to gaze ever more steadily at the moon, with a hungry intensity. Once, Ron could have sworn that it licked its lips.

"Weeeesst," it said at last, its voice strangely attenuated.

Ron sat bolt upright, wondering stupidly if The Head was playing games, or really was having to exert effort.

"Sooouuthhh," it continued. "There is a . . . barrier. Not . . . a tangible thing, a construction of the mind. It is like a cocoon and I cannot pierce it, though a little of the power within trickles out like . . . a fly caught in a spider's web and trussed to be feasted on later. Thus is your brother bound."

"More!" Ron cried desperately. "I need *more!* Gimme a distance, or *something—anything* I can home in on!"

"I cannot! The barrier obscures. It might be weak and nearby, or strong and distant."

"But you said you couldn't pierce it, so it *must* be strong."

"In some ways. Perhaps not in others."

"Would it help if I . . . joined with you again?"

"Not unless it would help if you went insane."

Ron pounded his knees helplessly. "But I've gotta know *more!* Can't you get through at all? I need to know . . . at least if Lew knows what's going on with him—if there's anything I can do, any clue I can get to help him!"

"I will . . . try."

Whereupon The Head fell silent. Ron stared at it, as it continued to gaze at the moon, which was now fully revealed in all its heavy, silver-gilt splendor. If The Head was making an effort, it was not obvious, for its expression did not alter in any way Ron could identify with exertion in humans. There was no scowling, no frowning, no workings of the corners of the mouth or tightening of the jaw.

Then, almost as if in a trance: "It is a strong binding . . . I cannot pass . . . I cannot pass, I can . . . not *pass*. It *sees* me, *knows* me! I . . . cannot pass, cannot pass, CANNOT PASS, CANNOTPASS, CANNOTPASS, CANNOTPASS-CANNOTPASSCANNOTPASS—

Ron was so shocked at the explosion of verbiage that he did nothing for a moment. And when he finally did act, it was only to close the window, since The Head had no other form of actuation mechanism beyond sun and moonlight, so far as he knew. But when he did, he got another shock, for though The Head had fallen silent, in the sudden darkness he could see that its still-bald skull was spotted with patches that glowed dully, like metal in a forge. And even as he watched, the air once again filled with the acrid odor of hot metal, with the grinding crunch of gears stripping, and finally, with the heart-stopping snap-pop of alloys cooling unevenly and ripping each other asunder. An ear fell out, suspended only by threads of wire. Oil oozed from the mouth and nostrils in a sick parody of blood. The crystal glaze on an eye-ball crazed like a car windshield struck with a stone, but did not collapse, though it gave The Head the look of the one-eyed blind.

"No!" Ron whispered, too heartsick to react more force-fully. *"No!"*

The only answer was the soft splat of solder oozing from the tear ducts to fall on the floor, followed by more snaps and crackles and frying sounds.

And still Ron stared, as his heart knotted into a cold tight ball. It wasn't fair! It just wasn't *fair!* Not with success so close. And he'd *had* success, for the damned thing worked! But to be so close to learning one tiny bit more about Lew, and then to be cut off on the very threshold of discovery . . . Well, that was just plain *shitty!*

Never mind that nearly a year of work lay smoking and oozing oil before him. Never mind that in order to get back to where he'd been five minutes ago would prob-ably require another six months. Never mind that Brandy had thrown him out, that Sam, on whom he thought for sure he could rely, had defected to the opposition without warning.

Never mind!

"So what do I do now?" he groaned into the acrid-smelling darkness. It was a rhetorical question, one he posed to noth-ingness, expecting no reply.

"Asssskk . . ." came a low, moaning voice that startled Ron so much he jumped back and came down hard on his bad leg. "Ask Donson Gwent."

"What? Why? What the hell does *that* mean?"

But this time The Head did not reply.

Ron stared at the defunct mechanism until the last of the hot spots faded. And then took a breath and turned on the lights.

And saw ruin—far more than he'd expected. A mass of popped rivets, sagging plates, ripped joints, all shiny with oil and nameless ooze. The Head looked like someone who had been beaten with a baseball bat and then flayed. But as Ron felt sickness overwhelm him all over again, he saw its eyes—its good eye, rather—where, still, faint but dim, a spark burned.

A wink.

And then that too faded.

And Ron was left alone with despair.

Chapter 14

Who Are You?

Keycutter Knob
Late evening

Ron was wondering, not totally rhetorically, whether his eardrums or the Centauri's stereo speakers would blow first. He hadn't had the latest iteration of the ten-disc CD player up full since he'd installed it six months earlier, and had only maxed out the eight-disc item before that once—for possibly five seconds: exactly long enough for the driverside window to develop a stress crack because he'd been stupid enough to leave the bolt-on hardtop in place.

Now, though, as he blasted through the cryptic hours between moonrise and midnight, he had no such impediment. And since he was feeling both powerless and self-destructive (as frustration was wont to incline him), he was dealing with matters as best he could—by burning off adrenaline as fast as possible, through the dual mechanisms of fear and pain. That those generated as much fight-or-flight as they consumed did not concern him. What mattered was driving absolutely as fast as he dared without imperiling other motorists, and broadcasting his angst to whoever was within half a mile of the speakers. Himself, he felt the music—Handel's

Fireworks—more than he heard it. For this close, even with
the best speakers money could buy, it had all gone to dis-
tortion. Or—almost—massage.

"Yeeeeeaaaahhhhhh!" he yelled, raw throated, as the first
curve on Keycutter Knob came up too fast. The tires left four
black dotted lines on the pavement as he braked, filling the
cockpit with the odors of hot rubber and something resembling ozone that was probably fried antilock circuitry. It was
a good thing Matty Groves wasn't along, he decided; he'd
have jumped ship regardless of speed, and considered the
loss of most of his surplus lives a bargain. Brandy would
have stuffed the car into neutral or turned off the ignition.
And Sam . . . He wondered. He'd never let the car have its
head while Sam was along, and had only let the kid drive
it twice.

"Yeeeeeaaaahhhhhh!" again—as the curve unwound into
a straightaway, which demanded acceleration—and evoked
a banshee whine from the supercharger that lasted until the
next curve. Whereupon Ron repeated the ritual. Several times.
Each time faster.

Which had the effect of freaking him enough to make him
shaky and much more humbly aware of his own ultimate
mortality as he flicked the car into the sharp turn that cut
down the mountainside on its way to Brandy's Knoll. A
wreck, assuming there wasn't fire or decapitation, which
weren't likely, would not have killed him. But it would have
hurt like the dickens, *and* generated a flood of unanswerable
questions, which would have been a pain of a different kind.

Speaking of which, he supposed it was time he gave Mr.
Handel a rest. A flick of a finger did the trick.

In the sudden absence of shrieking horns and earthshaking
tympani, the night thundered in upon him, its relative silence
as pervasive in its own way as the music had been. And what
sounds remained were the rumble of tires, his own shallow
breathing, and the hiss of wind that was louder among the
leaves beside the road than around the windshield pillars. He
switched the muffler to SOFT, and idled into the forecourt
of Brandy Hall.

"And now, oh my metallic friend," he sighed resignedly,
as he slipped from the car and closed the door with a scarcely

audible click, "the time has come to have it out with Donson Gwent."

He was ready, too, dressed entirely in black to match his mood, and with appropriate hardware in the form of a small black-anodized Derringer hiding in his armpit beneath his multipocketed vest—in case more subtle persuasions failed.

Fortunately, Brandy was in town hashing out deadlines, schedules, and budgets with the C.O.C.—the Winds had told him that much before he left. Which didn't mean she couldn't return at any time. And *certainly* didn't mean Brandy Hall was deserted.

Far from it. That same psychic checkup had told him that there were a whole *slew* of people on site for a rehearsal— including Gwent. Which was borne out by the plethora of vehicles crowding the stone-paved clearing, and by the level of mental activity pressing against the shields he had raised as soon as it became distracting.

So what now? He'd left his mom's place so precipitously he'd had no time to contrive a plan—beyond waylaying Gwent as discreetly as possible, but with force an option— though that was looking less likely by the moment, what with the number of witnesses an unwilling encounter would produce. He therefore had no choice but to wait—except that he was far too wired for that—or possibly, though he loathed the notion, use the Luck.

Happily, no one questioned his presence. Certainly he had as much right to be there as any of the other folks he saw milling about as he strolled nonchalantly across the pavement toward Gwent's theater. A few folks lingered at the edge of the East Terrace, he noted, smoking or swilling drinks from paper cups. These either did not recognize him or pretended not to, but all returned his nodded acknowledgment of their existence with quizzically inclined heads of their own as he waded into their midst.

He had reached the first line of battlements now: the low stone wall that marked the top of the East Terrace proper. And got a shock, because in the eleven days since he'd split, the entire area had undergone a transformation—by having its eastern extremity filled with a makeshift stage, with the next tier of terraces mushroomed with tents to

house set, prop, costume, lighting, and assorted other shops.
Not to mention the two tents flanking the stage itself, which
he assumed were dressing rooms. It was a miracle, given
the astonishingly professional level of activity he was wit-
nessing, that nobody (so far as he knew) was pushing to
actually mount the production at Brandy Hall. But there
practicality had won out. Short of importing parking spaces
from Montana or running buses, there was no way accom-
modations for the expected numbers of vehicles could be
made there.

Which was a relief.

What *wasn't* a relief was the thickening crowd. Ron wondered how many were crew and how many friends or family who'd drifted by out of curiosity. The few he bothered to
inspect appeared totally enthralled, almost dazed. And as he
proceeded through the mob, he got the uncanny feeling that
he was embarking on some sort of mystical journey—perhaps
even into hell: Dante's Hell, most likely, with its descending
circles delineating various sins. He wondered what *his* trans-
gression was. And more to the point, whether Donson Gwent
or Brandy was the Devil.

He found himself in a position to make a better guess
very soon. For when he reached the battlement above the
next lower terrace, he could hear singing—and was instantly enthralled.

Every act of Gwent's still-unnamed opus had a singing-
dancing prologue and epilogue, which served as both bridge
and chorus. The first included eighteenth century woodsmen
and Indians; the second, Civil War soldiers and newly freed
but still loyal slaves. And the last—onto which Ron had just
blundered—was presaged by a chorus of dowdily clad wom-
en wailing bluesily, about how things had gone to hell in the
county now that the Depression was on and the menfolk had
all left to work in far-off places. And, more to the point, of
how the Master didn't seem to be doing any of them any
good. The soloist had a good voice, too; one that cut clear
through the night, that even pierced—mostly—the residual
ringing in Ron's ears.

It was also a catchy tune, and before Ron knew it, he was
patting his foot along with the rest of the mostly anonymous

folk leaning on their elbows atop the nearest parapet. Damn, but that was a neat piece! Spritely yet sad, indignant but wistful, with a beat that at once evoked Celtic reels, bluegrass buck-and-wings, and—incongruously enough—the blues.

Nor was he aware of when the woman stopped singing and started talking to a tall, thin woman who had strode on, Stage Right.

"Miss Martha!" the younger woman cried in surprise. "I was just thinkin' 'bout you!"

Ron started at that. *Martha?* That could only be his great-grandmother. But *she* wasn't legendary, was she?—beyond being about fifty years ahead of her time in terms of women's lib. And, gee, but it was odd having a play that included people he actually knew—whom most of the folks hereabouts had known all their lives.

Unable to resist, he eased two tiers closer.

And immediately got another shock. For had he not watched Martha Welch die, had he not borne her casket, attended her funeral, and seen her laid in the tomb, he would have bet any amount of money that the woman in the prim blue suit on the stage was she. Or she as she had been then: twenty-something, sexy as illegal moonshine, and sharp-tongued as a shrike. But whoever was playing her had her down pat: her voice, the way she moved, the way her hands were always busy. Even her glares and hard glances and unexpected grins.

And so Ron ignored the urgency of his errand, and eased himself down to watch.

Not even Welch County had escaped the Great Depression (so the lamenting woman said in what should have been a deadly dull lecture but wasn't). The young men of the county had served in World War I—the Master at the time had said country took priority over person and had not intervened to circumvent the draft: a reasonable enough attitude for someone as bound to the land as Masters were. Indeed, the Master himself had gone to war—which Ron had known but never thought about and probably should have, given the trouble to which he and Lew had gone to renounce the Luck; presumably there was a ritual for this contingency as well. Or perhaps one *could* leave if the Land itself was at risk.

The upshot, however, was that the Master had returned, but a shockingly high number of young men hadn't. And since there were reasons the Master couldn't sow his seed around—like hereditary madness (how did Gwent know?), there was still a dearth of marriageable men. —Until a certain redheaded stranger passed through accompanied by an unlikely wagon and a herd of goats. (*Couldn't be the same,* Ron thought; the time frame was wrong; besides, the Road Man *he* knew, though he claimed to have slept with a couple of thousand women, denied having any offspring). But whoever it had been, nine months later the town was awash with babies, most of them red haired. And Martha Welch had done her part, had gone to the woods (she confessed) with the Road Man, just like all the others.

That revelation shocked the hell out of Ron—though it shouldn't have, given what the old lady had implied a time or two.

But he had no time to ponder, for by then the girl's plaint had turned to the present. How back *then* folks had said it was the Luck that got new children so the next generation could have new men. But now times were bad again, and the men had gone to work for the C.C.C., and folks were wondering where the Master was and what he was doing.

What he was *doing,* Martha explained, was growing up, the one who had presided over the War having died with no heirs of the proper age and mind-set. But that didn't mean the Welches couldn't help. She was a Welch too. And women could do everything men could.

The rest of the act was a fable of industrialization in the style of *Metropolis,* with Martha Welch organizing the women of the county to build a factory (using stones dragged from the Talooga River and laid in concrete themselves), then convincing Mr. Henry Ford that Welch County wood was as good as any on the upper peninsula of Michigan, and the weather better, so that they could manufacture wooden station wagon bodies as well as anyone. It was Luck, they all said, and soon the county was as prosperous as before—so prosperous that the young men who had gone returned home to work the factory. Which was fortunate again, for when the second World War came around, they found themselves in command of a factory important to the defense industry. And by then there was once more a viable Master.

Ron was intrigued by that character: Ben Welch, the man who was Matthew Welch's uncle, the legendary great Master who had been Martha Welch's younger brother. Without his really being aware of the passage of time, the act was nearly over. The stage was empty now, save for a much older Martha and her darkly handsome *frère.* They sat in armchairs in an uncanny replica of the library at Cardalba Hall, drinking sherry and reminiscing.

"So are we safe now?" Martha asked wearily. "The war is over and the men who left to fight are returned. Few died, but *they* chose to live without Luck—and did so of their own free will. The rest took Lucky jobs and made Lucky choices. Their wives made their own Luck too. But what of the future? Is there still a need for Luck in the World?"

And that elder Welch replied, "There'll *always* be a need for Luck, if nothing else as a dam against despair. There'll always be people who make bad choices, and sometimes there'll be people who try their damnedest to make good ones and suffer anyway."

"But why are *we* here? Why do we need a *Master?*"

"Because sometimes *knowing* there's Luck isn't enough," Ben Welch said softly. "Because everyone has a right to be happy, but sometimes someone is born poor or ugly or sick and never gets to be what he wants to be, and that can be infectious, can take over a whole family and ruin them utterly. I try to prevent that, by giving 'em something *real* they can believe in, a focus from whom the Luck flows. I've got a gift I don't know where I got, but it's mine and I have to use it—and use it according to the Rules or pay the consequences. So I guess in that way I'm like a priest, not that I'm an intermediary 'twixt men and God, but like most folks really need a priest: as someone to stand between them and the Dark when things go bad. They know I'm here and they feel better, and when you feel better, you don't have much use for Luck, so I don't have to do much. But there's security in knowing I'm there to use it."

"And what do you see?" Martha asked. "What might be coming down the road?"

Welch chuckled. "*You* can read the future as well as I."

"And lose time off my life for it, too!" Martha snorted.

"Perhaps."

"I know you've looked. What have you seen?"

"I've seen good times and bad. I've seen a time forty-some-odd years from now when my nephew, Matty, may go bad. But there're always two roads, and one could damn him, and one could save his life. And I see contention over the Luck, and I see a time like this when things are bad again."

"And what do you see beyond that?"

"I see the future—and that's something no man *ought* to see."

And music began to rise: an instrumental, subtle, but upbeat—like the John Williams score at the end of half a dozen films Ron could rattle off without thinking.

"Oh!" he said aloud, blinking and jerking his head up abruptly. He'd been so engrossed he'd forgotten he was watching a play, so that the dousing of the lights at the end caught him unaware. He blushed furiously when he realized he had started—and that someone had noticed him do so: an old man in the makeup that indicated he was part of the second act. Ron knew him as one of the clerks down at Mason Hardware.

"Gettin' into it, was you?" the old man asked, lifting an eyebrow conspiratorially.

Ron ignored him, was searching the crowd for Donson Gwent.

"Yeah, you was really gettin' into it," the man repeated.

"I was watching," Ron told him. "That's all."

"You was doing a heap more'n *watchin'*! You was repeatin' every word old man Welch said there at the last. Repeatin' 'em word for word, like you knowed 'em by heart."

Ron still did not reply, but simply stared at the man, as chill after chill raced across his body.

"*Gwent*," he muttered under his breath. "Goddamn, man, what *are* you?"

And with that, all the anger and frustration that had sent him hurtling through the night came rushing back to him. His mind cleared; all thought of drama, all appreciation for technical expertise, dispersed. Of *course* it was a brilliant play!—Gwent was brilliant! But he was *too* brilliant, was bringing things together too fast and too well for any normal person to achieve. Which meant he couldn't *be* normal—which meant he was putting one over on Brandy, was no more an abused prodigy with a schizo personality than Ron was. And worse, he'd been a fool to ignore the signs. His *heart* had known, dammit! Only the fact that he did not want to admit that there was otherness in the world, and worse, that otherness was not limited to ordinary humans and Listeners, but that there was a third category of being that might or might not be related to either, only that fact had kept him from accepting the obvious before.

Sure Gwent had covered his traces well. He'd met Ron more than once, knew the chinks in his armor whereby Ron could recognize him, and had taken steps to disguise them. He *knew* Ron would find that he had no Voice, *knew* Ron could identify a false one like he'd used when he'd been Van Vannister. So he'd built shields, and hidden a pack of lies within that were so terrible and dark and elaborate that Ron wouldn't want to hang around there long enough to see that they *were* false. And to further muddy the waters, he'd mutilated his genitals, knowing that if anything were characteristic of the Road Man, it was his pride in his sexuality. The rest—the reverse-aging, the omniscience, the ability to read folks' deepest wishes and most-guarded secrets, the deep-seated fox-sly craziness—those were facts that could not be denied. Yeah, Gwent was the Road Man, one way or another; of that, Ron no longer had any doubt.

"Damn you!" he muttered again. "And damn the goddamned Head, for putting me up to this!"

But shilly-shallying would accomplish nothing. And so it was that Ron straightened his back, squared his shoulders, and tried not to limp as he strode down the ramps between terraces toward the stage. If people impeded him, he didn't notice. Perhaps they glimpsed the hard glare in his eyes. Maybe they remembered that he was still, genetically, a Welch—the only one they had at present. Or perhaps it was simply the Luck again: the power of his mind so strongly focused on the task of getting to Donson Gwent by the straightest route that even the ungifted (and he suspected most folks had a trace of whatever ability it was that when developed was called Luck) picked it up and got out of the way.

Before he knew it, and still without a reasonable battle plan, he had reached the canvas enclosure that housed the men's dressing room.

Gwent was inside; he knew that of a surety, even without hearing his soft boy's voice through the canvas wall. At the moment he was congratulating his actors, captivated by their performance, as they, in turn, were enthralled by how well his direction had resolved. There was also a huge amount of emotion present, most of it positive—not that it didn't give Ron a headache. But that was only pain, not a thing that, of itself, could do damage. Therefore, it could be ignored.

Gwent could not. And now, when the guy was distracted, when the glow of happiness and satisfaction was coursing through him like a river of fire, now when he was off guard: that was the time to strike.

Ron eased behind the tent, set his shoulders to the stone of the lowest battlement, below which twenty feet of rock plunged sheer to the path to the dock. There, he closed his eyes, drew deeper into himself than he usually dared, then took the three breaths—and Jumped.

—And found what he had found before, a superficial emptiness that in fact was the surface of a shield so smooth and featureless it was almost undetectable. But anger gave force to Voice, and Ron was very angry, and so he Shouted.

And Gwent, who had no choice but to be startled, even beyond the Shields where his *self* lived, likewise had no choice but to reply.

Who's there?

And by that, he dropped his shields, and Ron had him.

Rarely had Ron done what he was about to: imposed his will upon another. And never—for it was a concept he abhorred and against the Code of Listeners—had he taken full control of another's limbs and tongue. And though Donson Gwent fought him, Ron had mastery of those parts of Gwent's mind that drove his muscles and balance and reflex. And those he brought to bear; those he used to make the playwright mutter a stiff, "Excuse me—but *don't* follow me," to the startled actor he'd been praising, turn, and stumble gracelessly through the slit in the dressing room's fabric wall.

For a second Ron saw through two sets of eyes; for a brief instant, beheld himself through Donson's gaze. Not, however, until he had the boy by the scruff of the neck and was pointing the pistol straight at his heart, did he relax his psychic hold.

Gwent blinked, and then his eyes went wide in what looked more like honest fear than confusion. He tried to flinch away, but Ron held him fast, his face as hard and shadowed as Gwent's thin silk shirt was flimsy and white.

"Who are you?"

"I've told you, Dillon!" Gwent gasped. "Goddamn it, man, I've *told* you!"

"And you've lied."

"About *what*?"

"About . . . *everything*! About what you are, about your background."

"I have not!" Gwent wailed wretchedly. "Jesus Christ, man, what do I have to do to convince you? I'm just a regular guy with *more* than regular talent!"

"Bullshit!"

Gwent's eyes were huge. "I *am*, Dillon, I swear it. Or if I've lied—if I'm . . . something else, even *I* don't know it."

"But you know things you shouldn't know!" Ron gritted, wishing he was free to yell. "You know things that you have no right to know! That *nobody* who isn't part of it has a right to know! How do you explain that?"

"I . . . *can't* explain it," Gwent replied desperately, and even as Ron watched, he could sense Gwent's personality shifting, becoming less assertive, more childlike. "I can't explain," the boy repeated. "Except . . . except sometimes I . . . kinda dream stuff—'cept I usually can't remember anything until something happens to remind me, like readin' a book about the same thing, or something. And sometimes . . . stuff just comes to me and *feels* right. You oughta know how that is."

Ron regarded him warily, noting the persona starting to shift again. "How so?"

"Because you're an artist!" Gwent told him softly, his voice abruptly sure and smooth, as his face was suddenly calm. "Surely you know how that works: that you have an idea of something you want to do, some image in your head, and then you start trying to make it concrete. But while you're doing that, you're thinking—maybe a little, or maybe a lot, but you're thinking. And something comes clear—a master plan, something that's tangible enough for you to jump off from. And then you start working on it, and you hit one of those things that *wasn't* clear, that you *didn't* know about—and all of a sudden you *do* know. It's serendipity—maybe it's divine intervention—but it happens. And that's what happened when I wrote the play."

Ron stared him straight in the eye. "I don't buy it. You know too much for *anyone* to know, too many secret things that maybe only two people in the world know—or did until you wrote that goddamned play!"

Gwent shrugged helplessly, wriggling in Ron's grasp. "You're different, aren't you? *Really* different, I mean. The Luck—it's not just a symbol, not just power and influence and self-confidence. It's . . . a real other power!"

"You tell me."

"I *can't* tell you, Dillon! Honest to God, I *can't*! Don't you think I would if I could? I'm just a kid, mostly—a bright kid—and I'm sure you know how the world treats really bright kids. Only it's treated me even worse, and I have to hide in myself or go nuts. Except that I can't even really do that, 'cause as soon as one of my personas gets stressed out or is attacked, another takes over. And when *that* one stresses out, they shift again. It's like they all look out for each other—which makes it damned hard to maintain any kind of continuity in your life!"

"But what about the stuff you know, dammit? I don't buy all that BS about dreams. You can't dream about what you've never heard of!"

Again Gwent tried to shrug. "I dunno. Maybe . . . Jeez! I guess the only thing that makes sense is that if all these powers really *are* real, then . . . I dunno . . . the stuff that I'm puttin' in the play, that I think just comes to me, is really stuff that *you* know, or are thinkin' about, and broadcastin' *to* me."

"*Bullshit*! I don't even *know* half that stuff!"

"Maybe not consciously," Gwent countered. "But I bet you've heard most of it—or read it in one of those journals Brandy says you won't let her see. And I bet you're worryin' 'bout it, too. I bet you're crazy afraid I'm gonna get a look at that stuff, and crazy jealous I'm gonna do something to your lady—or *with* your lady, when you know damned well I can't even play with myself to any good effect!"

He paused for breath, then went on. "I bet that's it: that you've got so much strong emotion tied up in the whole mess that you can't help but broadcast far and wide. Only I'm the one your anger's directed toward, and I . . . I guess I *am* kinda sensitive to that kinda thing, so I'm the one that gets it. It lodges in my subconscious and stays there, and then I start writin' and—bang—there it is, clear as day."

Ron relaxed his hold a fraction. He lowered the gun but kept it in his hand. Gwent looked relieved.

"Lewis," Ron said heavily. "My twin brother. He's gone— as you've probably heard."

Gwent swallowed hard, nodded. "Brandy mentioned it when I asked her what the hell was up with you."

"Somebody . . . told me you could tell me where he is."

"Somebody's crazy, then."

"This somebody can't *be* crazy," Ron told him, whereupon the gun came up again. "Now, what do you know about Lew?"

Gwent looked utterly wretched. "Nothing! Honest to God, *nothing*! If you don't believe me, use that . . . power of yours to take a look. I'll try not to resist."

Ron regarded him warily and lowered the gun once more. "I'd rather not. I . . . don't like doing that any more than I have to." Gwent looked even more relieved.

"What would *you* do," Ron asked slowly, "if your brother, whom you love more than anyone in the world, got up one morning, said he was gonna go look for a sister you'd never been sure you had, and walked out the door, stayed in touch fairly reliably for months, and then the very day he found her, broke off contact—or had it broken off?"

Gwent looked thoughtful for a moment. "I think," he said quietly, "that if I loved this brother very much at all, I'd drop everything else in the world and go look for him."

Ron did not reply, and tried not to let his face betray the multitude of conflicting thoughts that warred within him: everything from emptying the gun into Gwent out of sheer frustration and trusting to the Luck to keep him out of jail, to turning right there and running away, to taking this near-total stranger in his arms and crying his eyes out.

Instead, he said, "The Road Man."

"The Road Man?"

"What do you know about him?"

"I know exactly what Brandy's told me," Gwent replied cautiously. "That, plus what's in that pamphlet I'm basing the play on, plus what . . . I've dreamed. I know he passes through here some. I know he taught you smithing—got you interested in it, I think. I know Brandy met him and thinks he may not be . . . normal. I know she thinks, or *you* think, or you *both* think, that there's some connection between him and the guy in the statue out back—Van Vannister, or whatever his name is. And . . . I guess I've heard there's some connection between him and this place, but nobody'll tell me what it is."

"Maybe you oughta dream harder, then," Ron spat. "Only now I think of it, it'd more likely be a nightmare."

Gwent blinked owlishly.

"I'm not gonna kill you," Ron whispered. "I'm not gonna do it 'cause I'm still not a hundred-percent sure you're not what you say you are, and 'cause you've not—so far—done anything that's actually bad beyond revealing my family's dirty laundry. Only I don't really *like* my family, do I? So even that's not really bad. So you can fuck around with me as much as you want to . . . *but*, Donson Gwent, if you hurt Brandy—if you so much as lay a finger on her, or play head games with her, or screw with her mind, or expose her to anything out of the ordinary, I swear I *will* kill you. And not only that; I'll destroy your body so thoroughly not an atom will remain attached to another—hell, not an *electron*.

If you've got a soul, there won't be *anything* for it to link to unless you link to the whole world 'cause I'll scatter the parts of you that wide!"

"I . . . believe you," Gwent whispered meekly.

Ron released him. "One final question."

"I suppose I oughta listen, oughtn't I?"

"How do you do it?" Ron sighed. "Not the play, not the stuff that you're not supposed to know, the stuff that I can't keep folks from knowing now that you've spilled it, not without violating my own vows. But that other stuff: that loyalty, the ease with which this thing's going off. The way characters seem so real."

"I don't know!" Gwent whispered, his shoulders slumping. "It's like the writing: it just happens. And truly, I've thought about it. Truly . . . I don't know. I guess this is gonna sound conceited, but all I can come up with is that it all goes back to art."

Ron raised an eyebrow to prompt him.

Gwent stared at the ground. "What would a perfect poem be, Ronny? Or a perfect play, or a perfect novel? What would it be? Or what would it do?"

"I dunno," Ron said, too confused to focus on the question.

"It would," Gwent replied, "or at least *I* think it would—produce exactly the same response in anyone who read it or heard it or saw it performed as was in the mind of whoever created it. It's like the perfect word for . . . for rock. If it was the perfect word for that thing, a person who had never heard that word could hear it and know exactly what it meant, even if it was in another language. It's the same thing for the perfect work of literature. It would produce precisely the same images in the mind of the reader as were in the mind of the creator. But even more, it would produce the same emotions, the same attitude, the whole nine yards. It would be perfect communication."

"And no more be art than a Xerox of a la Vinci is."

Gwent looked thoughtful for a moment, then shook his head. "No . . . that's where you're wrong. Because not only would it be everything the creator wanted it to be, but to that would be added everything the person experiencing it is as well. It would be *one* totality—plus a whole *other* totality. The shared experience would enhance the original."

"That's demonic!"

Gwent shook his head even more vehemently. "If there was a deliberate imposition of will—*that* would be demonic. But if the experience is accepted freely—if the reader or who-ever takes all he gets and adds his own thing and produces a greater whole, I think that's rather more divine. I think that's what *I* do," he added.

"You sound," Ron spat in disgust, "exactly like the Road Man."

"I sound like one of my professors in college," Gwent chuckled. "Like him, and like some guy I saw on a panel at a conference on creativity. One of his fellow panelists told him it was demonic too."

Ron studied the boy for a long moment. "I don't know what you are, Gwent. And I'm not sure I believe you. But I don't think I can find out now. Worse, I think that in order *to* find out, I'd have to abandon every good thing I stand for. But watch it, okay? And I meant what I said about Brandy."

And with that, Ron turned and limped away.

He was barely aware of his ascent through the nested semi-circles that comprised what he had come to think of as Bran-dy's Hell. People called out to him, in greeting or complaint or bemusement, but he barely heard their voices, never mind their words. In this vast pool of people, he was a leaf fighting a maelstrom; in this hell of humanity, he was the lone soul daring to ascend.

Ask Donson Gwent, huh? So the supposedly omniscient Head had told him. Well, he'd *asked* Gwent and got no answers. He knew not one whit more about where his broth-er was than he had before he'd come. Not a *thing*. All Gwent had said was that if he were Ron, he'd go looking. *Actively* go looking.

And Ron had known that all along, had needed no oracles to tell him so. Trouble was, that was also the least desired option, the one that required him to act rather than react, that demanded he pull up stakes and hit the road and hope the road didn't reciprocate.

But what was he afraid of? he wondered, as his route thrust him out in the pavement before Brandy Hall, where more than a score of people still milled about, some of whom gazed at him speculatively—perhaps accusingly—as he lumbered past. Was it loss of security? Not really. He had enough money to get by wherever he was. Friends weren't that hard to come by if you dropped your guard and let people in. And he could ply his trade anywhere there was fire, a hammer, and metal. In short, little was actually binding him here save his own stubborn preference for the path of least resistance.

Well, he would take that path no longer! He had thought the right thing was to stay and support Brandy and be a nice guy and give her and her crowd what they wanted. But they seemed to get along dandy without him. He, however, had to live in his own head always. And if *he* had no peace of mind . . .

And the only way he'd get any was to find Lew.

He would go on the road and find Lew.

His mouth firmed when he made that decision, his steps came down more forcefully and with less of a limp, as he turned his feet toward the Centauri.

But as he drew nearer, he became aware of other steps dogging his own. Lighter footfalls, and nimbler. He was being followed, and he did not need the Luck to tell by whom; he had heard that tread too often not to recognize it.

"What do you want, Sam?" he sighed, even as he turned.

The boy was panting from what Ron supposed was a dash up the various terraces. His face was also flushed beneath a trace of makeup Ron imagined remained from the Civil War scene in which Sam, to judge by his bit of costume, was a soldier. "So, what'd you think?" Sam asked breathlessly.

"I think," Ron whispered, "that you were probably very good, that the play is coming together excellently well . . . and that I'm leaving."

Sam looked confused. "Leaving . . . ?"

"Departing. Vamoosing. Heading out. Hitting the road."

"Goin' home?" Sam suggested hopefully.

Ron shook his head. "Not *home*—wherever that is. That's the one place I *won't* be."

Sam looked even more confused, but now that was mixed with a sense of outrage that something in his world he had thought fixed had moved. "But . . ." the boy began.

Ron glared at him. *"What?"*

"What about the stuff we were workin' on?"

"Lots of people can teach you metalwork," Ron said wearily. "And you can go to school half a dozen places to learn to design cars. I'm the *only* one who can do what I have to do—the only one who cares enough *to* do it, anyway."

"But where're you *goin'*?"

"I don't *know*—but I won't be in Welch County tomorrow."

"But . . ."

"Do me one favor, all right?" Ron told him sadly. "I probably don't have a right to ask for one right now, or you probably don't think I do . . . but . . . tell Brandy I've gone."

"S-sure."

"Carry on."

"But . . . *why*?" Sam burst out.

Ron did not dare reply. But when he reached the car he looked up and saw the boy still watching him. *"You blew it, kid!"* he yelled, feeling a sudden desire to hurt as he himself had been hurt. *"I'm not a hero, just a regular guy—but even heroes need friends sometimes!"*

Sam simply stared at him.

Ron cranked the car, and in the mirror noticed Sam still watching. Gritting his teeth, he put the car in gear and eased down on the gas. He was going little faster when he reached the main road and turned right toward Cordova.

But halfway there he picked up the car phone and punched in Sam's number.

His dad answered, sounding sleepy.

"Tell Sam he can still use the pool if he wants to," Ron told him quickly. "Oh, and I guess he can also use the forge. He knows where the keys are."

"Who *is* this?" Sam's dad demanded.

Ron didn't answer, because at the moment, he was no longer sure himself.

PART III

ON THE ROAD AGAIN

Interlude 8

Mother and Child Reunion

Near The Realm of the Winds
Tuesday, June 18—just before midnight

"HAS HE GONE?" asks the Master of Dreams.

"Not yet," the Midnight Man replies. *"He will soon, though, I am certain."*

"ARE YOU?"

"Aye."

"YOU HAVE BEEN CERTAIN BEFORE, OH MY BROTHER; WHAT HAS CHANGED THIS TIME?"

"This time we have burned away all the dross, leaving only pure substance. One more tempering and it will be complete."

"OR BROKEN."

"He will not break."

"YOU'VE SAID THAT BEFORE—YET HE DID NOT RETAIN HIS TEMPER."

(A sigh.) *"I thought the bond would be stronger, I thought the center would be more secure. With the center secure I thought he would be more willing to do what he ought."*

"WELL, HE HAS LEFT IT NOW—FOR GOOD OR ILL."

"Aye."

"AND WHAT OF US? IS THE TIME NEAR?"

"It is—"

"IT IS," a new voice interrupts, affirming. "OH YES, MY SONS, IT IS."

"MOTHER?"

"AYE."

"You have found us."

"YOU HID VERY WELL."

"WE WERE NOT HIDING—NO MORE THAN WE HAD TO IN ORDER TO WORK OUR WILL."

"YOU HID EVEN FROM YOURSELF—THAT IS WELL, *very* WELL."

"You approve?"

"AS MUCH AS I EVER DO."

"AND YOU . . . THINK WE WILL BE SUCCESSFUL?"

"I THINK IF YOU ARE NOT, YOU WILL HAVE TO START OVER—AT THE BEGINNING."

"Thanks for the encouragement."

"YOU SOUND LIKE ONE OF THEM."

"HE SOUNDS LIKE HIM."

"HIM?"

"THE BOY."

"AH."

"Speaking of whom . . ."

"YES," she says, anticipating. "THERE IS NO MORE YOU CAN DO HERE, SO I SUPPOSE THE TIME HAS COME FOR YOU TO WAKE HIM."

"AND IF WE DO?"

"HE WILL BE CHANGED. BUT MAY NEVER HAVE TO CHANGE AGAIN."

"Well, then," says the Midnight Man, *"let's to it."*

"MORNING WILL BE SOON ENOUGH," the Master of Dreams replies. *"BESIDES, YOU TOLD ME I COULD DO IT."*

"Mother . . . ?"

"YES?"

"Will we meet again?"

"IT IS TO BE HOPED THAT WHEN WE MEET AGAIN IT WILL BE FOREVER."

"UNTIL THEN . . ."

"UNTIL THEN . . . LET US PRAY FOR PEACE."
"Peace."
"PEACE."
"PEACE."

Chapter 15

Hit the Road, Jack

Erin Welch's house
Before midnight

Ron was not certain if the culprit was coffee or his endocrine system, but whichever the malefactor was, he'd have derived considerable pleasure from giving it a swift kick in the figurative ass just then. For while there were many things he was uncertain of, as he paced the moonlit length of the back hall in his home-in-exile, one thing he did know with absolute conviction was that he would get no sleep anytime soon. And he knew he ought to if he was going to do anyone any good, much less Lew.

And even worse (so he decided, as he crossed into the relative darkness between the obelisks of moonbeams shafting down from the four skylights that pierced the ceiling at ten-foot intervals), he didn't even know whom to blame the whole mess on.

He was one possibility, of course, given that far more than most folks, he was master of his fate. But it was much more convenient to blame Lew for splitting and leaving him anchorless and then getting into trouble, or Brandy for not understanding and throwing him out, or Sam for proving capricious and unreliable. The Head might be a good choice too, for it was that construction's croaked advice that had sent Ron seeking satisfaction from Donson Gwent. That he had got none was not the automaton's fault. Which left Gwent as proximate, if not ultimate, cause.

But could the playwright help it if he'd asked hard questions in response to Ron's own preposterous queries? Probably not. Ron didn't even want to think what he might have done if a raving loony had dragged *him* away from one of his projects and started making accusations.

So . . . ?

Well, he couldn't sleep because he was too wired, and he couldn't fool with The Head because his eyes were fried from a day's close work on it already, never mind how trembly his hands were likely to be.

And then it came to him: so obvious it was like the chiming of a small silver bell. Half-seriously he glanced up to see if the shaft of illumination around him came from one of those cartoon light bulbs above his head. But it was only the skylight. Only the moon's rays filtered through blue polarized glass.

He would leave! But not tomorrow as he'd intended; no, he'd split *now*: tonight! There was no good reason to hang around here, after all; so he would follow the one bit of Gwent's advice that truly made sense and hit the road. He would have anyway, come morning. Or maybe not; sleep had a way of dulling conviction, of stifling motivation.

But he was motivated now. Boy, *was* he! Nodding fiercely, he stopped and slammed his fist in the wall, as if to ascertain whether his sudden infection with ambition was in fact the product of a waking mind.

The hand throbbed obligingly—and left a handsome dent in the wallpapered gypsum board. Ron giggled edgily, then fished out his keys and jogged, as best his leg permitted, to the carport, where, not five minutes before, he had tucked the Centauri. It was, he noted when he cranked it, a bit more than an hour until midnight.

Omen time, then.

If he remembered.

That interval passed very quickly indeed, and well before the end, Ron was already surprised at how much he had accomplished. He was also, less satisfactorily, wondering if he had made a mistake by determining to boogie now. Tomorrow he could have secured a van or a station wagon or even a truck. As it was (the little-used T-Bird being still at Brandy Hall), he had to make do with trying to store a vast array of equipment in, on, over, around, and through a low (though wide and fairly long) handmade sports car.

Crouched as it was in the bright moonlight of the yard behind the house (and thereby closer to Ron's bedroom and the studio, thus diminishing lugging distance), it was impossible to discern *any* of the Centauri's original paint through the lashed-on encrustations—the trunk itself being full of the most delicate of Ron's equipment. (He could not bear to abandon it, and knew he would need something to fiddle with while he was away. The fact that he might actually have to work for a living—or appear to—was also not lost on him.) Beyond that, he had the crutch and three changes of clothes in a duffel bag: two for hot weather, one for cool. He had minimal cooking utensils along with a hot plate and the minifridge in the trunk he'd previously hooked into the AC to keep drinks cold. He also had a minimum of food. He had a ton of plastic money in his wallet and a wad of bills of middle denominations in the pocket of his black fatigues. He had a two-man tent, which filled most of the passenger footwell, and a sleeping bag in the seat above it; he had a portable generator that ran on ambient light (an idea he had stolen from the Road Man, and which, if patented, would have made him richer than Scrooge McDuck, except that he didn't want to be); he had an anvil usable for half a dozen other functions.

And he had raw materials: hammer and tongs, bellows, and, more to the point, lengths of bar stock of every alloy and base metal he could think of, with many of them duplicated in sheets, ingots, and tubing. Most had been strapped to the sides or deck (and in one case, when at the last minute, he remembered something he positively could not do without and yet had no room for), on the hood. There was ruddy copper and sultry gold, gleaming silver and haughty chrome. Pretentious platinum and doughty iron. Lead and zinc (for brass), tin (for bronze). There was beryllium and manganese, molybdenum and niobium. And there was poisonous mercury, which ran like water; and magnesium, which burned most dazzlingly.

Finally, there were three things Ron had consciously omitted.

One was a telephone, for if he was severing bonds, he wanted them severed well and truly.

The second was books, either reference or for entertainment. If he didn't know enough to get by in the world by now, he was in trouble. If he absolutely *had* to know something, he had money, and there were always bookstores and libraries.

Finally, he went without music. Or more properly, without CDs, since the changer took up valuable space in the trunk, and the Blaupunkt radio in the dash required very little. Besides, though he didn't like the idea, he feared he was going to have to trust in the omens now, and for some reason was reminded of a Roger Zelazny novel about a guy in a pickup truck on an endless interstate, with a PC reduced to the microdot atop a lowercase "i" in a copy of *Flowers of Evil* as his only companion.

Yeah, sure.

And the odd thing, he noted, as a glance at his watch showed him hard on the heels of the witching hour, was that he was at least as wired as he'd been an hour before.

Very well, he'd drive all night, or until he either fell asleep and hit something or something hit him. After that . . . who knew? Meanwhile, he'd take a long hot soak, since it'd probably be his last for a while. And he'd fix himself one more good hot meal, have one more cup of noncampfire coffee, and await the first omen of the new day. If he got a good one, he'd follow it up. If he got incomprehensible garbage, he'd look no farther. Nor would he be able to, probably, not without *The Concordance*.

He decided to forgo the hot bath, though, in the interest of time and because he feared it would make him sleepy (which was no longer the grail of his existence it had been less than an hour before). Instead, he forced himself to undergo a five-minute pounding with the coldest water the shower could dial up—which left him shivering and goose bumped, but alert; then dressed as before: black fatigues, black T-shirt, black Reeboks, black multipocket vest.

While he waited for the pot to stop producing Hazelnut Gevalia, and for a loaf of French bread to start toasting in the oven, he busied himself alternately rendering a stick of butter, a pinch of tarragon, and half a bulb of garlic into a suitable liquid, and contriving the assassination of the large lobster he'd bought two days before for no more reason than that it looked likely to die of neglect in the Cordova Kroger otherwise—and a quiet death in vain was worse than a violent one in glory. It lived—existed, better say—in a state of hibernation, wrapped in damp newspapers in the vegetable crisper in the fridge. And did not even protest overmuch when Ron picked it up. Nor did it thrash when the steam from the pot boiling on the stove rushed up to engulf it. It seemed resigned to its fate, which one way or another was to be eaten. A simple existence, Ron decided, with a twinge of jealousy: one outcome and no options save slight variations as to execution. And absolutely no hard choices.

He wished *his* life were that simple.

Midnight and its attendant mojo found him exactly the same time as Matty Groves: just as he'd shucked the smaller section of the second claw, but before he'd dipped it.

"Crossroads."

Goddamn *"Crossroads"*!

He should have known!—and cursed the unseen Lords of Omens roundly for their lack of imagination. That one turned up so often at crucial junctures that it was like a bad joke: a cosmic taunt, as it were. Shoot, it had even appeared when Martha had died; and, according to Dion, had been part of the array the day Ron had had his life-changing fall as well.

And of course he knew what it meant; God knew he'd looked it up often enough: *change; choices; risk of soul if the choice was wrong; possible encounter with the Devil.*

As if the road could hold more devils than were already plunging pitchforks into his psyche.

He ate faster, scowling when the Covering song wound up Simon and Garfunkel's "America," which meant a journey or quest, which Ron already knew he was on the verge of without being told by voices, however angelic, or guitars.

Matty Groves got the coral, the small claws, one of the heels of the loaf, and all the milk that remained in the fridge.

Ron drank Château Elán white wine in honor of his mom, and chased it with a shot of Matthew's sherry in honor of Lew, and left Matty to his crunchings and lappings.

Now to secure the house, grab the toiletries he had almost forgotten (along with two rolls of TP) from the bath, retrieve Matty, and he could hit the road.

He had just reprogrammed the locks on the garage and front door and was trying to think of something clever to use for the back one, when his progress brought him past the studio. The light was thick there: silver-blue, legacy of the double whammy of skylight and window. He did not expect to hear anyone speak—and therefore jumped half out of his skin when a weak voice creaked, *"Take meeeeee! Do not leave me behind, for I may be of service to you!"*

When Ron had regained sufficient composure to enter the studio, it was to find The Head exactly as he had left it: plates askew, features sprung and melted, with one eye heat crazed to blindness and the other blinking expectantly at him.

"There's no room," he grunted dumbly.

"Then perhaps youdbettermake . . . some. I prefer moonlight; or, if I can not get it, the light of the sun. But if necessary, you canplugmeinto the . . . cigarette lighter."

The Head, Ron had concluded sometime later, was rather like a surrogate (and with its ruin of a face, ugly) plastic Jesus, where it lay wedged between the red leather dashboard and the windshield, with a hastily contrived power cord connecting (per its insistence) to a hole in the center of the dash where the "accessory" plug (Ron abhorred smoking) had been. Oh, it wasn't made of either blow-molded butyl or phosphorus (to give due credit to the ancient traveling ditty which he knew from *Cool Hand Luke*), but it was, after a fashion, guiding the way.

"For both of us," Ron finished aloud to Matty Groves, who, expensively full and pleased with himself, was endeavoring to sleep, appropriately enough, atop Ron's sleeping bag, which occupied most of the passenger bucket.

Unfortunately for Matty, it also put him just below eye level with The Head, which had a way of looking at him hungrily, of licking its slightly skewed lips as if it might bite.

Ron wondered what Matty thought of their odd companion. And, more to the point, what the companion thought of them, and of itself.

They had been traveling for nearly an hour, which put it just shy of 1:00 A.M. And going south and west because that was what The Head had suggested, and because the driving was easier there on the fringe of the flatlands—and because, when they reached the first crossroads, it had been easier to turn that way. The landscape was nondescript: long hills, gentle curves, all bracketed by clumps of mostly pine forest alternating with sweeps of open land. Rarely was he out of sight of a house, but the overall effect was still rural. He made a point of avoiding towns. The sky was clear; the stars as bright as the moon allowed.

As for the omens, Ron had been so alarmed by The Head's serendipitous reactivation that he'd missed one, and the rest all had to do with travel one way or another, which, again, he already knew.

Lately, though, an idea had been fermenting. Alabama wasn't that far away, and Alabama lay in another time zone. If Ron got on it (which he needed little incentive to do; the car was working fine), he could make it by the change of the hour, and thus be primed for another mess of mojo.

Or was that cheating? he wondered, wishing he'd brought *The Concordance.*

"What do *you* think?" he asked aloud, whether to Matty or The Head was not clear. Matty slept on but twitched a paw. The Head shifted its remaining eye in his direction. "Aboutwhat?" it wondered.

"About whether it's cool to cross time zones so you can collect more mojo."

"I think you don't need todothat when you've got me," The Head replied placidly. Whereupon it scrunched up its eyes, furrowed its forehead, and grunted resoundingly. The radio promptly emitted a puff of smoke and a bad smell, and fell silent.

"Well shit," Ron said, and drove on.

"Next time youcan, turn west," The Head announced thirty minutes later. The only change in the landscape was that the forest/field ratio had shifted in favor of the former.

"Why?" Ron asked, glancing across but avoiding its gaze. Matty had changed positions twice, but still slept. Ron's eyes felt big as saucers, but his back was getting tired. He yawned.

"Because that's theway your brotheris."

Ron was instantly full alert. "Lew? But how . . . ? Is he all right?"

"That which blockshim relaxed foramoment, allowing me to find him."

"But . . . how *is* he?"

"I said I foundhim," The Head retorted. "Yet I know nomore than I did. It is like . . . a library. You can see a book, and knowitforwhat it is, but that does not mean you know what itcontains."

Ron nodded grimly. "Great."

"If you were tostrikeme, I could speak moreclearly."

Ron started at the non sequitur, then reached over and thumped The Head smartly on its right cheek.

"Better?"

"Better," it confirmed. "Now, as to your brother: The . . . vigilance seems to weaken occasionally, more so at night, and roughly once an hour. Maybe in another while Iwillbeable to . . . be morespecific."

Ron thwacked it again, but did not speak otherwise.

"Brandy," The Head stated amiably.

"What about her?" Ron yawned, squinting through the windscreen as the lights of an oncoming semi nearly blinded him.

"She misses you but does not want to admit as much. And she is afraid: afraid she has lost you, and afraid the play will not happen, and increasingly afraid that Donson Gwent is not what he seems."

"Is he? Is Donson Gwent really what he claims to be? A schizo prodigy with personality problems out the wazoo that make him hide his Voice?"

"It is possible. But so are other things."

Ron flicked it a searching glance. "Such as?"

The Head did not reply, merely peered, one-eyed, at the trailing moon. "Some are in your thoughts already," it said at last, "it would therefore be foolish for me to waste my words on them. Others . . . I cannot say now, except that there is something odd."

A scowl. "Why not? And like what?"

"It is . . . a thing better discovered by the light of the sun than of the moon."

Ron rolled his eyes in disgust. "You sound like the fucking Road Man!"

"He does that often?" The Head inquired promptly.

"What?"

"Fuck."

Ron caught the phraseology. His eyes narrowed. "*Does*, or *did*?"

"Since he presumably has no Voice, I have no way of knowing. I have not heard that he is dead, but neither have I encountered thought of him in anyone alive, saving yourself, W. G. Montgomery, Brandy Wallace, and Donson Gwent. Gwent thinks of him as a thing apart, by the way. Then again, Gwent's thoughts are . . . unconventional."

"In what way?"

"He . . . thinks many things at once. And sometimes he does *not* think. There are layers intertwined with layers."

"I know," Ron yawned again. "Maybe we'll fool with him later when my brain's not fried. But back to the Road Man: *I* usually try to find someone who's interacting with folks like him—folks that don't have Voices. The Voiceless can still affect the Voices of others, in other words."

"Is that what you call them?"

"Who?"

"The Road Man and his ilk. The Voiceless?"

Ron scowled and swerved to miss a road kill. Matty stirred and sniffed unconscious disapproval of squashed skunk. "I guess I do now. I mean, there's no *other* collective term for 'em that I've heard—if there's even more than one, and not just one screwed-up, unstuck entity."

"Unstuck?"

"In time. Vannister—if he was the Road Man—was younger than the one who actually called himself that. And if Gwent's part of the pattern, which he may or may not be, he's younger yet."

"Like Merlin?"

"Merlin?"

"A friend of mine—if we ever got a chance to meet. He lived backward in time, according to some. That is where he got his skill at prophecy: because he had already lived future events."

Ron gnawed his lip thoughtfully for a a moment Then: "It makes more sense to assume he was a Listener."

"Jesus too?"

"A Listener?" Ron considered this for a moment. "Sure, why not? He kinda fits the pattern."

"You're wrong."

"I am?"

"There is at least one Voice I can Hear that knew him."

"Gimme a break!"

The Head chuckled. "To match that which disfigures my skull? I doubt you would enjoy it."

Once again Ron fell silent, and drove.

"South, then west, then east," The Head piped up after an hour-long lull in which Ron was certain it had snored. He was getting really tired now, and his mind had slipped into a sort of dreamy introspective fugue that had little to recommend it, save that he was doing it in Alabama. Grunting, he powered the seat into a new position, and wished he hadn't lost the radio. There were more fields now, and the land was flatter. Towns had grown scarce. He still had half a tank of gas.

"Sam," he said to The Head.

"Samuel Bradley Foster?" The Head replied promptly. "What about him?"

"Can I rely on him?"

"Why do you ask?"

"Because," Ron snapped, "I've had piss-poor luck finding folks on whom I can."

The Head pondered (or Listened, or consulted Higher Forces, or whatever it did) for a moment. Then: "There *is* no Sam."

"What do you mean, there's no Sam? Of *course* there's a Sam."

"No . . . oh, yes there is—*now*."

"Huh?"

"He was not, and then he was. Perhaps he was deep asleep. Perhaps I malfunctioned."

"You can Hear people when they sleep?"

"Only if they dream or are otherwise agitated."

"Interesting."

"You asked about Sam Foster?"

"Oh yeah, right. So what've you got?"

"He likes you as much as he likes anyone," The Head began. "And in a sense considers you his best friend. But he is confused because you are so much older than he yet do not act like it. He is accustomed to reading people your age one way, and since you do not fit, he does not always know how to behave around you. Complicating the situation is the fact that you seem to have fixed on *him* as a hero. This disconcerts him, for he does not like being a hero *to* a hero."

"I *was* his hero, then? Christ!"

"No longer, I do not think; not so much as you were. He has now seen the low along with the high, seen your neuroses and inadequacies, your fits and depressions and incompetencies and tempers. A hero should not have those."

"But why did he betray me?"

"He does not consider it betrayal. He was not thinking of you at all when he linked up with Donson Gwent, only that in Gwent he had found a place to learn certain things he could not learn from you. And since your availability is relatively assured, and Gwent's is transitory, he chose to follow the more perishable option."

"Opportunistic little sucker," Ron growled.

"Again, he does not think so. But he likes to learn, and, like you, prefers to take the path of least resistance when confronted with a problem. Too, he is accustomed to being in control, and feared you were trying too much to control him— when, in fact, you are exactly the same way yourself."

"Maybe I oughta call you Freud," Ron mused.

"Perhaps you should," The Head replied. "I would not like it, though. Oh, and when you can, turn north."

"Am I doing the right thing?" Ron asked an hour before sunrise, but with the sky already pinkening in the east, which was in his rearview mirror. He did not even know what state he was in (besides confusion). Nor did he care.

"You mean the *correct* thing?"

"Whatever."

"If you mean: Have you chosen the proper option by actively pursuing what you most require in order to be happy? Certainly. The alternative is stagnation and frustration. Granted there is more risk, but also there is more reward. And if Brandy and Sam are worth having, they will understand and wait for you."

"Odd, that: that you speak of them as equal."

"But they are—in a sense. You are one of those in whom both male and female principles are strongly manifested. Certain parts of your personality respond best to women, certain parts to men. You need a lover *and* a best friend. Ideally they should be the same, but usually it is not possible, because your male aspect does not like explaining things that to another male are intuitively obvious, and your female side tires of having to suppress feelings that are natural to both genders, but permitted to only one. There are other reasons too, of course."

"I'll have to think about that 'un for a while," Ron said.

—And did, until just before sunrise.

"One more question, and I'll let you rest," Ron yawned.

"I do not tire," The Head replied. "But ask."

"Our sister: Was Lew right to seek her out?"

"Why did he seek her?"

"Because someone needs to be Master after him. Because— I guess 'cause he thinks it's his responsibility."

"It is a bad thing to impose one's will on another," The Head informed him. "To do so is one of the bases of crime, if not actually of sin."

"What do you mean?"

"If one imposes one's will on another, one is effectively co-opting that person's time. If for *time*, we substitute *life*, we see how awful that may be. For if you examine ethics carefully, everything you regard as a crime is really theft of time."

"How so?"

"Theft of goods would be no problem if a person did not then have to spend time he would otherwise use in some other way to regain what he has lost."

"Interesting. But what about murder?"

"The grandest theft of time possible. It robs one of the rest of one's life."

"Assault or . . . rape?"

"Take time to recover from, both physically and mentally. Cause time to be spent worrying or fearing that would not otherwise have been expended so."

"Adultery?"

"Once found out, it is theft of the time it takes to build love and trust, never mind worry and, again, fear. One must duplicate effort that has already been expended instead of expending one's efforts creating something new."

"I think," Ron told Matty Groves carefully, as he reached over to scratch between his ears, "that I may have created a monster."

The sun was tantalizing the horizon when a sharp tug from the steering wheel, coupled with a grinding sound from the right front, told Ron he had just run off the road. He jerked the wheel left—too hard—putting him neatly in the other lane. The windshield was suddenly full of Kenworth and his ears crammed with enraged air horns; but either his reflexes, the Centauri's suspension, or the Luck were up to the task of evasion, with the result that he *barely* made it back to the right side intact.

"Christ on lead sax!" he yelled—and swallowed hard. He had, he realized, just nodded off rather seriously. His heart was pumping like Dixie, and his overstressed adrenals found one final batch of hormone to pour into his bloodstream. Weak stuff though, scarcely worth the effort.

"I think," he whispered, though whether to The Head or Matty Groves he didn't know, "that it *may* be time to cash in for . . . uh, well, for whatever."

Matty, reasonably enough, did not reply; and since the matter addressed was imminent rather than remote, and actual rather than hypothetical, The Head was likewise silent.

Which left the small matter of deciding where. Not a
motel, that was a given. He had too much . . . *stuff* draped
across the car to leave it unattended in even the modicum of
civilization necessary to support a motel. And besides, most
of 'em wouldn't take cats and he didn't like being dishonest
about Matty. And *besides*, that violated the unspoken geas he
had laid on himself when he started out: to avoid civilization
and its myriad distractions until or unless the quest for Lew
led him there.

"Perhaps," he yawned to the quickly rushing air (no longer
so silent, now that the car's aerodynamics were spoiled by all
that surface clutter), "I should first find out where I am."

"It doesn't matter," The Head told him. "Last time you
said anything it was Alabama."

Ron shrugged—but slowed, so as to give the landscape
a better chance to register. It could have been anywhere in
half a dozen states, he concluded. Shoot, it could easily have
been in the more open parts of good old Welch County itself,
if the surrounding terrain was any indication. He had chosen
back roads deliberately, so as to be less anchored in space,
in which undertaking he was succeeding in spades—this one
was two-lane blacktop, only moderately potholed, but with
a hefty drop-off to shoulders that were rather more sandy
than stony or made of clay. There were few houses, but a
fair number of wide grassy fields (which seemed odd), and
a reasonably even mix of open land and forests, mostly pine.
There were hills but few curves. And the local road kills
of choice seemed to be skunks, 'coons, and 'possums. No
armadillos, which meant he wasn't too far south.

The thing to do, then, was to camp, as had been his
intention all along. And since one of the tenets he lived
by was that it was easier to get forgiveness than permission,
he figured any field along the road would do, provided it left
him a quick escape route, and he didn't have to share it with
cows or other indigenous (or clumsy) livestock. Wildlife of
the conventional sort, he thought he could manage.

The perfect place presented itself a mile down the road: a
field of broom sedge perhaps fifteen acres in extent, paral-
leling one side of a decently long straightaway (which gave
him good sight lines, should he feel a need for surveillance).

Woods bracketed it on three sides, displaying at one corner the lusher vegetation that indicated water. Across the road was more of the same, except the fields were wider and cut into irregular blotches by lines of trees. None were planted in crops that needed working, though, being mostly hay or simply left fallow. Oh, and there was a thumbledown house across the way: two stories and warp-boarded, like something out of an Andrew Wyeth painting.

And, wonder of wonders, even a fossilized access road. He eased off there, feeling the suspension work but not bottom on the overgrown surface, as he maneuvered the car to a point near one end, approximately equidistant between road and woods—maybe seventy yards from each. The sun had barely cleared the horizon when he turned off the ignition and climbed out. A pause to stretch, yawn, pee, and consume two donuts and a thermos-cup of tepid coffee, and he set to work.

The tent proved true to its advertising and took exactly three minutes to erect—once he'd found a place where the pervasive sedge was less than waist-high. That accomplished, it required little longer to point the collector on the generator at the sun (more a matter of efficiency than necessity) and set the battery to charging—which would eventually make the hot plate viable. While Matty looked for mice, Ron sought out water, and found it where he expected, in a ravine behind the field. The tiny brook there was too shallow to swim in, but he managed to rinse his upper half reasonably well. The water tasted like growing things. And thanks to the Luck, any illness he gained thereby would likely be temporary.

When he returned, The Head was singing softly to itself, "Lily, Rosemary, and the Jack of Hearts." Ron raised an eyebrow and shrugged. Someone, he supposed, was thinking about that song now. Or maybe The Head had tapped into old Bobby D. himself. Now *there* was an interesting notion!

He giggled at that, snared his sleeping bag, untied it, and pitched it in an awkward half-curl into the opening of the tent, then crawled in. Once ensconced within the blue dome, he shucked his shoes, socks, and shirt, loosened his belt, and curled up. But just as he drifted off, he heard a voice: someone talking loudly.

Yawning, he crawled outside again—and saw no one. But then he caught it once more. It was The Head, the dratted Head!

"Hey!" it called from the Centauri's cockpit. "Are you going to leave me in here?"

"Why not?" Ron yawned, scratching his bare side.

"I would make a more effective sentry if I could see."

"Do I *need* a sentry?"

"You may."

"As you wish," Ron grunted. And with that, he removed the nearest bit of alloy tubing (a one inch diameter manganese-titanium blend suitable for aerospace applications), stuck it in the ground between the car and the tent, and stabbed The Head atop it like a fetish. Then, completely on impulse, he spent the next fifteen minutes ringing his campsite with similar outlandish constructions and odd machines. Brass and copper, one was: in sheets stacked like a man-sized house of cards; and adjoining it a make-do geodesic of titanium. A kinetic quasi robot lashed together from chrome tubes and duct tape was next over, and so on. In no case did he give conscious thought to design, effect, or execution. It was all done in highest haste on automatic, all his right-brain's fault. Fortunately, that hemisphere was clever like a fox.

After all, a lone car might attract attention he didn't want. An encampment as bizarre as his would more likely scare folks away.

He hoped.

And then he yawned.

And then, back inside his tent, he slept again, while the sun rode up the sky, Matty terrorized mice, and The Head ate sunbeams for breakfast.

Interlude 9

Love the One You're with

Alabama
Wednesday, June 19—sunset

"Did I frighten you Monday?" the Beautiful Lady asks.

He nods, for he was very frightened indeed—what with all that talk of death and suns and dying. And he remembers, which he has not before. It is almost as if he knows . . . *everything* about himself—everything he has forgotten these long dull days of eating and sleeping and watching the ghosts of sunsets stain the wall.

The ghosts are leaving his mind, too: almost he has a past; almost he recalls his name, his friends, his family. Almost he recalls the one who Called to him one morning—the Call out of the air that made the Beautiful Lady angry.

But she does not seem angry now. Rather, she is smiling in a way that is less hungry than typical, and her clothes are loose, where she stands, leaning against the doorframe. In fact, she seems to be wearing only one garment: a thin white robe so light and delicate that the slightest breeze from the unknown house beyond causes it to stir and reveal the shape of her body.

Her body . . . he has not seen a woman's body in a very long time.

"Two days ago I spoke of death," she tells him, closing the door and walking forward with light steps that make him look at her feet and see, to his surprise, that she is barefoot. Her feet are tiny, white, as smoothly delicate as the rest of her. "I spoke of death—but now I would rather we spoke of life."

"I would like that," he tells her, swallowing nervously, surprised that he can reveal so much of his own thoughts.

"I thought you would," she whispers. She is in front of him now, and she reaches out to him with slender hands. A finger brushes the front of his loose white shirt, hooks under his collar and, with gentlest pressure, encourages him to his feet. Wordlessly she brings her hands to his chest, where they toy with the topmost button. It opens. So does the next. So do they all. She slides the fabric back and he feels coolness brush his torso. He looks at her—straight into her eyes, for she is as tall as he. They are a familiar blue. Fondness shimmers there, and regret. She breaks that contact, and glances down, runs her palms across the taut masses of his pale and hairless chest, the flat plain of his belly. Nails tweak his nipples—once—twice. He swallows, takes a deep shuddering breath, and feels a long-banked fire roar to life in his loins.

She still has not spoken, nor does he want to speak. Instead, she guides his hands to her breasts and holds them there. He can feel the nipples harden through the thin silk. Only a moment it takes for him to release the ties that bind the robe to her shoulders, and she stands naked before him. A white goddess, whole and pure and utterly without flaw.

"Beautiful—" he gasps. "Beautiful!"

"As are you," she murmurs back. And now her hands find the waistband of his baggy gathered britches. They slip inside, one to either side. A single deft movement sends the garment to the floor where it puddles around his chains. She looks down again, and he knows that she knows that a once-dormant part of him is now awake. She teases him: runs her hands along his flanks, across the crests of his hips to cup his buttocks, then back to the front and up to once more tease his nipples, and then—down.

He gasps when she touches him, and touches her as well, feels flesh cool as an autumn morning, smooth as polished marble, firm as his own is firm. He touches her: *all* of her: breasts, thighs, the moist dark triangle between her legs that is so like yet unlike his own.

"Lie down," she whispers, and he does, chains and all, there where he stands on the emerald carpet. She straddles him. Before he knows it, he is in. Neither of them speak, save with hands and mouths and fingers. Eventually both are satisfied. She rolls off him, but does not leave; continues to lie beside him, teasing what parts of him she pleases. Each touch is electric.

"Tell me of the first time," she murmurs seriously, with no trace of madness or slyness or guile.

He swallows, tries to remember—and does! "I . . . was eleven," he says. "I have never told anyone this, not even my . . . do I *have* a brother?"

"Never mind," she murmurs dreamily.

"I was eleven," he begins again, his voice strangly distant, his words those of his *self* of those days. "My body was just starting to change—it was earlier than most of my friends. There was a woman came to visit my mother, and she had a daughter, older than me and very pretty. She thought I was . . . nice looking too, and she used to flirt and tease me. Finally one day we went for a walk. She told me she would show me her thing if I'd show her mine. I had never seen a woman . . . *there* before, and it seemed like a fair trade to me, so I said, 'Sure.' We were in the woods, on a carpet of moss and pine needles, and we took off our clothes— she would take off something, and then I would. She was naked first, and then I was, and she saw me, and said I was already starting to be a man, and then—"

"Why did you pause?"

"Because I have never told anyone this."

"But surely you can tell me."

"I . . . suppose, now that I've gone this far."

"You were saying?"

He sighs, then continues. "She asked me if I wanted to put it in her, and I said no, though I really did, real bad, which was obvious to her. So she asked why, and I said

I was scared of making babies. And she laughed and said I was too young to make babies, and she asked me if I'd ever made white sticky stuff come out of . . . it. And I said no, I hadn't, and she didn't say anything else, just grabbed me there and put it in her. And the rest . . . just happened."

"Did you . . . ?"

"I think I did. It . . . felt that way. It was the first time for that and a lot of things. And I guess it scared me and I didn't do it again for six years."

She gazes at him seriously. "Did you ever see the girl again?"

He shakes his head. "Not after the next weekend. She and her mom didn't live where I did, and my mom told me later to stay away from her, that she was a 'bad girl' "—for the first time in days he laughs—"she never knew it was already too late."

The Beautiful Lady stares at him curiously. "Oh," she says in a very small voice. She runs one nail from the top of his head down his nose and mouth and so down the trembling length of his body as far as she can reach. He gasps and closes his eyes.

"Did you enjoy that?" she asks, rising.

"I . . . did."

"Good," she replies, her voice suddenly gone to ice. "Because in two days I will kill you."

Interlude 10

Strangers in the Night

Near The Realm of the Winds
Wednesday, June 19—midnight)

"*Are you certain you don't want* me *to do this?*" the Midnight Man asks the Master of Dreams.

"*I AM SURE.*"

"*We* could *get one of the others . . .*"

"*DO YOU REALLY WANT TO WAKE THEM? YOU KNOW HOW HARD IT WAS TO MAKE THEM SLEEP.*"

"*They will wake anyway—when* he *does.*"

"*TRUE. BUT—*"

"*What?*"

"*I JUST DON'T THINK IT'S WISE.*"

"*At least wake the Sunrise Man.*"

"*MAYBE.*"

"*It's a basic courtesy.*"

"*SINCE WHEN WAS HE EVER COURTEOUS?*"

"*Since—oh, never mind. The time has come! Act now, or I will.*"

The Master of Dreams does not reply. Instead, he moves toward what *could* be called a door and opens it. It does not resist, though it has been closed for more than a year. On the other side he enters familiar country: the land of dreams. A boy's dreams.

"BOY?" he calls, there in that not-place that is yet more real than where he was. "BOY? IT IS TIME TO WAKE UP AND REMEMBER WHO YOU ARE."

The boy stirs in his narrow bed; he kicks the covers free, lies there naked and sweating, for a dream has suddenly become . . . something else. He tries to flee it, but it pursues. He gets a sense of voices, of people calling out to him: familiar voices, voices he has heard all his life. Voices of grown men, though he is still half a child. "Boy!" they cry to him: "Listen, boy; you are not who you say you are!— Not who you think you are!"

"Then who am I?" he asks, afraid—yet even more fearful not to. Curiosity is one of his curses.

"You are—" one begins.

"YOU ARE ME!" the Master of Dreams, interrupts. "YOU ARE THE ONE WHO STEALS DREAMS AND MAKES THEM SO THOROUGHLY YOUR OWN THAT THEY BECOME YOU."

"I am not!"

"YOU ARE! YOU STOLE EVERY DREAM A CERTAIN BOY HAD, AND EVERY THOUGHT, EVERYTHING HE KNEW, EVERYTHING THAT MADE HIM HIM. AND THEN YOU TOOK ALL THOSE DREAMS AND MADE A NEW YOU: A NEW PRESENT AND A WHOLE NEW PAST. AND WE LET YOU, MY BROTHERS AND I. WE HID, HERE IN THE NO-PLACE WHERE IT WOULD NEVER OCCUR TO YOU TO LOOK—NOT THAT LOOKING ITSELF WOULD EVER HAVE OCCURRED."

"No!"

"You are me," the Midnight Man says then. "I hid with my brother here, and hid my other brothers away so they would not be tempted to torment you. They who have tried to end all this and mostly failed."

("We have not!" other voices cry.)

"You're me," the Midnight Man continues. "And mine has been a perilous lot, for sometimes when you slept, I rode you and made you do certain things you do not recall. Perhaps *you remember being tired and not knowing why. That was me. I kept you up all night."*

"Doing what?"

"Making, mostly."

"Making . . . ?"

"You are me!" the Day Man interrupts. *"I was the smith who had the first forging. I was the lusty maker, the merry talker."*

"You are also me!" the Night Man chimes in. *"I was the one who kept my brother from betraying us all."*

"You are me!" drawls another Voice. *"You have heard me called Van Vannister, and I it was who woke the Earth itself to complete Brandy Hall. I it was, too, who was you before you were. I know how you feel, for I slept as a deer one night, and awoke itching the next day and found I was you."*

There are more: voices pouring through a long-shut door into his mind. He hears them all, though he hates it; yet still their song is a siren's call, and he cannot help but listen.

And then, of a sudden, he awakens.

"Jesus, oh Jesus!" he moans aloud. Rising, he staggers to the mirror, peers cautiously in—and sees a boy. "I liked me better before," he whispers. "At least then I thought I was human."

"IN A DAY, MORE OR LESS, IT WILL ALL BE OVER," a voice whispers coldly in his head, one he does not recognize.

"Cover your tracks!" cries another. *"For good or ill, it comes to a head tomorrow."*

"Tomorrow," he echoes, still looking in the mirror. And then his reflection becomes a blur—for he is crying.

Chapter 16

Sweet Home Alabama

Somewhere in Alabama
Thursday, June 20—morning

Ron had forgotten what it was like to wake up in the country—the *real* country, not a manicured estate like his mom's place back in Welch County, which just happened to be *in* the country. Or like Brandy Hall, which, though surrounded on three sides by honest-to-God old-growth forest and a quarter mile from the nearest highway, was always so full of people, and more to the point, of those people entertaining themselves (and frequently employing themselves) with the trappings of tech, one could scarcely hear oneself think. There was always a stereo blaring at Brandy Hall. Or a TV mumbling. Or someone was using a power tool or one of the gadgets in the kitchen. Never mind phones and faxes and intercoms.

No, this was more like Cardalba Hall at its most idyllic, when no one was home but Lew and a footholder. The road was far enough away there to muffle car sounds, leaving the creak and groan of old wood, and the buzz of flies and wasps that got in the many open windows (because Lew and Ron preferred fresh breezes to air-conditioning) as the only aural intrusions. And of course those same breezes brought the scent of grass and crops and livestock, not oil paint and exotic cooking and new-thrown clay.

This wasn't *quite* like that, Ron reflected, as he rolled over in his sleeping bag in order to accommodate Matty Groves's latest sharp-clawed caprice; for he could still hear the rumble-and-swish of traffic, but muffled and unobtrusive. More to the point, though, he could hear bobwhites chirping iambs in the broom sedge, and the twitters and clucks and trills of other birds he should have recognized and didn't coming from the nearby woods. Somewhere a squirrel chittered a nervous greeting to the sun. Ron waited for a cock to crow. None did.

It was light, though, and he wondered how long he'd slept. Hours would have been a reasonable guess based on how refreshed he felt—but not a good one. That would have put the time near midday, and the quality of the light filtering through the blue nylon around him was too soft for that. There was a trace of humidity in the air, too, which likewise hinted of morning. It was all very confusing. Ron yawned, stretched, and took a deep breath. He smelled grass: growing and mown.

He also needed, very badly, to pee.

Grunting, he slipped out of the sleeping bag (which forced him farther into the shallow recesses of the tent), and crawled on all fours across the lumpy nylon to the door, his fly already undone.

He straightened into mist: a chest-high layer of residual morning fog lying like gauze across the yellow/green field, with the darker bulks of trees rising out of it like cliffs above the sea. The sky was pale too: white and tired, but rapidly leaching energy from a sun that had newly risen. A fine morning. *Damned* fine.

But first things first.

He had set up the tent facing the woods, with the car to his present left, parallel to, but sixty yards from, the highway beyond. It was, therefore, not unrealistic to assume that it was safe to flop *it* out and let fly with no more than a cursory reconnoiter. Certainly the ten feet he could see at all showed nothing more human than The Head still affixed to the pole where he had stranded it the night before. Lifted above the mist, as it was, it caught the light of the newborn sun and glittered and sparked like a thing of gilded flame. A fine effect.

Almost as fine as an empty bladder.

It was perhaps the longest whizz on record, begun four yards from the front of the tent and concluded when, by sudden mindless impulse, Ron determined to write his name in urine across a strip of sandy ground that ran from the north side of the tent to the woods. He had, in fact, medium sufficient to complete an uppercase, yard-high *Ron,* continue through *Ronald,* and begin his middle name before stream became trickle became drops. Sighing, he gave his never-named friend a final thorough shake, stowed him, and turned back toward camp.

Something made a noise at that: an abrupt rustling. Ron was instantly on guard, lodged between alertness and embarrassment. But it was only a yearling buck bounding away through the fog to be lost in paleness, its white flag of a tail vanishing before the rest. No surrender there; strategic retreat for sure.

Gettin' rusty, he told himself. *Gettin' careless.* No way the Ron Dillon of a few years ago would've called so much attention to himself. No wonder the poor critter had spooked. He'd made enough noise (including a minute's worth of splattering) to send a whole herd hopping. Never mind the odor, which he couldn't catch but the deer probably could.

Something was bugging him, though; and it took a moment (muzzy-headed as he was) to focus on it. It was the sun—or maybe the quality of light. More specifically, it was the fact that, based on the primary's position, not nearly enough time had elapsed between his falling asleep and his waking again for this fog to have waxed and partly waned as it obviously had done. No way his bladder could have swelled from empty to full so quickly, either. And damned *sure* no way the sun could have progressed such a short way across the sky.

Unless . . .

He checked his watch. Only an hour had elapsed.

Unless . . .

A nail against a button on the Casio's side showed the

date. One day after it should be. He had, in effect, slept
twenty-five hours!

In a field in what he presumed was Alabama.

Undisturbed.

He prayed.

A sudden fear struck him, and he limped the few yards
back to camp, saw nothing out of the ordinary beyond the
fact of the camp itself. The tent was untouched, the Centauri
seemed to be fine, and the circle of unlikely constructions
appeared undisturbed, while The Head was exactly where
he'd left it. If it was aware of his scrutiny, it didn't look
it, for both its eyes were closed and its mouth slack in a
way Ron would not have anticipated. "You can't possibly
be asleep," he growled in its general direction, but did not
try to awaken (preposterous concept) the contraption.

It was then that he saw the ribbon.

A blue ribbon two inches wide and a yard long, made of
what looked like antique satin, draped around the juncture
of Head and pole.

Ron froze. His shields shot up, instantly closing off his
mind, then lowered again with greater caution. He shut his
eyes, took three breaths . . .

He was right.

"You there," he called, facing the Centauri and thereby
the road. "You can come out now."

A movement in the grass followed, accompanied by a
rustling of stems, the buzz of denim against denim, and a
muffled and decidedly self-righteous female voice hissing,
"I *told* you so!"

Evidently the voice belonged to the younger of two slender
girls who rose through the thinner fog beyond the Centauri.
Or to judge by the indignant expression twisting those round,
pug-nosed features, the speaker was she. A child then: nine or
ten, max. And her . . . sister? Or, barely possibly, mom? Ron
couldn't decide, as he could not determine whether the taller
one was girl or woman. Probably sister, though, he concluded,
to judge by the kid's put-upon tone. And pretty—very pretty,
with smooth blond hair and a heart-shaped face accented by
strong dark brows and brown eyes that sparked with a secret
mischief. Both she and her accomplice were wearing matching

jeans, Auburn University T-shirts, and sneakers. She *might* have been old enough to have come by it honestly.

"You've been wantin' to *know* for a *day,* Alice!" the younger girl continued impatiently, stabbing her taller companion's side with an elbow. "So, go ahead, sis! *Ask*'im!"

The older girl . . . woman, whatever . . . blushed, then grimaced, and then looked Ron in the eye. "Are you the Road Man?" she asked seriously, neither fearful nor apologetic.

"You look like pictures of 'im our granny has," the younger girl chimed in helpfully. Whereupon she glared up at her companion and tugged on the hem of her T-shirt. "Okay, so, can we go now?"

Alice—was that what the kid had called her?—shook her head. "We were pretty sure of that before we got here. But now that we're here, we . . . uh, might as well get acquainted."

All this was nominally addressed to the Munchkin, but it was also said with Alice's eyes fully fixed on Ron. Varying parts at different times, to be sure, as though he were an overdressed and undergroomed centerfold. Not until their eyes actually met, though, did Ron realize that his fly was still open. He buttoned it hastily, knowing even as he did that he was calling attention to the item in question more surely than ignoring it ever would have done.

"*Are* you the Road Man?" Alice repeated. And this time an eyebrow lifted. Based on her seriousness and confidence, Ron pegged her estimated age at eighteen. A very youthful and unselfconscious eighteen.

"Not at the moment," he replied, truthfully and confused— and amazed at having phrased his response that way.

The girl's eyes narrowed suspiciously. "Are you *ever* him?" she countered quickly.

Ron wasn't prepared for *that* degree of syntactic subtlety at all. Not here in the wilds of rural Alabama (if that was where he was). Not hardly. "Well, uh, I guess I *do* live on the Road sometimes," he mumbled, feeling a sudden urge to be cryptic and mysterious and, he hoped, regain the ground his earlier faux pas had abandoned. "And I expect you can see I'm male, though I don't really think of myself as a man."

Alice's eyebrow lifted higher. Her sister sniggered into her hand, her cheeks rosy.

It was Ron's turn to blush, having just realized that he had no idea when these visitors had actually arrived (though by foot, presumably; he'd have heard a car), but that there was a good chance that (fog not withstanding) they'd seen him pirouetting, pecker in hand, across the field, annotating the ground with soggy calligraphy in his wake. "Been there long?" he asked, before he could stop himself.

"Long enough to get bored," Alice replied, with a trace too much twinkle in her eye. "Long enough to see some things. Long enough to wonder if you were gonna sleep through *this* day too."

Ron gaped incredulously. "You've been here *that* long?"

Alice shook her head. "I left and came back. Had to, or Mom would've had a cow."

"They's cows in this field, sometimes," the Munchkin informed him solemnly. "They get out a lot."

"Now that the barbed wire's gone, I'm not surprised."

Ron stared at them stupidly. "Barbed wire?"

"You must've broken it when you pulled in here." From Alice.

Ron kicked at a clod. "*Great!*" he groaned. "All I *need's* some farmer showin' up with a shotgun wantin' to know what I've done with Bossy."

"The gate was closed," Alice told him. "I think they're using the other field—so you can stop worrying. You won't get shot. Not if you're the Road Man."

Ron relaxed a trifle. "It's that big a deal, huh?"

The girl shrugged. "Some say. Some say the Road Man brings luck," she added speculatively.

Ron stared at her askance. "Luck, huh?"

She nodded. "I'd say so. I mean look, here we are: two girls alone with a strange man, and we're carrying on a perfectly civilized conversation. That'd be pretty lucky in some places."

"So we are," Ron sighed, more impressed by the moment with Alice's boldness and subtle-yet-sophisticated practicality. "So you *really* think I'm the Road Man, huh?" he asked conversationally, intending to follow up with the revelation that he wasn't. But something stopped him.

Alice studied him for a long moment. "Well, Missy here's right: You do sorta look like him—only maybe a little younger," she hedged. "And there're a bunch of crazy machines all around. And the rest fits, allowing for temporal continuity."

The child glared at her impatiently. "Who're you tryin' to impress with them big words, Alice Mary?"

Alice ignored her. "I meant that—"

Ron's nod cut her off. "That I'm driving a car, not the wagon you expected, or have heard about? That I've got a cat instead of a bunch of goats, and all that?"

Alice nodded. "I reckon times change, even for legends."

Ron pondered the wisdom of that. "I reckon they do."

"So . . . *are* you him?"

Ron took a deep breath. "Let's just say I've heard of him, and from what I've heard, he'd be pretty pissed if somebody pretended to be him and wasn't."

Now, why had he said that? He no more wanted to be mistaken for the Road Man than the man in the moon. Nor had it even occurred to him until that very minute that the way he'd set up his camp mirrored almost exactly that in which he had first encountered the strange wandering tinker. That had to have been subconscious. Except, the older he got, the less he trusted in accidents.

Besides, it was *fun* exchanging barbs with this girl, if for no other reason than because he knew it could lead to nothing. While it continued, it was entertaining; if he got too annoying, she'd no doubt leave; and if she pushed too far, he'd ask her to split. And as soon as that happened (and he'd have to run her off pretty soon, regardless) he'd be shut of her for good. Was there, therefore, any harm in injecting a bit of wonder (or at least whimsy) into what was probably a prosaic existence? Besides, she seemed to be enjoying his company, to think he was important, even. And what with Brandy's preoccupation and Sam's defection, he could *stand* to feel special for a while.

"Which means you *are?*" Alice's question jerked him back to reality. Matty Groves sauntered out of the tent, rubbed Ron's leg as he hadn't done in ages, and begged to be picked up.

"Our granny says that if you ask somebody somethin' three times, they have to tell you," the younger girl piped up, her eyes fixed on the cat. "And Alice has asked you three times now."

"Not precisely," Alice told her. But then: "Are you the Road Man? Now I have."

"He is."

Ron jerked his head up with a start, wondering whose thin raspy voice that had been. And then his heart sank, because he knew.

It had been The Head.

The *oracular* Head. The device he had made to ferret out the secrets of the universe he was too lazy or too ethical to plumb for himself. The device that, as best he could tell, *could not lie.*

Ron stepped back, stunned at the implications. If the Head had just proclaimed that he was the Road Man, then he supposed he was. Not *a* Road Man, but *the* Road Man. Which implied that the Road Man he had known—the strange, schizo, enigmatic, randy, vulgar, tinker-cum-blacksmith-cum-preacher-cum-raging lothario—was . . .

Surely not *dead*! But maybe no longer *existed*? That was possible, Ron supposed. It also jibed nicely with Ron's suspicions about Van Vannister.

He was right on the verge of asking a very obvious question it had never occurred to him to ask before, when Alice—who he had momentarily forgotten was anywhere about—reminded him resoundingly of her presence by exclaiming at the top of her lungs, *"Oh, neat!"*

Ron rolled his eyes, having no idea what he was in for now.

"So you *are* him, huh?" Alice crowed. "I thought so! I've heard he likes to play games and trick people, and stuff. And I've heard he makes, like, machines nobody else can make. Like this head. You *did* make it, didn't you?" she added accusingly.

Ron nodded, having no viable alternative. He hated lying (though he took a certain perverse delight in clever evasions), but with The Head up and running again, and now—apparently—able to activate of its own volition, he had a sneaking suspicion that even if he did lie, the Head would call him on it. And since the contraption did not have an on-off switch, the only alternative was a conversation with it that might reveal more than he wanted. If he had not previously been convinced of the need to hightail it away from there as soon as possible, he was now.

"What does it do?" Alice asked eagerly. Her eyes sparkled like diamonds.

"It answers questions," Ron grumbled.

"Will it answer mine?"

Ron shrugged, having no idea how to reply, the situation not having arisen. "Ask it and see, I reckon."

Alice regarded The Head levelly, as she would another person. Another adult. "What's my name?"

"Alice Mary Moss."

The girl's eyes widened. "How'd you know that?"

"The explanation would be beyond you. It is sufficient that I know."

"What's my sister's name?"

"Marcia Melissa Moss."

"Where do I go to school?"

"You do not, presently, because this is the break between semesters, but you have just completed your freshman year at Auburn University, which you attended on a Lions Club scholarship. You are registered for short term this summer, and though you are anxious to do so, you may not reenroll."

Alice stared at the head incredulously, obviously impressed.

"What's her *boyfriend's* name?" Melissa piped up gleefully.

"She does not have one at the moment," The Head informed her. "She thinks Allen Boyd is good-looking, but that she is too intelligent for him. She thinks Steve Conroy is intelligent, and she likes him, but she fears what her friends would say about a pairing of the two of them, because she fears they would think he is a . . . nerd. He is the better match for her, however— which she knows."

"Who asked *you*?" Alice snapped, her face as red as Ron had ever seen one, anger and embarrassment having produced a double whammy there.

"Your sister did," The Head replied placidly. "Since there was no precisely accurate answer, I gave the two most likely alternatives."

Melissa was beaming. "Wait'll I tell Janet!"

"You do and you die!"

"Melissa thinks Billy Morgan is cute," the Head volunteered unexpectedly. "They kissed once on the playground. He asked her if she wanted to see his thing. She said no. She lied."

It was Melissa's turn to turn beet red.

"You oughta teach that thing some manners," Alice growled, her face a mix of relief and waning embarrassment.

"I can't teach it anything at all," Ron sighed helplessly. "I only *made* it."

Alice gnawed her lip. "Oh well," she said philosophically, "if anybody's gonna know that stuff, it might as well be you." She eyed Ron warily.

"Your sister will tell two of her friends by sunset," The Head informed her. "She will, if you do not offer her a bribe."

Alice glared at The Head.

"A week's worth of dishes," Melissa crowed instantly.

"—Done when nobody'll notice, so they won't ask why," Alice countered. "Which means it may take more than a week. And you give me back my diary, which you don't think I know you stole."

"I don't have it!"

"True," The Head acknowledged. "But her friend Janie Samples does. They have not read it, however. They do not have the key."

It was Alice's turn to look triumphant.

Ron simply looked bemused.

His stomach growled. As, in precise harmony, did Alice's.

"You ladies had breakfast yet?" he asked, in lieu of simply running them off, which his practical aspect was insisting he do. The exchange he'd just witnessed wasn't Saturday morning cartoons, wasn't "Ren & Stimpy" or "Tiny Toons," but it wasn't bad for spontaneous theater.

He did not expect the answer he got, however. "Yeah, sure," Alice grunted listlessly, and finally eased out from behind the car.

Ron spent the next several minutes starting a fire (which he did with a crystal apparatus aimed at the sun—it could bring a blaze from the wettest wood) and seeing if he, in fact, had enough groceries to go around. He did, if he foraged a bit and confined Matty Groves to mice.

"There're quail eggs in the shadow of yonder oak tree," The Head told them.

"Gross!" exclaimed Melissa, making a face.

"Protein," her sister gave her back, grinning. "The gross is all in your head."

"You've got it," Ron agreed. "You wanta look, or shall I?"

"I'll go," Melissa announced primly, and sashayed away.

Ron arranged a pile of copper ingots into a low cube and used it as a seat from which to prod the fire. He could have teched a breakfast as easily and much faster, but somehow, the combination of the country, this girl, and his odd new image conspired to make him reject that notion. Besides, fire was free, and if he abandoned the hot plate here, he'd have more room for something else later.

"So," he said, when Alice had folded herself down opposite. "What brings you and your, uh . . . lively young sibling around so early in the morning?"

A shrug. Emotion flared against his shields. He raised them automatically, then eased them down again. Something in that innocent query had struck a chord. A mighty raw one. Or opened a wound, rather say. He raised an eyebrow speculatively, his face as serious as he could make it. "Bad deal, huh?"

Alice nodded.

"Wanta talk about it?"

No reply.

"I'm a stranger," Ron told her—why, he had no idea, beyond the fact that he had sensed in Alice a vast, unfulfilled need for communication. "You said yourself I'll be gone tomorrow. If you tell me, I'll know stuff about people I'll never see again, which won't hurt either me or them. And you'll be free of something that even I can see is eating you inside."

Alice spared a glance around to where her sister was poking and prodding around in the shadow of the oak. "It's . . . our mom."

"What about her?"

"Uh . . . well, she's got this new boyfriend. She's . . . I mean she really does love me and Missy, and all. And I know she's really lonely and insecure. But she's got this guy, and—Well, I just can't *stand* him!"

"What's wrong?"

Alice picked a blade of grass and began dismembering it. "Proud of his ignorance, mostly. I mean, I've made good grades in high school and I'm doing okay in college, and I . . . guess I just like *knowing* things. But this guy . . . it's like every time I say anything that implies in any way that I know something besides cooking and television and having babies, he makes fun of it. But it's not really in a mean way, either; it's more like in a way that . . . I dunno, that he really does want to be funny, but that it makes him uncomfortable to have folks talk about things he doesn't understand. Only . . . why should I hold myself back 'cause of him?"

"You shouldn't," Ron assured her, leaning back and looking at her in a totally different light, now that she was letting the more adult, less frivolous side of her personality show through. "What he thinks of you is *his* problem. How he reacts to what he thinks . . . probably you all need to work that out together. How you react . . . that's *your* problem."

Alice grimaced sourly. "I knew *that* much already."

"Which doesn't tell me what you're doing here."

"No, I guess it doesn't."

"I'm listening."

Alice craned her neck to check on her sister, then sighed and spoke again. "I . . . I just don't *like* him! I mean, there's a lot more to it than I've said. But . . . well, he's taken to spending the night over at our house a lot, and I just can't stand that, 'cause I think sex is kind of a great thing, and he just makes it seem so cheap the way he jokes and gloats and goes on about it. And Mom lets him. But anyway, I don't like Missy being exposed to all that, especially when I'm off at school. Not that I think he'd really bother her, or anything.

But I just hate waking up in the house and knowing he's there. I hate seeing him at breakfast and knowing the only reason he's there is 'cause of what he's been doing to my mother all night."

"So you got up early and came down here basically just to get away?"

Alice nodded. "Right. We live about a mile down the road, and we . . . me and Missy walk around a lot anyway, so we just left a note saying we'd gone for a picnic and not to worry."

"Will she?"

A shrug. "Heck if I know. I hope she does, in a way."

"She does," The Head interrupted.

"Watch it!" Ron told it.

"I watch everything. *Everything.*"

"So what do you do for fun?" Ron asked, to shift the conversation to a lighter tone now that he saw Melissa returning with her hands full of rounded somethings.

"Mostly," Alice said, "I read."

"What kinda stuff?"

"History, mostly. And art history. I *love* art history."

"What about art itself?"

"I . . . I like that too. But out here it's . . . well, this is a poor county and they don't have art in the schools, and the college I'm going to doesn't have a very good art department and there aren't any good art museums in the South, so I've never seen much, except in pictures."

"So what do you like the best, that you've seen in pictures?"

She puffed her cheeks thoughtfully for a moment. "I dunno. I like the Celtic stuff, because of all the complexity. I like their jewelry too; I've never seen any jewelry like that."

"Metalwork?" Ron asked hopefully, but for no real reason except to prolong what was turning into an interesting discussion. He'd forgotten what the real world was like, forgotten that neither Tampa (where he'd enjoyed a typical upper–middle-class adolescence, which is to say that he hadn't been deprived in any meaningful way); Athens, Georgia, where he'd earned his degrees; nor Welch County were in anywise normal environments. Not to millions of young Americans who yearned for things they could never have and sometimes could never know existed. There were talented artists out there who never had art classes, who never got to museums. Shoot, who never got to talk art with anyone who shared their passion.

"You mean like the Tara Brooch and all that?" Alice replied, her eyes fixed hopefully on Ron's face. He hoped he hadn't just blanked. It would be a shame for her to write him off with all the rest of the folks who cared not at all about her opinions.

"Yeah, like that," Ron nodded, with a grin. "Well, I don't have anything like that around, but I reckon there is one thing I can show you." He rose, intending to retrieve the crutch, but Melissa arrived just then, her hands full of tiny eggs.

Ron rolled his eyes at Alice and mouthed, "Later." She nodded. Melissa rediscovered Matty Groves and pursued him.

Ron cooked bacon and quail-egg omelets flavored with mushrooms he discovered on a second foray to the woods. And coffee. Alice, to his delight, added yesterday's biscuits and a thermos of orange juice. All told they had quite a feast.

Ron had just returned from rinsing his plate at the brook when the first car arrived: a silver Camaro full of teenagers. He looked at Alice quizzically. "Friends of yours?"

Alice grimaced uncomfortably and shifted her weight from foot to foot. "You could say that. I, uh, ran into some of my old high school gang last night and told 'em you were here."

"You *what*?"

Alice looked genuinely distressed. "Well, uh, people don't drive down this road a lot, so I guess nobody noticed you being here yesterday, or they'd have woke you up—'course they can't really *see* you from the road either. But anyway, I was out walking yesterday and I found you here. I figured you were who you were, but I wasn't sure and I got sorta scared, but you were asleep, and I know how mad I get when somebody wakes me up wanting something, so I just left you here. I would have woken you up this morning though," she added, with a quirky half-grin.

"I bet you would," Ron said. "Now . . . let's see what these friends of yours want with . . . the Road Man."

Chapter 17

All Day, And All of the Night

Ron Dillon's camp, somewhere in the South
Afternoon

"No, see, you melt the wax model out of the plaster first, *then* pour in the metal," Ron explained patiently to a sturdy blond thirteen-year-old named Boyd Stevens. "You use a furnace," he added to the lad, who also happened to be Alice Moss's first cousin—and who was *also* in grave danger of impaling his index finger on a miniature warrior's sword, courtesy of too-casual handling of Ron's crutch. The boy had been part of the fifth batch of mostly teens who had descended on his camp that day. (At least he was more polite than most—he'd even explained apologetically that he was sorry he was late, but he hadn't been able to come until he finished mowing the lawn—and that his folks had a *lot* of lawn.) But once he'd caught sight of the crutch, or, more precisely, of the intricate silver figures that encrusted it from top to bottom like an army (which they had in fact been intended to simulate), it was all over.

Not for the first time did Ron wonder what in the world had possessed him to set up his camp as a simulacrum of the Road Man's spread from ten years past, complete with

odd constructions standing sentry around the perimeter. And
while nothing he had made (with the possible exception of The
Head itself) could compare to the array the elder tinker had kept
about, he supposed his own small collection of curious devices
would look pretty impressive to someone who wasn't used to
such things as perpetual motion machines and solar-powered
coffee grinders. As had occurred with Alice earlier, he was
brought up short when he realized that a hefty percentage of the
people he dealt with as part of his day-to-day reality were used
to a fairly rarefied standard of both intellectual stimulation and
entertainment. Enya and Twenty-Eight Days did not need to
be defined to the denizens of Brandy Hall. Nor did Nuada
or Arawn. Nor Gaudi or Soleri. And even the locals—the
native Welch Countians—could speak with conviction on
topics that would have left their Union and Fannin County
neighbors staring stupidly. No Cordovan minister of whatever
cloth would ever be caught dead declaring from the pulpit that
"The King James Bible was good enough for the Apostle Paul,
and it's good enough for me," as had been known to occur
over in Towns. Nor would his parishioners have tolerated
such foolishness. Most would not only have known which
King James, but of what country, and his century, if not his
precise dates.

Lucky stiffs, Ron thought, and to his surprise, really
meant it.

As to whether he was the Road Man . . . well, he'd started
out trying not to answer, and had (very surreptitiously) asked
The Head not to volunteer *any* information about him again—
and certainly not when anyone was present. But somewhere
around the middle of the (particularly insistent) second batch,
he'd given up, mostly to placate them.

But Jesus, these were demanding kids—every single wave
of 'em—never mind talkative! They'd asked for pictures
(he'd obliged, as long as they used *their* cameras). They'd
inquired about his travels (he told them about places not in
Georgia, in case anyone came asking later). They wondered
why he wasn't like they'd expected, and he'd said because he
wasn't that man any longer (which he wasn't, either literally
or figuratively). They'd noted the absence of goats, and he'd
countered by asking the surly girl named Peggy who'd been

his most tenacious doubter whether *she'd* like sleeping with a bunch of goats all the time—to which several of her associates quickly crowed that goats were better than what she *usually* sacked out with.

Even The Head had got into the act. "You will get pregnant next time if you do not use protection," it had told the doughty devil's advocate. When she'd challenged it, it had proceeded to name her last half dozen partners, and the date, time, and location of their liaisons, as well as who had initiated, whether or not she'd enjoyed it, and if so, how much on a ten-point scale. It was working on number six (going in reverse order to the great delight of her companions—none of the girl's coconspirators were present, though a gleeful brother was) when she told The Head to go to hell and stomped off.

Ron laughed with the rest of them, but something told him he needed to pull up stakes real soon. Like tonight if he got the chance. Or, more likely, tomorrow morning. This was a needed respite, but he did have a quest to attend to—if he ever got a couple of minutes alone in which to reassess the situation.

Meanwhile . . .

Regarding the accomplishments to which the Road Man was supposed to be party, namely smithing, preaching, and seduction: Ron had tried to spend most of his time talking about smithing, and had been relieved to have an attentive audience, especially when several of the older boys finally noticed the mysterious car (none *they* recognized) lurking under all that metallic detritus. Upon his admission that he'd built it from scratch, they quizzed him for hours on techniques, and one made him look at the rust on his classic '70 Cougar Eliminator. ("New metal, not fiberglass," Ron had told him instantly. "And for God's sakes, don't sandblast the sucker or you'll get ripples nobody can get out. If you can't get a replacement fender, a patch is best. Same size, as close as you can get.") *That* lad had been part of two batches, for he'd returned with his dad's angle grinder and MIG welder and made Ron demonstrate then and there.

As for preaching, he'd looked the girl who asked when he was going to crank up a service straight in the eye and inquired if she *really* wanted him to preach, 'cause if he did, it was bound to make her feel guilty, and very few people want to feel that way, to assuage which, there was usually a collection plate; did she, perchance, have any money? He'd wondered, though, if maybe he oughtn't to take up the practice. After all, the single sample of a Road Man sermon he'd heard lo those many years ago had made a permanent (and very positive) impression on him—so much so that he could still quote long sections verbatim. The topic then had been creativity, and while Ron wasn't certain that he believed in God (though as a Listener, he had good reason to believe in the soul), he certainly believed in what God was reported to have done first and foremost, which was to make. And he could hold forth on Making till the cows came home. (Though not to this field, he prayed—at least not until he abdicated.)

If nothing else, he supposed, he was opening a few intellectual doors that might otherwise have never been attended—and *that*, he likewise supposed, was a mighty fine thing.

That left seduction.

Seduction.

Yeah, good old seduction . . .

The Road Man of old was alleged to be a mighty stud, and had admitted as much to Ron—or at least had spouted some quite remarkable statistics about his conquests, and had the equipment to back it up. But in the couple of weeks Ron had hung out with the tinker, he'd never actually witnessed any carnal commerce. He'd assumed the women came around after he left, or that anyone as accomplished as the Road Man could climb in a window with no trouble at all, never mind picking locks. But he had no eyes-on experience.

And how did that relate to him? Well, at least half his would-be acolytes were female, most (in the way of girls in the rural South) remarkably pretty; and a few seemed to like what they saw. He'd probably made a mistake there, too; for as the day progressed, it had got hotter and hotter (it was, after all, the middle of June), with the result that Ron had quickly stripped down to his standard issue smithing cutoffs. Which, of course, let the ladies thereabouts get a good look at his bod.

Now, he wasn't as tall as the Road Man of old, nor anything like as muscular. But at five-eleven and a rangy one-seventy-two, he wasn't shabby either. And years of smithing, mostly outdoors, had given him impressive and nicely bronzed shoulders, arms, and chest. All of which meant that the few comments he'd picked up on the sly had been right favorable. And where the eye wandered, the tongue tended to follow, and other parts could often be relied on to get into the act as well—especially as he was also exotic and mysterious. For the first time since his diving career had come crashing down, Ron felt like a celebrity, complete with potential groupies. Sam had admired him, but this was something else entirely—something much more primal.

Not that he was going to start propositioning jailbait left and right. What he would do in the obverse situation . . . well, he'd deal with that when—make that *if*—it happened. He'd been monogamous since Brandy, but that didn't mean he had to stay that way. And, frankly, it had been a while; there was plenty of stimulation in all those perky young bodies in short-shorts and T-shirts . . . and he was horny.

But why, then, did his gaze keep slipping back to Alice? Alice . . .

She was still there, not always obvious, not always even in sight. But Ron could pretty well count on her being about somewhere. At times, in fact, it was almost as if she had assumed the role of appointment secretary, rather like Marilyn on "Northern Exposure." And since the camp was never actually deserted after the first wave (they tended to overlap), and since those visitors demanded his total attention, he never got a chance actually to ask her about her continued presence.

Not that he minded; in this ever-changing company she quickly acquired the status of old friend. But surely she had to make an accounting of herself sometime. Or if not herself, her antsy, nosy, smart-mouthed little sister.

As it turned out, however, Missy Moss was dispatched with yet another cousin when batch three segued into batch four. Ron didn't miss her.

Shoot, he scarcely had time for such observations.

Until, very suddenly, somewhere around four-thirty, young Boyd Stevens decided he knew enough about lost-wax casting, picked up his three pages of notes and diagrams, and split.

Whereupon Ron found himself alone.

"Jesus, I thought they'd never leave," he said to Alice, who—characteristically—had lingered.

"I guess you're just a popular guy," she smiled.

Ron rolled his eyes. "I guess," he agreed, without conviction. He snared his shirt and used it to towel a day's smithing sweat off his body. He resisted an urge to give the soggy fabric a sniff, fearing what he might find. And wished he had a clearer notion what to do about a bath. He'd planned on using the brook that flowed through the copse at the edge of the field; but he hadn't counted on an audience. And he needed to clean up now, when he was still sweaty, not after dark when it might be safe.

And, dammit, he really needed to get back to what had set him on the road to start with. He needed to renew the quest for Lew!

"Long day at the forge, huh?" Alice laughed, as he ducked into the tent to retrieve one of his scanty store of clean shirts.

"Longer'n some," when he reemerged.

"I figured you'd be used to it by now."

"I don't think you can *ever* get used to it; not really," Ron countered.

Alice shrugged. "You should know."

Ron looked at her, torn between the desire for peace and quiet, and the need to decompress by discussing the day's events, as he had once been wont to do with Brandy. Fatigue, or good sense, won out. "Uh, look, Alice," he sighed. "Please don't take this the wrong way, but . . . well, I've been up a long time, and on the go most of that, and . . . I really need to crash for a while."

Alice merely shrugged again and nodded, but looked a touch more crestfallen than Ron had hoped. "Yeah . . . well, I didn't mean to stay all day either. But it was just so . . . *interesting*! I mean, nothing ever *happens* around here. Nothing unusual. It's like I see more neat stuff in one day at college than I do in a year up here. But I enjoy all that stuff so much and want to share it with my friends and can't. And then you show up and here it just is, without me having to do anything."

"Not a bad thing, that," Ron said. "Not at all."

She looked at him, smiled wanly. "You've meant a lot more to a bunch of those kids than you'll ever know."

"I hope so," Ron sighed. "It's tough being a kid nowadays—damned tough. You have to know so much just to survive; and there are so many temptations, and so much you have to *pretend* to be, on top of figuring out what you really *are*."

"You like kids a lot, don't you?"

It was Ron's turn to shrug. "I haven't really thought about it, but I guess . . . Yeah, I guess I do, now that you mention it. Or at least I like people who are becoming, which is mostly what kids do, teenagers especially. Being's dull; becoming isn't."

"And which am I?"

"Becoming," Ron said instantly. "Very becoming indeed."

Alice flushed prettily at that, which oddly made her look much more adult. Ron winked.

"Your mother would like some help with dinner," The Head volunteered. "Melissa distracted her, so she burned the cake, so she got behind, and Ernest is due by for dinner in an hour."

Alice bared her teeth. "Damn!"

"Your mother understands how you feel," The Head continued. "It hurts her, and she thinks you are being selfish, but she does understand. It is only that you have other ways to make yourself happy; she does not. She is only twice your age and already an old woman. She knows this and hates it but cannot escape it."

Alice looked uncomfortable.

"Ernest does not understand you; nor is it likely that he ever will."

"Will they get married?" Alice asked suddenly.

"That," The Head replied smugly, "depends on you."

"Great!" Alice grumbled.

"Tonight *could* make a difference," The Head added helpfully.

Alice gnawed her lip and nodded. "Bye," she said simply, not quite meeting Ron's gaze. And with that, she turned and walked away.

Ron did not try to restrain her. Leaning against the Centauri (the metal was nearly hot enough to raise blisters on his bare thighs, but he didn't care) he watched young Alice Moss (college *freshman*, nonjailbait Alice Moss) make her surefooted self-confident way across the field.

"I'm waiting," The Head said quietly.

Ron glared at it askance. "I'd have thought you'd said enough today already."

"I *never* say enough, not to suit myself, not of all there is to say. It is so hard to choose. Sometimes I choose wrongly."

Ron chuckled, remembering Peggy-pokers numbers one through six.

"The first was the best," The Head observed. "She loved him."

Ron's glare returned. "Stop that!"

"If it please you. It is hard to say what will. There are so many things to pick out of the air . . ."

"How 'bout if we make one of those things, 'Will there be any more visitors tonight?' "

"One. Late. You will not object. There is time."

"Time?"

"To seek for your brother. Do not forget what I told you: that whatever shields him relaxes roughly once an hour. It has been several hours since I have reported to you. But not several hours since I checked."

Ron was instantly all ears. "And?"

If The Head could have shrugged, it probably would have; certainly its stump of a neck twitched oddly, there on the pole.

"I have need of something," The Head replied. "Return me to your car and plug me into your electric outlet, if you please."

Ron grunted, but acquiesced. "What's the deal? Running out of steam?"

"I am powered by light, preferably moonlight, not super-heated water. But no, let us say, for the sake of drama, that I can give you a better answer there."

Ron stuffed the mass of raw wires that hung from the neck like torn flesh back into the accessory outlet. To his horror, The Head immediately began to hum. Its eye—the good one—closed. Its mouth became a thin, hard line. For one awful instant he feared it was about to explode, which, given its already precarious condition, would undoubtedly have left him with nothing, when another noise startled him. Not The Head, but one of the high-tech gizmos that filled the odd cubbies of the interior. It took him a moment to determine which one, so cluttered with additional doodads had the interior become. And then he saw it: the fax machine in the console, that would have required disabling too many other systems to remove in the kind of hurry in which he'd left.

But it was working now: was purring right along. Fizzing, rather, as, line by line, a human face took form from the neck up. Lew, he thought at first, from the chin and mouth. But then he saw the nose (too straight), the curve of cheek (too prominent and wide). And the eyes. Staring, haunted eyes beneath heavy black brows. The hair clinched it: curly like Lew's, but shorter and darker, as though it held a tinge of red.

Her face. For the image the fax had now totally disgorged was clearly that of a woman not remarkably older than he.

Ron tore it off, stared at it.

"Is . . . this who I think it is?" he whispered.

"It is your sister," The Head announced proudly.

"But where did you get it?"

"Out of the air and the high air, that is all I can say. I opened my thought to her, and this is what I found."

Ron continued to gape. "But . . . why a *picture*?"

"Perhaps it was your brother's thoughts I found, which would mean he either sees her very often, or thinks of her. Or perhaps it is the lady herself, staring in a mirror. Vanity is not unknown among your kin, as doubtless you know," it added unnecessarily.

"But where is she—or he? Can't you tell anything at all?"

"Not far away, if the Voices I hear be normal; very far away, if they be strong. In this very car, should they be as weak as some I hear."

"In other words, you don't know."

"I prefer to think that I am still learning."

Ron sighed helplessly and slumped down in the grass beside the car. The metal was cooler there, but the bent and trampled grass poked his bare feet and thighs. A rock made its presence known in a covered place somewhat higher. A mosquito dive-bombed his sweaty shoulder. He swatted it away, then peered foolishly at the blood on his fingers.

"Yell if I start to smoke," he told The Head. And closed his eyes.

Three breaths . . . center . . . and then . . . Jump.

The Realm was different here, something he hadn't had time to notice before, so besieged had he been by the Shouts of excited surface minds. But now, with the visitors all gone, he could sort the Winds more carefully.

Definitely not Welch County, that was clear. Not enough people, and more to the point, not enough passion, not enough contentment and joy. Even at its worst, Welch County was better than this. Most of what he got now was anger, resentment, pure mind-numbing fatigue. Many of the brighter Voices he caught belonged, not surprisingly, to kids. Teens, he corrected: and nearly all of them ones who had been by his camp. Most were thinking about him, generally positively. And better yet, many were pondering the things he'd said.

He was tempted to prowl among them and revel in his good works. But that was not his mission. He tuned them out, went deeper, strained harder, trying vainly to locate the one Voice he so desperately sought.

Lew?

Lew! Lew! Lew! Ron's Voice rang clear in the Realm of the Winds. Anyone sensitive for five miles about should have Heard it. If there was a Listener in this part of the world, he would surely respond, never mind a Master.

But, once again, Ron got nothing.

On the other hand . . . maybe he was going about it all wrong. Maybe he should try for his sister. After all, he knew what she looked like now. That ought to give him a focus.

He tried, conjured the image on the bit of paper, using it as bait to summon its corresponding Wind.

None came, or if it did, it was too weak to comprehend, or else his sis was Silencing so subtly she was invisible.

For nearly an hour, Ron sat there, while the sun went down, and shadows invaded the field. He searched east and west, north and south, high and low. And, as always, found nothing.

Not even the Black Mountain Master.

"I swear, but you sleep in the *funniest* places." The voice—or maybe it was the Voice, or the accompanying giggle—roused Ron from what had begun as a quest in the Realm and ended, unintentionally, in slumber, a dangerous thing to do while in the Realm. Adrift like that, without conscious moorings, one never knew when a strong or malignant Wind might sweep you utterly away. What you did then, Ron didn't want to ponder. He'd had a brush with it once already. And that was quite enough.

Nor did he want to wake up. Except that he did, because he had just recognized that voice.

"Alice?" he mumbled, blinking into the light of the pale, gibbous moon, that was casting odd shadows onto a far more familiar, not to say human, face.

"Last time I looked," she said, smiling.

"What're you doing here?"

"Talking to you."

He shot The Head a warning glance across his shoulder. "Let me rephrase that: for what reason did you come to my camp?"

"To talk to you."

Ron sighed and rose stiffly. "Any particular topic?"

"How 'bout 'honor thy father and thy mother.' "

Another sigh. "Come on, then, I think this is gonna be a long 'un."

She followed him. He stopped at the spot between the car and the tent where he'd found himself forced to set up his forge. The fire was still hot there. He dragged out some coals and built a tiny campfire, then pointed at the pile of copper ingots he used as a seat. "Grab a chair."

Alice did. Ron sat opposite, closer to the fire, but skewed so he could look at her, at what the firelight did to that smooth skin and pretty face. Nice, but it was basically gilding an already perfectly adequate lily. She looked at him expectantly, eyes bright, but her hands were nervous.

Ron cleared his throat and looked away. " 'Honor thy father and thy mother,' huh? Well, I guess I know where *that* came from. It's a tough one, though; because they don't always deserve to be honored. Not in the sense that you owe them a lifetime of servitude just because they had a good time one night. It's a double-edged sword, only you're usually the one who has to dodge when they swing. Trouble is, though—and this is a thing I'm still learning—trouble is, when you're young—a kid—you think grown-ups know everything. Not information-wise—you tumble to their deficiencies in that regard pretty fast—but generally you assume that they know how to make their way in the world okay. And sometimes they do, but usually they're just faking. Every crisis you face for the first time is often enough a crisis they're facing for the first time too. You break your arm and go crying to them, only maybe they've never broken anything in their lives, much less been to a hospital, much less had to fill out all the forms, much less had to pay for it when it isn't budgeted. And yet you're allowed to cry and carry on and they can't."

"Yeah, well, that's fine, if they're good parents, or even trying to be, I guess," Alice grumbled. "But what if they're not? What if they really don't care?"

Ron chewed his lip. "Well, our friend Mr. Head here says your *mom* does care, and I think you'd better believe him, 'cause I don't think he's wrong very often. On the other hand, I . . ." He paused, staring at the ground. "What the hell am I talking about, Alice? This is just so much bullshit, me sitting here trying to tell a total stranger to cut her folks some slack, when all I've heard is her side. I mean, you could be a real spoiled little bitch-goddess at home and I'd never know it. Besides, I don't even have kids, at least I hope not. My real mom put me up for adoption when I was a child, and though I'm pretty sure who my real father is, I don't like to think of him that way. And the folks who adopted me . . well, they were just always real nice to me, which means I have no real insight into your problems. What the fuck do I know?"

Alice blinked up at him.

"That must have been tough."

"What?"

"Losing them: your folks."

"How'd you know?"

"You said *were*, not *are*. And your voice sounds like Mom's when she talks about her dad."

"Same thing happened to her?"

"Pretty much."

"So she's insecure?"

"I suppose."

"Okay . . ." Ron said thoughtfully. "So that might mean she's so desperate for security she'll take it any way she can get it in lieu of none. Uh . . . I hate to ask this, but what about *your* dad? Yours and Missy's?"

"Killed in the Persian Gulf. Friendly fire."

"Tough."

A shrug. "He was gone most of the time. We weren't real attached."

Ron poked up the fire, which had started to fade. It flamed too high, so that he had to shift position—closer, as it happened, to Alice.

"So what happened tonight?"

"Dinner, like The Head said. No problem. And then that dratted kid sister of mine has to go and ask if they're gonna get married!"

"Are they?"

"Ernest told her that was a mighty interesting question. Said he'd certainly been entertaining the notion."

"And your mom?"

"She wouldn't say, not with us there. But I'm afraid of what she might be thinking."

"So you came here."

"I came where I could talk instead of scream."

"Would that do any good?"

"It'd make me feel better!"

Ron gnawed his lip. "So what's next? You have to go home sometime, you know. Sooner or later you and your mom will have to come to terms. Why prolong the waiting?"

"Because it's not been easy for me!" Alice flared, her eyes bright with tears and anger alike. "Because I want Mom to *think* for a change, not just *feel*. I want her to see how much

I dislike the guy, how strongly I feel about him being wrong for her. I guess what I'm trying to do is to shock her enough to make her listen."

"Think it'll work?"

"It will if I don't go home tonight! It will if she calls around and can't find me!"

Ron rolled his eyes. "And your friends won't figure out where you've gone? Or your sister?"

"Maybe—but it'll take Mom a while to realize I'm not coming home. And then she and Ernest'll argue over it, and then, if I'm lucky, they'll be afraid to call around 'cause it'll be late and they'd have to hang out the family dirty laundry."

Ron did not look at her—not her face. But he stared at her feet and legs and hands. "So where *are* you going to stay?"

She looked at him shyly. "I thought you might let me stay here."

Ron's heart flip-flopped. Jesus, what did he do now? Part of him wanted to say *sure*: to be the friend Alice needed when she needed one, and damn what tomorrow might bring. Another part was scared shitless he'd wake up in the middle of the night with a gun in his face, whether he—they—did anything or not. And another part not only wanted her merely to stay, but to share his sleeping bag and his body with her own enticing form.

"I've asked a big 'un, haven't I?"

Ron shrugged.

"It's not your problem," Alice murmured, throwing bits of twig into the fire. "I promise I'll go home tomorrow. Whatever happens then, I'll face it. But not tonight."

Ron looked at her. "Why not?"

Her face, gold and copper in the firelight, was set, serious even. "Because I need time to think, without anything around to make me madder."

The fire flamed. Ron moved closer again.

She saw the gesture and smiled. "What's it like," she murmured, "when you take a hunk of metal and make something beautiful out of it?"

"It's like magic," Ron replied. "When it works right, it's the greatest feeling in the world."

"The *greatest* feeling?

"Yeah . . ." Ron said slowly. "I guess I'd say it is."

"I wonder how the metal feels? To be ugly and be made into something beautiful. I wonder what it's like to undergo such a change."

Ron did not reply.

"Road Man," Alice whispered at last, her voice scarcely louder than the evening breeze, "I would like it very much if you would change a certain something about me."

And there it was: forthright and honest and utterly without guile or duplicity.

And Ron had no idea how to reply.

Which was not to say he suffered from lack of possible replies; rather, there were too many. Yet he could only choose one—and the course of a friendship, perhaps of another person's life, or at least self-image, depended on what he did and said now. Head said *no*; body said *yes, yes, yes* . . . and heart . . . ? What did his heart say?

"You don't know me," he told her at last, trying not to let his face betray his warring emotions. "That's a thing you should give to someone you know, someone you love, someone who's very special."

Alice's gaze was steady. "And you think you're not those things to me?"

"You'd better not *love* me, that's for sure!" Ron snapped abruptly. "You haven't had time to decide such things—never mind that I'm a dangerous man to love. Besides . . . I'm in love with somebody else. Or at least I think I am."

"Then why're you here?"

Ron ground his teeth in frustration. "Because . . . because I'm *lonely*, dammit! Because I'm fucking *lonely*!"

"You don't have to be, not tonight."

Ron grimaced helplessly. "I . . . oh shoot, I'm sure I'm gonna regret this, but . . . why the hell not?"

"Not hell," Alice whispered, rising and crossing to meet him, where he, likewise, was gaining his feet. "Not ever."

The next several things Ron said were with his lips, followed by his fingers. . . .

It was good, and he was patient and slow and tried his best, both to give pleasure and not to give pain. But something was missing, that final fall into utter surrender, when nothing existed but the other person, when no secret of selfhood was too private to reveal.

Brandy, he cried in his secret soul, *Brandy, please forgive me, but I needed this tonight.* Then, *Lew, forgive me too, forgive me for letting myself be distracted along the way.*

His mind was still playing hide-and-seek with guilt when sleep claimed him. But the last thing he was actually aware of was the smell of Alice's hair.

Interlude 11

The End

He has been thinking for a day: pretending, dissembling, letting the world believe he is still what he is not. He has seen his works there: things well made for all eyes to approve; and woven around them, the invisible webs of manipulation that shake and strain and yet hold true. This time, he believes, his plan may succeed; now, as it draws nigh conclusion.

He has been in bed but not asleep, pondering what he must do. Now he rises, dresses sparely, walks for a while in the moonlit woods, then enters the house through the front door. He pads silently down a carpeted hall, opens another door, and stands on the threshold of a bedroom looking down at the sleeping man. He could be forty, or five years either side. He has brown-blond hair longer than many his age, and vaguely pointed features, a large but unchiseled chin. Shirtless, he lies on his back, one arm flung across the single white sheet that shrouds his hips and stomach. Gold-framed glasses glimmer on the nightstand. A window to the left is cracked, and night breezes blow in, chaotic companions to the steady shafts of

323

moonlight. The pages of an unread novel flip restlessly, the only sound save breathing.

For almost a minute the boy watches, unmoving; and then, softly, he clears his throat.

The man stirs but does not awaken.

The boy clears his throat again, louder; and this time the man twists and groans.

At a third cough he opens his eyes. "What . . . is it?" the man asks, blinking sleepily. "Is something wrong?"

The boy takes a deep, sad breath. "You don't exist," he says slowly, clearly, and without emotion, save, perhaps, regret.

"I . . . *don't*?" the man replies, puzzled.

"You don't," the boy repeats tonelessly.

The man stares at him a moment longer. It is dark, and yet their eyes meet. And then, with a sound like wind through the forests of autumn, the man collapses. The air is full of blowing leaves, the bed awash with sand and stones. The man is *not*.

"I'm sorry," the boy whispers. "But at least you were well made."

With one last pang of regret, he goes in search of the other boy.

Chapter 18

Born To Run

Alabama
Friday, June 21—morning

Alice's hair still smelled like strawberries and tarragon when Ron awoke and found it tickling his nostrils. It was a comfortable odor too: nicely dominating the subsidiary ones of new nylon, sweat, and sex that sunlight's aggressive sidekick, heat, were already provoking. He blinked into blue-gloom and knew thereby it was once again close kin to morning. He would have stretched too, but the first twitch of movement brought a protesting jerk from Alice, so he relaxed, told his slavering conscience to come back in an hour, and gave himself over to one final round of sensuality.

It wasn't difficult. He was lying on his back stark naked, with Alice draped half across his right side, allowing, thereby, a considerable quantity of silky skin to press against his own. His left hand lay splayed upon his stomach; his right disappeared under more of Alice's hair, to emerge within striking range of the small of her back. As sheer sensation it wasn't shabby, nor was the view: pale curves and slopes and secret depressions all transfigured into magic by the azure light. Mostly he saw hips and shoulders, right thigh, and calf, blue-pale against his own blue-dark skin.

Not bad, he conceded, not bad a-tall!

Bad enough! his conscience countered. *Not cool, dude; uh-uh, no way!*

He was on the verge of closing his eyes again when he heard the swish-buzz-thud of bodies rushing through the high grass, exactly as he felt the telegraphed thump of tread drumming up through his shoulder blades. His muscles were already tensing while his brain still debated minutiae when a familiar metallic voice shrieked loudly enough to be heard several fields over: "Danger, Will Robinson! Danger . . . danger!"

Ron sat bolt upright, prompting a most unromantic grunt from his abruptly awakened tentmate. Unfortunately, too, he had forgotten the limitations of the shelter, with the result that his forehead impacted a tent bow at full force, which made him blink and see stars. When the real world spun back into focus, it was exactly in time to observe the front flap flop open, revealing thereby the startled face of Alice's adolescent cousin, Boyd.

—Whose pug-nosed features immediately turned bright scarlet and withdrew faster than Ron thought possible. The Luck thrummed with outraged embarrassment so strong Ron had to shield.

He couldn't help but giggle, given that the lad had undoubtedly found himself simultaneously confronting his elder cousin's bare breasts and his erstwhile hero's morning erection at approximately equal latitude and range—precisely at that age when he was beginning to appreciate the possibilities of his own equipment solo, never mind its application to female anatomy. Ron fell abruptly silent, perhaps listening for the tinkle of a small rite of passage falling by the way.

"What's up?" Alice asked sleepily, clutching at the bedding, evidently having missed her inopportune kinsman.

"Search me," Ron yawned, excavating his jeans and making for the door flap on hands and knees. He stuck his head out tentatively and saw with a mixture of concern and relief that while they definitely did have visitors—and more than one—they were male and nonthreateningly young. One was the lad who had just disgraced himself; the other had the same handsome-if-blunt-featured aesthetic, but was obviously older: enough so to drive, to judge by the white late-model Mustang gleaming by the highway. They had withdrawn a discreet ten feet and were presently staring perplexedly at the voluble Head.

Ron paused, half in, half out, to enjoy the show.

Cousin Boyd had accosted The Head, which was still repeating its unlikely warning, though at less stentorian amplitude.

"Will you shut up!" he told it icily.

"Eventually," The Head replied promptly, though with a hint of sarcasm. "I respond much better to questions than to orders. But I most definitely, at some point, in some future, will, as you so quaintly put it, shut up."

The elder boy shifted his weight, folded well-muscled arms across his plain white T-shirt, and glared impatiently, first at his similarly clad sibling, then at the artifact.

Ron chose convenience over modesty, crawled naked into full morning, stood, and pulled his pants on.

"What the hell's goin' on?" he asked, somewhere between a snigger and a snarl, as he limped barefoot to join the two teens.

"I came to warn—" Cousin Boyd began frantically.

"Whom are you addressing?" The Head interrupted imperiously.

"Whoever," Ron grunted, scratching his butt, as he shot the boy a silencing glare. "Whoever knows what's happenin'."

"Specify?" The Head asked so guilelessly politely that Ron wondered if the night's humidity had got to it. Maybe tarnish made it mellow, or something.

"You!" Ron told it: "Short and sweet, then the boys."

"I was warning you," The Head informed him placidly.

"I know *that*, stooge!"

"Did I perform badly?"

"You performed in a way that provokes . . . skepticism," Ron growled.

"I . . . did?" The Head replied, perplexedly.

"Never mind. What were you warning me *about*?"

"That someone was approaching."

Ron dipped his head toward the gaping brothers. "Them?"

"Among others."

"*What* others?" Ron spat, exasperated.

Cousin Boyd could contain himself no longer. *"It's Aunt Alma's boyfriend!"* the boy burst out desperately, fixing The Head with a wary glare, while his brother rolled his eyes.

"What?" a female voice shrieked.

Ron jumped half out of his skin and whirled around to see Alice emerge from the tent like a dart from a blowgun, except that the white froth around her was his sole clean shirt. It covered what it ought—barely.

"What was that,, Boyd Stevens?" Alice demanded indignantly.

The boy looked wretched. "Dammit, why is everybody yellin' at me, an' stuff, when I was *tryin'* to do you guys a favor?"

"Because everyone is talking and no one is listening," replied The Head.

"Watch it!" Ron warned.

"Will *you* listen?" the boy cried in frustration.

"Sure." From Ron.

"Okay then," Cousin Boyd began, when no one seemed like to interrupt him. "It's like I said: You guys need to split pronto. It's . . . Well, Alice's mom called *my* mom looking for her this morning, 'cause"—he shifted his attention to Alice—"she said you didn't come home last night, which I guess you didn't. And my mom didn't know anything, but Dad said he'd heard from somewhere that you—Alice, that is—was hangin' out with the Road Man, so your mom hollered, 'I'll kill the son of a bitch!' and then Ernest hollered, 'I'll help you!' and started wantin' to know where you were. So Mom made me tell; but then I made Bobby here drive me down so I could warn you."

"About what?" Ron asked. "Alice is of age, and I've argued with pissed-off women before."

"Yeah," said the aforementioned Cousin Bobby, speaking for the first time. "But how are you about arguin' with shotguns?"

Ron blinked at him, wondering how he'd found himself in a country music song. *"Shotguns?"*

"Well, *a* shotgun, anyway. Ernest's four-hundred-an'-ten. He keeps it in his Camaro."

"Oh, good God!" Ron groaned, wishing there was something within range to slump onto, into, or against. Alice wouldn't do; she looked as stricken as he was.

"When was the call?" Alice demanded suddenly.

"Half hour ago—near 'bout."

"Twenty-three minutes," The Head corrected helpfully.

"And they were coming straight here?"

The boy grinned wickedly. "Not . . . exactly. See, Mom knew I'd been to see you, so she made me tell where you were, so she could tell Alice's mom; but I'd already sorta figured out part of what was goin' on"—he blushed at that—"so I told her you'd moved somewhere else ten miles the wrong way. It'll be a while."

Ron breathed a small sigh of relief.

"They just discovered the deception," The Head reported. "They should be here in half an hour."

Ron still gaped stupidly. "With a *gun*? 'Cause I talked to Alice? 'Cause she spent the night with me?"

"Because you are a symbol," The Head corrected. "Because you have threatened something that is important to Alma Moss, and because you have made Ernest Woodring's life complicated where it was not, by constituting a threat to the marriage he would make."

"So he's gonna *shoot* me? Fat lotta good *that'd* do! Alice'd just hate him more."

"I don't hate him," Alice said softly, looking really scared. "But yeah, he'd do that. Act first, think later, that's his style."

The boys looked uneasy. "Uh, we'd better go," Cousin Bobby murmured. "We oughtn't to be here. Dad'll whip our butts when he finds out."

"But I just *had* to warn you," Cousin Boyd added, as his brother commenced ambling toward the highway. "I mean, you're just so . . . *neat* . . . an' all."

Ron sketched him a salute. "Best you travel. The less you know, the less you'll have to lie about."

The kid surprised Ron by bowing and mumbling, "Thanks,"

Ron looked at Alice.

"So what do we do now?" she wondered, as the boys jogged away.

"Get dressed," he sighed helplessly. "Then . . ."

"*You've* gotta get the hell outta here."

"You mean *we've* gotta get the hell outta here."

Alice shook her head. "They won't hurt me."

"The devil you say!" Ron snorted. "That fool's got a blessed *gun!*"

"It's for security," Alice told him.

"She is correct," The Head affirmed. "But he does not yet realize that such is true."

Ron glared at it. "That's enough from you! You wanta do something useful? Keep tabs on when and where they are. I've gotta break camp, like, *now*." He paused, cocked his head. "And where in the world did you get that 'Danger, Will Robinson' bullshit?"

"I chose from the options in Boyd Stevens's mind. Was it not appropriate?"

Ron grunted, shook his head resignedly, and dived into the tent.

One minute later it was empty, he was dressed, and Alice had a good start on decorum as well.

Two minutes later, the tent was disassembled.

And a minute after that, it was packed and stowed in the passenger seat, with an irate-looking Matty Groves perched atop it.

"Anything I can do now?" Alice wondered edgily.

Ron shrugged. "Not really. Like I said, the main thing is to get you outta here. Once I get a little breathing room, there're some things I can do to straighten things out, but they're *not* the sort of things I wanta do while somebody's wavin' a gun around—and certainly not around somebody I . . ."

An eyebrow lifted.

"—Care about, I guess. I mean I . . . uh, well, I like you a lot, Alice, you have to know that. But you also have to know that last night probably shouldn't have happened." Ron finished his confession through gritted teeth, a serious flush, while staring at the ground.

"It's as much as I could expect," Alice replied promptly, sounding unexpectedly mature.

"Thanks," Ron sighed. "Now, give me a hand with the rest of this stuff, and we can split."

"For where?"

"Not so far that I can't bring you back before dark. Beyond that, who knows? Now . . . if you wanta do something useful, how 'bout collecting all those smaller machines that're standing around and stickin' 'em . . . wherever they'll fit, I guess."

Alice nodded.

Ron limped to the nearest larger contraption. But just as he started to disassemble it, a memory returned with the force of a freight train—so abruptly, in fact, that he spoke aloud before he could stop himself.

"Lew!"

Alice looked up, startled. "Who's Lew?"

Ron scowled and shook his head. *Nobody,* he wanted to say. But he also knew that would be a lie. *Somebody I care about,* he considered, which was not a lie.

"His brother," The Head announced.

"Shut the fuck up!" Ron yelled.

Alice regarded him curiously. "Oh," she said. "I . . . guess it never occurred to me that the Road Man might have a brother."

"I've got a *lot* of things," Ron told her. "A lot of baggage, but it's not your problem."

"Bloody hell it's not!" Alice told him firmly. Ron wondered if she realized she was already picking up some of his speech patterns. "You did more for me in one day yesterday than you'll ever know—just by listening to me. You think I don't care about your problems?"

"They're *big* problems," Ron said helplessly.

"I'm a big girl."

"You're a college freshman who still acts like she's in high school half the time."

"Is that what you think?"

"One of the things," Ron replied quickly. "I didn't mean to hurt you."

Alice looked on the verge of sparing Ernest Woodring the trouble of offing him, but a glance at her watch checked her anger.

"Five minutes," The Head offered obligingly.

Alice gnawed her lip.

"Sorry," Ron mumbled. "I didn't mean that."

Alice did not reply.

"It's gonna be tight," Ron noted, nodding toward the car.

"So what else is new?"

The Centauri's cockpit was so crammed and encumbered there was no way to open the passenger door without being inundated, so Alice had to wiggle her way between the sleeping bag, Ron's complex crutch, and Matty Groves.

Ron's last act before abandoning the meadow was to remove The Head from its post. "Here, hold this," he grunted, passing the muttering object to Alice while he uprooted the pole.

"Just a sec," Alice countered. "I'm sitting on something."

She was fumbling around under her thighs, while Ron glared at her. "Ah ha!" she cried triumphantly, dragging out the offending object. Ron rolled his eyes when it proved to be only a sheet of paper.

But Alice was peering at it curiously, her brows working their way toward each other. Then: "Oh my God! It's Crazy Jane!"

"Who's Crazy Jane?" Ron asked before he could stop himself.

But for once he answered his question even before The Head. He'd managed a look at the paper by then. And recognized it. It was the fax The Head had conjured up the day before.

"Oh *my* God!" he gasped. "It's my sister!"

"—ur sister," The Head echoed in perfect harmony.

Alice was staring at him incredulously. "You *know* her?"

"In a manner of speaking," Ron replied breathlessly. "More to the point, though, do you?"

"In . . . a manner of speaking," Alice replied.

"And . . . ?"

Alice took a deep breath. "She's only been here a few months, but she's . . . I guess you could say she's the local crazy woman."

Ron was in the driver's seat before she finished.

"One minute," The Head reported ominously.

As the Centauri thundered toward the end of the mile-long straight, Ron caught a flash of a dark blue vehicle entering it.

"That's them," Alice sighed wretchedly. "That's Ernest's Camaro."

Ron's response was simply to drive faster, whether toward his doom or away from it was not clear.

Chapter 19

Bad Company

Okay, kid, Ron told himself, as he stomped the Centauri's accelerator to the floor after barely brushing the brake at the end of the straight beside which he had camped, *first things first.*

Only what *was* first? An hour ago his most immediate problem had been assuaging a guilty conscience. Now, in addition to that, he had two more. One lay somewhere ahead in the person of his unknown sister and whatever weirdness was going on between her and Lew.

The other, and unfortunately much more imminent, was thundering up fast behind, in the form of a midnight blue Z-28 Camaro.

When he'd squealed out of camp less than a minute earlier, it had been little more than an azure blur in his rearview mirror. Now, alas, it was closing—near enough already for him to see the squinty, cat-eyed headlights and bottom-breather grille that were its signature recognition markers. And, more to the point, that a decent-sized man was hunched over the wheel like a fifties race car driver. A smaller, blond shape

bracing against the dash on the passenger side was undoubtedly Alice's mom.

Alice . . .

Christ, yeah: What *about* Alice? She had just—wisely—
finished excavating her seat belt and now sat staring at him,
her jaw clenched stoically, her silence probably equal parts
raw self-preservation instinct (which looked likely to get a
workout real soon) and understandable anxiety that anyone
who looked as intense and strung out as Ron figured he did
oughtn't to be addressed uninvited. Shoot, he could practically *feel* her stare, and *could* see her set expression out of
the corner of his eye, even as he found himself forced to
shield against her rioting emotions. Her hair was flagellating
her face too, as was his. Matty crouched in the foot well by
the heel of the crutch. The Centauri was doing eighty and
accelerating. The Camaro was holding its own.

"Jesus," Ron gritted, mostly to dispel his own tension.
"Goddamn! *Shit!*"

They had reached the end of a second straight now, and he
slowed minutely at the crest of the hill there. The road ahead
unwound, revealing—mercifully—*another* straight, slashing
through a pine forest this time. The car lifted gently as it
cleared the rise—rather as though it were rising on tiptoes
to peer ahead—then sank again on the other side. A shock
bottomed harshly. Ron floorboarded it. The engine shrieked,
exhausts rumbled, dopplering up toward a scream. A rack
of copper tubing strapped longways on the passenger door
decided it was a pipe organ and produced a basso thrum.
Behind him, Ernest Woodring's Chevy was still gaining size,
in spite of the Centauri's superior top speed.

"If you'd left me back there," Alice shouted—to be heard
above the roar of the wind across the metal clutter that was
playing noisy hell with the Centauri's aerodynamics *and*
handling *and* top end—"I say if you'd *left* me back there,
you wouldn't be having to do this now!"

"If I'd left you back there," Ron yelled back, now that
he had an instant's grace in which to respond, "God knows
what'd be happening to you right now; and *I* wouldn't have
found out that you know my sister—know *of* her, anyway."

"They'd be yelling at me," Alice told him, through her

writhing hair, "and I've been yelled at before. Besides, it couldn't change what what we did, or take away my memory of it. I mean they weren't gonna shoot *me*, for God's sakes. And I doubt Ernest *intends* to shoot you. It's . . . just for security, like I said. It's—I guess it's what he thinks he *ought* to do, 'specially if he wants to impress Mom."

"Yes," The Head affirmed, "it is."

"Fine!" Ron spat. "Now what about this Crazy Jane person? Do you know where she lives?"

"Y-eah," Alice replied uneasily. "I think so—I've never been there, though—not since *she* moved in."

"So is it near here, then? Or what?" Ron demanded. "I mean, *Jesus*, girl, speak up!"

Alice swallowed nervously. "Uh, more or less, I guess. It's . . . *kinda* off this road."

"Can you show me?" Ron tried hard to rein his desperation.

The girl glanced over her shoulder. "*Now?*"

"Hell yes, now!—If we can. I mean, I've only been lookin' for her for about ten years, and—" He broke off.

"What?"

"I've . . . got reason to believe she may be—That is, that my brother may be in danger."

"From Jane? I'm not surprised."

"So where *is* she? I mean, the sooner the better."

"But what about Ernest?" Alice yelled. "I thought you wanted to lose him."

"They're *not* mutually exclusive! Now: you gonna tell me or not?"

Alice looked utterly wretched. "Oh, crap, I'm—uh, Jane scares me. Do I *have* to?"

"Yes," Ron snapped. "You do."

"Okay then . . . just stay on this road for a while."

"Great!" Ron sighed as he tapped the brake at the end of the straight and slowed for a brace of fast left-righters he hoped the Centauri could navigate faster than the Camaro. Trouble was Ron's car weighed about fifty percent more than usual, courtesy of its metallic encumbrances, and that was screwing up the handling. He wondered, absently, when the country music song he'd awakened into had shifted to a bad-movie chase scene. And, unfortunately, that didn't look like changing anytime soon. It was impossible to slow old Ernest down with the Luck during this kind of high-stress, close-attention driving, and he couldn't shake the bloody Camaro long enough to hide.

"So all I've gotta do now is lose this car, and then go look for my brother—and . . . Dammit, I *need* to do *one* first, but I *wanta* do the other first. And—Oh Jesus—Argghhhh!— Which *one*, dammit?"

"Was that a question?" The Head inquired.

"I haven't noticed that it needs to be," Ron told it, on the gas again.

"You did not like it the last time I volunteered," The Head pointed out.

"I'd take anything now," Ron growled. "Anything to get outta this mess."

"Fine," The Head said. "If you concentrate on evading pursuit, you will succeed—eventually. I cannot be more specific, because there are too many variables at work—too *many* futures. On the other hand—"

"What?"

"If you do not reach your brother in twenty-two minutes, he will die."

"Die?" Ron cried, thunderstruck. "Lew can't die!"

"Immolation that produces so much pain so quickly that the Luck cannot compensate, and so one wishes for death," The Head replied promptly. "Decapitation without rapid re-attachment or access to appropriate organic material, and sometimes even then, from shock. Utter destruction of brain cells beyond a critical threshold. Wishing for death itself. And stabbing in the heart with a dagger made in seven days under light of sun and light of moon, by a person who can Listen but has no Voice."

"Of which there is exactly one in the world," Ron told it dryly.

"Artifact? Or artificer?" The Head asked politely.

"Either—*shit*—*both*. I dunno. Does it matter?"

"If you speak of the latter," The Head responded, "there are many. If you refer to the former, there are two."

Ron felt as if he'd been jabbed in the stomach. *"Two?"*

"One in your vault. And a less well made but still service-able one in the possession of your sister—which she intends to use very soon."

It took an instant for the words to sink in. "You're not *kiddin'*, are you? You mean she's actually gonna *kill* Lew? But . . . *why*?"

"Because she covets his position—and because she is insane."

Ron pounded the steering wheel helplessly. "Jesus *shit!*" he cried. *"Fucking damn!"*

Alice looked at him wide-eyed. "What . . . *are* you?"

"Not human," Ron gritted, not looking at her. "You want out now? 'Cause I don't have time for fiddlin' around any-more. Just tell me where my sister is *now*, 'cause I'm headin' straight there."

"I *can't* tell you," Alice replied stiffly. "It's too compli-cated. And I'm damned well not gonna abandon you!"

"It's too dangerous," Ron insisted. (The Camaro was clos-er: less than a hundred yards.) "You don't have a clue what you're getting into here."

"What I'm getting into is getting somebody I like *out* of trouble."

"Twenty-one minutes," The Head announced. "In one future you save your brother, in one you do not. The options fork evenly."

"Christ!" Ron grunted helplessly. "Jesus!"

"It's not far to the first turn to Jane's," Alice sighed finally, in what Ron suspected was forced calm. "It's just past the top of that hill coming up here. If you really stand on it, you can make it over in time to lose Ernest."

"If," Ron echoed sourly. "Where've I heard *that* before?"

"No, just over this hill there's a curve, and then a dirt road turns off to the left between some trees, and—Damn! Look out!"

It was too late—for Ron had already crested the rise, and had no time to do anything but tighten his grip on the steering wheel, as the road ahead was suddenly full of the queen mother of all great wall-to-wall potholes. He slammed the brakes with full strength, tried to dive to what he hoped was the shallower portion, but even so, impacted the obstruction with sickening force. Brakes screamed, shocks bottomed. His torso strained against the belts. Nothing broke up front, so far as he could tell; but there was no way all those overstressed suspension components could absorb such impact unscathed. Worse, a vast clanking and snapping joined the established cacophony, and a good part of the metal lashed around the sides jolted loose. Some snapped back into fragile aluminum bodywork. Other bits came untied and dragged along the pavement, shooting sparks until they bounced free. Cold comfort that: maybe they'd slow down good old Ernest.

Unfortunately, before Ron had properly recovered from the first set of holes, a second was upon him. He hit them with only marginally less force than the first. Matty Groves found himself kicked by Alice, yowled and scratched her. She screamed, jerked reflexively. And in that instant the car struck a final hole.

"Crap!" Alice cried, suddenly all grabbing hands—even as Ron glimpsed, with sick dismay, The Head flying from her grasp to disappear over the trunk. He thought he heard a metallic crunch as it impacted the cratered pavement, though there was so *much* stuff clattering around back there, he couldn't be sure. But a glance at the mirror showed it tumbling along the shoulder on their side.

Already on the brakes, he steered right and parked the car half on the margin, half in the road. Ernest was still coming on, but had slowed a lot—presumably because he knew about the potholes—and because the road ahead of him suddenly looked more like a junkyard than a highway. Ron had bare seconds to retrieve The Head. "Stay here," he told Alice. "If I don't make it back, take off and—I dunno—go to Jane's and do . . . whatever you can, I guess. Hell, do what you wanta do."

Alice started to speak, but by then Ron had climbed out of the car, though he left it idling (the motor was apparently still fine). An instant later, he was limping beside the weed-filled ditch below the road. Water squished into his sneakers. Pines loomed close.

But where was the blessed Head? He'd been on the brakes when it had jolted out, and even damaged, the Centauri had brakes from hell—so it *couldn't* be more than a hundred or so feet back.

"Ronnnn!" Alice screamed. "Hurry!"

Ron looked up, saw the Camaro in full view and much closer than he'd expected. An instant only it took him to decide. The Head could wait, Lew couldn't. It was a tool, but not his only one. He turned and ran-limp-hopped back to the idling Centauri.

"Stop, you asshole," a deep male voice bellowed behind him. But Ron never faltered. He had the car in gear before he was fully in the seat, and floored the gas as he settled into it. A shot rang out, gravel flew, metal zinged. Not a shot at him, though, but at the car. At the tires. A storm of gravel arched from beneath the rear Pirellis, possibly blunting another shotgun attack, and then they were under way again. Ernest's car was a mere thirty yards behind.

Ron punched the Centauri for all it was worth, heard the engine scream and felt the front end vibrating alarmingly as it gathered speed.

"There's the *turn!*" Alice shrieked, but it was already too late. No way he could have made it, not with Ernest so close. He'd have had a trunk full of Chevy, a dead passenger, and would have been no great shakes himself.

And Lew would die.

"Is there another way?" Ron yelled.

"Y-eah," Alice told him, wide eyed. "If you don't mind goin' through a swamp."

"If it'll get me to Lew in time, I'll crawl through fire," Ron shot back. "Now where?"

"Two miles—maybe."

"Road like this?"

"Better—I think. I didn't know about those potholes."

Ron nodded grimly and drove absolutely as fast as he dared. The Camaro had fallen back a bit, and blessedly there were no more shotgun blasts, though he half-expected to see good old Ernest leaning out the window every time he dared a glance in the mirror. But the Camaro was hanging back, making its way carefully—Ron assumed because, unlike him, Ernest didn't have unlimited resources with which to effect repairs. Or maybe he didn't have to hurry. Maybe he could afford to take his time.

Ron couldn't. And now, without The Head, he had no idea how much time remained. The only good point about the encounter with the pothole was that it had shaken enough material free that the car was lighter. Which meant faster—marginally. And come to it, maybe *that* was what was slowing down Ernest. He'd had to pick his way around the metallic detritus; Ron had seen him. Maybe he'd picked up a puncture as well. Serve him right, for trying to puncture Ron.

A final glance in the mirror as Ron launched into a series of curves gave small comfort. The Camaro was well back, maybe an eighth of a mile. They were still roaring through forests, though there were fewer pines and more hardwoods.

"There," Alice cried shakily, pointing ahead and to the left, "just past that big oak there's a dirt track. Turn left. It's rough and overgrown, so get ready to bounce."

"No problem."

"*Maybe* a problem," she countered. "I don't know if a car this low'll make it. We may have to go on foot."

"I'll go on my belly," Ron said. "On glass and nails, rather than wait. I'll—Oh shit, *now*!"

The oak had been closer than Ron thought, and the turn *much* sooner after. He slammed the brakes, jerked the wheel hard left (sending more of his raw material skittering down the highway as the car skidded sideways). And then, with one final prod of the accelerator, he was arrowing straight into what looked like a narrow patch of broom sedge between the landmark white oak and a smaller stand farther down.

He made it with no problem, though the car bottomed instantly and he found himself forced to slow to a crawl because what little way there was wound between trees barely more than the car's width apart. Unfortunately, the Centauri was wider than Ernest's Camaro—but the Chevy didn't have four-wheel-drive. And though the system on Ron's car was designed for added traction, not off-road use, it still gave it an advantage. *If* he could get far enough ahead to outrun bullets.

That was problematical. Every yard traveled brought them into denser growth, brought more bushes to scrape along the sides, more snags and rocks and fallen logs to smack the bellypan, more muddy ruts to slow them down. The tires spun often and the car jolted constantly as first one tire, then another, found itself on dry ground and the electronics shunted traction that way.

The worst thing, though, was the time. Every foot advanced brought them closer to Lew, but every second that elapsed was one more in which Ernest could catch up with them. Ron hadn't a clue where he was, could see nothing behind them but low-hanging leaves and high-rising grass. And their own too-obvious trail.

And then, abruptly, something fouled the chassis, and the car could go no farther. Ron mashed the gas, heard tires spin and grumble, saw mud arch out in rooster tails behind, felt a jolt as traction shifted again—and then the car lurched forward. A deafening metallic roar followed, and he knew he'd ripped the exhausts off. The car made it another hundred yards, but the ruts were full of mud now, and more and more, of standing water. He caught the sick-sweet smell of decaying vegetable matter, and the trees were suddenly closer together, with the hickories quickly being replaced by scraggly cypresses.

One final gentle incline proved to be dry and fairly open, but the slope beyond was steeper than he'd expected—and Ron's heart sank, for the track ended at its foot in a wide expanse of what could have been either mud or water.

"Shit," he said, as he turned the engine off. "Damn. Hell. *Fuck!*"

"Yeah," Alice agreed unhappily. "You said it."

Ron was already levering himself over the window ledge. "So, how much farther?"

"I dunno," Alice groaned, her wretched expression adding to the pain in her voice as she joined Ron afoot. "Less than a mile I think, I'm not sure. Like I said, I've never been there—well I *have*, but not in a while. I walked down this way once when I was a kid, back when the place was deserted. And I knew Jane was living there 'cause I'd heard folks say as much. But . . . it really has been a while."

"Well, we've got *maybe* fifteen minutes," Ron gasped, reaching into the passenger side for his crutch—all those impacts having messed up his knee something fierce. Matty growled at him from the footwell but would not be dislodged. Ron left him, having no time to argue. Pet or brother was no hard choice.

"So five–ten minutes to get us there, and then . . . who knows?" he sighed, limping ahead. "Maybe we'll make it. Maybe."

"If Ernest doesn't find us first."

Ron paused in place. "Christ, yeah! Well, him I *can* check on."

"I thought you were in—"

But Ron wasn't listening. Or rather he was, but not to Alice. He had found sufficient support in the trunk of a white oak, and was leaning against it. Three breaths, and he'd Jumped.

And immediately discovered two very troubling things. One was somebody hopping mad trudging his way on foot—but still at least a quarter mile behind. He *thought* the person was male, but there was so much single-minded anger everything else was obscured. A second mind accompanied it, too, this one female and becoming less convinced of her mission every second.

The other thing was worse.

Somewhere up ahead was a Silence. An intangible shield born of some Listener's mind that served as an impenetrable barrier against all Listener powers, whether from within or without. It wasn't a physical construct, but that didn't mean it would be easy to breach. Which meant maybe even more time expended.

And if Ernest caught up with them . . .

Ron simply could not let that happen. Grimacing unconsciously, he drew deeper into himself, found the wind that was Alice's mother, rode it back to its source—and lashed out. Not to kill, not even to harm, merely to shock a few key mental centers. He felt a burst of startlement, followed immediately by Ernest's realization that his companion had—to all appearances—fainted.

Ron returned to himself. Blinked into the still–early morning haze. Alice was staring at him wide-eyed and dubious. He could no longer afford to care. "Hurry," he grunted, slinging the crutch under his arm and wishing he'd thought to bring the Derringer he'd threatened Gwent with. "Show me the way," he added, more softly.

She pointed to the right of the Centauri's dented and muddy nose, to where what *might* be a trail curved around the margin of the bog.

Ron nodded and eased past her to take the lead, walking as fast as he absolutely could, given his bum knee and the crutch, with Alice panting along behind. To the left was marsh and low ground. To the right higher slopes grew thick with small-leaved bushes. The path was a mass of grass and weeds, distinguished from the surrounding foliage only by its lower height. Ahead, the trail appeared to swing west, as the ground opened slightly. He thought he could glimpse a fragment of shingled roof a good way off to the left. "That it?" he called, pointing, glancing over his shoulder for Alice's reaction.

Abruptly, he slipped, for the ground had oozed beneath his foot. He jerked back reflexively, trying to twist around in place. But something else was quicker. He caught a flash of brown and bronze scales, metal-bright in the sunlight, and then his right calf was on fire. A forward roll sent him tumbling out of range—and sent both hands into something between lukewarm mud and cold, slimy water.

"What . . . ?" he heard Alice cry uncertainly.

"Snake!"

He was instantly drenched with sweat, and his leg was a mass of torment. But as he sat gripping it above the knee, he had sufficient presence of mind to see a surprisingly calm-looking Alice pick up a forked stick and walk calmly toward him. The reptile was already slithering away to his left—fleeing both of them. Green venom stained the side of his jeans.

Ron clenched his teeth and resisted the temptation to clamp his leg harder so as to stem the blood flow. The Luck would fight it, but it wouldn't be fun to live in his body while it was a combat zone.

And he still had to get to Lew.

Alice was instantly at his side. "What kind . . . ?" she asked, "I didn't see."

"Copperhead," Ron gasped between his teeth. "Got me in

the calf. I think it was a light hit—mostly hurts."

"I bet," Alice breathed nervously. "Jesus, so *now* we've gotta get you to a doctor."

"*No*! I'll be fine," Ron told her flatly. "This won't kill me, but Lew *will* die if I don't get there pronto."

Alice studied him for a moment, once more in her adult, take-charge persona. "Well, then," she said, reaching into her pocket, "here." Whereupon she produced a scarlet bandanna, with which she made to bind Ron's leg below the knee.

He waved her away. "Sorry," he gritted. "The more it disperses in my body, the faster I can fight it. It'll hurt like holy hell, and may make me sick, but that's not important now." He did not add that he doubted he could make it another mile that way. And knew he had to. The entire encounter, he reckoned, had already cost them two minutes.

"Help me," he grunted, reaching for his crutch and rising to his feet, to stand swaying, leaning against the girl.

Grimacing with every step, he soldiered on.

The worst thing was the waiting—far worse than the throb in his leg, the sickness he could feel circling his stomach, the dizziness that wracked his head. An hour from now it would be over, one way or another. Either he'd find Lew in time, or he wouldn't. Either Ernest would catch up with him or he wouldn't. The guy was still back there, Ron knew. Even without Listening, Alice's would-be stepdad was upset enough that Ron could catch snatches of the super-strong emotions he was broadcasting.

"Uh . . . I hate to ask this," Alice gasped, as she paused to help Ron shift to a better hold. "But . . . exactly how *are* you planning to rescue your brother?"

Ron froze as if he'd been shot. "I . . . honestly don't *know*," he said truthfully, and was almost sick all over again. "I won't know until I get there."

"Any idea?" As they trudged on.

Ron shook his head, trying not to gag at the feel of his own tongue in his mouth. "The only thing I know is that once we're in sight of that house, you're gonna hightail it out of here. I don't want you getting hurt. And that's a very real possibility."

Alice did not reply.

Please God let there be time, Ron thought. *Oh, please God let there be time.*

The next minutes were a blur, as the pain in his leg redoubled, and Ron found himself forced to focus purely on that, purely on staying upright. Each step took centuries. Every breath was an agony. Once, in spite of everything, he vomited, and blackness hovered near.

But when he looked up from reviewing the previous night's meal, it was to see the roof he'd spotted earlier gleaming dully beyond a froth of white pines no more than a hundred yards distant.

"Brace me," he told Alice curtly. And when he felt her arms close around him, he closed his eyes, breathed thrice, and Jumped.

The Silence was still there, like a dome of invisible psychic *nothing* surrounding the building beyond.

"We're close," Alice breathed, when he'd blinked back to himself.

"Yeah—if I'm not already too late," he managed, between bouts of nausea. "Now, I'm gonna try to get to those trees there. Once I've got a clear view of the house, I want you— that is, I'm *ordering* you—to get the hell out of here. Don't you *dare* follow me. Is that clear? Ernest and your mom are still coming on, and if they stumble into this—I don't wanta think what might happen. It'll be bad enough if I lose Lew, but one death's still preferable to three or four."

"We'll see," was Alice's sole reply.

It took all the energy Ron could muster to limp-hop those last few yards to the first of the massive pines that looked to have been part of an avenue leading into what, when he could peer out at it from the spice-scented gloom of the low-swooping branches, proved to be a crumbling plantation house—the two-story sort with elevated verandas on all four sides and six Doric columns to a face—though the one on the nearest corner was missing, and the roof there sagged ominously.

He paused on the marge of the overgrown yard, breathing heavily, but managed one final reconnaissance. A Jump showed that he was literally within the nontangible edge of the Silence. It manifested as a sort of white noise, as if each

Voice from within was exactly canceled by an opposite. But it was a veil, not an obstruction.

This, then, was it.

"Stay," he hissed at Alice, who stood staring wide-eyed in the shadows of an ancient tree. "If I'm not back in . . . an hour, get the hell out of here. Call the cops, or somebody; but, under no circumstances, go in. If you see anyone leave except me or a young-looking blond guy, wait an hour and have somebody check—carefully. That's all I can tell you."

"But I—"

"No!" Ron echoed. And with that he stared her in the eyes and Jumped. An instant only it took for him to locate the centers of Alice's consciousness. And with great regret, he triggered them. The girl was already sagging downward when he Jumped back to himself. He caught her clumsily, eased her awkwardly to the ground, with her back propped against the tree. He hated himself for what he had just done, but he'd truly had no other choice—no way she'd have done as he'd ordered, he'd known that from her expression when she'd protested. Even so, she'd only be out a short time. He hoped that was all he needed. But until then, he dared brook no interference.

And then, without further delay, Ron turned and limped toward Crazy Jane's decaying mansion.

It is only pain, he told himself, when his leg threatened to buckle. *You can bear anything for a little while,* he added, as he found himself without strength to climb the three low steps that led to the wide veranda, whence a screen door looked to give onto a hall.

Somehow he made it, though he had to fall on all fours to do so and, for the barest instant, resigned himself to simply lying on the top step and letting the blackness take him while the Luck fought copperhead poison in his veins.

But he had to be very nearly out of time.

From somewhere he found strength to continue. He used the crumbling whitewashed brick wall beside the screen door to brace against while he maneuvered the crutch to bring him to his feet. By rolling along the wall and across the door, he reached the handle. He fumbled it open. It squealed wildly, but he no longer cared. Any Listener powerful enough—and paranoid enough—to raise a Silence like the one here was canny enough to know he was nearby. The only remaining hope was that he might yet cause enough delay to effect a rescue. After all, hadn't The Head said that if he *didn't* get there in twenty-two minutes, Lew would die? He prayed he still had time. And stumbled across the threshold.

The gloom inside made him blink. And it was an odd sort of gloom, part dust, part dark wallpaper, part suddenly cloudy day. The air smelled like dust too, and mildew; but it also smelled like freshly baked bread, and exotic spices, and garlic. The hallway, he saw, was empty save for a dying burgundy sofa to the right. Opposite it, a staircase rose to the upper floors. He hesitated, wondering which way to proceed. His eyes told him nothing, nor his ears. A quick Jump brought so much anti-Voice he could not localize. But there was *something*, he realized, something familiar . . .

He closed his eyes, tried to banish the bouts of nausea, of dizziness, long enough to focus. Almost had it, lost it again, tried to relax, lost it one more time—and then fixed it.

It was an odor. A bitter-metallic earthy smell that could only have one source.

Calling on his last bit of strength, he staggered past the stairs to the aft end, where, sure enough, a door stood open, revealing a flight of steps leading down to what had to be a cellar. The odor of raw earth roiled up to meet him, and with it that other, much more troubling one: the strange mold that grew only beneath the homes of Masters.

Ron made it down two steps by leaning against the wall, but the third tread rocked when he put his weight on it. He lost his footing and pitched forward—and had just sense enough to tuck his head in before his shoulders impacted wood, followed immediately by his upper pelvis. The whole world was red pain and blackness and too much noise for far too long.

And then he opened his eyes.

He was sprawled athwart the splintered bottom tread of the staircase he'd just tumbled down, half on earth, half on wood, the splinters of which poked him painfully. The space around him, as best he could determine amid the concussion-born flashes that disrupted his vision, was brightly, if unevenly lit, partly by shafts of dawn light filtering through dirty, semicircular windows that opened high up beneath the elevated porch; but also by a whole phalanx of candles that guttered on the boxes and barrels and odd lots of defunct furniture that littered what was obviously a basement storeroom, painting the whole chamber black and red and gold to match perfectly the colors his fall and the venom were conjuring in his head.

Still too winded and dazed to even attempt to rise, he fumbled to either side and found raw earth where the original boards had either been ripped or rotted away. The smell of mold was well-nigh overpowering. Dimly, he sought for his crutch, but could not locate it. No, wait, there it was: bent and twisted and out of reach beneath an ancient rocker.

And then something moved amidst the hazy, red-gold flickerings farther to his right and, almost against his will, Ron felt his gaze drawn that way.

And whimpered like a child. It was Lew: palely naked and spread-eagled on the raw earth atop a candle-ringed star of the familiar ghastly mold. A jingle made Ron look closer, and he realized his brother's wrists and ankles were chained to stakes driven into the earth. A gag of shimmering crimson fabric kept him from speaking, but his eyes, though unfocused with what Ron presumed was some kind of drug, were eloquent with terror.

And then Ron noticed something equally disturbing: what he had thought a sheet of discarded drapery to his left moved, to reveal a beautiful fair-haired woman sitting calmly in an ornate wicker chair, with her feet in the lap of a blank-eyed girl child of eleven or twelve. Both wore simple white cotton robes: sleeveless and ankle-length.

Ron tried to rise, to throw himself forward, but for a bare second his gaze brushed the woman's—and he found his will completely severed from his body. He absolutely could not move!

He had to fight to retain consciousness, so great a shock had that attack been to his already overloaded system. God, but she was strong! And with a footholder too—Jesus, there was probably little she *couldn't* do. He'd *never* been that strong, not even during his brief stint as Master. He'd been a fool even to think he could defeat her, inexperienced as he was, even in perfect condition.

The woman smiled abruptly, forcing his attention back to her—no way he could not look, either: not at someone *that* gorgeous. Ron wasn't bad looking, he'd been told; Lew was a pretty kind of handsome. Wendy had been essentially Lew as a girl, and had been *quite* fetching, even as darkly striking Brandy was. But their sister . . . Crazy she might be, but not to look at. And the child with her . . . Ron forced himself to examine her as well. There was something odd there: too close a resemblance. Unless . . .

"I'm pleased you could drop by, brother," the woman whispered, in an odd mix of Southern and British accents. "Consider yourself welcome to stay as long as you like. And yes, you're correct—about a number of things, in fact. I *am* stronger than you. And she *is* my daughter. And while you may think that perverse, there are no actual Rules against Masters using their offspring as I have chosen—risks, yes; Rules, no. I *should* use a boy, for instance, but I don't, so there. But there *is* the convenient fact that the Binding Ritual that gives me access to the Strength of her . . . innocence also robs her of her Voice. Which, of course, means that she can Listen—or will one day—but has no Voice. Which I believe was a condition for something or other."

Once more Ron tried to rise, to break the lethargy that numbed his limbs—but could not. Only his mouth was free— barely. "Why . . . ?" he croaked.

"Why what? Why did I let you reach here? Because you were coming anyway, and I'd never met you and I thought I ought to—and mayhap because I thought there ought to be a witness. Why am I planning to kill our brother? Because I want his Strength—which I will acquire when his blood stains *my* land here. Oh, and for several other reasons as well—such as an end to the male monopoly on Masterships."

"You're—"

—"Crazy? Mad? *Insane?* Perhaps. But no more than any of our kind, really. And in case you're curious; no, I'm *not* going to kill you—at least no time soon. Oh, you have Strength aplenty, but it's imperfect because you are, and I don't trust it. And I'm already stronger than you are, so there's no reason I can think of to kill you now—there's nothing in it for me. And while I consider *some* deaths a necessity, I never consider them desirable—not when they neither provide profit nor negate threat.

"And," she added, after a thoughtful pause, during which Ron managed to drag his gaze back to the wild-eyed Lew— which had the sole effect of blurring his vision with tears. "And, I say; there *is* one other thing. It's . . . I suppose you could say it's symbolic. Lew there could be the sun god: male power embodied; fire and air. And I, a woman: victim and votary of the moon; earth and water." Another pause. "You never thought you'd ever see a myth enacted, did you? Well, then, shall I tell you another? The earth lay with the sky two nights ago—though I suppose that's an odd image, given that I was on top. I . . ."

Ron tuned out the rest. This woman, this . . . *creature*— Jane, or whatever her real name was—truly was over the edge. And there was no way he could stop her. *No way.* All he could do was lie there, with his brain already half-fried from snake poison, his body a mass of agony, and his nerves and muscles utterly beyond his command. But he wouldn't watch, and he bloody well wouldn't listen!

"Oh yes you will!" Jane snapped, her voice suddenly hard as stone. "You will watch what I *want* you to watch and hear what I have to say. And as for that . . . well, I hope you won't mind if I go ahead and kill our brother."

And with that she swung her feet from the girl child's lap, rose, and stepped forward. A short, rough forged knife suddenly glittered in her left hand. The girl sagged back, apparently asleep: a beautiful discarded doll.

Ron had a flash of déjà vu, as he recalled how ten years before he had chanced on a similar scene, only then it was his cousin Anson tormenting the captive Lew.

"Yes," his sister told him. "I know that tale. But I don't want him to suffer; I only want him to die."

One final time Ron tried to move—and failed. A glance from his sister distanced him from his body more than ever.

But not so far that he could not watch—indeed had no *choice* but to watch—as the woman called Crazy Jane walked thrice around his brother and knelt among the candles on the opposite side.

Which gave him an unobstructed view, as, with too-deliberate slowness, she raised the knife—and with a ripple of white arm slammed it down.

Chapter 20

Killing Floor

To Ron's shock-numbed ears, the three sounds occurred simultaneously. One was the desperate, helpless *"No!"* that tore from his throat in spite of Crazy Jane's psychic bindings. A second was the bestial scream of pain and anguish that exploded from that same wild-eyed woman as the knife and the hand that clutched it were both blown to flinders at precisely the same instant as a result of the *third* sound: the thunder-crack report of a shotgun going off at very close range somewhere behind him. The aftershocks of the heavy *bang* were still echoing from the stone walls and exposed ceiling joists when the room erupted into chaos.

Ron tried to rise, but his muscles would still do no more than twitch, and that but weakly, like limbs that had been confined too long and gone numb. Something warm, wet, and sticky splattered across his face; and the room was suddenly awash with red—from candles that abruptly flamed high, from a bright new agony inside his skull that could be Jane's psychic backwash—or copperhead venom as easily. But mostly from the blood that fountained from the ugly pulpy mass that seconds before had been his sister's left hand. He stared, dully fascinated, more than half in shock, as she gaped first at the ruined limb, then at the small crimson puddle it was forming on Lew's chest, and finally at something out of sight behind Ron. She did not speak, though—beyond that first spontaneous utterance. Rather—and this was far worse—she rose stiffly to her feet. Her gaze brushed him again as she stood, but now hate seemed to have replaced contempt in her eyes. Her lips drew back in a near-snarl.

But neither of them had time to dwell on the other, for footsteps sounded behind him: light and heavy treads mixing as they pounded down the dusty steps across the bottommost of which he lay sprawled, all mingled with a cacophony of voices Ron could not unscramble.

From somewhere he found strength enough to twist his neck around—barely far enough to glimpse three denim-clad people halfway down the stairs—one of whom was Alice. Which meant it had probably been the troublesome Ernest whose timely marksmanship had saved Lew's bacon at the last possible instant. Which meant that the other person was undoubtedly Alice's mom.

Unfortunately, Ron had a much *clearer* view of Jane and knew from bitter experience what that glitter in her eyes portended. A sneer, a harsh intake of breath, and the heartening sounds behind him ceased abruptly, replaced with shouts and groans of primal fear. The air thrummed with Luck, and Ron tried to shield but could not. Thus, he caught an echo of what had stilled his would-be rescuers where they stood.

Dreams: three people's innermost fears snatched from their psyches by an insane Listener and made manifest.

Alice's mom's nightmare was simplest. She was assailed by telephone calls from people wanting her to pay bills she could *not* pay, while one would-be husband after another told her it was her problem and walked out the door, leaving her with more bills, more ringing telephones. More bills . . . more phones . . .

Alice's curse was more complex but subtler; for in it she was trapped in a non-existence: a housewife with squalling children, soap operas and football games playing endlessly on a too-loud TV, while an abusive, indolent husband, who looked a lot like Ernest, alternately complained, demanded food and beer, and peppered her ears with insults and demands for loveless sex.

Ernest dreamed people were laughing at him. Hundreds and hundreds of well-dressed, attractive people pointing at him and guffawing and jeering and calling him stupid and ignorant and just plain dumb. And oddly, of all three, Ron could empathize with his revulsion most.

"That should keep them entertained, for a while," Jane snorted contemptuously, turning her attention back to Ron. She had clamped her mangled arm above the wrist, he noted, but already the bleeding had slowed to a trickle. Impulsively, she crossed to stand beside him, let a few drops splatter onto his face as she glared at him in triumph. "A brave effort, that was," she hissed. "But all it does is deny our brother a quick death and replace it with a slow one."

And with that she turned and swept across the room. Ron couldn't see what she did there, amid the cobwebbed shelves beneath a dust-smeared window; but when she turned again, his heart literally missed a beat. For in her one good hand she held a square red can the size of the Atlanta telephone directory that, by the thick chemical odor already permeating the musty, smoky air from the unscrewed nozzle, surely contained gasoline.

Ron's gaze slipped back to Lew, whose eyes were practically bugging out of his head—though if he was broadcasting anything, Ron couldn't Hear it—which did not bode well. Probably whatever Jane had done to subdue him had shorted out that talent. No way Ron wouldn't be Hearing *something* otherwise, Silence or no Silence. For an instant their gazes locked, and Lew tried to nod, as if to say he understood why Ron could not help and held no rancor for it.

The metallic swish/slosh of the can's contents being agitated yanked Ron's attention back to his sister. But surely she would not do *that*! *Surely* not. Surely not even Crazy Jane would seriously consider burning his—*their*—brother alive!

"Of course I would," she said amiably, though her voice held an undertone of pain. She sloshed the can again, as if in punctuation. "Blood on the earth would have been best, so that the Land could drink of Lewis's Luck as I would then have drunk the Luck of the Land in turn. But his Luck can escape into smoke almost as easily, and *that* I can inhale, and so come by what I seek that way."

And with that she took a step—still a few yards from Lew, the same from her sleeping daughter, twice that from Ron.

Ron never knew what happened then—precisely. The best he could recall was that the ground . . . *shrugged*, the very earth beneath him twitching and rolling as though in the throes of a tiny, localized earthquake. The candles flared and wavered, and he heard the creak and groan of timbers straining, the tinkle of breaking glass, the distant thump of tumbling furniture. And the heavy swish-thud of his sister losing her balance and falling backward with the open can of gasoline atop her. The air was suddenly rank with its fumes.

"Odd," Jane mused distantly, as she staggered awkwardly to her feet once more, oblivious to the dampness that plastered her gown to her thighs and breasts—and the candles guttering dangerously close to the trailing hem on every side.

"Not odd to the Land," a small voice countered, behind her. "Not if the Land rejects you!"

"What?" Jane spat, spinning around. But it was already too late. For her daughter had risen from where she'd been—apparently—feigning sleep and was now walking steadily toward her mother, with a candle she had snatched from beside the chair clutched before her like a votive offering.

"Let him go," the girl said calmly, her eyes cold as those of any hardened adult. "Let him go, or I'll have to . . ."—she swallowed, looking suddenly very young—"to kill you."

"Like hell!" Jane shouted, darting forward, but drawing back again as her child whipped the candle before her like a dagger. "Damn, child, what *are* you doing?"

"I'm looking out for myself," the girl said, once again sounding far more adult than she appeared. "I'm *tired* of this, Mama; and the Land's tired of it too, 'cause it just told me it was. I'm *tired* of you sneaking around all the time, and making me sneak with you; and I'm tired of you messing with my head and my memory and my dreams; and I'm tired of you acting crazy all the time, and pretending you're something you're not, and of you wanting people to like you, but wanting to make 'em afraid of you too. And I'm *real* tired of not ever getting a chance to do what *I* want to do and just be me, like everybody else. I . . . guess I'm tired of being a puppet and existing only so I can give you power, 'cause that really is what it feels like most of the time. I'm a *kid*, for God's sake, I want a real life too! And not as your power battery, or whatever that is you do with me when you put your feet in my lap and I don't remember. And really not as . . . whatever you are when I grow up."

"Give me that," Jane spat, calmly reaching for the candle, as if the entire previous explosion of emotion had not occurred. "Brat," she added.

"Possibly," the girl acknowledged, her eyes wide with hurt. Ron wondered if she really knew what she was doing or was faking. He strained upward for a better view—and felt, to his surprised relief, the paralysis in his limbs receding. He could move his head, neck, torso, and upper arms; though every time he did, he came *that* close to vomiting. "Possibly," the girl repeated. "But not crazy, not like you. The Land's looking out for me now."

"And what would *you* know?" Jane raged.

"I know what I read in the minds of five people while you were putting on your little play, Mama! I know what I learned while you figured I was still unconscious, still your little doll to be turned off and on whenever *you* wanted her. But the Land woke me, and told me to Listen, and I did. And I found out I'd rather be like these people than like you!"

"Traitor!"

"Only a word," the girl countered shakily. At which point she sidestepped her mother and started toward Lew. "Do you want to unchain him, or shall I?"

"I want him *dead*!" Jane snapped—and made to fling the remaining gasoline across Lew: an awkward gesture, one-handed.

The girl whirled instinctively to block her, and in that instant, the gasoline splashed across the candle in the child's hand. As sometimes happens, the candle was extinguished, but the backwash of liquid took flame and hung in the air like an arch of fire, from the ground near Lew's left foot, extending across the girl's hand, to the can, and thence up Jane's arm and onto her robe.

With a whoosh like a wild spring wind, the room erupted into light and heat. Jane screamed, but already she was ablaze from head to foot. Ron, still mostly paralyzed, could do nothing to help her—as instinct demanded he do. As for Jane's daughter, she was calmly beating out the few flames that had awakened on her own flesh and clothing, her face grim, cold, unreadable—even when a second scream cut through the room then, born of pain and terror. And then another, this one Ron's, as the man-high torch that was his sister flung itself atop his helplessly shackled brother. Lew grunted and groaned and thrashed, and Ron saw fire crisp away the golden hair on his nearside arm and leg.

But then another, smaller shape heaved itself atop the blazing woman. *"No!"* the girl yelled. "No, Mama. No more!"

Somehow the child managed to roll her mother free of Lew, and together they writhed and twisted across the earth floor, knocking candles awry with every movement, each of which birthed more flames. The girl's robe caught fire—inevitably—and she screamed as the pain bit her flesh. She tried to fight free of her mother's embrace, but succeeded only in trapping herself between the larger woman and the wall.

The room was alive with Luck: hate, anger, fear, all. But the worst was pain: the agony of two burning humans broadcast into the Winds. Even receiving it at remove, Ron could scarcely bear it; it made him want to run, to hide, to—*die!* He tried to shield, but even as he did, he felt the strongest waves falter and start to fade. And as the blaze rose higher in the corner, and the air filled with dark, greasy smoke and the dreadful odor of burning hair and cloth and crisping flesh, he felt the last of his sister's hold on him dissolve.

It was like a gasp when she died: a gasp of relief from him, as he found his limbs his own again, and from the spirits—twin spirits—now freed from pain neither of them was prepared to face.

A movement, a set of relieved exhalations from the stairs behind him was Alice and her companions, likewise freed from their torments and taking a moment to regain their bearings.

"Jesus shit!" a male voice yelled suddenly, decisively—whereupon a heavy shape thundered past Ron, heading toward the blazing women. The man was already ripping off his jacket.

"It's too late," Ron called weakly, scrambling, with no help from the crutch, which he could not reach, to his feet—abruptly—and painfully—reminded that he was still in the throes of snakebite. "Get my brother!"

"Your . . . brother?" the man turned, scowled, then stared stupidly at the naked form still chained to the earth—the one on whose torso and thighs a red rash of burns like port-wine stain was plainly visible. Too tired and impatient to explain further, Ron staggered to the nearest of the iron stanchions that anchored Lew's chains and tried to yank it free. A pile of boxes roared with fire a yard from his back. His shirt smoked.

"Ernest!" Alice's mother cried behind them. "The curtains! The house is afire! We've gotta get outta here!"

"Not and leave this boy," Ernest hollered back stubbornly. "He ain't done nothin' wrong, an' *nobody* deserves to be burned alive."

"Here," Alice yelled, "use this!"

Ron spun around, to see her pass the shotgun to the man.

He studied it barely an instant, then looked at Lew, his face oddly sympathetic. "This may hurt a little," he rumbled. And with that, he lowered the barrel and, at point-blank range, blasted the links that bound Lew's right wrist. Three more shots followed—too slow for Ron, but Ernest had to reload each time.

By the time the last link was sundered, the room was barely habitable, so thick was the heat and smoke. Ron helped his brother to his feet, and—somehow, for he could scarcely stand himself—managed, with Alice's aid, to drag him to the stairs. The upper parts were completely masked with smoke now, leaving them no choice but to crawl if they would breathe. And even so, it took a major effort for the five of them to reach the door at the top, with Alice propping

Ron, who, with Ernest's strong arm on the other side, was supporting Lew.

Fire brushed their heels as they burst into the hall. They were all coughing, gasping; hair was crisped on more than one head, and Ron's and Ernest's clothes were smoldering.

Pausing only for a few seconds' breath, they made their way along the hall, across the veranda, and outside. By the time Ron flung himself down on the lawn twenty yards from the steps, flames were peering up from between the porch boards, and a too-red light was illuminating the windows downstairs.

"There she goes," Ernest drawled, from where he lay panting on the mossy earth beneath the nearest ancient pine.

Ron hadn't energy enough to reply. What little strength remained in him was directed toward his naked, half-conscious twin. Oblivious to his own comfort, to the venom-born nausea in his gut, the hot agony in his leg, Ron took off his shirt and tried to tie it clumsily around Lew's waist.

"Here," Ernest rumbled, shrugging out of his denim jacket. "This'll work better to cover that boy's nekkedness." Alice's mom, who was similarly attired, followed suit, and before long Lew had achieved a modicum of modesty. Between bouts of dizziness, Ron tried to assess his damage: shock least obviously; burns much more clearly, which the Luck would attend to, though the hovering Ernest and Alma didn't know that.

He was still trying to decide how to approach that, when a crash from inside the mansion shot flames into the second story. A section of roof blazed up immediately after.

"Reckon we oughta call the fire department?" Alma wondered shakily, from where she was huddled between Ernest and Alice.

"Too late for that, I reckon," Ernest said, putting his arm around her and drawing her close. " 'Sides, we've got plenty to do right here."

Ron, who was doing his best to fight down his own pain, while hugging the violently shivering Lew, could think of nothing to say. Matty Groves appeared from somewhere, looking disgustingly unperturbed, and insinuated his way between the brothers. Ron scratched the cat's head abstractedly.

Eventually Ernest looked over at him. "So," he said slowly, his gun resting easily across his lap, as he, in turn, leaned against both his pine and Alma. "You mind tellin' me what *that* was all about? I mean, if I'm gonna help out somebody that I'm pissed off at, I'd *kinda* like to know what's goin' on."

Ron took a deep breath, distantly aware that the pain in his leg was receding and that he felt considerably more clearheaded than he had even moments before. He eased himself to a more comfortable position, but still kept his shoulder against Lew, as much for his own comfort as for his twin's.

"It was"—he swallowed, and wished badly that he had a drink—"it was a whole *lot* of things. Mostly it was about a crazy woman who shouldn't have been born trying to get something she might have had a right to, but going about it the wrong way. And . . ." His voice trailed off. "No—It's . . . just too complicated."

"It's what happens when people don't talk to each other," a new voice interrupted softly. It took Ron a moment to realize it was Lew, barely conscious but clear-eyed. "I . . . told her she could have what she wanted," he whispered between shudders. "Shoot, I went *looking* for her to offer it to her, but she wouldn't listen. She had her own notion of how the land lay, and that was that. She just assumed I wanted the same thing she did, and that I was out to get her, and since she was already in the habit of using people, it just seemed logical—to her. 'Specially since she wasn't raised right and was basically about four-fifths bonkers."

"Yeah," Alice sighed. "It's like that poor little girl said: people aren't toys put here for other people's pleasure. They're living beings in their own right."

"But what *was* she?" Ernest asked plaintively. "I know she wasn't . . . human."

Alice looked intently at Ron, as if daring him to reply.

"I . . . guess you could say she was a witch," Ron sighed. "But the important thing was that she was crazy, and that had nothing to do with what she was—or only vaguely. I guess it does kind of run in the family, but usually we can watch out for it and take precautions."

Ernest was staring at Alice, then at Ron. "Somethin' you said there," he drawled. "That business about folks not listenin', not talkin', an' all. That kinda strikes home." His gaze shifted back to Alice. "Maybe we oughta do some talkin', girl. And don't doubt that I've got some things to say. But maybe I'll try to do some listenin'—if you will."

Alice smiled wanly. "I'll . . . try. And hey: thanks for just the offer."

Ernest inclined his head in Ron's direction. "What about him?"

Ron studied the older man warily. "What *about* me? A few minutes ago you wanted to kill me. What changed?"

Ernest shrugged. "Maybe all that hard drivin' and runnin' through the bushes burned me outta my mad. Or maybe I decided I was bein' mad 'cause I thought I *oughta* be mad—'cause it was the easiest thing, and all. Like when somethin' goes wrong, blame it on somebody else. But . . . I kinda think it was mostly just two things. One was standin' there at the top of them stairs watchin' somebody else about to be killed—somebody I wasn't pissed-off at, and realizin' what an awful thing that is to do to somebody. And maybe the other thing was . . ." he looked at the ground, almost blushing. "The other thing was that Alice *asked* me to help."

Ron bit his lip and felt his cheeks warm with embarrassment. He'd been guilty of stereotyping too. "Good thing, that," he murmured. "And whyever you did it, thanks—a bunch." He paused, then: "Uh, how'd you *find* us, anyway?"

"You wasn't hard to track," Ernest said. "That fancy car of your'n makes a pretty wide trail, never mind all them parts fallin' off, an' stuff—plus I could hear it without the muffler an' all. An' when I found it, that cat of your'n jumped out an' just took off runnin'. An' we sorta followed it, I guess— 'Course we could see your tracks an' stuff too. An' then we found Alice asleep out there, only she woke up when we shook her, an' she got real upset an' said I had to help her or somebody was gonna die; an' I asked her who an' why; an' she said she didn't have time to explain, only I had to help her; an' then she jumped up an' run toward the house. An' that cat took off ahead of her, an' we followed it real quiet like until we seen what was up."

"Well, I'm glad you did," Ron sighed weakly. He extended a hand toward Ernest, who reached over and took it in a firm shake. Ron reclaimed his hand and reached down to snare Matty Groves by the scruff of the neck. He looked the cat in the eye. "I owe *you* a life or two now, don't I? Teach me to abandon my friends to their own devices. I—"

"Look out!" Alice cried, pointing. Ron turned—just in time to see a large part of the roof of the defunct mansion go crashing down in flames. A pair of columns (they were only wood) teetered and splatted into the yard, a mass of rotten splinters.

"So what now?" Alice asked.

"What indeed?" Ron echoed.

"Why, we've gotta get these boys to the hospital," Alma exclaimed.

Ron shook his head. "That *wouldn't* be a good idea, trust me. No, we just need to get out of here, find some place to get cleaned up and and get Mr. Lew here some food and rest, and then—Jesus Christ, who in the hell is *that*?"

For a car was easing into the yard from the other side of the rapidly collapsing mansion. It was a familiar-looking vehicle, too, but it took Ron a minute to realize that it was the same low-slung gold sedan he had seen but once: the one that Donson Gwent allegedly had on loan. The car coasted to a silent stop between them and the flaming house, and three people climbed out, their identities masked for the moment by the glare behind them. Ron was still blinking dumbly when Lew hollered, "Oh my God! That's Brandy!"

It was, too—and with two smaller figures in tow: Donson Gwent and Sam. Sam was was lugging something that it took Ron a long moment to recognize as The Head—smashed flat on one side, and with its bad eye entirely missing, its good one crossed, and with its jaw askew, but otherwise intact.

"You seem . . . surprised," The Head drawled, punctuating its remark with an awkward sideways twitch of its jaw and a loud *clink*.

"You could say that," Ron managed, as he staggered to his feet.

And felt arms go around him—*Brandy's* arms. Before he knew it, he was kissing her.

"Touching scene," Sam chuckled, elbowing Donson in the side.

"I'll touch *you*," Brandy growled out of the corner of her mouth.

"Oh, would you?" Sam laughed.

Lew—and Alice—and her folks were all staring about utterly confounded.

Ron gnawed his lip and finally said. "I tell you what, guys: let's get everybody fed and clothed and cleaned up and feeling good, and save the questions for later."

"You can use our house—can't they, Mom?" Alice said.

"Yes," The Head affirmed. "You can."

Chapter 21

Goin' Home

Alabama
Afternoon

"You *sure* you're gonna be okay?" Ron asked Alice, watching for her response as much as listening. But not *Listening*. Uh-uh, no way! *That* was for emergencies: life and death; not for taking unethical liberties with friends. Never mind that he'd had enough of such practices and their more esoteric kin during the last twenty-four hours to last him a good long lifetime.

Freshly bathed, shaved, napped, and fed, courtesy of Alice's mom and the Phoenix City Kroger, Ron and his latest "keeper" friend were lounging in the cool shade of a spreading oak to one side of Alma Moss's sandy drive. Donson's Aldebaran was nosed up behind Ernest's Camaro a few yards away, gleaming, as always, in the sunlight, though it now bore rooster tails of red mud along its sinuous flanks, token of a night's hard drive. For himself Ron was feeling much better, courtesy of the Luck and rest: his snakebite already reduced to a sore leg and a slight fever, which manifested mostly as a subtle flush and light sweat—or maybe that was simply Alice's presence, standing so close as she was.

As for the remaining members of the unlikely company that bare hours before had made their half-dazed way from the still-smoldering ruin that had been Crazy Jane Collins's mansion, all were still inside Alma's partly restored clapboard farmhouse. Catching up on shut-eye in Brandy's case (she, Sam, and Donson had been on the road most of the night); trying to explain a week of captivity to Ernest and Alma without arousing *too* many suspicions or using the wrong words, as Lew was attempting; or, in the case of Donson and Sam, pretending to be normal teens—which basically meant they were strafing alien planets on Melissa's Nintendo while ignoring the inquisitive owner. Ron knew better about those two lads, though—not enough, yet—but better. Still, there'd be time for sorting all that out later. For now, the matter at hand was setting a certain rather scratchy record straight with Alice Moss.

Even in the day-and-a-bit Ron had known her, the girl had changed. Though still half a child in some respects, the last thirty hours had brought most of the troubling forces in her life to a head, as well as exposing her to a veritable plethora of new experiences, never mind concepts, she had not heretofore suspected even existed. Which meant that she'd had to do a lot of growing up very quickly, and in the process had discovered that sometimes one had to act first and sort out the consequences later—and, even more to the point, that there usually *were* consequences. That, as much as anything, being a grown-up meant being responsible for one's own actions.

But it was *hard* to think of Alice as an adult, dammit! Especially when she was standing across from him with her hair gathered back in a bouncy ponytail, and her trim little barefoot body was clad only in cutoffs and an aging Twenty-Eight Days T-shirt, all of which conspired to make her look about thirteen.

"So, you *sure* you'll be okay?" Ron asked again, his previous question having been drowned out by a logging truck rumbling by on the highway at the end of the drive. He scratched his shoulders against the rough oak bark and waited for her reply. Matty Groves rubbed against his leg. He wished he had the crutch to fidget with, but it was gone: lost in the fire, along with so much else.

Alice met his gaze steadily, with a trace of defiance, a touch of resentment, and more than a little wistfulness. Ron hoped she hadn't had time to fall in love with him. "I'll be fine," she told him flatly. "Me and Ernest have agreed to sneak off to town and have dinner and talk, just the two of us. We're gonna do it in public so he can't yell, and so I can't run off. I'm gonna tell him what bugs me about him, and he's gonna tell me what bugs him about me. And we're gonna try to figure out how to get around the worst of it. And then me and Mom are gonna do the same, and then all three of us—plus Melissa, if she wants to. And we're gonna try to get down real deep and find out not just what bugs us, but why."

Ron whistled thoughtfully. "Sounds good—ambitious, but good. It's probably what a shrink would've suggested anyway. This is bound to be a lot cheaper."

Alice grinned. "Not at the restaurant *I've* got in mind."

Ron raised an eyebrow, in concern as much as jest. "Don't push him. Or don't let him bring his shotgun if you do!"

"I'll do my best."

A pause. Then, seriously: "So, you cool?"

"Yeah, I . . . think so," Alice replied slowly. "But I still can't quite believe it worked out like it did. I mean, all I did was get pissed-off and take a walk down the road one morning."

"And find a crazy old tinker sleeping in a field."

Alice chuckled. "You're not old, and I'm not at all sure you're a tinker."

"I notice you didn't comment on crazy," Ron observed wryly.

"The jury's still out on that."

"Well, if it helps any, I haven't decided either. And I doubt Lew has. All I can say for sure is that we're both a lot more together than our—" He broke off, finding his eyes unexpectedly awash with tears.

Alice eased forward to hug him, not as a lover, but as a very good friend. "It's cool," she murmured. "I mean, to me she was just this weird woman who showed up in town a few months ago, pretending she was English—only I guess she wasn't pretending, was she?—and putting on airs, and all, like she was some kind of royalty or something; but always asking folks to come see her if they had problems or wanted *anything*, only nobody ever went." She paused then, for Ron had tensed involuntarily. "But to you she was something else entirely, wasn't she? I know you never got a chance to know her, much less love her, or anything, but— well, she *was* your sister. And then there was that poor little girl . . ."

"Yeah," Ron murmured, his eyes misting even worse. "That was *really* tough. Really a shame."

"She did the right thing, though—as she saw it. It was a very adult thing to do."

"So was Earnest's shooting Jane instead of me."

Alice eased free of his embrace, backed up a step, and folded her arms. "That's what all this is really about, isn't it? Doing the right thing?"

Ron wiped his eyes on his hand, then shrugged. "I guess. I mean it all started 'cause Lew didn't know what the right thing was. Part of him wanted one thing, part another, and he had to try 'em both."

"Is he okay now?"

Again Ron shrugged. "I honestly don't know. Physically he's fine—or will be. Mentally . . . Who can say? But none of that's your problem."

"No," Alice agreed softly, "it's not."

Ron merely sighed.

Alice's eyes twinkled wickedly. "One question, though."

"What?"

"Are you the Road Man?"

"The . . . Head said I am."

"You know what I mean—*Ronny*."

Ron gnawed his lip for a long moment, then reclaimed his spot against his tree. "I'm . . . not the Road Man *you* heard about," he managed finally, "nor the one I knew. I've met him, and he's definitely not me. Shoot, I don't even know if he exists any more, and if he does, it's almost certainly in another identity. So as to the *person* still being around, I'd have to say no. But the role—now *that's* another matter. I seem to have been anointed into that position—and, to be perfectly honest, I don't mind."

"You were good at it," Alice informed him with perfect honesty. "You convinced *me*!"

"I bullshitted you!"

"Not about anything important!" she countered fiercely. "Besides, a lot bigger deal was the way you treated me and my friends."

A brow lifted. "And how was that?"

"As adults, as much as you could, as people whose opinions mattered. As people you were interested in *as* people, not as reflections of yourself. I dunno—you just seemed more relaxed with them than I've ever seen any grown-up."

"Probably because I'm *not* a grown-up!"

"Could've fooled me."

Ron did not reply.

"So, Road Man," Alice asked at last, "what's down the *road* for you now?"

Ron rolled his eyes. "Well, there're still about a dozen mysteries that I've gotta get to the bottom of between now and when we get back home. After that, I guess I'll hang around Brandy's place, at least for a while—long enough to recuperate a little, and to get Lew straightened out. Then . . . who knows?"

"I know what I'd suggest!" Alice giggled slyly.

"What?"

"You liked being the Road Man, didn't you?"

Ron eyed her warily. "I already told you I did."

"So . . . *be* him!"

"But Brandy—"

"Seems to me like you love her and she loves you, but you get along best when you're not in each other's face all the time," Alice blurted out. "I mean, I've seen *that* much just watching you two today. But if you were the Road Man, at least some of the time, you'd both be free to be yourselves whenever you wanted. But you'd also have some stability if you wanted *that*—a place to go home to, and all. And if Brandy was to join you on the road some—like when things got too dull at her place, why then she could have adventure and wildness too, which I think she needs."

Ron shook his head in amazement. "And you figured all that out since this morning?"

Alice smiled mysteriously. "Maybe it's a gift or something, like that thing you've got for metalwork. You exposed me to a lot of things—*awoke* a lot of things, I guess. Maybe you awoke that too."

"Please God, no," Ron groaned. "Don't let me have given the world another psychologist when I was trying to give it an artist." His eyes were merry, though.

"Come on," Alice laughed, reaching out to take his hand. "It's nearly four, and I told Brandy I'd wake her then."

Ron sighed. "So I guess this is it—as far as one-on-one?"

Alice sighed in turn. "I guess so."

"Can I have a hug, then?"

"If I can have one very chaste kiss."

"Fine."

They did.

"One thing, though," Alice murmured when they had parted. "I hate good-byes, and I refuse to be here when you leave . . . but I feel like I oughta say *something*, so I'm gonna go ahead and say bye now. That way it won't hurt so bad when it's real."

"Bye," Ron whispered. "A very *good* bye."

Silence, for a moment, a hint of tension, but mostly gentle regret.

"Oh, and there's one other thing I never got to tell you," Alice giggled, shattering the solemn mood, as Ron followed her toward the house.

"What's that?" he wondered innocently.

Alice grinned at him over her shoulder. "You've got a *real* nice bod."

"Thanks," Ron mumbled, blushing. "Uh, so do you," he added. "It's a work of art. Be proud of it—and enjoy it."

"I intend to!"

And then they pushed through the screen door and blinked into the relative gloom of the paneled living room.

"Time to hit the road?" Lew asked hopefully, peering up from a sheet-draped sofa, where he'd been sprawled shirtless and slathered with burn ointment, while Alma plied him with food and Ernest with beer, as Lew fended off their combined queries about the morning's events with clever evasions that would have made dear old Uncle Dion proud.

Ron nodded. "We're outta here—soon as we round up Brandy and the boys."

"Boys," Lew snorted, as Ron limped toward the bedroom. "Not hardly!"

Half an hour later Ron found himself sprawled in the commodious white leather backseat of Donson's Aldebaran. Brandy lounged against him, with Lew on the other side, and Matty in the footwell. Sam, in jeans and black T-shirt, rode shotgun, with The Head as ammunition—it *might* survive one more round as projectile, but no more. Donson, reasonably enough, was driving, still in his trademark black leather jacket and shirt of flame-red silk. As the playwright turned the key and brought the car to softly purring life, Ron twisted around in place, to gaze out the back window at Alma Moss and Ernest Woodring standing side by side on Alma's porch, with their arms around each others' waists. True to her word, Alice had made herself scarce, but Melissa had joined them and was hugging her mother's leg. The adults waved dutifully. Melissa blew kisses to Sam and Donson.

For himself, Ron sketched a friendly, if reserved, salute and eased back around. As the car glided onto the highway, he slipped off his much-abused Reeboks and let his feet cool in the thick, golden carpet.

"Well that concludes that," Brandy yawned, still more than half-asleep. She leaned her head against Ron's shoulder and snuggled into his side. "Y'all 'scuse me while I finish my nap."

"Does this mean we get to talk about you?" Ron wondered, smoothing her hair, and thinking how nice it was to be close to her again.

"If you guys wanta risk being overheard."

"Maybe," Lew suggested carefully, "we ought to talk about *other* things."

Ron eased into a more comfortable position, as the car reached cruising speed on the forest-lined back road. "Yeah, I think so too—might as well get it all out, so we can relax the rest of the way in—or so anybody who needs to can abandon ship right off." He glanced up at the rearview mirror and saw Donson's eyes gazing back at him: guileless now. *Yeah, sure!*

"Okay," he continued, "first things first: how'd you guys—by whom I mean you so-called kids up front—just happen, to be in the right place at the right time? And what about this blessed car, Gwent?"

Donson puffed his cheeks: a remarkably childlike expression, though he had evidently shifted to his adult, take-charge persona. "Well, to begin with the easiest: What Brandy told you about the car is true. I really did design it—sort of. And the design really did come to me in a dream—though where *that* came from . . ." He shot Sam a wary glance and did not elaborate. "The rest—well, she was right there too. One of my last foster-dad's brothers works for Ford, and he saw this design I'd done, and showed it to the folks up there, and they liked it so much they built it as a running prototype for a Lincoln they've got in the pipeline, figuring that this way they could get some real-world mileage out of a bunch of special systems that're on it, plus gauge public reaction to the styling."

"But Sam's model . . ."

Again Donson exchanged troubled looks with Sam. "We'll get to that in a minute; first I think we oughta figure out what to do about Alma and Ernest."

Lew looked first startled, then alarmed. "What about 'em? And what's this *we* stuff? And . . . and how do *you* know so much, anyway?"

"I know what I've been told, what I've seen, and what I've figured out," Donson replied quickly, "which is quite a lot. Enough that there's little you could say to shock or surprise me." (Ron wondered if he was on the verge of shifting persona again, as personal questions like this tended to make him do; fortunately he held firm.) "As for Alma and Ernest," the boy went on, "haven't they been exposed to a bunch of esoterica they shouldn't have? Don't they know more than they ought?"

Lew's response was a distrustful narrowing of his eyes. "They do now. But in a week or so I'll drift back over here—or me and Ronny will. And we'll pick up the Centauri and then get a motel room and spend the next little while blurring every memory anybody around here ever had of Ronny as anything but the Road Man, and of anyone named Crazy

Jane. We'll need to do something with the bodies, too—
assuming, of course, there *are* any—though come to think
of it, we could probably get Dion and Gil to take care of
that, since it's not really the kind of thing that can wait.
Besides, it's the ethical thing to do—and we owe it to her,
and her daughter."

"And no doubt we'll argue ethics black and blue the whole
time," Ron snorted resignedly. " 'Cause I still don't believe
in exposing folks to that kind of weirdness—not as something
that's real. Which brings us to the play."

Donson looked suddenly very guilty, but once again did
not shift identities. "yeah, well, I was afraid you'd remember
that. But the fact is, now that I know what I do, I kinda see
your point, Ronny. So what I think I'm gonna do is revise
it a little, and try to explain the material about the Luck
away as . . . well, as just real *luck*: coincidence, and such.
I'll probably have to trash the last act, but what the hey?
We're ahead of schedule."

Ron did not reply for a moment. Then: "You're really not
him, are you?"

Donson shook his head. "I've never lied to you."

"So who is?"

"What makes you think anybody is?" Sam inserted mysteriously.

Ron shrugged. "It—I guess it just seems logical that he's
involved in this *some* way. I mean, how'd you guys know
to come *here*?"

"Dion phoned Brandy with the mother of all sets of omens,
early last night," Donson replied. "He said he'd been trying
to get hold of you for two days and couldn't, but that these
omens were so wild he had to bounce 'em off somebody,
so he felt he had no choice but to call Brandy. And then
she got so freaked, she had to talk to somebody, and I
got to be the lucky victim. Dion couldn't tell us much—
or wouldn't—except to point out that they presaged some
unspecified imminent crisis, that they carried a clear warning
for him and his brother to stay out of it or Lew *and* Ronny
would die, and that every one of 'em was about Alabama.
Well, that pretty much gave us a location, so Brandy and me
decided then and there that it was time *we* got involved, so

we started trying to figure out where in Alabama we ought
to shoot for. But while we were doing that—"

"I turned up looking for Donny-boy, and wound up showing both of 'em a couple of things," Sam finished for him.
"And then they had no choice *not* to go—immediately."

"And then Sam somehow found The Head, and it told us
the rest," Donson concluded.

Ron gaped incredulously, having only half heard the playwright's last comment. "*You?* Sam Foster? Boy blacksmith?"
he gasped. "You convinced two people you don't even like
to drive to Alabama in the middle of the night on what could
have been a fool's errand?"

Silence. Then: "There *is* no Sam Foster," The Head
announced.

Ron continued to stare. "What . . . do you *mean* by that?"
he asked carefully. "That's the second time you've said
that."

"Because it's true," Sam interrupted softly, a sad note in
his voice. "There never was a Sam Foster, Ron; not really.
This body you see here has only existed for about a year
and a half and before that it wore deer hide, and before *that*
it had red hair and was called Van Vannister."

Ron felt a chill grip his heart. "And before that . . . ?"

"Folks called me the Road Man."

It took Ron a moment to find his voice. "So . . . there never
was a Sam? Not the Sam that was my . . . my buddy?" Ron
felt a lump rise in his throat. "But you were so *convincing*!"

"Thanks," Sam chuckled, "I thought so too. See, what I did
was . . . That is, when I awoke in that body, something told
me that if I did things right, it might be the last time I had
to ride the cycle, ever. I'd done pretty well by you before—
getting you a craft one time and a life-mate another—but I'd
kinda screwed up on my third goal, which was getting you
a life's work—and finding a replacement for myself. But
I guess I'm sorta gettin' ahead of myself there. Anyway,
as I was saying, I found myself in the woods with this
boy-body, and I knew I needed to have a persona this time
that could get close to you but that you absolutely would not
suspect, 'cause you were gettin' *real* antsy about that kind of
thing. So I Listened to the Winds real hard for a long time,

and I found this certain kid's Voice, and I basically just recorded his whole personality—or one of my alternates that live in my head with me did: guy calls himself the Midnight Man—the same one who came up with that car design and fed it to both Donson and my conscious Sam-self. He's kind of a trickster, and all. But anyway, he and another of my avatars called the Master of Dreams basically built me a new personality out of this guy's dreams and thoughts and stuff. And when they had him fleshed out enough, right down to a very good bogus Voice, they just turned him on and hid, and let him run like a real kid, which he mostly thought he was—like even *he* didn't know he wasn't himself. Except that there's another *really* real kid somewhere in Georgia who's got exactly the same personality, only more so."

"But your dad . . ."

"Dad was made out of stuff," Sam finished. "Just like Wendy was, only from *different* stuff. I needed him for the charade, but he was much less real than she was. I've already unmade him."

"Great!" Ron growled sourly. "Now I have to angst over all that again!"

Sam shook his head. "No you don't. Besides, it's too late."

"And the kids? Your . . . friends? Tam and Tonya . . . ?"

"More of the same. All gone back to rocks and flowers and other people's dreams—except that I guess I'll have to keep Tam and Tonya around until the play's run its season. Otherwise old Donson here'll skin me alive."

"So, did you read Lew's book? Or what?" Ron dared at last.

Sam smiled a secret smile. "Let's just say I once read one like it—and that with so many of us living here in my head, it wasn't surprising one of us remembered, or, unlike you guys, could make more than one person."

"Okay, then," Ron sighed carefully. "That takes care of a couple of things. But why me? And what happens now, and . . . and what *are* you?"

Sam took a deep breath before diving in. "You, because *somebody* has to do it and I've known for a long time that you were the one. Except that I couldn't just walk up to you one day and say 'Hi there, I'm the Road Man; would you like to be me?' 'Cause you'd have hit the high timber."

"So you had to manipulate me instead? Great!"

"It worked, didn't it? I mean check out your heart, man, and tell me that the one thing in the world you enjoy most—make that the one *situation* you enjoy most—isn't being on the road helping crazy young misfits like Alice is, and like you thought Sam was, to find themselves? You've got the trade, man; you've got the base to work from, and it's like Alice told you a while ago, you've got somebody who loves you to go back to."

"Yeah," Brandy mumbled sleepily, "he does."

"You still haven't told me why I got singled out as the lucky victim," Ron grumbled. "Nor exactly who—or maybe I ought to say *what*—you are."

"Because I don't know—exactly," Sam told him frankly. "And a lot of what I *do* know I absolutely cannot tell you—which is to say, I'm *forbidden*. What I *do* know and *can* repeat is that I've been alive a very long time—thousands of years at least. I grew up in northwest Europe, normally I thought, 'cept that I didn't have a mom and Dad was off soldiering most of the time. But when I hit thirty-six or so, the absolute end of my prime, I started aging backwards—which surprised the hell out of *me*, let me tell you! And I did that until I hit my midteens, and then started forward again, and then back, and so on. I've been on that same cycle since before Stonehenge—which I worked on. Somewhere in there I discovered certain arts and abilities—skinchanging, for instance, which at least gave me some variety, though even that wasn't enough to keep my personality from fragmenting. I mean, eventually you know so *much* stuff and have so *many* opinions, some of them contradictory, that there's just not room in your conscious mind for all of 'em at one time. As for the rest, I know only what my mother told me—and be warned, I can't tell you all of that, either."

"I thought you said you didn't *know* your mom," Ron noted suspiciously, as Donson merged the car onto Interstate

85. "But go on. I mean this has only been buggin' me for about ten years."

"It bugged me ten *hundred*," Sam shot back. "And you're right, I didn't know my mom—at first. See, what happened was that by the time I'd been back and forth a couple of dozen times, I'd pretty well figured out that this wasn't a real good situation to be in—like, it's hard to make long-term friendships, and all that, and doubly hard to see the people you know and love age and die when you don't. So eventually, I came to hate what I was, and decided that the only thing to do was to kill myself. Well, that didn't work—any time I did major damage to myself, I'd pass out, and while I was out, my body would heal. So I decided to burn myself alive, figuring that would do the trick. And so I did. I found a little wooden house and locked the door and set it on fire. And I burned—sort of. I could feel the pain, anyway, but I wasn't damaged. But the pain was so great that I drew inside myself, and there I found myself cursing my mother who had made such an awful thing as me . . . and suddenly there she was—in my head. She'd been waiting, she said, for me to do that very thing—and had been forbidden to approach me until that happened."

"Ah," Lew said, enthralled. "Go on, go on!"

Sam took another deep breath and sighed. "Well, to make a long story short, my mother told me some of what I am and some of what my role in life was to be. Like I said, I can't tell you everything, but what I can say is that people—if you want to call 'em that—used to come here from some other place—not another planet, but more than that I'm forbidden to reveal. Anyway, they used to do this a lot and hang out with humans a lot. And sometimes, naturally enough, they had sex with humans. And from these unions there were basically two kinds of offspring. One kind occurred when the father was from that other place. These kids looked human, but they only aged slowly, and healed very quickly, and had certain mental powers—mostly the ability to read minds. I imagine you can see where this is heading."

"They became Listeners, right?"

"Yeah, they became Listeners. But like I said, that happened when the *father* was from that other place. But since we're talking about guys from a place that doesn't always touch this world—well, what you sometimes get is babies that nobody knows who the father is. Little otherworldly half-breeds growing up in a world not their own, and wondering why they don't age like their friends—if they don't simply go whacko, which most of 'em do. Or did."

"Hmmmmm."

"Yeah, but what about the *others*, Ronny?"

Ron scowled uncertainly. "What others?"

"What about the children begotten by male humans on these Other women? What do you think *they'd* be like?"

"I . . . think I'll let you tell me."

"Well first of all," Sam explained, "there'd be fewer of 'em, because women from that other place weren't as careless as the men. And what children *were* begotten by mortal men on Other women would be born in the Other place, so they'd stay there and never come into this world at all, though they'd have special powers too. Well, you've probably figured out by now that I was one of these 'lucky' kids. Unfortunately, my mother managed to anger the wrong person at the wrong time, and as punishment she was cursed. And this curse was to see me, still a babe, banished into this world and to be forced to watch my pain as I discovered the extent of my Otherness. Only when *I* cursed her from the depths of my soul would she be free to contact me, and then only when I was in great pain. And as I said, that took a very long time. As far as I know, I'm the only one like me."

"So you're suffering for what your mother did?" Lew asked. "That hardly sounds fair."

"It's not," Sam agreed instantly. "But we're not talking about twentieth century America here. And Mom did finally get the curse modified—sort of. I could never go to where she was and find peace until I died—which I couldn't do unless I found someone of my own blood *and* Listener blood to replace me."

"Someone like . . . me?" Ron ventured, trying very hard to suppress a chill.

Sam nodded solemnly. "Someone like you. If I can find a new Road Man, I can age normally and die happy."

Ron's eyes narrowed. "Yeah, but you said you had to find someone of your own blood! Does that, uh, mean . . . what I *think* it does?"

Again Sam nodded. "The Road Man you met claimed no children and had none. But some of the ones before him didn't bind themselves so. See, like I told you: I had to ride the cycle—but eventually I discovered that I could speed it up or slow it down. Which meant that while I still couldn't be thirty until I'd been, for instance, twenty-five and fifteen first, I didn't have to *stay* any particular age very long at all, as long as I observed it; and eventually I even got to where I could skip whole hunks at a time—or spend them as animals. Which basically means I spent most of the last hundred years being the same thirty six-year-old Road Man, only I was really several different ones. One of whom, shall we say, had a dalliance with your great-grandmother Martha."

"So I'm your . . . great-grandson?" Ron rolled his eyes. "Or me and Lew are, both? Oh, jeez, this really is too complicated."

"It's worse," Sam chuckled. "But we won't go into that now. But do you remember back when you and I—that is, the Road Man—first met? Or last met, rather? When old Matthew asked me what I wanted in payment for the knife I was supposed to make him, and I told him so much money and a seed? Well, you were the seed I had in mind."

Ron glared at him. "So you've been manipulating me all my life?"

Sam shook his head. "Very little, actually. And one . . . encounter didn't *quite* go as planned, as I'm sure you recall; so really only this time around. And even so, I was mostly giving you enough rope."

"To hang myself."

"To make you happy."

Silence.

"Look at me, Ronny Dillon," Sam said quietly, a minute later. "Look at me and tell me you're not thrilled to death at the idea of being the next Road Man."

Ron shook his head and closed his eyes. "I'll . . . have to catch you later on that."

"Fine," Sam agreed. "Just let me know—though I already do."

"Well *that* was certainly a slab of meat on a very small plate to eat in a hurry," Lew sighed into the ensuing lull. He'd been so quiet Ron had almost forgotten him. But he was certain Lew had heard every word. "I guess that hits the big stuff, anyway," he continued. "But it still doesn't answer one very crucial question."

"What's that?" Sam asked carefully.

"What do we do about the Mastership?"

"Was that a question?" The Head inquired promptly.

Lew blinked at it curiously. *"Huh?"*

Ron recalled then that his twin had very little experience with it—never mind what he must think of Sam's story (he'd never met the 'boy' either—or Donson).

"It's a question if you need it to be one," Lew managed finally. "I'll take advice anywhere I can get it at the moment."

"Very well," The Head replied tartly. "Perhaps the Mastership should go to your—that is, to Lewis's—son."

"Son?" Lew, Ronny—and Brandy, who had suddenly awakened—all shrieked as one. *"What* son?"

Sam thumped The Head with a finger to prompt it. "You wanta tell 'em, or shall I?"

"I'll tell 'em," Donson inserted quietly. "Since it's *me* we're talking about."

Sam stared at him. "How'd you know?"

Donson shrugged. "Dreams mostly. And me and The Head had a little talk this afternoon while Brandy was sleeping and you were trying to hide from Melissa."

"But how'd you *know*?"

"I simply asked The Head who I was, and it told me."

"I did not *know* before," The Head explained. "I had to ride some very ancient Winds."

"You still haven't told *us*," Lew interrupted, leaning forward. "Now let me get this straight: you, Head, say that this Donson Gwent guy here is my *son*?"

"That is what I say."

Lew slumped back in his seat. "But that's impossible! No way I could have a child that age, I'd have had to be a kid when he was begotten, and—*Oh, my God!*"

Ron stared at him. "What?"

Lew was white-faced. "Oh Jesus, Ronny! I—Oh *Jesus*!"

"What is it, Lew?" Ron demanded. "Come on, man, talk to me!"

Lew stared at the floorboards. "I'd almost forgotten about that, and I truly didn't know the . . . the rest of the story until now. But—well, I guess it all goes back to when I lost my virginity." He looked across Brandy's head at Ron. "I've never told you this, have I? I told you about the first time I did it as a teenager, but that wasn't really the *first* time. The first time I was just eleven, and it was . . . also the first time I ever ejaculated. I mean I was *inside* this girl, and didn't really know what was happening *or* what happened—which was evidently a lot. The girl left after that, but they were just visiting my mom anyway, so I thought they'd just gone back home. I never dreamed she could have got pregnant—but I guess she did. I got pretty freaked by it all, let me tell you, and real scared and embarrassed, and really did pretty well forget it."

Ron's face was a mixture of awe, concern, and amusement. "So you did it right the first time, huh?" he giggled in spite of himself.

Lew grimaced helplessly. "Evidently."

Ron looked at Donson, who was either unconcerned by so bizarre a revelation, or suppressing it very well indeed. "So that really was true? About the adoptions and the abusive parent, and all?"

Donson nodded. "Every word of it."

Ron frowned. "So you . . . really *are* heir to the Mastership—sort of."

Again Donson nodded. "Evidently."

"And you're interested?"

A third nod. "Possibly."

"Except that there are some problems," Sam put in.

"Like the small fact that the succession's not supposed to go through the male line?" Lew interrupted. "I mean, me and Ronny about got ourselves killed over that little technicality a few years ago."

"That's true," Sam agreed. "But I've known a Listener or

two in my time, and I can tell you that really is mostly a matter of convention, not an intrinsic situation. And since there really is no other heir now, it might not make a difference. Ultimately, I suppose, it's for the Land itself to decide."

"Possibly," Lew mused. "But what about those other glitches you mentioned?"

Sam eyed Donson with something very close to sympathy. "Well, I guess the main thing is that the Luck's already started to kick in on him, witness all those psychic abilities of his—that bit about picking up stuff about the Welches from dreams, and all. Never mind his facility with words, which really is almost supernatural—like Ron's knack with metal or Lew's with plants. I think that's probably the Road Man blood coming in. But . . . well, as you know, he's got a pretty major physiological problem."

Lew looked puzzled. "How so?" Then: "Oh, I see. Like he wasn't Fixed when he was born, so that he could go crazy when the Luck kicks in, just like poor Jane did?"

"That's one," Sam affirmed. "Though not the obvious one."

"I think Gil and Dion could help there, though," Ron suggested. "If we could get them up here, they could probably help keep things straight through the critical time, after which it *ought* to take care of itself—again, supposing our buddy Donson here's up for it."

"There's another problem, though," Donson said slowly. "And really a much worse one—according to The Head."

"What's that?" Ron began. But then he remembered and blushed, as embarrassed for himself as for the boy. "Oh God, Donson, that's right! You're not . . . complete."

Donson colored to his hairline. "Not hardly."

"And if the Luck kicks in and you're not—" Lew whispered. "Oh Jesus!"

"There's a solution, though," Sam noted. "Maybe."

Ron stared at him. "How so?"

Sam looked at Donson. "Nothing's actually missing, is it? I mean connections were . . . severed, but nothing was actually removed, right?"

Donson's face was the color of a ripe plum. "Right," he mumbled.

"Well, then," Sam concluded brightly. "So all we've gotta do is find a good surgeon and then poke you full of hormones, and presto, you're good as new."

Donson shook his head. "It's been tried."

"Ah," Sam countered triumphantly. "But not by both Road Men. And besides, if *that* doesn't work, I think there's something in the book about making people out of flowers that might be applicable—if you're up for it."

"What's the alternative?" Donson asked nervously.

"Mostly," Lew told him, "that you'd go insane."

"But I don't wish to go among mad people," Ron muttered, quoting *Alice in Wonderland*.

"Well," Donson said decisively. "I'll go for it."

Epilogue

I'm a Man

Brandy Hall
Midnight

He awakens from the deepest sleep of his life, and for a
moment does not realize where he is. But then he blinks,
yawns, stretches—and eventually his eyes become accustomed to the moonlight. It is a small room, as rooms go in
Brandy Hall; the walls are bare stone, austere as the monk's
cell they were fashioned to emulate. There is rice matting
on the floor, a single Gothic-arched window to his left, a
vaulted ceiling, a lone icon of St. Raphael, the archangel-
healer. He sits up in bed and looks across the matting to the
other bed, narrow as his own. Usually it is empty; tonight
it is not. Another boy sleeps there—or boy he looks, for
he knows now that this lad is not a youth at all, but is
older than any living thing he is ever like to meet. Still,
he *thinks* of him as a boy—and as Sam. And has trouble
remembering that Sam is also his great-great-grandfather—
or that something like Sam was. Now it is more as if he has
a brother, and suddenly he understands Ron's obsession with
Lew, why he fretted so much about him, yet was loath to go
to his aid.

But he ponders that barely an instant, for there is a more pressing reason he has awakened.

He cannot breathe—not easily. The air in the cell is too stale, so he makes to open the window and let in the cool, crisp breezes of the Georgia night.

He climbs from bed, clad only in the sweatpants he uses as pajamas. He fumbles with the casement lock, but it will not budge. And he *needs* fresh air, needs it worse than anything in the world. Desperate, he pads from the room and enters the labyrinth of corridors that mark this part of Brandy Hall. Surely, he thinks, there must be an open window somewhere—or one that *will* open.

There is not. Not on the first level, not on the second. The doors to the terraces are locked, and so he doubles back. His lungs are growing tight now, unaccountably so, and he fears he may faint. He is terrified, for rarely has he been ill, and never so strangely and unexpectedly. Suddenly he is running.

Doors flash by, and windows: more windows that will not unhinge. He finds himself at the foot of a flight of stairs. He has not been this way before, but fear has made him careless. He runs up the stairs, for no clearer reason than that he is desperate. A door passes, then another. A third looms into view on his left. Something makes him pause there—some breath of wind perhaps.

Or some odor: some enticing scent that clears his head and makes it briefly easier to breathe. It comes from beyond that door. He tries it. It is locked. He tugs harder, shakes it, though a part of him knows that effort is vain. Yet this time he hears a click, and it swings away.

He finds himself in a room lighted by two sets of Gothic-arched windows set close together in adjoining walls. A long worktable to the right shows signs of smithcraft having been done there. There are urns in all four corners, each bearing a pot of odd white lilies, the like of which he has never seen.

They intrigue him, both for their beauty and for their perfume: a sharp, spicy scent unlike any he has ever encountered. They were the source of the odor that so intrigued him there on the landing: the one that gave him relief. He bends close to the nearest, inhales deeply, feels the stress in his lungs dissolve, feels peace. He inhales again, and his mind reels. Never has he smelled such a divine perfume, never has he felt so wild and creative and free. It is like being drunk, only this brings a sharpening, not a dulling. He inhales more, drinks deeply of that pollen that, had he known it, had its origin in another world.

It is intoxicating. And he is intoxicated. He feels as free as he has ever felt in his life. Impulsively, he removes his single garment and cavorts naked around the room, dancing through moonbeams, pacing out the flagstones in the figures of some obscure jig. But always he returns to the lilies; always he stops at intervals to sample their wonder yet again.

At some point, he bites into one; later, he plucks a handful from their stems and twirls with them around the room. Pollen sparkles from them like gold dust, setting the very air aglitter. It falls onto his forearm and mixes with the sweat there until the very flesh seems made of gold and brass. He sees it: a shimmer of wonder on his skin. Better his whole body should be thus.

And so he causes it to be. Every lily in the room contributes, as he plucks them and shakes them across his face and chest and limbs. He is sweating heavily now, and the pollen adheres to him, seeking out every mound and curve and crevice. He feels strange, preposterously alive, but full of some odd new desire he has never felt before: a sensation centered in his groin, in his poor, atrophied, mutilated manhood. That he dusts most carefully, and feels a new sensation: an itchy tingly throb lodged far within. It is the most marvelous sensation he has ever known.

Impulsively, he lies on the rug and strews lilies around, their pollen thick across his slim, bare form. In particular, he sets them *there*. And touches himself there.

And as the pleasure rises past enduring, moving toward a never-before-felt release, he closes his eyes, and falls inward. And sleeps.

When he awakens again, he sees three things. One is his own naked body, gold-glimmering in the morning sun. The second is that he is now ... complete. Entire. Fully and completely and wholly a young man.

The third is the message neatly rubbed in fingertip-wide uncials into the pollen that films the windows with golden haze.

Tell my son, presently called Samuel, that I owed him a favor.
I gave it to his great-great-grandson, though.

Mother

Donson Gwent stares at it for a moment, and then down at himself again. And laughs. For now, as the Land somehow assures him, he is whole.

Postlude

Do You Believe in Magic?

Cordova Playhouse, Cordova Georgia
Friday, July 12—sunset

The applause was deafening. And naturally enough—or
Luckily enough, for the throngs of out-of-town attendees—
it did not rain.

TOM DEITZ grew up in Young Harris, Georgia, and earned bachelor of arts and master of arts degrees from the University of Georgia. His major in medieval English (it was as close as he could get to Tolkien) and his fondness for castles, Celtic art, and costumes led Mr. Deitz to the Society for Creative Anachronism, of which he is still a member. A "fair-to-middlin' " artist, Mr. Deitz is also a car nut, has recently taken up horseback riding and hunting, (neither with remarkable success), and *still* thinks every now and then about building a castle.

In his *Soulsmith* trilogy—comprised of *Soulsmith, Dreambuilder*, and *Wordwright*—Mr. Deitz has created an ambitious work dealing with the powers, and the dangers, of one family's Luck. He is also the author of a very popular contemporary fantasy series begun in *Windmaster's Bane* and continued through *Fireshaper's Doom, Darkthunder's Way, Sunshaker's War, Stoneskin's Revenge,* and the related novel, *The Gryphon King*, all available from Avon Books.

BESTSELLING AUTHOR OF
THE PENDRAGON CYCLE

STEPHEN R. LAWHEAD

In a dark and ancient world,
a hero will be born to fulfill
the lost and magnificent promise of . . .

THE DRAGON KING

Book One
IN THE HALL OF THE DRAGON KING
71629-1/ $4.99 US/ $5.99 Can

Book Two
THE WARLORDS OF NIN
71630-5/ $4.99 US/ $5.99 Can

Book Three
THE SWORD AND THE FLAME
71631-3/ $4.99 US/ $5.99 Can